REALMS OF THE ROUND TABLE

REALMS OF THE ROUND TABLE

THE SECOND GREAT BOOK OF

THE ONCE AND FUTURE KING

✠ ✠ ✠

Part 2 of the New Morte D'Arthur

Compiled & retold by
JOHN MATTHEWS

Foreword by
SIR JOHN BOORMAN

Illustrated by
JOHN HOWE

HarperCollins*Publishers*

HarperCollins*Publishers*
1 London Bridge Street
London SE1 9GF
www.harpercollins.co.uk

HarperCollins*Publishers*
Macken House, 39/40 Mayor Street Upper,
Dublin 1, D01 C9W8, Ireland

First published by HarperCollins*Publishers* 2025

1

DEDICATION

———— ✠ ————

To the memory of Henry Treece (1911–1996),
another who trod the roads of King Arthur's Realm
and wrote many wonderful stories of it.

ACKNOWLEDGEMENTS

First and foremost I want to thank my wife, Caitlín, for reading every one of these stories – sometimes three times! – and offering her invaluable suggestions and corrections, and for her suggestion to include the ballad that became 'The Sweet Sorrow of Sir Gawain'. Also to my friends Dwina Murphy-Gibb and David Elkington, for their enthusiastic and eagle-eyed reading and corrections. Special thanks to my agent Peter Buckman, and to my amazing editor Chris Smith, who made the whole operation so much a pleasure. And of course, as with the previous volume, a huge thank you to John Howe for the fabulous and beautiful illustrations (illuminations?) which bring my text to life in so many ways. An equally huge thank you to the great Sir John Boorman, for his lovely Foreword. I would also like to pay tribute to the legion of Arthurian scholars and translators whose efforts have opened the vast library of Arthurian texts, many of which provided the source materials for this collection. I would especially mention my friends, Nigel Bryant, who has single-handedly translated some of the most important texts available, and Maarten Haverkamp, whose translation of the *Prophecies of Merlin* enabled me to write a fitting closure to the collection. The publisher D.S. Brewer also deserves a mention. More than half the original texts included here in my own versions were published by them – indeed a good part of my Arthurian library bears their imprint. Everyone who studies this subject should be grateful to them. Thanks also to Glyn Hnutu-Healh for a timely reminder about the story from *Perlesvaus*, which I might otherwise have forgotten, and to all the readers of the earlier collection who wrote words of appreciation. Lastly, to the owners and staff of the Beirut Restaurant in Oxford, for friendship, great food and encouraging words.

John Matthews,
Oxford 2025

CONTENTS

BOOK THREE: GUARDIANS OF THE GRAIL

POSTLUDES

PLATES

FOREWORD

We must be grateful to John Matthews for unearthing these marvellous stories surrounding the Knights of the Round Table and I look forward to immersing myself in their glories as they swirl about the figure of King Arthur.

In my researches for the film *Excalibur*, I kept colliding with John Matthews. From his great knowledge of the Arthurian legends, he gave me notable advice as I researched my story. His writing about the Arthurian legend is enjoyable as well as authentic and this book of new stories is as surprising and enthralling as you would expect.

When I was working on *Excalibur* I researched all these legends, and I went with a slightly different focus – I had Merlin as the central figure for my film, and he and his magic help in the quest for the Holy Grail. Arthur and the knights assemble at the Round Table and go off on their different adventures and come back and speak about what they have learned.

Having arranged his marriage to Guinevere, Arthur later sends his friend Lancelot to escort his future bride back to Camelot, and of course what happens is they fall in love. Lancelot is attracted to her but his love of the king is strong, and he delivers her to Arthur. But her heart was by then with Lancelot and his with Guinevere…

These stories about Arthur and the Knights of the Round Table have been published in many versions for hundreds of years and one of the reasons it interests me, and many others, is that it runs very deep to our core. It is the central myth of Britain… The stories have been told in many different ways – my version was to do with the recovery of the Holy Grail and that the king and the land are one. If the king gets sick, the crops suffer.

The only thing that will save the king and the land is the Grail. Many knights go to try and find it and fail, until Arthur sends a knight who is but a boy. The boy discovers all the knights who had left on the Grail quest hanging dead from a tree. He is attacked and his knightly clothes are torn from him. He is thrown naked into a river and his weapons are all gone. He is washed downstream and comes to a bridge leading to a castle and he climbs up naked and a voice says: 'What do you want?' He replies: 'I want the Holy Grail.' He climbs up to the castle and successfully answers the question – that you can only see the Grail when you are stripped of everything, just as the boy is. The Grail Cup fills up with wine and he feeds this to Arthur. Upon receiving a sip from the cup Arthur is immediately restored to full strength. This is the essence of the great myth.

John Matthews's knowledge of the Arthurian legend is unsurpassed and anyone attempting to reimagine them must go to him. My success in finding the Holy Grail and making *Excalibur* owes a great deal to his advice, knowledge and help.

Sir John Boorman
Annamoe, 2025

INTRODUCTION

Further Forays into the Great Wood

A number of people have asked me, before and since the collecting of these stories, what it is about the Arthurian world that keeps us coming back for more? The answer, to me anyway, is simple: they contain virtually every aspect of our lives; they show the best and worst of us; they are, by turns, exciting, powerful, funny and full of sorrow. We may live a long time after they were written, and chivalry is certainly not what it was then, or still might be; but there is enough love, anger, peace, bravery and fear, truth and falsehood in these tales to satisfy most people. We can learn from them.

I began reading the stories of Arthur and his knights over fifty years ago when I discovered T. H. White's extraordinary telling of the epic of Camelot, *The Once and Future King*. White's witty and erudite take on the epic led me to the inspiration for his work: Thomas Malory's retelling of a cycle of stories, which resulted in *Le Morte D'Arthur*, published by William Caxton in 1485.

Since then, I have continued to read every original medieval Arthurian story I could find – including many that form part of this collection. Many more are available in English than there were all those years ago, and I must pay homage to the legion of scholars and translators who fed my love of the vast panoply of tales, dating for the most part from the twelfth to the fifteenth centuries. But it was Malory's work that has always meant most to me, as it does to the fictional scribe in this book, and I would like to take a moment to consider what we know about the life of this great author.

When Sir Thomas completed his book, then still titled *The Whole Book of King Arthur and His Knights of the Round Table*, he was held captive in Newgate Prison on a variety of charges – some undoubtedly made up, others not – which gave him the time to compile and write his mighty book. Fortunately for Malory, as for those who love his work, he was allowed to have books brought to him in the prison, and he may well have had access to the Whittington Library, established by the fabled Mayor of London, Richard (Dick) Whittington (*c.* 1354–March 1423).

Almost everything we know about Malory is what he tells us within the pages of the original manuscript of his epic, where a number of colophons are included which appear to have been written by him personally. Several prayers addressed to the readers of the book appear, requesting their attention to the plight of the author. At the end of 'The Tale of King Arthur' (Caxton, Books I–IV) we read:

> And this book endeth whereas Sir Lancelot and Sir Tristram came to court. Who that would make any more let him seek other books of King Arthur and of Sir Lancelot or Sir Tristram; for this was drawn by a knight prisoner Thomas Malleorre, that God send him good recovery.

A second prayer, coming at the end of 'The Tale of Sir Gareth' (Caxton, Book VII) reads:

> And I pray you all that readeth this tale to pray for him that this wrote, that God send him good deliverance soon and hastily.

Later, at the end of 'The Tale of Sir Tristram' (Caxton, Books VIII–XII) comes:

> Here endeth the second book of Sir Tristram de Lyones which was drawn out of the French by Sir Thomas Malleorre, knight, as Jesu be his help.

Finally, towards the end of the whole book, there is a reference to:

> The Most Piteous Tale of the Morte Arthure Sanz Gwerdon par le shyvalere Sir Thomas Malleorre, knight, Jesu aide ly pur votre bon mercy [Jesu help me of your great mercy].

All of these pleas were omitted from Caxton's printed text, but were replaced, as a final colophon to the work, with the following:

> I pray you all gentlemen and gentlewomen that readeth this book of Arthur and his knights, from the beginning to the ending, pray for me while I am alive, that God send me good deliverance, and when I am dead, I pray you all pray for my soul. For this book was ended the ninth year of the reign of King Edward the Fourth by Sir Thomas Maleore, knight, as Jesu help him for his great might, as he is the servant of Jesu both day and night.

Taken with the other references, it is clear that the author is writing in prison, from which he hopes to be released soon. The last statement was augmented in 1934, when the only surviving manuscript was discovered in the Winchester

Cathedral library. This is the closest we can get to Malory's original, which has never been found, and it led various scholars to put forward a whole range of identities for the 'knight prisoner' whose name, as was common in the medieval period, appears under so many variable spellings.

On the balance of evidence, the most likely contender is Sir Thomas Malory of Newbold Revel (or Fenny Newbold) in Warwickshire. He has proved the longest lasting and most popular claimant of all, and a huge amount of research has been done into his life. For many, this is *the Malory* of *Le Morte D'Arthur*, though his life seems at times greatly at variance with the personal statements contained in the book. Noted medievalist, H. Oskar Sommer, was the first to mention this Malory in his 1890 edition of the book, but it was the distinguished Harvard Professor, George Lyman Kittredge, who outlined the evidence relating to the Newbold Revel Malory in 1897. Deriving most of his information from a book by Warwickshire antiquarian Sir William Dugdale, Kittredge presented this Malory as a soldier and parliamentarian who had fought at Calais with Richard Beauchamp, Earl of Warwick, one of the truly great chivalric figures of the fifteenth century. This Malory died in 1471 and was buried at Greyfriar's Church in London.

This discovery created sufficient interest to provoke several other scholars into researching various documents, including legal rolls contained in the Public Record Office in London. The information thus gleaned revealed a very different figure from that suggested by Dugdale. Most of the records concerning the career of Thomas Malory of Newbold Revel were concerned with his criminal record, which included several periods in jail for crimes including theft, grievous bodily harm and even rape. A somewhat sensational biography called *Sir Thomas Malory, His Turbulent Career*, by Edward Hicks, appeared in 1928 and promoted still further investigations, which gave a full and rounded portrait of Malory as a thief, bandit and rapist – scarcely reflecting the high chivalric standards contained within the book of which, it was claimed, he was author.

His parents were Sir John and Lady Phillipa Malory, the former originally of Winwick, the latter heiress to the estate of Fenny Newbold. Thomas, their only son, was born somewhere between 1393 and 1416. According to Dugdale he became a professional soldier and served under Richard Beauchamp, but even here the dates are vague and we have no idea how or if he distinguished himself. In 1442 he acted as an elector in Northamptonshire, but in 1443 he was accused, together with one Eustace Burnaby, of attacking, imprisoning and making off with goods to the value of £40 belonging to a Thomas Smythe, of Sprotton in Northants. Nothing seems to have come of this charge and shortly after we hear that Thomas Malory married a woman named Elizabeth, who later bore him a son, Robert.

In 1443, Malory was elected to parliament, and served at Westminster for the rest of that year, being appointed to a Royal Commission charged with the distribution of monies to the poorer towns of Warwickshire. We may judge by this that whatever the truth of accusations made against him the previous year, Malory remained in the good graces of his peers.

This was to change in 1450, when we learn that Thomas Malory, knight, was accused of lying in wait, along with 26 other men, to attack and rob Humphry Stafford, the Duke of Buckingham, one of the richest and most powerful men in the country. The reason for this remains unknown, and the accusations were never proven. Various suggestions have been made, including the possibility of Malory's involvement in a political plot organised by Richard Neville, Earl of Warwick. Whatever the truth, Malory seems to have been bent upon a life of crime from this time onwards. In May of the same year he is accused of extorting with menaces the sum of 100 shillings from Margaret King and William Hales of Monks Kirby, and, the following August, of engineering the same injury against another neighbour, John Mylner, from whom he allegedly stole 20 shillings.

Somewhere between these two events Malory was accused of an even more serious crime. Around June of 1450, aided by three other men, Malory is said to have broken into the house of Hugh Smyth of Monks Kirby and to have stolen goods worth £40 and raped his wife. It is important to understand that, at this point, the word 'rape' did not always mean the same as it does today. Rape in medieval terms meant 'to steal or run off with', so that we may choose to see Malory's crime to be more one of thievery than assault. Nine months later, on the 15 March 1451, the arrest of Sir Thomas Malory of Newbold Revel, along with nineteen others, was ordered. Once again, however, nothing seems to have come of this, and in the ensuing months Malory and his 'gang' went on a spree of robberies. At one point Malory was arrested and imprisoned in Maxstoke but he escaped almost at once, swimming the moat and rejoining his band at Newbold Revel.

Finally, on 23 August 1451, the matter came to trial at the Nuneaton assizes. The list of charges was extensive and included both Malory and several others who, according to the legal system of the time, may or may not have been present to answer their accusers. In any event the judgement went against Malory and by January of 1452 he was imprisoned in Marshalsea prison in London, where it seems he remained for at least a year.

His response to the judgement against him was to plead 'not guilty' and to demand a retrial with a jury of men from his own county. This never took place, but Malory was released for a time. In March he was arrested again and returned to Marshalsea, from where he escaped once again some two months later, possibly by bribing the guards. Less than a month later he was back in prison again, and this time he was held until the following May, when he was

✦ *Sir Thomas Malory* ✦

released on bail of £200 – a considerable sum at that time. However, when the date arrived for Malory to answer for his crimes, he could not be found. The reason for this was that he was already in custody at Colchester, where he was accused of still further crimes involving robbery and horse-theft. Once again, the ever resourceful Malory escaped, and remained at liberty until November, when he was apprehended and returned to Marshalsea, this time under the huge penalty against his escape of £1000.

During the next few years, we hear less of Malory. For much of the time he was imprisoned, either in Marshalsea or Newgate, though he seems to have obtained bail on at least one occasion and this time to have returned on the date appointed and been duly locked up again. The worst crimes of which he was accused on this occasion were failure to pay back loans made to him by various people for his bail payments.

In and out of prison again over the next few years, Malory served as a soldier for a time in the armies of both York and Lancaster during the Wars of the Roses (1455–1487). His name finally appears on a register of captors pardoned by King Edward IV in 1461. He may well have been detained for longer than other men who took part in the conflict, very likely due to his habit of changing sides.

Unfortunately for him, he ended up on the losing side and seems to have been held longer than most because of his attacks on Humphry Duke of Buckingham, whose influence with the king was considerable.

Sir Thomas Malory, knight, died on Thursday the 14th of March 1470, and was buried in some splendour at Greyfriars Chapel, London, in the shadow of Newgate Prison, where he had spent so much time as a prisoner. The fact that his mortal remains were interred here suggests that not only were his old misdeeds forgotten, but that he was also possessed of some wealth. This may have been the result of his misspent life, or because he had a wealthy patron, whose possible existence has been surmised as a reflection of the number of times he was set free or granted bail. Who this patron may have been, if he existed, is a matter for speculation. It has been claimed that it may have been Richard Neville, the Kingmaker himself, and that Malory may have spent time in his pay as a spy; but in a life already crowded with events, this may be stretching the evidence too far.

Malory's tomb bore the inscription:

HIC JACET DOMINUS THOMAS MALLERE,
VALENS MILES OB 14 MAR 1470 DE PAROCHIA
DE MONKENKIRBY IN COM WARICINI

[HERE LIES SIR THOMAS MALLERE,
VALIENT KNIGHT. DIED 14 MARCH 1470 IN THE PARISH
OF MONKENKIRBY IN THE COUNTY OF WARWICK]

Though he seems to have died in his own home, Malory was buried in London. His grave was lost for ever when Henry VIII dissolved the monastery of Greyfriars. But of Thomas Malory of Newbold Revel nothing more is currently known. He remains an enigmatic, and in some ways unlikely, author of the *Le Morte d'Arthur*, although in other respects he lived a life every bit as colourful and dramatic as some of the characters in his book.

✢ ✤ ✢

I am not the first to have fallen under the spell of Thomas Malory's work. Another book which I devoured when I came across it in the 1980s is John Steinbeck's *The Acts of King Arthur and his Noble Knights of the Round Table*. The American novelist clearly loved Malory's work in the same way that I do, and set out to create a modern language edition. In fact he did not live to complete it – in part because, as he wrote, the book gradually ceased to be Malory's and became pure Steinbeck. The result is a wonderful mix of fifteenth- and twentieth-century writing.

I realise that my own efforts, both in this collection and the previous volume (*The Great Book of King Arthur and His Knights of the Round Table*) have followed a similar path. Beginning from a desire to retell as many of the additional stories not included by Malory as possible, I soon found that I was adding details not in the originals. This was in part due to the need to make sense, for a modern audience, of these medieval stories – but also because, having adopted the persona of a scribe who loved Malory's work, I found that his voice spoke in my ear so often that I realised I was adding to the original works, just as Malory and Steinbeck had done. This has enabled me to impose some unity on the wondrous complexity that created the *Realms of the Round Table* – stories composed by so many different hands, making them a cycle of tales rather than a loose-knit collection.

So these are not exact retellings, though I have tried to follow the originals as far as possible. There is perhaps a little more of my own imaginings in this new selection than in the first. Often I felt, as I wrote, that I was almost taking dictation, so swiftly the words flowed from my hands. Throughout, I kept in mind that certain concepts and ideas would not have been used by the authors of these works, but that to copy the medieval style exactly would not really work for a modern audience. So I chose to aim for something halfway between. At the same time I had to make the hard choice of having to omit many details and episodes from the longer texts in order to keep within the dimensions of this book. As I did with the first collection, I have provided details of the originals whenever possible, so that those seeking to know what I left out can do so by seeking out the volumes I utilised in making my own versions.

Characters and situations wove into and out of the growing mountain of texts, and I found that including internal references within my own tellings made the collection into something more. Thus it can be said that these are versions based upon the originals. The words are thus all my own. I have given names to characters who were anonymous, and drawn out narrative threads that are scarcely there in the originals. If this approach requires an excuse I could only say that Malory himself did this – putting words into the mouths of his heroes and heroines and constantly referring to 'the French book' (now known as the *Vulgate* or *Lancelot-Grail Cycle*) the source of much of his own vision. Malory's own presence is as much in his book as is the nameless scribe who stands as an alter ego for myself in this.

Most people who know of the Arthurian legends know of *Le Morte D'Arthur*, but few are aware that several hundred other texts exist which broaden the landscape of the adventures of the Round Table knights and of the king and his immediate family. Most of these, unlike Malory's book, were written in other languages: French, German, Italian, Dutch and Spanish. Quite a large number of them have yet to be translated, while those that have remain unfamiliar to those who only know Malory and possibly the works of Chrétien de Troyes, whose cycle of French romances widened the range yet again. There are many clues scattered throughout these medieval tales of Arthur and his knights which refer back to a much older stratum of stories, mostly now lost. In particular the many references to what might be considered a state of warfare between Arthur and the realm of Faery, implying that this was once a much more developed strand of the myths. This is referenced clearly in the final story of the book, 'King Arthur and the Dragon of Normandy', in which the king is stated to be the leader of the Faery Hosts. I have done my best to identify these details and to place them where they may be seen in the stories told here.

There are many other regular patterns within the medieval tales. The basic standard story is the coming of a supplicant (usually an attractive woman) who requires one of the Round Table knights to defend her, rescue her mistress, avenge her murdered lover, or obtain for her rare magical items. The knight is then dispatched and encounters a number of adversaries along the way, most of whom will be dispatched or captured and sent to Camelot to swear allegiance to Arthur. I have done my best to create variations to the countless battles, jousts and rescues undertaken by the likes of Gawain, Lancelot, Meleranz and others, both less and more familiar.

I have once again adopted Caxton's device of adding what we can term 'ends and beginnings' to each book: thus, *Explicit liber Primus* (End of Book 1) *Incipit Liber Secundus* (Beginning of Book 2), and so on, for each of the individual stories as well. I have included these here to add to the links between Malory's book and my own.

As the Foreword to the first of these collections stated: '. . . *these tales feel like they still exist in a glorious present, as if one could travel to King Arthur's court simply by walking, and find oneself in Camelot.*' This is true of most of the original romances, of which I have gathered as many as I could that seemed worthy of retelling for a modern audience. In retelling these, I have drawn not only on the stories themselves, but a lifetime of reading, research and writing about literature of the Arthuriad in all its many forms. Nor should I forget the work of my old friend, Sir John Boorman, whose film, *Excalibur*, is still the finest retelling of the central myth I have seen, dramatising the story with such power and energy, and who so generously provided a Foreword to this collection.

Not everything within these pages will chime with modern sensibilities, but they are true to the time in which the originals were written. Here we are in a world of chivalry, knightly adventure, random love triangles, war and peace, magic and reality. A wonderful tapestry of a time that never really was, but which invites us into its wild forests, soaring castles and magical islands. I hope the work will inspire my readers, and that, when you have read them all (and there are still others not included here) you might go in search of your own discoveries. I promise you that the journey will be as exciting as any adventure undertaken by King Arthur's knights in the realms of the Round Table.

John Matthews
Oxford 2025

A WORD FROM THE SCRIBE
OF THESE STORIES

Thus I continue, beyond the beginning, with these tales that Sir Thomas Malory did not include in his great work which master Caxton named *Le Morte D'Arthur* when he published it in the year of Our Lord, 1485. As he tells us in the beginning of that book, many people came to him asking why he had not printed tales of the mighty King Arthur, and so have others come to me, asking if I had further tales than those I compiled and wrote in the collection which I named *The Great Book of King Arthur and His Knights of the Round Table*. As I write, further tales have come to light, some brought to me here in my lonely cell in the wilderness by those who, like myself, love the writings of Master Thomas and long for more. So I have made here a second assembly of tales from that distant time, when King Arthur ruled from Camelot the Golden. Many I have only lately come to hear or read, and all are as full of wonder as those previously brought together by my humble pen. My wish, as named before, is that these tales be remembered and told again in whatever time to come, when they are needed.

It is said that in those times, the great trees walked, and that they came together in a mighty assembly that became the wood that is named Broceliande – a place that I believe lies between the worlds of humankind and Faery. I cannot say if this is true, but for those who have walked the avenues of that uncanny place, or even just its margins, the whisper of voices can still be heard. Some have even seen where the Lady dances on the greensward. These are the stories told by the Great Wood itself. Thus, I am able to satisfy the requests once again to enter there, where the Knights of King Arthur rode in search of wonder.

Sir Thomas wrote often of knights who went forth in search of adventure, and were lost in the thousand pathways of the Great Wood. These were quickly forgotten by the tale spinners, but here I have sought to recover them amid the broken littoral of text and tale, and have gathered many that I believe deserve to be remembered and rediscovered. These then, are the tales of the lost and chivalrous knights within the Realm of King Arthur.

A WORD FROM THE SCRIBE OF THESE STORIES

The first shall be the story of 'The Perilous Cemetery', and several other tales of the noblest of knights. And after that shall come some stories of love, including that of 'The Sweet Sorrow of Sir Gawain' and 'The Tale of Tandereis and Flordibel', such as may warm the hearts of all who delight in such tales.

BOOK ONE

THE BOOK
OF THE KNIGHTS
ADVENTUROUS

ARTVS·REX

1: THE PERILOUS CEMETERY

⊹

MANY TALES I HAVE FOUND OF SIR GAWAIN OF ORKNEY, NEPHEW TO KING ARTHUR AND THE FIRST OF THE BROTHERS BORN TO KING LOT AND THE LADY MORGAUSE. IN ALL OF THESE, I HAVE FOUND NONE THAT FAIL TO PRAISE THE GREAT KNIGHT AS ONE OF THE FIRST AMONGST THE ROUND TABLE FELLOWSHIP. ONLY SIR LANCELOT OUTSHONE HIM, AND THERE ARE THOSE WHO SAY THAT THE KING'S NEPHEW WAS INDEED THE GREATER OF THE TWO. OF THIS I MAKE NO CLAIM TO KNOW THE TRUTH, ANY MORE THAN THOSE WHO FIRST SET DOWN THESE STORIES MAY DO – BUT IN THE TALE THAT I SHALL TELL HERE SIR GAWAIN IS SHOWN TO BE A VERY PILLAR OF CHIVALRY. ALSO, THERE IS A GREAT MYSTERY, FOR HERE IT IS SAID THAT GAWAIN DIED, AND YET THAT HE WAS NOT DEAD. AND SO, ALSO, THAT HE MET AND DEFEATED A DEMON OF HELL IN THE NAME OF OUR LORD JESU, AND SAVED A LADY WHOSE PERIL WAS PERHAPS THE GREATEST EVER ENDURED AMONG THOSE WHOM THE KNIGHTS OF THE ROUND TABLE HELPED.

⊹ ✠ ⊹

THE STORY BEGINS at Pentecost, when King Arthur held a great feast to which many knights, ladies and damosels came from all quarters of the kingdom – for to be seen at such a gathering was reward enough, and many of the women hoped to encounter one of the great Knights of the Round Table and to find favour with him, while the men sought to prove themselves in the lists and so perhaps become part of the Fellowship.

The first two days of the gathering passed as they were wont – with tournaments and hunting and games, as well as feasts serving only the best of repasts. Then, around the hour of *nones*,* when the king and queen and their guests were enjoying refreshments in the great hall, there came in a most beautiful damosel, clad in a scarlet gown trimmed with fur. She rode her palfrey right into the hall and

---

* Nones. The Ninth Hour, approximately 3 p.m. by current reckoning.

3

only stopped when she came before the king himself. There, she greeted him with great solemnity.

'Sire,' she said. 'I come to ask a boon that only you may grant. I swear that what I will ask be neither base nor unjust.'

'Tell me what it is that you desire,' said the king. 'If it is in my power I will surely grant it.'

'I ask only that for the duration of this feast, that I, and I alone, may be your cup-bearer and serve you faithfully at every repast. And one other thing I crave – that the bravest and greatest knight in this gathering will be my protector while I am here – for otherwise I may not stay.'

'Damosel,' answered the king. 'Both requests are fairly spoken and shall be granted. However, I do not know whom I may in fairness name as the greatest amongst this company. Is there perhaps one that you would yourself choose?'

'Sire,' replied the damosel. 'I cannot do as you wish. Surely you of all must know who is the best amongst your own knights.'

The king thought for a moment. Then he said: 'It is surely not right that I name one of my own kin as the noblest or best of my Fellowship. Yet there is one here who is handsome, brave and courteous to all. Many adventures has he undertaken and there are none in which he has failed that I know of. So if it please you, I ask that you accept my nephew, Sir Gawain, as your protector.'

To this the maiden responded that she was well pleased and, from the blush upon her cheeks, it was clear that the king's choice met with her wish. And it must be said that when Gawain saw the damosel, he was glad enough to accept the task, for she was indeed a most lovely maiden.

✣ ✣ ✣

ALL WAS WELL on that evening, and all there enjoyed the best of suppers, especially Gawain, who sat next to the damosel, whose name was Blanche, and who in turn served King Arthur nobly at the feast.

Next morning, all that were there attended mass in the great minster, and then returned for further feasting and games. But there the joyful meeting was broken by the arrival of a knight of unusual tallness, who rode into the hall, just as the damosel had done, and before anyone could do or say anything, seized the damosel Blanche from her place beside Sir Gawain and flung her across the crupper of his saddle.

So sudden was this action that all remained still, while Gawain struggled to know whether he should leap up, as he was given to do, or remain in his place until the king gave him leave to do so. Thus was his nobility proven, but by his action, a long and burdensome adventure began.

As all sat as though enspelled, the tall knight spoke haughtily: 'King Arthur, my name is Escanor. I am come to take away this lady, who is my sweetheart, and whom I have loved this long while. If any knight here is brave enough to fight for her, you should know that I shall be on the northern road from this place, and that I shall ride slowly enough to be easily overtaken.'

Without further ado the bold knight turned his horse about and galloped out of the hall, leaving all there amazed and wondering. Indeed, so angered by this was King Arthur, that he drove his knife deeply into the table, so that the blade broke. When they saw this many looked to Sir Gawain, who in turn looked towards the king. But before anyone else could speak, Sir Kay the Seneschal cried out that since none there – looking towards Gawain – had the courage to accept the knight's challenge, then he would do so. At this, Gawain could no longer keep silent. He rose to his feet and looked to the king. 'My Lord, the maiden was in my care. I beg you therefore to allow me to accept this challenge for the honour of the Round Table.'

'Go with my blessing,' said King Arthur, at which Sir Kay sat down unhappily, while Sir Gawain called for his armour and his great steed Gringolet. Then he set out, following the road to the north from Camelot the Golden. Soon he entered the Great Wood, but had not gone far when he heard an outcry coming from close at hand. Amongst other things he heard the cries of more than one woman, and a great lamentation from all.

Without hesitation, Gawain turned aside from the road and plunged into the trees. He quickly found himself in a clearing where a terrible sight met his eyes. Two maidens were gathered around a youth, who was not dead, but whose eyes had been blinded.

'Who has done this deed?' demanded Sir Gawain.

'Two knights were here,' said one of the ladies between her sobs. 'They killed a brave man and did what you see to his page!'

'That is nothing,' cried a second lady. 'We saw a far worse act that this!'

'Tell me,' said Sir Gawain grimly.

'We were accompanied by the brave knight whom this poor youth served. Our guardian was enjoying the morning and but lightly clad, without his armour. The two craven knights attacked him and though he fought bravely they slew him.'

'Alas!' cried the first damsel. 'When they had finished they cut up his body and took away the parts – as trophies they said. One took the head and limbs, the other the trunk. Alas that this should happen to one of the greatest knights of the Round Table, and that we were witness to it!'

'Which knight was it that was so vilely treated?' demanded Gawain. 'Be sure that I shall hunt down those who did this and end their lives.'

'Ah, fair sir,' the first lady said, wiping the tears from her cheeks. 'It was Sir Gawain who fell here. The bravest and most handsome of men.'

Astonished, Gawain said: 'I assure you that the knight you name was this very morning seated in King Arthur's hall.'

'That cannot be,' said the ladies. 'We have seen Sir Gawain before and recognised him, and the youth here once served as his squire and remembered him also.'

Gawain, feeling a cold splinter of fear in his heart, wondered greatly at this. His first thought was to pursue the knights who had done this deed and to prove that he was very much alive, but then came the memory of his appointed task. Though it was hard for him to leave the women and the wounded page, yet he could not ignore the task appointed to him by King Arthur.

'This shall not go unpunished,' he said. 'I must depart upon an urgent matter, but rest assured that I shall return and seek out those responsible for this barbarous act.' Then he added: 'I shall not give you my name at this time. Indeed I seem to have lost it.'

So saying, he mounted Gringolet and made his way back to the road, spurring his great steed to a gallop as he sought to overtake Escanor and the damosel Blanche.

After a while he saw a rider in the distance, and hastened to overtake him, but night was falling, and he soon found himself in a narrow valley at the head of which was a castle with mighty walls and a gatehouse huge enough that an army would have found it hard to overcome it. Gawain rode up to the gate and used the butt of his spear to hammer upon it. When he received no answer, he called loudly upon the porter to admit him. Finally, a voice spoke from behind the gate.

'I am sorry, Sir Knight, if such you are, but I cannot open the gate to you now that darkness has fallen. The lord of this castle is given instruction to this end, and I may not gainsay him.'

'It is late and the night is cold,' said Gawain. 'If you cannot let me in where else may I find hospitality nearby?'

'I fear there is no other place for many miles in any direction,' the porter answered. 'You may need to wander the forest and the moorlands throughout this night.'

No more would he say, so Gawain turned Gringolet about and rode back the way he had come. Less than a league hence he found himself outside a gracious chapel with a walled graveyard. No lights shone from within but the door opened to his touch and Sir Gawain entered.

The air was still and quiet within, so Gawain took off his armour and laid his shield and spears against the wall. Then he took the saddle from Gringolet and set him free to crop the grass. As he was doing this, he heard a rider approaching, and in the dim light of the risen moon saw a finely dressed young nobleman riding by, his horse laden down with the body of a freshly killed deer.

Gawain greeted him politely. 'It is late to be abroad,' he said.

When he heard this the man started and crossed himself several times.

'Lord Jesu defend me from such demons as you!' he cried.

'I am no demon,' replied Gawain. 'I am a knight of the Round Table who has taken refuge here this night. Tell me, in God's name,

why were you so fearful when I greeted you?'

When he heard Sir Gawain call upon the name of God, the man turned his horse and drew near. 'Do you not know?' he said, glancing all the while on every side as if he expected to be attacked at any moment. 'This is the Perilous Cemetery. None who enter here have lived to tell the tale.'

'How may this be?' requested Gawain.

Still glancing to every side in great fear, the nobleman told his story.

'Long ago a demon came to this place, some say more than one, but the truth is that no man who spends the night in this chapel has ever been seen again. Sometimes their bodies are discovered, rent in pieces, but mostly they are vanished away. So I beg you, good sir, return to my home, the castle which is but a short distance away, and I will see to it that you are well housed.'

'I have already tried to gain admittance,' said Sir Gawain. 'But it was refused to me – I assume because of fear for this demon you describe.'

'That is so,' answered the young nobleman. 'It is my home, and that of my sister. I set out early this day in search of game, but it took much longer than I had expected. My servants will be fearful for my safety, but they will not open the gates. However, they will let down a ladder from the wall. Come with me and you will be safe for the night.'

'But what of our horses?' asked Sir Gawain.

'They can be left to fend for themselves outside. The demon will not harm them and we can bring them in on the morrow.'

'My steed does not know this place,' answered Gawain. 'He may wander too far and be attacked by wolves. I cannot leave him thus. I will remain here this night and take whatever comes to pass.'

'Then I fear this may be the last words we

exchange,' said the young nobleman. 'May I at least know your name, so that I may tell others who come seeking you how you perished.'

'I am Sir Gawain, King's Arthur's nephew.'

'Then I am doubly sorry,' said the nobleman. 'For such a brave knight as you deserves a better end.'

'As to that,' replied Sir Gawain, 'what shall be, will be.'

When he saw that Gawain would not change his mind, the young man prepared to depart. But before he did so Gawain told him the story of Escanor and the damosel he had stolen. 'I am come to rescue her, but since I may not enter the castle, where I am sure they have taken shelter – may I ask that you and your sister protect the damosel from her captor this night? If I am alive on the morrow I will come to win her back myself.'

To this, the young nobleman agreed, adding that Escanor was well known in that part of the land as a dangerous man. Then he bade farewell to Sir Gawain, and set off at full speed for the castle.

When he arrived there, as he had promised, the young nobleman's servants were watching out for him from the walls, and at once threw down a ladder for him to climb. Thus he entered the castle and went immediately to speak with his sister. He explained how Sir Gawain had come to rescue the maiden – who had indeed taken shelter with her abductor for the night – and that Gawain had begged that she should be cared for and kept apart from her captor. Then he summoned their guests and demanded that the tall knight give the damosel into their keeping.

Angrily, Escanor refused, but the young nobleman made it clear that if he did not do as he was requested he would be thrown into the dungeons for the night.

So it was that Escanor was given a room and placed under guard, while the damosel Blanche was taken to a chamber where the lady of the castle took care of her and saw that her every need was fulfilled.

Meanwhile, despite the encroaching darkness, Sir Gawain spent some time exploring the chapel and the graveyard, and though he saw no sign of any demon, he felt the cold and unchancy air of the place, and donned his armour again and drew his sword in readiness for attack.

When none came he seated himself on a mighty stone sarcophagus to await whatever might come. Soon he felt a stirring of the air, then the lid of the tomb on which he rested moved beneath him, so that he sprang off it and raised his sword. The lid of the tomb lifted further and fell back upon the ground. Then out of the grave came a most beautiful maiden, who seemed to Sir Gawain far from dead. Here was no corpse wrapped in a winding sheet and stinking of rottenness, but the most womanly maiden, who smiled upon him and greeted him by name.

Gawain made the sign of the cross, but the lovely woman showed no fear at this and begged him not to be afraid.

'I am no demon,' she said, 'but one who has suffered greatly.'

'How do you come to be here, sleeping in this tomb?' asked Gawain.

'My name is Alisand,' said the lady, and tears coursed down her cheeks as she told her story. 'My mother died when I was still a child and my father married again, a lady of greater station than himself. She was fair to look upon, but her heart was black, for as I grew to maidenhood she became jealous, and used spells and incantations to make me appear mad. For several years this continued, and many of these I spent locked away to hide my seeming sickness from the world. Then, one day when I was deemed well enough to go out alone, I went for a walk in the forest, and as I did so I met a man along the way. He seemed of gentle nature and when he learned of my story, promised that he would cure me of all the dark things my stepmother had forced upon me. In my desperation I agreed to allow this, and in truth he carried out his promise, but only then did I learn that he was in fact a demon from Hell. Since then I have been his prisoner, his plaything, and every night I am forced to sleep in this stone sarcophagus.'

Gawain, deeply shocked by this, put away his sword.

'How may I help you, my lady? For this is indeed a dark tale that you tell.'

'I fear there is only one way you may do so,' answered the Lady Alisand. 'The demon will have sensed your presence, and will be coming to destroy you – as he has all of the other knights who dared to spend the night in this haunted place. If you can defeat him, then I will be set free.'

'Then I shall do what I can,' said Gawain. 'Though if I can kill a demon or not, I do not know.'

'While the creature is in human form, it is vulnerable,' the lady answered. 'I have seen those who fought with him inflict wounds upon him – but always he has been victorious.'

Even as she spoke, there came the sound of hoofbeats on the road and next moment the demon himself appeared. Though he seemed human in appearance, armed and accoutred like a knight, Gawain saw that the eyes that looked at him through the slits of its helmet flashed red, and the voice, when it spoke, seemed to come from a far-off place.

'Who is this that dares challenge me?' demanded the fiend. 'Who dares even speak to my lady, who belongs only to me?'

When Gawain answered with his name, the demon laughed aloud. 'So, I have at last a challenge worthy of my skill!' it cried, and at once leapt from its horse's back and unsheathed its sword. Gawain seized his shield and drew his own sword, and there in the graveyard, while the lady from the tomb looked on in fear, began the most terrible fight of Sir Gawain's life.

Again and again he struck out at the demon, only to find his weapon seemed not to have any power, while his opponent's blows opened several wounds on him. And all the while the demon laughed and seemed not to tire. Sparks were struck from their armour, and both their shields were soon in ribbons. Harder and harder Sir Gawain fought, but each time he was driven back. Summoning his greatest strength he hewed and hacked, at last landing a blow that seemed to shake his opponent, and all the while Gawain felt his own strength diminishing.

At last, as he was once again driven back against the wall of the graveyard, the Lady Alisand called out to him: 'Do not forget you are fighting a demon. Call upon God to give you strength!'

At that moment, Sir Gawain looked to where the figure of the crucified Christ was carved above the door to the chapel. From this he drew fresh strength and renewed his attack upon the demon knight.

At last he beat back his adversary, striking him with blow after blow. Both had now lost parts of their armour, broken or hacked into pieces by the ferocity of their attack. Now, Gawain delivered a blow which cracked the helm of his adversary and sheared away the visor, revealing the ugly face beneath. At that

PLATE I: *'The lid of the tomb lifted further and fell back upon the ground. Then out of the grave came a most beautiful maiden, who seemed to Sir Gawain far from dead'*

moment, Gawain made the sign of the cross and struck one more time. His blow cut away half the demon's face so that it screamed and fell back. Gawain followed up his advantage, striking blow after blow until at last the fiend's head was severed from its body. Dark smoke escaped from the creature's form and with a dreadful cry it expired upon the earth.

Gawain, in his weakness, almost fell there himself, but the Lady Alisand, weeping for joy, brought him water to drink, all the while praising him and thanking him for setting her free.

With her help Gawain was able to get back upon his horse, and with the lady sitting before him, he made his way to the castle. By this time dawn was breaking and those who had kept watch through the night cried out in wonder as Gawain and the Lady Alisand approached. Not one in a hundred knights had survived their encounter with the demon; to see how Sir Gawain, though wounded, held his head high, and how the lady clung to him, filled all with joy.

The young nobleman whom he had met the night before came forth to greet them and invited Gawain to rest and recover from the battle. Everyone there praised his courage and strength.

Sir Gawain thanked them all, but asked if his request that the damosel he had come in search of had been given into the keeping of the young nobleman's sister, as he had asked.

He learned that she had indeed been separated from her captor, but that in the morning he had reclaimed her and that they had departed at sunrise. Once again Escanor had warned that anyone who came near the damosel would need to fight him, and none there had taken up his challenge, so that he had departed unchecked.

'Then I must follow him,' said Sir Gawain.

Though in truth he was weary unto death by his combat with the demon knight.

'That you most assuredly must not do,' said the young nobleman. 'I know where Escanor can be found, and I can bring you there when you are sufficiently healed. If you encounter him now you will surely die.'

So Gawain agreed, though in his heart he longed to depart at once. The party returned to the castle where a surgeon searched and dressed his wounds and a bath was drawn for him, and fresh clothing brought. Once he had eaten, Gawain was shown to a great bed in which he could rest, and he fell at once into a dreamless sleep.

In the morning he woke refreshed and called for his armour and weapons. But so battered and dented were his breastplate, greaves and helm, that he looked on them in dismay. At once the young nobleman proclaimed that he would not permit any knight, especially one to whom they owed so much, to depart without being properly accoutred. Then he called for fresh armour of the finest kind, and with gratitude Sir Gawain donned it. He then received a fresh shield and helm, and several strong spears.

Meanwhile, the Lady Alisand came to him and begged him to allow her to go with him in search of Escanor. At first Gawain was reluctant, but she pleaded with him so eloquently that at last he agreed. Thus they set off together, accompanied by the young nobleman, who knew where Escanor had gone.

It was not long before they reached the castle which belonged to the tall knight. Scarcely had they arrived at the walls before Escanor himself appeared, clad in rich armour and ready for battle. When he saw Sir Gawain, he laughed aloud. 'At last, we meet! I have long wished for this moment.'

'I was many times in Camelot the Golden,' answered Gawain. 'Why did you not seek me out there?'

'I preferred to challenge King Arthur and all his knights,' answered Escanor haughtily. 'I sent my own lady to the court and then stole her from under the very noses of the famous Knights of the Round Table. Soon, perhaps, I shall add a second lady to my house,' he added, looking at the fair Alisand.

At this Sir Gawain frowned. All the adventures leading to this moment had been to enable him to recover the damosel placed in his care. Now he understood why she had not cried out or indeed struggled when Escanor abducted her. All this time, she had been a willing part of the tall knight's plot.

The realisation of this trick raised Gawain's ire. 'I am glad the time has come for us to test each other,' he said, and prepared himself for battle.

So the two knights came together with all the might of their steeds. Both shattered their lances upon each other, and both fell back almost unhorsed by the power of their clash. Sir Gawain, still weakened by his recent battle with the demon, felt Escanor's undoubted strength, while the tall knight was forced to acknowledge the prowess of his opponent.

Two more spears they broke before they drew apart and Gawain said: 'Let us continue on foot for the sake of our mounts.'

'I am ready,' said Escanor fiercely, and dismounted, drawing his sword.

So they came together again, and little there was to hear but the clash of sword against sword, sword on shield or hauberk – the clang of the weapons almost drowning out the quick, rough breathing of the two men. For several hours longer they fought and Sir Gawain began to tire. His recent wounds burst open and blood ran down his armour. As for Escanor, his confidence waned as he felt the determination of his opponent. His shield was shattered and his breastplate so dented that he felt shaken, while his strength diminished with each passing moment.

At length, Sir Gawain renewed his attack and delivered such a mighty blow to his adversary's helm that the sword cut through the metal and deep into Escanor's brainpan. The knight fell dead in an instant, while Gawain stood still, almost too weakened to move.

The Lady Alisand and the young nobleman both cheered the king's nephew and came forward to help him. At this moment the damosel Blanche, who had been part of the dead knight's scheme, came from the gates of the castle, wailing loudly for the death of her lord.

Gawain, when he saw her, pulled off his helmet and approached her. 'I am sorry that you have lost your love,' he said. 'It is unfortunate that you chose to be part of his plot. He could have challenged me at any time by coming to King Arthur's court.'

The damosel continued to weep, and in response Sir Gawain promised to bring her back to Camelot the Golden and there to find a knight who would accept her as lover or wife, for she was indeed a most beautiful maiden. And the Lady Alisand agreed to return to the castle where they had spent the night, and to comfort the Lady Blanche.

So the party made their way back to the young nobleman's home. There Gawain was given time to recover from his second great battle, but his mind was already turning to the women and the grievously wounded squire, whom he had left behind in the Great Wood while he sought out Escanor and the damosel.

As soon as he felt well enough, he took his leave of his new friends and set off back to where he had last seen the sad party. His mind was much occupied with the mystery of his own reported death, which, for all his strength, and the fact that he was very much alive, troubled him deeply.

First, he returned to the place where he had encountered the women and the wounded page. But of them there was no sign, nor did anyone that he met upon the road know anything of them or where they might be found.

So Gawain began a long search. For many weeks he travelled back and forth through the forest where he had met the ladies, but no one knew of them or had any knowledge of the two knights who had claimed to have slain the great Sir Gawain.

The true owner of that name continued his search – until one day he met a knight named Sir Tristan. The story tells us this was not the famous hero who loved the Queen of Cornwall, and who became one of the greatest of the Fellowship of the Round Table. This man was named Sir Tristan Who Cannot Laugh (though I cannot say why this was so) but on the day they met he offered Gawain the hospitality of his castle, and that night, as they sat at table, the host told a tale that, he claimed, was the most sorrowful thing he had heard for many a day.

'There were two fine ladies who lived not far from here,' he began. 'They were deeply loved by two knights, one named Sir Gomeret, the other who goes by the name Orgueilleux* – though I believe this is more a description of his nature than his true name. The two women were loved by these men, and again and again they tried to plead their suit to them. Each time the ladies refused, saying that they were already in love with one of the greatest knights of all

of King Arthur's kingdom, and they would give themselves to no other but him. When the men demanded to know the name of this knight, the women told them: Sir Gawain – the most peerless knight of all. And if it chanced that he chose only one of them, then the other would consider only the Red Knight of the Red Launds, of whom it is told, in another tale, that he stole a cup from King Arthur's table and spilled wine into the lap of the queen.[†]

'When Gomeret and Orgueilleux heard this, they were beside themselves with jealousy, and swore that they would seek out Sir Gawain and the Red Knight and kill both of them – for only thus could they win the love of the two ladies.

'Now it is known that the Red Knight had been already slain by Sir Perceval, he who seeks the Grail with Sir Galahad, Sir Bors, and many other knights of the Round Table. So the two men sought only Sir Gawain, and finding him riding with his squire – both of them only lightly armed – they attacked and slew the great knight, and inflicted a terrible wound upon the squire. I have heard it said that the ladies found the wounded youth – but they did not find the body of Sir Gawain, for the two knights had cut his body into pieces and carried them off to different places.'

All of this Gawain heard in wonder. Finally he broke in upon Sir Tristan's narrative. 'This is the very adventure I have sought these long weeks. Tell me, how did you hear of this, and do you know anything of the whereabouts of these two dastard knights.'

'I heard this story from Sir Gomeret and Sir Orgueilleux themselves,' the host replied. 'They came here seeking shelter and bragged

---

* Prideful.

† See *Perceval ou le Conte du Graal* by Chrétien de Troyes for this story.

11

❖ *The Demon Knight* ❖

that they had slain Sir Gawain. Indeed, they had parts of the body with them. In their pride they offered to show me one of the arms of the dead knight, and this I allowed them to do, for scarce could I believe Sir Gawain was truly dead.'

'And did you see the arm?' asked Gawain.

'Not only that, but I begged them to give it into my keeping, and thanks to their pride they felt at having slain one of the greatest of the Round Table knights, they agreed.'

'Do you have this relic here?' demanded Gawain.

'I do indeed,' replied his host.

'Then if you would show it to me I would be most grateful, for I swear that I have seen Sir Gawain only recently, and that he was alive!'

So Sir Tristan had the severed arm brought to him, all wrapped in silk, and showed it to Sir Gawain as though it was a holy relic. 'Be

sure that I am determined to have it encased in gold and silver,' he said. 'The best that any goldsmith may accomplish.'

Gawain looked at the arm, all the while giving thanks to God that he was fully alive, for all his sadness that another had died for him. At last, he asked: 'Tell me if the two ladies were persuaded by this deed to accept their suitors?'

'I believe they were not,' answered his host. 'When they heard that the famous knight whom they loved had been slain, they were so distraught that they fainted and were speechless for several days. When they recovered they swore they would rather kill themselves than have anything to do with Sir Gawain's killers.'

Gawain was silent for a time, staring at the grisly relic. Then he said: 'Sir, if you know where I may find these knights whose heinous deeds you have related, please tell me.'

'I will do so gladly,' said Sir Tristan. 'Had I

12

known who they were I would not have given them shelter in my home. Sir Gomeret has set up a pavilion not far from here in the forest. There he awaits anyone willing to dispute with him for being one who helped kill Sir Gawain. Orgueilleux has retired to his own castle, to which I can also guide you. He, too, lets it be known that he will do battle with anyone who contests his part in the death of King Arthur's nephew.'

N EXT MORNING SIR Gawain set out, accompanied by his host for the first few miles. They spoke little along the road, for each, in turn, had much to think about – Gawain of the dark deed that the two jealous knights had undertaken; Sir Tristan, concerning the truth or otherwise of the story he had believed.

After a time Sir Tristan turned back for home, leaving Gawain to continue alone until he came to where Sir Gomeret had pitched his pavilion in the depths of the Great Wood. Within moments, the knight arrived, already clad in black armour and riding a horse of the same midnight colour.

'Be careful, Sir Knight!' he cried. 'Before you approach me, know that I am one of those who killed the great Sir Gawain!'

'Stop telling your baseless lies,' answered the true wielder of that name. 'If that knight of whom you speak were to encounter twenty men like you, he would slay them all before noon!'

'Nevertheless, I have the body of he whom we killed, that proves otherwise!' answered Gomeret angrily. 'Orgueilleux has the limbs and the head.'

'Then defend yourself,' said Gawain. 'For I swear that I have seen the king's nephew many

times of late, and so I shall disprove your false claim with the strength of my body.'

So the two knights came together, and fought – oh, how long and hard they fought! – until Sir Gawain at last felled his opponent and stood ready to slay him. Gomeret begged for mercy, and Gawain, despite his anger against the knight, granted it, ordering his fallen foe to swear that he would attend King Arthur's court within the next week. 'There you shall see the one you claimed to have killed,' he added, and Gomeret grew pale when he heard this, and began to doubt his own story. Nevertheless he gave his word that he would go to Camelot the Golden in the next few days.

Sir Gawain now followed the way his host had told him, until he reached the castle where Orgueilleux dwelled. Gawain rode up to the gates and demanded the knight to come forth. Orgueilleux did not need any encouragement. He was soon ready, armed and accoutred and prepared for battle.

The two engaged at once, and such was Gawain's skill and strength, doubtless increased by his anger towards the false knight, that he quickly brought Orgueilleux to his knees. When the fallen man begged for mercy, Sir Gawain asked why he should be spared. 'For you have killed at least one man in unknightly fashion, and blinded a page. Also you spread a lie that has caused much pain for those who believed it.'

'I sought only to persuade the lady with whom I was in love to acknowledge me,' cried the fallen man. 'Just as did Sir Gormeret.'

'Then I shall tell you the truth,' said Gawain. 'I am he whom you claim to have slain.' So saying he removed his helmet so that Orgueilleux could see his face.

The knight turned pale at this. 'I promise you the man I helped kill looked much like you.'

'That may be so,' answered Gawain. 'But still you attacked both men while they were yet lightly armed, which is a most unchivalrous act.'

'I can only swear that I was driven mad by my feelings of love, and cared for nothing else,' said Orgueilleux. 'I appeal to the mercy of the Great King Arthur.'

At this Sir Gawain sheathed his sword and helped Orgueilleux to stand.

'It is for the king to decide your fate. As Sir Gomeret has promised, so I now demand of you. Attend the court at Camelot the Golden within one week and all shall be decided there.'

Orgueilleux gave his word, and Sir Gawain took leave of him and began his journey back to the court. You may be sure that when he arrived, all of those present came out joyfully to greet him, for word of his death had reached there in the last few days and all had been prepared to mourn him.

King Arthur embraced his nephew. 'This story is one that must be told this day, before all,' he said.

And so it was. The Fellowship, the Queen's Knights, and the Lords of Britain were gathered that night, and all listened to Sir Gawain as he told, with great modesty, the story of the Perilous Cemetery and the rumours of his own death. Even in that great assembly, few had known such adventures, and Sir Gawain was even more praised than before. The next day, the Lady Alisand arrived at the court and was required to tell her story again. Soon after this, Gomeret and Orgueilleux arrived, both still nursing their wounds and greatly chastened. King Arthur heard them speak of their actions, both claiming that love had driven them mad.

The king then summoned the two ladies who had promised only to wed Sir Gawain, and of them he enquired of their feelings at this time. Both hung their heads in shame, and gave their apologies to Gawain, who granted them forgiveness, believing them to have suffered enough. Then the king bade the foolish ladies to face the two knights, and this they did with much sadness upon both sides.

First the king asked the knights if they were still in love with the ladies, to which both assented. Next he asked the ladies what their feelings were towards the knights. Both, with great timidity, confessed that, while they deplored the actions of the knights, they felt they had learned their lesson and had earned their affection.

'Only one thing would cause me to allow you to live,' said King Arthur. 'If you were able restore the sight of the youth you so grievously wounded.'

At this Orgueilleux spoke up. 'Sire, this I may do, for I am partly of Faery origin and have been granted powers not available to humankind.'

And as the court looked on in wonder Orgueilleux made an incantation that summoned the page, who of a sudden stood among them all, blinking in the light and marvelling that his sight was restored. Then King Arthur pardoned both Gomeret and Orgueilleux, though insisting that they should do penance for the deaths of the unknown man and the pain they had caused to the page. Further, the king commanded that they bring the scattered parts of the dead knight to Camelot the Golden, so that he might be properly interred. This they did, and it is said that Sir Gawain looked upon the face of the unknown man and saw there some likeness to himself – though not sufficient to be the cause of his death. Not long after, word came that established the dead man's name as Sir Courtois of Huberlant, so that his grave could be marked with his true name.

Within a year of this, the two maidens who believed themselves to be in love with Sir Gawain married the knights who had fought so hard for them, and the tale tells that Gawain himself was present at the ceremony and smiled upon them all.

At this time also, Sir Tristan (Who Could Not Laugh) came to Camelot the Golden, and with him the Lady Alisand and the damosel Blanche. As he had promised, Gawain presented her to the court and made it known that she sought a man to love and protect her. Nor was it long before such a man came forward, though his name is not told, and their alliance was soon celebrated. Last of all, it transpired that the Lady Alisand had fallen in love with Sir Tristan during their time together, and so they too were married. And it is said of the Lady Alisand that she was never again troubled by a demon of Hell.

✢ ✠ ✢

SO IS THIS story of Sir Gawain told – how he was believed dead but yet lived; how he fought and defeated the demon of the perilous cemetery; and how his fame grew from that moment onward.

———— ✢ ————

EXPLICIT THE STORY OF THE PERILOUS CEMETERY.

INCIPIT THE TALE OF HUNBAUT.

2: THE TALE OF HUNBAUT

THERE CAN BE LITTLE DOUBT THAT OF ALL THE KNIGHTS OF THE ROUND TABLE, SIR GAWAIN WAS THE MOST LOVED AND THE MOST PRAISED. SIR LANCELOT AND SIR GALAHAD, SIR TRISTAN AND SIR PERCEVAL HAVE THEIR PLACES IN THE ROLE OF HONOUR, BUT GAWAIN OVERTOPS THEM ALL. SO IT IS PERHAPS SURPRISING THAT THIS CURIOUS TALE THAT I RETELL HERE, DRAWN FROM FRAGMENTS OF A WORK THAT LAY FORGOTTEN FOR MANY YEARS, PLACES THE GREAT KNIGHT IN A ROLE THAT IS LESS HEROIC AND LESS WORTHY OF CELEBRATION THAN MANY OTHERS. INSTEAD WE ARE OFFERED SIR HUNBAUT, A KNIGHT WHOSE NAME BARELY APPEARS UPON THE ROSTER OF THE ROUND TABLE FELLOWSHIP, BUT WHO IS SHOWN HERE AS ONE WHOSE GENEROSITY OF SPIRIT FAR OUTWEIGHS THAT OF SIR GAWAIN. I INCLUDE IT HERE BOTH FROM A SENSE OF FAIRNESS, AND BECAUSE I DOUBT NOT THAT HAD HE ENCOUNTERED IT IN HIS READING, MASTER THOMAS MALORY WOULD HAVE READILY ADDED IT TO THE ADVENTURES HE SO WISELY NARRATED.

✠ ✠ ✠

WHEN THE FEAST of Pentecost arrived each year, King Arthur let cry a great celebration which included tournaments, feasts, and the coming together of as many of the Round Table Fellowship as was possible. On the occasion of which I speak, many of the greatest knights and the most beautiful of ladies were present, including Sir Gawain, Sir Sagramore, Sir Galyhodyn, and Sir Grummor Grummerson, as well as the ladies Elaine, Morgana, and Sir Gawain's sister, Helice. Together these mighty heroes and their beauteous ladies celebrated the festival, led by King Arthur and Queen Guinevere, and others close to them. They attended mass in the great minster of Camelot the Golden, and feasted each night in the vaulted hall.

Despite the presence of so many noble lords and ladies, King Arthur was especially glad when the bold knight Sir Hunbaut, who had been absent in search of adventure for more than two long years, arrived in time to join the company in celebrating the holy feast and the many great deeds of the Round Table.

King Arthur and Sir Hunbaut spoke together into the deep of the night, and amongst other things the knight raised the name of the King of the Far Isles, who, despite many requests to do so, refused to bow the knee to the High King Arthur, and to serve him as did the greatest of the Lords of Logres.

'I have heard it said that the king mocks you, sire, and speaks openly of his defiance of your desire to have him join with the other nobles in offering service to you.'

When he heard this King Arthur frowned. 'Perhaps it is time to send another envoy to the Far Isles, to request yet again that their king join with the other nobles in acknowledging my overlordship.'

Next morning the king spoke to his nephew, Sir Gawain, charging him with the task of bringing this rebel lord to heel. Gawain readily agreed to undertake this task, and begged that his sister, the Lady Helice, might be allowed to accompany him. She was, he said, wishing to journey to visit her cousin in the country of Strathclyde, which lay far from Camelot the Golden on the road leading to the Far Isles.

To this King Arthur agreed, and Gawain and Helice prepared to set forth. Only when they had departed did Hunbaut approach the king, and with all gentleness and good intent, ask if his nephew was indeed the best choice for this task.

'Sir Gawain is one of your greatest knights, my lord,' he said. 'But you know that he can be hot-tempered and less gentle than might be wished.'

King Arthur thought for a moment, then nodded his head. 'You speak truly, Sir Hunbaut,' he said. 'I am mindful to send you after my nephew to join with him. Your more temperate ways may avail us better in this task.'

So it was that Hunbaut set out at once, and by dint of riding full pelt, overtook Sir Gawain and his sister upon the road. Gawain was, indeed, most glad to see his fellow knight and the three made an excellent company as they continued upon their way.

Soon after, they entered a part of the Great Wood that seemed especially dark, and then it was that Hunbaut began to question if it were wise to bring the Lady Helice into a place where many kinds of danger could threaten her, even with the presence of the two knights.

At first Sir Gawain questioned this, while the lady herself protested that no one would dare attack her while accompanied by the finest of the Round Table Fellowship. But at that moment there came in sight another knight, who greeted the companions graciously and without challenge. The three men fell to talking, and he who had joined them, his name was Gorvin Cadrus. He, who as you shall see, fought long and bitterly with Sir Meraugis de la Portlesguez for the hand the Lady Lidoine,[*] hearing of Gawain and Hunbaut's concern for the Lady Helice, at once offered to escort her to her destination, which lay upon his own road.

To this the Round Table knights agreed, and the lady also, since she saw how pleasant the knight was. And it may seem to those who read this tale that Gawain and Hunbaut acted carelessly in agreeing to let her go with an unknown man, but it should be understood that such was the power of the Round Table Fellowship and the excellence of King Arthur's rule, that neither considered for a moment that their companion might act in an unknightly fashion.

---

* See 'Meraugis and the Wounds of Love' pp. 132–146.

Gawain, especially, should have remembered that Gorvin Cadrus had acted in an unknightly fashion against Sir Meraugis, but such was his eagerness to continue on his way to the Far Isles that he failed to recognise one who had once been an enemy of the Round Table.

So it was that the two parties went their separate ways, Gawain and Hunbaut following the road to where they could take ship for the Far Isles, while the Lady Helice went in the company of Gorvin Cadrus. What happened to her we shall wait to hear, as the story here follows the two great knights upon their way.

☩ ☩ ☩

THEIR WAY LED them through a many changing land, and I believe they met with more than one adventure as they journeyed north. But as the first day of their journey drew to a close, the two knights found themselves near a castle, where they prepared to seek shelter. Before they did so, Hunbaut spoke to Sir Gawain. 'I have stayed in this castle before,' he said. 'Its lord is a noble and honourable man, but he possesses a daughter who is beautiful to look upon and as sweet as the birds in the trees. Be careful not to pay her too much attention, for her father makes every effort to protect her from any man who casts his eyes upon her. I have heard of men blinded or even hung for daring to look too fondly at her.'

To this Sir Gawain assented, though it must be said that his interest in the damsel of the castle was immediately piqued.

The knights were well received at the castle and were soon seated in the hall before a most noble feast. As they were about to enjoy this, the noble lord's daughter, whose name was Elin, entered, accompanied by her ladies.

In accordance with her father's wishes she was seated between the two visiting knights. As he looked upon her Sir Gawain at once thought that she was one of the most beautiful maidens he had ever seen (which, considering the many faery women whom he had loved, was surely a sign of the damsel's beauty). As the meal continued, he began to talk with her at length; nor was the lady herself immune to the charms of the handsome knight, whose fame had gone far before him and whose gentle speech soon captured her heart.

Hunbaut, who sat close with them, saw how things stood, and did all that he could to distract the lord of the castle by engaging him in conversation about the deeds and triumphs of the Round Table.

So it was that the evening passed pleasantly until the time came for those who wished to retire for the night. Elin herself rose and bade the company goodnight, but before she could depart her father reminded her that she should bid the two great knights a gentle repose, and that, in the name of hospitality she should kiss each one of them.

This the Lady Elin did, but while she kissed Sir Hunbaut but lightly on the cheek, Sir Gawain she kissed not once but four times upon the mouth, and with more enthusiasm than seemed right.

At once, the lord rose up in rage and called for Gawain to be seized and thrown into the dungeons. Only Hunbaut's knightly speech calmed him, and Gawain himself praised the nobility of the lady and her gentle greeting. Thus mollified, the noble lord was calmed and allowed all present to retire, which they did, undoubtedly glad that the evening had ended without further quarrel.

However, though she bowed her head before her father's wrath, once the castle fell silent and all were abed Elin made her way quietly

→ *A dog-headed creature* ←

to the chamber given to Sir Gawain, and there, to his great delight, she joined him in his bed and the two enjoyed great disports throughout the night.

Before dawn the lady left to return to her own chamber, and soon after, without any sign of hostility from their host, the two knights left the castle and once again took to the road. There, Hunbaut reproved Gawain for ignoring his warning, to which the great knight responded: 'I am not made of wood,' and that the damsel's beauty had overwhelmed him. But of this liaison, the story speaks no more, and it is not told if the lady ever again laid eyes upon the king's nephew.

✠ ✠ ✠

THE REMAINDER OF the day passed pleasantly enough, though the two knights spoke little as Sir Hunbaut brooded upon the events of the past night. As dusk began to settle over the land the knights saw where a fire flickered between the trees, and both smelled the aroma of roasting meat. Gawain, who had also spoken little that day but spent much of it thinking of the damsel of the castle, smiled and said: 'Let us have some sport!' Then he spurred his mount into a gallop and rode into the clearing where several men had set up camp and were about to eat.

Roaring loudly and waving his sword, Gawain scattered them all, and while Hunbaut watched, drove the party off into the forest. Then, laughing, Gawain plucked meat from the deer roasting over the fire and called out to Hunbaut to join him.

This the knight did, though with some reluctance, and not without words of warning that those who had made camp there must soon return and would feel no friendship towards those who had so rudely interrupted their feast.

Gawain waved away all such concerns. 'They will not begrudge a small part of their meal to two hungry knights, I am sure,' he said.

Soon after, Hunbaut's warning was fulfilled

when a dozen men, armed and accoutred, rode into the clearing. The leader, clearly a knight from his shield and weapons, demanded to know by what right the two men had attacked them and stolen their food. Hunbaut, anticipating an angry response from Sir Gawain, at once begged their forgiveness. He had recognised the knight whose camp this was and addressed him by name. 'Greetings, Sir Landunas. We were but jesting and meant no harm. See how little of your food and wine we have enjoyed.'

The knight thus allowed his anger to be assuaged, and when Sir Gawain himself joined in asking his forgiveness for their behaviour, swords were sheathed and spears laid to one side, and the three knights and the rest of Sir Landunas' company settled down to enjoy their feast in a companionable manner.

It fell out that Sir Landunas was lord of a nearby manor, which guarded the only port offering access to the Far Isles, and once having become friends – despite Gawain's bold entrance – both he and Sir Hunbaut were invited to rest in his home that night, and to take ship with Landunas's blessing on the morrow.

N EXT DAY, THE two knights crossed the sea to the Far Isles without incident. When they stepped ashore, they found their way blocked by a powerful knight who guarded the entrance to the Isle. Gawain was ready to fight with him, but Hunbaut engaged him in conversation and in this way avoided direct confrontation, allowing them to continue on their way.

Soon they came within sight of the grim fortress where the King of the Far Isles had his court. As they rode towards it they saw a narrow bridge that stretched across the moat. There stood a powerful man with a club who defied them to cross. Gawain, without hesitation, spurred his mount forward and rode at the man full tilt. He, leaping to one side to avoid the mounted knight, fell from the bridge into the water with a great cry.

Hunbaut followed Gawain and together they rode through the gates of the castle and into a wide courtyard. Here they were met by a dwarf who called out to Sir Gawain, calling him a ruffian and a fool. 'Did you not know that the man you almost killed by riding him down had a leg made of wood?' cried the dwarf. 'You are no knight – more of a churl than a nobleman!'

At this Gawain became enraged, and before Hunbaut could restrain him drew his sword and struck the dwarf down.

In truth, Sir Hunbaut was shocked by this show of rage, and even Gawain himself regretted his hasty action. But since there was nothing that could be done for the dwarf, the two knights made their way to the entrance to the keep.

There they were met by a well-spoken seneschal, who nonetheless looked askance when he learned that the knights came from King Arthur's court. Despite this they were shown into the presence of the king, and Gawain, as abruptly as ever, told him that he must pay a tribute to King Arthur or suffer the consequences.

The King of the Far Isles showed his displeasure at this, threatening to have the two 'insolent' knights killed. At the same time a messenger came post haste and told how Gawain had ridden down the guardian of the bridge, and then slain the dwarf. At this the King of the Far Isles summoned his guards and Gawain and Hunbaut drew their swords and held them at bay with mighty strokes and great bravery. But at length, so greatly outnumbered were they that Hunbaut said: 'Come. We have delivered the words of King Arthur. Let us leave this place until its lord decides whether he will acknowledge our noble sire or not.'

Reluctantly, Sir Gawain agreed, and the two knights retreated from the King of the Far Isles' guards and hastened back to the ship. They soon reached the mainland and set out upon the long road back to Camelot the Golden, but soon after they encountered the knight named Griflet le Fils le Do. He explained that after many weeks, when neither Gawain nor Hunbaut, and most concerning of all, the Lady Helice, had returned from their journey to the Far Isles, the king himself had declared that he would go forth, accompanied by a dozen knights, to search for the missing men and his niece.

Greatly distressed by this, Gawain and Hunbaut set out to look for Helice themselves, while Sir Griflet was sent back to tell King Arthur that the two knights were safe and well. At the first crossroads they reached they agreed to go separately so that they might cover a greater area. Hunbaut took the road to the east, while Gawain rode west in search of his sister, but found no sign of her.

Turning back at last from his fruitless quest, he came to the bank of a river and saw there a ferry large enough to carry twelve men and their steeds. There, he met Sir Kay the Seneschal, Sir Sagramore and Sir Brandelis, who were about to embark. But as they were preparing to go aboard, the ferryman came to them and told them of a strange enchantment upon the craft. If an odd number of passengers were aboard at one time, the craft would cross safely, but if an even number it would founder.

Since Sir Gawain would have made them an even number, and since he was so urgent in his desire to seek for his sister, the other knights allowed him to go ahead alone. As he reached the further shore and rode off into the forest, King Arthur himself arrived and by dint of dividing into two groups, both he and his men were able to cross the river.

Seeking to overtake his nephew, King Arthur and his men followed the path on which he had last been seen and soon arrived at a castle named Gaut Desert, whose lady very happily made them welcome. She only expressed her sorrow that Sir Gawain, whom she secretly loved, was not amongst the knights with the king, but Sir Kay spoke of seeing him at the ford and expressed his belief that the king's nephew would soon join them.

As the party prepared to go in to supper, Sir Kay happened to pass a chamber where he thought he saw Sir Gawain, but when he drew near he found that it was in fact a statue, carved from painted wood. Indeed, it so closely resembled Gawain that it would have been almost impossible to tell it apart from the knight himself. When Sir Kay hastened to tell the king of this, the lady of the castle, overhearing, blushed red as a sunset and confessed that she felt a great love for the king's nephew, even though they had never met, and that she had caused the creation of the statue, which stood by her bedside, and upon which she looked every night.

It is clear that Sir Gawain alone was not the only knight to act in an unchivalrous manner on this day, since the king's men were wont to mock this display of infatuation, but at this time Sir Hunbaut arrived, having sought in vain for the Lady Helice, and reproved the knights for their behaviour. King Arthur also rebuked his followers and as one they apologised to the lady before joining her at the table.

Sir Gawain himself, meanwhile, followed the

path that led ever more deeply into the Great Wood, and following the advice of those he met upon the way, at last found his way to a castle belonging to Gorvin Cadrus, the knight he and Hunbaut had encountered at the beginning of their journey to the Far Isles.

There Sir Gawain learned that Gorvin had taken the Lady Helice prisoner, and that the reason was because of the old rivalry between him and Sir Meraugis de la Portlesguez, one of the greatest of the Round Table knights and Gawain's great friend. Thus Gawain challenged the knight to release the lady or face him in battle.

Gorvin chose to fight him and the two men engaged in a mighty contest of arms, for both were well matched and willing to die if need be for the release of the lady. To begin with Sir Gawain led the conflict, battering his opponent with countless mighty blows. But to his surprise, Sir Gorvin fought back powerfully, and in the end it was only a misplaced step, which caused Gorvin to stumble, that enabled Gawain to inflict upon him a deep wound. When the fallen man begged for mercy and agreed to release the lady, Gawain spared his life, and so it was that he returned to Camelot the Golden

with Helice by his side, while Gorvin was made to do penance for his actions.

Gawain and Hunbaut recounted their adventures and learned that the King of the Far Isles had at last bowed the knee to King Arthur, following their visit. In the days that followed, so the story tells, the Lady Helice and Sir Hunbaut drew closer together, and finally declared their love. The pair were married in the spring amid great rejoicing.

The tale of the likeness of Sir Gawain in wood was spoken of often thereafter in the court, but of its fate I cannot say more, nor indeed if the lady of Gaut Desert ever met the bold knight for whom she felt such love. Nor can it be fully understood how the likeness was achieved, unless it was by some magic art. But we may see from this, that despite his plea that he was 'not made of wood' when failing to avoid the wiles of the Lady Elin, it seems that, in this fashion, he was!

Thus is the story told, and thus we may say that, for all his nobility and strength, Sir Gawain could not match that of Sir Hunbaut, whose gentle nature outshone that of the Round Table Fellowship at that time.

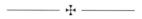

EXPLICIT THE TALE OF HUNBAUT.

INCIPIT THAT OF THE RED ROSE KNIGHT.

3: THE RED ROSE KNIGHT

───── ✛ ─────

IN THOSE TIMES OF WHICH I WRITE MANY KINGS AND PRINCES SIRED CHILDREN OUT OF WEDLOCK. IT IS SAID OF KING ARTHUR THAT HE HAD AT LEAST THREE SONS BY THE BEAUTIFUL WOMEN WHO CROSSED HIS PATH. YET THE SADNESS REMAINS THAT HIS TRUE WIFE, QUEEN GUINEVERE, BORE HIM NEITHER SON NOR DAUGHTER, AND THAT THE ONE SON WHO CAME TO BE RECOGNISED BY HIS FATHER WAS THE PRODUCT OF A DARK MINGLING WITH HIS OWN HALF-SISTER, MORGAUSE. BUT OF THIS SON, WHOSE NAME I WILL NOT WRITE HERE,* MASTER THOMAS HAS TOLD, AND HE IS THUS WELL KNOWN TO BE THE CAUSE THAT THE GREAT FELLOWSHIP OF THE ROUND TABLE WAS BROKEN, FOLLOWING UPON THE DAYS WHEN THE KNIGHTS WENT IN SEARCH OF THE GRAIL, WHICH TASK WEAKENED THE STRENGTH OF THE TABLE AND OF CAMELOT THE GOLDEN.

BUT THERE WAS ANOTHER SON OF ARTHUR'S WHO ATTAINED GREAT FAME IN THE WORLD, AND WHO WAS MADE A KNIGHT OF THE ROUND TABLE BY THE KING'S OWN HAND – THOUGH WHETHER HIS MAJESTY KNEW THAT HE WAS HIS SON IS NOT TOLD IN THE STORY I HAVE FOUND. THE NAME OF THIS CHILD WAS ANDRET, BUT TO MOST HE WAS KNOWN AS THE RED ROSE KNIGHT.

✛ ✛ ✛

THE STORY I shall tell here, concerns a liaison between King Arthur and a lady named Angelica, daughter of Earl Androgeus of London. This took place soon after the young king came to power, when he plucked the Sword from the Stone, and following his wars with the eleven rebellious kings who sought to prevent his wearing of the Crown of Britain.

The Lady Angelica was deemed by all who

---

* This clearly refers to Mordred.

saw her to be one of the fairest maidens in all of that land, so that it was perhaps no wonder that the young king should fall under her spell, and that she should return his love with equal ardour, since he was as handsome as she was lovely.

Since a marriage between them would not have sat well with the Lords of Britain, the couple arranged to meet in secret, and after a time Angelica was with child. The matter was hidden from both the maiden's family and the king's courtiers by dint of sending the girl to a convent founded by Arthur himself in the town of Lincoln. There, in the time appointed, Angelica gave birth to a son, whom she named Andret.

Only Merlin knew of this, and advised the king to let the birth remain secret, since it was better for the land that a legitimate heir be born to the king. In truth this saddened King Arthur greatly, but in that time such things were not as they are now, and thus he gave his consent that the infant should be placed into the care of another, who would not know its origins.

Less than three nights after the child's birth, one who served as handmaid to the Lady Angelica, took it away while her mistress slept, and went with it into the Great Wood. There, she laid the infant on a grassy mound, and withdrew behind a tree to observe what would occur. Around its neck she hung a small purse filled with golden coins, and wrapped the baby in a mantle of silk. To her astonishment, as the lady watched, she saw how a flock of birds flew down and encircled the babe, singing to it as if they were the very birds of Rhiannon,* until it cooed and waved its fists and then slept.

---

* Referenced in *The Mabinogion* as belonging to the goddess Rhiannon. They had the ability to enchant those that heard them.

In this way, it is held, was the significance of a future hero shown.

Soon after, there came an elderly shepherd named Alanus, making his way home in the evening sunlight. When he saw the child and the rich mantle in which it was wrapped, his eyes became full of wonder. Looking everywhere, but not seeing the handmaiden where she had hidden, the shepherd picked up the sleeping infant and carried it home – for he and his wife had long wished for a child of their own, but had not been so blessed. There, his wife took it into her arms and sang gently to it. And so she found about its neck the little purse of gold, at which both she and Alanus were filled with amazement, for this was surely meant to be. From that moment King Arthur's son became theirs, though not knowing his true name, they called him Tom.

The Lady Angelica suffered great sorrow at the loss of her child, which she was told had died in the night whilst she slept and been buried in haste. But thanks to the provision of the gold coins, the shepherd and his wife were rich, and if some murmured at their sudden wealth, yet they were known to be good and honest people, so that no one thought less of them. Thus the shepherd was able to purchase land of his own, and build a fair house, and he and his wife dressed themselves in fine garments. Upon their son they lavished every love and benefit in their power, and as he grew from infant to strong and generous-hearted youth, so he assumed the duties once followed by Alanus, watching over the sheep they now kept for their own.

But as he grew older, the boy became restless. Beyond doubt it was the spirit of his true parents that filled his mind with deeds he longed to perform. And in his heart he felt that some part of him remained hidden, and this in turn led him to follow a path that caused great pain to Alanus and his wife. For soon the youth began to assemble other youths from the lands around Lincoln, who made him their leader and followed his every command. Soon he led them into the Great Wood, where they lived as wildmen and outlaws, and began to rob travellers who journeyed there, and in his deep desire to live the life he could only dream of, he took the name of The Red Rose Knight – though he had yet to receive the buffet that would proclaim this status.

The shepherd and his wife were troubled deeply by this, and because of the great love they had for the boy they became fearful for his future. Thus it was that Alanus made his way into the forest in search of his wayward son, and being captured, as was any man or woman who travelled there alone, he was taken to the wildings' camp. There, when his son recognised him, he was at once set free and invited to remain with the band. But Alanus would have none of this, and spoke harshly to his son, who in turn grew angry and sent his father away with bitter words.

Heartbroken, Alanus returned home, and so deep was the wound to his soul made by his son's cruel words that within the year he was dead, his wife soon following him.

When word of this reached him, the youth greatly regretted his angry words, and used the treasure come by through his outlawry to build a noble tomb in the Cathedral of Lincoln. There he had his father and mother interred with great splendour, after which he returned to the Great Wood and once again took up his life as an outlaw.

✠ ✠ ✠

So it was that King Arthur himself heard word of the youth who called himself the Red Rose Knight, who at this time began to lead his followers out upon the land, seeking to right wrongs where he discovered them, behaving in all ways as a knight should. To each of his companions the youth gave a red rose and told them that they must hitherto call him the Red Rose Knight. Even though he took this title without right, they accepted his words and thence forward he was known by this name.

Wishing to know more of his story, the king sent three of his most trusted knights, Sir Lancelot of the Lake, Sir Tristan of Lyonesse, and Sir Triamour, to bring him to the court. He also issued a general pardon to the young outlaw and those of his followers who would swear allegiance to the crown.

When they came to the encampment of the Red Rose Knight they were splendidly received. They dined as well as they ever did in Camelot the Golden, and though they slept that night under canvas, they were as comfortable as they could have been in any castle or hall.

When the young outlaw read the letter sent by King Arthur, along with the pardon, he was most glad, and at once called out fifty of his best men to return with the three knights to Camelot. There, in honour of his good and noble deeds, King Arthur himself made him a knight, unaware that this was his own son – any more than the Red Rose Knight knew that the king was his father. When they saw this, the rest of the outlaws swore to serve King Arthur and to defend his kingdom against all-comers.

A great tournament was then declared to celebrate the joining of the Red Rose Knight with the Fellowship of the Round Table. In the lists at that time he proved his strength and prowess, overcoming all who rode against him until many of the king's knights swore that they had never encountered such a strong and bold warrior.

Yet there were those who murmured behind their hands concerning the knight's unknown parentage. For, they thought, he might well be of base stock and therefore unworthy of the honourable rank of knight. In this they proved themselves unworthy, for though the Red Rose Knight had been raised by poor folk, yet he was the child of two great houses, that of King Arthur Pendragon and of the Earl of London's daughter.

Hearing these rumours, it came into the mind of the Red Rose Knight that he would seek out his true father and mother, and to this end he begged King Arthur to give him leave to set forth on this task. The king, having no idea of their true relationship, allowed him to depart from the court, and gave him command of a fast ship – for surely, he declared, if any man in Britain knew of the Red Rose Knight's parentage, then they were sure to come forward to claim him, but if they had not, then it must follow that he seek them over the sea. Furthermore he gave the youth leave to select any of his knights to go with him. The Red Rose Knight chose Sir Lancelot of the Lake from amongst all the rest, which that knight was glad to accept, and together they set forth, swearing brotherhood to each other that should last all their days. So, too, several others amongst the younger knights of Camelot the Golden chose to go with them, so that there were a number of brave souls who joined their company.

They set forth with great gladness in the ship the king had given them, and sailed for many days and nights, following the patterns of star and wave, the transits of wind and water, the glory of sun and moon. They journeyed to many lands, and in each one the Red Rose Knight asked after any lord or lady who had lost a child in infancy. But though none gave answer that led to the discovery of the knight's family, upon the way they had many adventures that must one day be told.

Thus it was, that on a certain day their ship came to the shore of a great island in the Western Ocean. Not even the sailors knew of this place, and many were fearful that it might be the home of monsters or evil-doers. Both the Red Rose Knight and Sir Lancelot hoped this might be so, for thus would they find adventure, so they set out together, leaving their fellows behind to make camp on the shore, while they travelled inland in seek whatever might befall them.

Within a day's ride they saw before them a mighty castle that seemed to float upon the air, and as they approached, the gates opened and a band of richly clad ladies came forth. All wore armour that flashed in the sun, and carried swords and spears in such a manner that the two knights at once realised they were seasoned warriors.

Never had either man seen women garbed in this fashion, and both were filled with wonder. They removed their helms, and turned their shields to show that they meant no harm. At this two of the damsels rode forward and demanded fiercely to know who they were and why they had invaded their land.

At once the Red Rose Knight explained that they had sailed for many days and nights and that they had come to the island in search of food and water – and perhaps of adventure such as two Knights of the Round Table might wish to find. Also he asked why he and his companion should be so harshly welcomed.

One of the warlike damsels responded thus: 'This land was once ruled over by a king named

⇨ Approaching the boat ⇦

Larmos, a powerful overlord much given to making war with kingdoms across the sea. Finally, he gathered up all his best and strongest knights, soldiers and men-at-arms, and took ship to another land. There he spent the next few years in conflict, and laid siege to his enemies' castles and cities. When time had passed, the women of this country came together and declared that we would no longer live under such terms, and at once outlawed every man who remained here, setting them adrift in boats to go where they would or driving them out. Then we named the king's daughter, Caelia, our queen, and renamed this the Isle of Faerie, for so we wished to be like that place where all magic dwells. Since then, we have permitted no man to land upon our shores. Therefore we demand that you and any who came with you depart, or face us in battle.'

Then Sir Lancelot spoke: 'My lady, we are knights of King Arthur, on a journey of adventure. We seek no warfare with you, especially since we are sworn to protect all women.'

'It is as my comrade says,' said the Red Rose Knight. 'We landed upon your shore with no warlike intent, but simply to get fresh water and food before continuing our voyage. I ask that you return to your queen and tell her we mean no harm, but seek only rest and refreshment here.'

When they heard these words, and understood that the knights were of Camelot the Golden, the damsels bade them remain where they were and to come no closer to the castle upon pain of death. Then they returned to their kin and passed within the gates, which were firmly closed behind them.

The two knights made camp where they were, and awaited the word of the queen, all the while marvelling at the story they had heard. Lancelot recalled another story he had heard, of a land of women such as this, and how they were all fierce and warlike warriors, and The Red Rose Knight spoke of Amazons, such as had dwelled in the Greek lands in a distant time.

Meanwhile, when she heard from her lieutenants the identity of the knights and their avowed reason for coming, the queen went herself to the wall of her castle and looked upon the two men, seated peacefully in their camp. When she saw the Red Rose Knight she at once felt a stirring of love for him, while others looked well upon Sir Lancelot.

Taking swift thought, the queen commanded her lieutenants to bring both knights to her and treat them gently. So it was that Sir Lancelot and the Red Rose Knight were welcomed and given food and fresh clothes, while their steeds were groomed and fed with the best the castle had to offer. And when the Red Rose Knight saw the queen of that island he conceived a great love for her and desired to remain with her.

The remainder of the knights and sailors from the Red Rose Knight's ship were also invited to enter the castle, and all were well treated to the best hospitality they had known since departing from Camelot the Golden.

Thus they remained for some time, during which the Red Rose Knight and the queen grew closer together, and many of the knights from Camelot the Golden found love amongst the ladies of that city. So at last the Lady Caelia begged the Red Rose Knight knight to join his hand with hers and that they should rule over the land together.

Glad though he was in his heart to hear this proposal, the Red Rose Knight had begun lately to think again of the purpose for his journey – to discover his true parentage. Therefore with every courtesy and gentleness he told the queen that he could not remain there any longer, but that he would assuredly return as soon as his quest was ended.

The queen received these words with great sorrow, and that night she came to the bed of the Red Rose Knight and used all her wiles to persuade him to stay. And though the Red Rose Knight would not change his mind, yet he gave way to the queen's desire, and on that

night was conceived a child, though the knight had no knowledge of this at the time.

So the two knights and their men, many of whom were reluctant to leave having found love among the queen's ladies, prepared to continue their voyage. Those who wished were allowed to remain, but despite their newfound love all elected to continue their quest, and within two days all the company returned to their ship and set sail again – leaving behind many sorrowful damsels and many promises to return.

Thus they sailed onward for many weeks, and landed on shores both welcoming and inhospitable, until at length they arrived at a place of such beauty and nobility that they were amazed to see it. They docked in a harbour of great magnificence and looked upon a city of such glory that even Camelot the Golden seemed as nothing beside it. Everywhere the streets were broad and well paved, lit at night with a thousand torches so that it seemed as if it was always day in that place. At the centre, overshadowing all, rose a mighty palace, its walls bedecked with jewels and the great dome of its roof supported by pillars of porphyry and jade.

When he saw this the Red Rose Knight dispatched Sir Lancelot and three other knights to go up into the city and enquire of the ruler of the city and the nature of the country. This the knights did and received a good welcome from the people of the city, who lined the streets when they heard of the newcomers from across the sea.

The knights quickly learned that they had arrived in the lands of Prester John, a mighty and splendid emperor, rumour of whose rich and powerful kingdom had reached even into the shores of Britain. So famous indeed was this potentate, whose far off land had been

PLATE 2: *'They docked in a harbour of great magnificence and looked upon a city of such glory that even Camelot the Golden seemed as nothing beside it'*

mostly hidden from the Lords of the West, that all who heard of it desired to see it.[*]

Having thus been warmly welcomed, the knights returned to the ship, accompanied by a party of Prester John's own men, who on behalf of their master invited the Red Rose Knight and all his men to ascend into the city and to meet there with the emperor himself.

This they did, greatly marvelling at the richness and splendour upon every side. At the gates of the palace Prester John himself came out to meet them. Clad in robes of gold and wearing a jewelled crown, he shone like the sun. With great pomp the knights of King Arthur were conducted into the greatest hall any one of them had ever seen, and formally greeted. Chambers were allocated to them all and fresh raiment's provided, as well as wine and other refreshments. Then, as dusk fell across the city, they were led into the great hall again, where all were gathered for a great feast, and all Prester John's captains stood and applauded the Arthurian knights. There too was the emperor's daughter, Anglatora, who was judged to be the most beautiful woman any of the visitors had ever seen. The Red Rose Knight especially noticed her, and was glad indeed to be seated at her side at the high table. She in turn, feasted her eyes on the knight, and desired greatly to hear of his adventures.

All those there that night, long remembered the coming of the strangers from the West, for even here the name of King Arthur and the Knights of the Round Table had come to be heard, and all present hung upon every word as Arthur's men spoke of their deeds. Sir Lancelot alone was received with awe, such was his fame, but most of all the emperor, his daughter, and the Lords of the Kingdom sought to learn more of the Red Rose Knight and his journey.

They in turn, begged to know more of the great empire of Prester John, and learned that it was one of the richest and most powerful in all the world, which yet lay hidden from most other lands by the mountains to the east and the mighty and ever-restless sea along its coast. The emperor himself spoke much with the Red Rose Knight and told him, among many wonders, of a tree made of living gold that grew in his lands, and that each year gave forth golden fruit. 'But alas I can never taste of this, for a terrible dragon lives at its foot, and no one who dares approach it has ever returned.'

When he heard this the Red Rose Knight at once offered to go to the tree and to do all in his power to rid the emperor of this monster.

'If you succeed where all others have failed,' responded Prester John, 'you shall have the hand of my daughter as a reward.'

The Red Rose Knight looked upon the beauty of Anglatora and saw how she blushed, and his heart melted so that he could feel only love for her from that day forth. 'To this I pledge my strength and my courage,' he said. And all those in the hall raised their cups and blessed him for his bravery.

Soon after the knights of King Arthur were shown to their sleeping chambers, the Red Rose Knight and Sir Lancelot sharing one such. There the young knight asked his brother in arms if he thought the task he had taken upon himself was one of honour and renown. 'To me it seems an enterprise of death,' replied Lancelot. 'Did you not see how every man there this night, while they praised you, also believe that you had no chance to destroy the dragon, but sought only your own death?'

'Nevertheless,' said the Red Rose Knight, 'I shall not turn away from this, for I have given

---

[*] See also 'Titurel's Dream' pp. 239–244.

my word. And if it brings me to my death, so be it, for I shall die in the knowledge that I kept my faith and did as should all Knights of the Round Table.'

Though they knew it not, Anglatora stood outside the door of their chamber and overheard this exchange. As she retired to her own rooms, she lay awake many hours thinking only of the Red Rose Knight, whose beauty had already struck deep into her heart, and whose words to his brother knight, were the noblest she had ever heard. Then she slept at last, dreaming of the young knight and praying that he would survive the ordeal of the dragon – since this would mean their marriage, for such she longed for with her utmost strength.

NEXT MORNING THE Red Rose Knight dressed himself in his bright armour, and set to sharpening his sword until it was able to cut a hair in twain. Then he mounted his horse and set forth for the valley, which lay but two miles from the city, and where the tree grew, guarded by the dragon. As word of his departure upon this mission spread, the citizens climbed to the walls of the city, and the knights of King Arthur and those of Prester John ascended to the towers of the palace, and turned their eyes towards the valley, expecting never to see the Red Rose Knight again. Anglatora herself climbed to the highest point of all and there stood for many hours, praying for the safe return of he whom she saw as her future lord.

The Red Rose Knight came to the valley and there beheld the glory of the golden tree, already hung with glittering fruit. But as he dismounted, the dragon itself emerged from a cave and came towards him. It was more than thirty feet in length with a mighty tail and a great and noble head from which it blew streams of molten flame.

Caring nothing for his life, the Red Rose Knight raised his shield and advanced towards the terrible beast, which at once sought to overwhelm him with its fire. Still the knight approached, protected to some degree by his armour and shield. He struck a mighty blow to the dragon's head, striking it between its eyes. Roaring with pain, the beast opened its jaws and thrust forth not one but three tongues, one of which gave forth black smoke, which quickly began to choke the Red Rose Knight, while a second tongue spat poison and a third sent forth fire.

Despite this the Red Rose Knight was able to avoid all of these frightful things and delivered such a blow that he cut off all three of the dragon's tongues at the root. This caused the beast such pain that it screamed so loudly that those gathered in the city heard it and wondered greatly how the young knight fared.

Bellowing with pain and rage, the dragon turned away from the Red Rose Knight and swung its huge tail, flinging him through the air to land upon the earth. The dragon roared in triumph, but this was but short-lived as the Red Rose Knight got to his feet and with one great blow severed some seven feet of its tail. So angered and inflamed was the dragon by this, that it sought to crush the Red Rose Knight with the weight of its huge body, hurling itself upon him. The knight fell and seemed likely to meet his death by this means. But calling upon all his strength he drove his sword up into the dragon's body, piercing its heart.

Dying, screeching with pain and rage, the beast withdrew towards the shelter of its cave, but fell dead before it had gone more than a few paces.

For a time the Red Rose Knight lay unmoving on the earth, while he slowly recovered his strength. Then he rose at last and first took the dragon's tongues and stuck them on the point of his sword. Then he cut a branch from the golden tree, and found the strength to climb onto his horse and set it in motion towards the city.

When the crowds gathered on walls and towers saw him approaching, and what he carried, they were at first struck silent then, as they understood what this meant, they gave voice to their delight until the whole city rang like a great bell. From the height of the central tower Anglatora cried aloud in her delight and ran to tell her father the news.

At first Prester John was as glad as his people, then his brow darkened as he realised that the Red Rose Knight could now rightfully claim his daughter's hand. So confident had he been that no man could best the dragon, that he had made the promise without thought. Now he sought for a means to refuse the young knight his right. This he hid from Anglatora and showed only joy that the dragon was dead and the golden tree set free of its guardianship.

✣ ✠ ✣

THE RED ROSE Knight was received by cheering crowds and the sound of trumpets and drums. Prester John himself came forth to praise him, as did Sir Lancelot and his own companions, all astounded that he had prevailed against the monster.

The Red Rose Knight retired to his chamber to rest and dress his wounds. There Anglatora herself came, with a basin of fresh water and healing unguents with which to attend him. Nor could he pretend that the touch of her hands upon him failed to rouse him to great ardour, and thus he began to press his suit upon the damsel. She, being modest and well taught in such matters, spoke only of their coming marriage, and that she would keep her virginity until that time. To this the Red Rose Knight bowed honourably, and submitted to her gentle ministrations.

Next day he went before the emperor and reminded him of his promise. Prester John turned angrily away and swore that while he lived such a marriage would never be celebrated, and though the Red Rose Knight reminded him of his former promise, the emperor refused to discuss the matter further.

So things stood, and in his heart the Red Rose Knight believed that he would never seal the bond of love with Anglatora. He spoke at length with Sir Lancelot and his companions and all declared that they should depart from that place and continue their voyage.

When he learned of their intent, Prester John was glad and gave them many rich gifts. Of his daughter he spoke not again, but the Red Rose Knight secretly visited her and told her how her father had reneged upon his promise.

Fair Anglatora's heart seemed as though it might break, but she at once declared that she would come with her love to whatever part of the earth he desired, and when she saw how delight lit his face, she gathered together all her jewels and other treasures and together the couple stole away unseen into the Red Rose Knight's ship.

Without further delay they raised their sails and set forth. They were far from the shores of the emperor before Anglatora's absence was noted. Then Prester John wept for the loss of his child, and wished that he had kept his word. Beyond this the story tells no more of the great emperor or his land, but turns instead to a sad event.

For as the ship began to turn towards far off Britain, Sir Lancelot reminded the Red Rose Knight of his promise to Caelia, who it must be said he had forgotten once he set eyes on his new love. Yet, being of honourable mind, he declared his intent to return to the Faery Isle and beg forgiveness of the queen.

She, meanwhile, sorrowing for the loss of her love, had taken to standing for hours on the cliffs overlooking the sea, in the hope of seeing the sails of the Red Rose Knight on the horizon. But when the day finally came when she did indeed see the ship, flying the banner of King Arthur, to her dismay it did not turn towards the shore of the island, but continued onwards. In truth this was because of violent tides and furious winds, which drove the ship past, despite the best efforts of her crew to bring her into the safe harbour on the Faery Isle. To the queen it seemed to her only that the Red Rose Knight, if indeed he lived, no longer loved her.

Great was the regret of the Red Rose Knight that he was prevented from explaining all that occurred. Perhaps if he had known of the existence of his son by the queen he might have sought again to return, but she, broken-hearted by what she saw as his failure to remember her, threw herself from the cliffs to her death. And of his first son, born while he travelled far in search of adventure, the Red Rose Knight remained ignorant to the end of his days.

It fell out that the sea bore the body of Queen Caelia away from the shores of the Faery Isle and carried it by strange currents until it was washed up on the beach in another land. There came the very ship on which the Red Rose Knight and his companions were, and so it was that the young knight came on deck and beheld the body in the water. At once he demanded that it be brought aboard and so set eyes upon the dead face of his former love.

Then he wept most bitterly, and upon hearing this Anglatora asked him the reason for his sorrow. The Red Rose Knight told her of his past love, that now was dead, as were his own feelings for her, though he still felt sadness for her death. Anglatora understood this and looked with gentleness upon the body of the Lady Caelia, insisting she be brought home

✦ *The Dragon Guardian of the Tree of Gold* ✦

to Britain to be buried in splendour. To this the Red Rose Knight agreed, and so it was that Caelia was interred in great reverence and solemnity in the city of Lincoln. And indeed her tomb was close to that of the Red Rose Knight's own foster-father and mother.

Little remains to be told at this time of the lives of the Red Rose Knight, and the daughter of Prester John. When the ship brought them safely to Britain, the Red Rose Knight married his love, and it is told that they lived long and happy lives together, and that the Red Rose Knight became one of the great heroes of the Round Table. He never discovered the truth of his parentage, for his true mother had died before his return from his long voyage, having kept to the end the secret she had borne so long. Nor did Merlin ever speak of this to the king, and Arthur himself forgot his youthful liaison. I have heard tell that the son of the Red Rose Knight and Queen Caelia grew to be a fearsome warrior, known to men as the Faery Knight, and that his deeds are remembered elsewhere – but of these I will not write at this time as they do not form part of the story of King Arthur and his knights. So here I end the story of the rise of the Red Rose Knight, whose name was rightly Andret, but whom all knew as Sir Tom of Lincoln.

EXPLICIT THE TALE OF THE RED ROSE KNIGHT.

INCIPIT THE STORY OF SIR LANCELOT, SIR GAWAIN AND THE WHITE-FOOT STAG.

4: SIR LANCELOT, SIR GAWAIN, AND THE WHITE-FOOT STAG

MORE TALES OF SIR LANCELOT AND SIR GAWAIN THERE ARE THAN ANY OTHER KNIGHTS OF THE ROUND TABLE. JUSTLY SO, SINCE THESE WERE THE PEERS OF KING ARTHUR'S COURT. BUT WHAT SEEMS TO BE LESS SPOKEN OF, EVEN IN MASTER THOMAS'S GREAT BOOK, IS THE FRIENDSHIP THAT EXISTED BETWEEN THEM. THEY WERE FOREVER FRIENDS – UNTIL, THAT IS, THE SAD DAY WHEN SIR GAWAIN'S BROTHER WAS SLAIN IN THE SAVING OF QUEEN GUINEVERE FROM THE STAKE. ONE STORY, THAT RELATES TO THEIR COMRADESHIP, I HAVE FOUND AND WILL TELL HERE – TAKEN FROM THE LANGUAGE OF THE FRISIANS, BY ONE WHO KNEW THE STORIES OF THAT DISTANT TIME AS WELL AS ANY LIVING MAN.

✢ ✤ ✢

MANY OF THE tales collected here show that it was from within the Great Wood of Broceliande that the hardest tests of the Round Table Fellowship came. One such is this I tell here, which begins on a day in the heat of summer when there came a maiden who spoke on behalf of her mistress, Dame Blanche. With her came a little white dog, that rode on the cropper of her saddle and regarded all there with keen sight.

Standing before King Arthur and Queen Guinevere, the lady told her story. 'Not far from here there is a place where the forest fills the valley with trees. It is an enchanted place you may be sure, for there lives a mighty stag with a single white foot. It is guarded by huge lions, far greater in size than such beasts normally are. My Lady Blanche rules over this land as your vassal, lord King. She shines as bright as sunshine, and is much loved for her kindness and strength of will. Many noble lords and knights have come in search of her hand in marriage, but all of these she has refused. Not long ago she made a promise – that she would only marry he who could bring her the white foot of the stag. Many have tried but none have returned. Since my lady believes that only the best and most noble knights reside in this court, she sends me to request that if any man here would wish to undertake that test, he may do so.'

34

At once, Sir Kay, who was close at hand and had heard all the maiden said, came forward and begged to be given this task. King Arthur, doubtless remembering the many occasions when his foster-brother had failed in his attempt to prove himself worthy as a Knight of the Round Table, gave him leave to try this quest.

The maiden was delighted by this and told Sir Kay that the way to the part of the forest where the valley of the White-Foot Stag lay was to the South, and that the little white dog would lead the way. 'You will find a part of the wood that has a walled enclosure. There is a little gate that permits entrance to the valley. But beware, Sir Knight, of the lions. There are no less than seven there at this time.'

Sir Kay, full of pride at being given this task, scarcely listened, but donned his armour and followed the little dog from the gates of Camelot the Golden into the depths of the Great Wood.

In no time at all he came within sight of the wall enclosing the entrance to the valley. But there before it lay a wide and furious river. Kay reined in his steed and stared with dismay at the fast flowing water. There was no sign of a crossing place that he could see. The little dog, without hesitating, jumped into the water and swam swiftly to the further bank. There it waited for Sir Kay, but the knight, fearful of the river, would go no further.

As if to make him feel more foolish the dog swam back to him and sat, waiting. Then into Sir Kay's mind came a dark thought. He must find an excuse for his failure, and thus avoid shame, and if he killed the little white dog there could be no witness. At that moment, as if it knew his intent, the dog ran off, and Sir Kay spent the next hours fruitlessly seeking it through the depths of the Great Wood. At last he found that he was back on the road to

Camelot the Golden, and hanging his head, he entered the great city.

There he met with Sir Gawain, who expressed surprise that he had returned so soon.

'Alas!' said Kay. 'I had but followed the white dog a few miles when a great sickness overcame me. So weak was I, that I almost fell from my horse. I thought it best to return and try again when I am recovered.'

Scarcely had he uttered these words than there came a howling from behind him. The little white dog had followed him home, and now set up such a noise that Sir Kay was quite confounded and made off as quickly as he could, leaving Sir Gawain to smile as he went on his way.

NOW IT HAPPENED that Sir Lancelot came to Camelot the Golden at this time, though he was often absent on one adventure or another. When he heard the story, he at once prepared to go forth himself, calling for his armour and weapons, and his brave steed.

So it was that Sir Lancelot set forth, following the white dog, which had returned soon after Kay, and gave him a wide berth. As before, he led the knight through the dark wards of Broceliande until they reached the rapid river. Unlike Sir Kay, Lancelot did not hesitate, but gave his mount free rein. The mighty steed swam across the river and soon reached the other side. There, Lancelot rested awhile until both he and his steed were dry, then followed where the white dog led.

This part of the forest, walled in both with stones and the steep sides of the valley, had a strange feel to it. A strong scent of herbs that grew there filled the air, and where it should have been dark beneath the trees it was somehow light. Within the branches many birds sat and sang, and Sir Lancelot, happy to be engaged on a new adventure, sang with them, and followed where the little white dog ran before him.

There, amid the trees, Sir Lancelot saw where a great stag ran, its single white foot shining forth as if lit from within. But fast as the knight rode, the beast went faster. Then came the lions, of which the maiden had warned. They were in truth larger than natural size, and attacked Lancelot from all sides.

Drawing his sword, the great knight defended himself ably, while his steed kicked out at the savage creatures. Within a short time three of the beasts lay dead, but Lancelot had suffered several deep wounds. Nevertheless, he fought on and soon had dispatched all of the lions.

Once the battle was ended, Lancelot realised how deep and painful were his wounds, yet when he caught sight of the White-Foot Stag again, he gave chase. The little dog, which somehow seemed to have grown larger, also pursued the beast, and after a long ride through the trees caught and brought down the fleeing animal. There Sir Lancelot caught up with it and dispatched it mercifully. Then he cut off the white foot and wrapped it in a piece of silken cloth and placed in within a leathern bag.

By this time Lancelot was weak from loss of blood and could not even climb back onto his horse. The brave beast itself was sorely wounded, the blood running down its flanks. Breathing in the scent of the herbs helped Lancelot rally, but he was still unable to do more than sit upon the ground and do the best he could to staunch his wounds.

✛ ✛ ✛

AT THIS TIME, it chanced that another knight came this way, and seeing where Lancelot sat, and the blood upon him, reined in and dismounted, offering to help the wounded man.

Lancelot would accept no help, but he thanked the stranger knight and asked if instead he would carry out an errand for him.

'Within this pouch,' he said, 'is a gift for a lady who awaits it in her castle, which lies a little way to the north. If you will take it to her in my name, I am sure she will be grateful and reward you. Tell her that Sir Lancelot sends her greetings and will attend upon her as soon as he may.'

When he heard this, the stranger knight gave thanks that he had not attempted to fight with Lancelot, such as might have happened under normal circumstances, and learning the story of the White-Foot Stag, saw how he might benefit from this, especially that he might obtain the hand of the Lady Blanche whose wide lands lay all around the valley.

He took the pouch with the white foot and then, foul caitiff that he was, struck Sir Lancelot a mighty blow on the head, so that he fell to the earth and lay still. Expecting the great knight to die of this and his other wounds the stranger knight rode away as fast as he might towards the castle of the Lady Blanche.

Meanwhile, the lady who had sent her handmaid to Camelot the Golden in the hope of finding a matchless knight to become her husband, waited for news. She was in her garden when word came that a knight had arrived who wished to speak with her. Eagerly, she asked that he should be brought to her. When he arrived she was dismayed to see that, while he was tall and strong, yet his face was as ugly as any she had ever seen. Nevertheless, she received the man courteously. He sat beside her and drew forth the leathern bag and took from it the white foot of the Great Stag.

'My lady,' he said. 'You have said that you will marry the man who brings this to you. I found the stag and slew seven lions to obtain it. Now I offer it to you with my pledge of devotion.'

Though secretly dismayed, the Lady Blanche called to her women to care for the knight and see that he had all that he needed. 'For this man has fought bravely for me,' she said, 'and deserves to be well treated.'

Once the stranger knight had been led away to be given fresh clothes, food and drink, and a chamber to himself, Lady Blanche called her closest advisors to her and explained her quandary. 'I have given my word to marry the one who brought me the foot of the Great Stag, and this knight whom you have seen has done so. Yet I am fearful that his soul may be as ugly as his visage. What may I do?'

The courtiers spoke amongst themselves, then one of their number said: 'My lady, we cannot see any way to escape the promise you have made. All you can do is delay the wedding for two weeks more while you make preparations. Perhaps a solution will come to you in that time.'

With this the Lady Blanche had to be content, and though the knight frowned when he learned of the delay, yet there was nothing he could do but agree.

✠ ✠ ✠

So TIME PASSED, and meanwhile Sir Gawain, having heard nothing from Lancelot and believing his task light enough for one of his ability to have been soon dispatched, decided to go in search of his friend. He set off at once, though without the little dog to guide him believed that he had little chance of discovering what had happened to Sir Lancelot.

Fate had other intent. Gawain followed the road south into the forest, and came to a place where he found the remains of several knights who had fallen victim to the lions. Most were scattered and broken, their faces too damaged to enable the knight to see who they were. Even their shields were so battered that for the most part he could not read them. Then Gawain wept, believing his friend to have fallen here and to be beyond recovery.

However, something prompted him to ride further into the Great Wood, and there, by the kindness of fate or the will of God, he found where Lancelot lay – so weakened by his wounds, and the blow given him by the unknown knight, that he could scarcely move. Beside him lay the body of his brave steed, fallen from its wounds received in defence against the savage lions.

Rejoicing, Sir Gawain helped his companion to stand, gave him water and helped him onto his own mount.

'There is an abbey near here that is famed

→ *The lion attacks* ←

for its healers,' Gawain said. 'Let us go there and get help.'

Lancelot agreed, despite his desire to continue with his task. He told Gawain all that had happened, how the stranger knight had pledged to take the Great Stag's foot to the Lady Blanche, but had then struck him down and left him for dead.

When he heard this, Gawain's anger knew no bounds. Supporting the wounded Lancelot before him on the saddle, he made his way to the nearby abbey and left his friend in the care of the monks, who having searched his wounds declared that he would soon recover.

Gawain, meanwhile, set out for Camelot the Golden. On his way he met with others from the court and from them learned of the impending marriage of the Lady Blanche to a stranger knight who had brought her the foot from the Great Stag. They themselves were going to attend the forthcoming wedding, and invited Gawain to join them. He, with little more than a salute, turned his horse's head towards the lady's castle and galloped off, leaving the rest behind.

When he arrived all was in such a bustle that no one noticed him or even greeted him. Thus he made his way through the throng until he came to where the Lady Blanche was preparing to marry the stranger knight. She seemed, indeed, far from happy, and Sir Gawain pressed forward until he came to where the stranger knight stood. At once, Gawain challenged him.

'You have no right to claim this lady!' he cried. 'You stole the white foot from Sir Lancelot and left him for dead.'

'You lie!' shouted the knight. 'I fought with all my strength to kill the lions and brought the foot to my lady as requested. I have every right to claim her.'

'Not so,' Gawain insisted. 'I have spoken with Sir Lancelot, who is very far from dead. He has told me of your villainy. I challenge you to answer my words with sword and lance.'

Though he continued to protest his innocence, the stranger knight could not avoid the challenge. Many there believed the words of Sir Gawain rather than he, and so it was the two men faced off there in the garden, with the people of the castle, and Lady Blanche herself, looking on, joined by those who had arrived from Camelot the Golden.

THE BATTLE WAS short-lived. Though the stranger knight was a strong and adroit fighter, against Sir Gawain he stood no chance. A final blow left his helm and head both cloven, so that he fell dead. The story tells us that his body was tied to the tail of a horse which was then driven through the city. Whether this be true or not I cannot say, but such unchivalrous acts were part of that time, even when King Arthur ruled.

Everyone celebrated Sir Gawain's victory, most especially the Lady Blanche, who had watched the contest knowing that her fate was decided by its outcome. She came herself to thank and praise the great knight, declaring her delight that he had beaten her enemy. But Gawain, though he was glad that the lady had thus found her freedom, spoke his concern that since it was Lancelot who had followed the White-Foot Stag and had sent the sign of his victory, by the hand of the false knight, thus it was he who had won the right to marry the Lady Blanche.

She, in turn, asked to know more of her champion.

Gawain spoke of his friend in glowing terms, praising his strength and courage, his handsome features, and his fame. 'But I am concerned for his well-being,' Gawain added. 'I wish to depart at once to the abbey where I left him, and to establish his state of health.'

The Lady Blanche, who was in truth well pleased by the description of Lancelot, whose fame was well known in her own lands, begged Sir Gawain to remain there one night longer before he returned to the abbey. Gawain, ever courteous towards women, bowed to her wish, though he continued to feel concern for the fate of his friend.

That night he slept in the most rich and splendid bed he had ever known, and was treated like a king. In the morning he returned to the abbey and was happy to find that Lancelot was recovering well from his wounds. Gawain told him of the events at the castle of the Lady Blanche and of the death of the stranger knight.

'By right, it is you who should be free to marry the lady,' said Gawain. But he knew well what the answer would be. For, as all will know that have read Sir Thomas Malory's great book, Lancelot loved but one woman in his whole life, and that was Queen Guinevere. And even though that love remained unspoken between them for many years, yet the great knight was ever faithful to her name and thus would not even think of wedding the Lady Blanche.

Gawain remained at the abbey and richly rewarded the monks for their care of his friend. Then, when Sir Lancelot was recovered, the two men rode to the castle of the Lady Blanche and there Lancelot made excuses that prevented him from accepting her hand. From kindness, he begged her to wait until such time as he was free to return there, and though she barely hid her disappointment, she agreed.

So the two knights left to return home to Camelot the Golden. As for the Lady Blanche, she assuredly did not see Lancelot again, and since her future husband could no longer present her with the foot of the Great Stag, King Arthur proclaimed a tournament at which the most worthy winner might claim her hand. Whether she found a husband in this way, the story does not tell, though I have heard it said that Sir Gawain returned later to her castle and that the two were lovers for a time – but I have heard many such tales of Sir Gawain, so I cannot say if this was so or not.

EXPLICIT THE STORY OF SIR LANCELOT, SIR GAWAIN AND THE WHITE-FOOT STAG.

INCIPIT THAT OF THE BOY AND THE MANTLE.

5: THE BOY AND THE MANTLE

FEW AMID THESE TALES ARE MEANT TO BRING A SMILE TO THE FACE OF THOSE WHO HEAR THEM. YET ONE SUCH I HAVE HEARD MORE THAN ONE BRAVE SINGER RECOUNT, AND THOUGH IT MAY SEEM TO BRING NO GOOD ODOUR TO THE COURT OF CAMELOT THE GOLDEN, YET IT BRINGS A MESSAGE I CANNOT DISGUISE. THEREFORE, I SET IT HERE, IN THIS PLACE, TO SHOW HOW THE COURT OF KING ARTHUR COULD BE BROUGHT LOW YET RISE TO SHINE WITH THE LIGHT OF HONOUR DESPITE ALL. AS THE TELLER TOLD IT TO ME SO HAVE I WRITTEN IT HERE.

✛ ✛ ✛

I WILL TELL YOU the story of an adventure that took place one year in King Arthur's great city of Camelot the Golden. Never was there a more splendid place than this; nor could you find finer knights and ladies than those who attended at the feasts which King Arthur and Queen Guinevere held. Everyone was invited, from the four corners of the realm, for Arthur loved to know all that happened in his lands, and in this way, he learned of many things that might otherwise have passed unnoticed. To everyone who came he gave the richest gifts, armour and weapons to the knights, horses and hounds to the ladies. The queen likewise had all of the women visit her in her own suite of rooms, where she gave them fine silks and samites, as well as rich and costly jewels.

So it came about that on a day at the beginning of the feast of Pentecost, when the court was especially brilliant, the king and queen and all their guests went to hear mass in the morning, returning to the great hall for dinner. As was his custom, King Arthur refused to sit down and eat until he had heard of some new wonder. Sir Gawain, who was serving as chief steward at that time, did his best to persuade the king to dine, but Arthur was adamant. At that moment a young man was sighted approaching on a horse that had clearly been ridden hard.

'Well,' said Gawain, 'I believe we may be able to go in to dine; for unless I am mistaken, this youth is the harbinger of a new wonder.'

'We shall see,' said the king.

The youth entered the hall and was stopped by Sir Kay who demanded to know his business.

40

'As to that,' the youth replied, 'I shall speak to no one but King Arthur himself.'

'He is here,' said Sir Kay, and showed the youth where the king sat on his throne, dressed in splendid robes.

The youth made his way through the courtiers who thronged about the king, and made a gracious bow. 'Sire,' he said, 'I have come on behalf of a lady to ask of you a boon. But I must tell you that I may not say who the lady is or what it is she desires until you have agreed to grant her wish. Yet I will say that it shall bring no ill-repute to either you or your court.'

'That is well said,' replied King Arthur. 'Speak now, and tell me of your lady and her wish.'

By way of answer the youth took from a little pouch that he carried at his side a most beautiful and remarkable cloak. If I tell you that no finer had ever been seen in that hall then you will know that I speak the truth and that it was truly remarkable. It seemed to shimmer as one looked upon it, and where it was embroidered with a shifting pattern of leaves, they seemed to be living rather than made by human artifice. But the strangest thing was, that the harder one looked at the mantle to see how it was made the harder it became to see it.

'Sire,' said the youth, holding up the mantle. 'This is a magical garment, woven by an elf-woman in Broceliande. It has this property: let any maiden or gentlewoman wear it and, if she has done ought to be ashamed of, the mantle will reveal it in this wise: either it will become too long or too short. Only she who has the noblest and most innocent nature and is true to her lover will find that it fits her exactly. This is the boon I ask, for the sake of my lady: that all the women of your court be asked to try this mantle, and that they be not told about its properties until they have done so. For I have

heard that only the fairest and most illustrious of women are to be found at this court, and my lady would have me see for myself if this is true or not.'

At this King Arthur looked askance, as did many of the other nobles gathered about him who heard the words spoken by the youth. Only Sir Gawain laughed and said this test was surely worth the sport it might bring.

Though he was reluctant to play what seemed to him an unknightly trick, the king had given his word. So he sent Sir Gawain, together with a page named Meon, to the queen's rooms to summon her and all her ladies. This is how Sir Gawain spoke to her.

'Madam, the king asks that you join him in the great hall, and that you bring with you all your gentlewomen and all the noble ladies who are our guests. For there has arrived a handsome young man who has brought a wondrous gift, the fairest mantle that ever was seen. The king has promised that whichever lady it best fits shall have it to keep. It is my belief that it is made by no mortal hands.'

'Surely this is a great wonder,' said the queen, and without further delay she ordered all the ladies and gentlewomen to accompany her, and like so many lovely birds they made their way to the hall.

There the youth showed them all the mantle, which sparkled and shimmered with unearthly light. All who saw it desired it greatly, but the first to try it was the queen herself. Imagine her displeasure when, on settling it around her shoulders, it was too short by several inches.

At that the queen changed colour, and bit her lips with annoyance. Meon the page, who was standing by, said to her: 'It seems a little short, my lady, but here is the maiden who is beloved of the noble Aristes. She is less tall than you. Surely the mantle will fit her.'

The queen handed the mantle to the maiden who stood beside her; but when that lady put it upon her it seemed even shorter, barely covering her calves.

'Now it seems to me,' said Sir Gawain, straight-faced, 'that this mantle has grown shorter, even though it has not been worn long!'

'My lords,' said the queen. 'I am sure the garment was longer than this. Am I mistaken?'

Sir Kay said: 'I think you are more faithful than this other lady, at least by as much as a few inches!'

The queen turned to King Arthur. 'What manner of garment is this? It seems to me that it has some power of which you have not spoken.'

Then the king somewhat shamefacedly told her everything about the mantle. As she listened the queen went first white then red, but at last she laughed, turning her embarrassment to jest. 'Now surely,' she said, turning to the rest of the women who were gathered there. 'Every one of you will try this garment since I have done so first.'

'Then on this day shall the faithfulness of all of you be proven once and for all,' said Sir Kay spitefully. 'For I dare say there is not one of you here today that has not sworn that she was faithful, or chaste, or true to her lover.'

When they heard this there was not a single woman there who would not as soon have remained at home that day and kept her honour intact. None wished to go near the mantle or touch it.

Then King Arthur said that he would return the mantle at once to the youth; but he said that this was unfair, according to the promise the king had made. 'For neither I nor my lady shall be satisfied until every maiden or gentlewoman present has tried the mantle.

Such was our agreement, and I see no reason to break it.'

'You speak the truth,' said the king heavily. 'I am ashamed to have sought thus to avoid the matter. I promise that every lady here shall try the mantle.'

Then Sir Kay spoke up, addressing his own lady. 'Beloved, try the mantle, for I know of no one more faithful than you. Together we shall carry off this prize.'

But the lady looked at the floor and said that she would as soon not, for there were many more here whom she knew would fail this test if they were put to it.

'Ah-ha!' cried Sir Kay. "It seems to me you are afraid, and I would know why!'

'It is not that I am afraid,' replied his lady, looking up and blushing rosily. 'Rather it is that there are many more noble ladies than I who should try this first. I would not put myself forward ahead of them.'

'You have no reason to fear,' said Kay sharply. 'Since no one seeks to put on the mantle I am sure no one will object if you are the next to try it.'

Biting her lip, the lady took up the mantle and arranged it about her. But alas! – it came scarcely to her knees at the back and in front rode even higher.

Now it was Sir Kay's turn to change colour, while the lady herself fled from the hall, pursued by the laughter of both knights and ladies.

'Now I dare say,' said one of the knights to Sir Kay, 'that you may boast of your deeds done in honour of this lady (for Sir Kay was known for a braggart) as much as you like, for we know now that there is not another like you in all of Britain!'

Then Sir Yder said: 'Surely you have derided enough of us in the past; it seems only fair that such words should be said of you!'

Angrily Kay said to all who were present: 'Don't be so hasty to speak of my lady. It remains to be seen how your own loves will fare!'

Then one of the squires, a lad named Bodender who was known for his courtesy, said, innocently enough: 'Surely we are going about this in the wrong way, my lords. Sir Gawain's lady is by far the loveliest among us – surely she should have tried the mantle after our lady the queen?'

'I shall be glad to have that happen,' said Gawain at once, and called forth his own most recent sweetheart, who was widely believed to be faithful and true. However, once she had put the mantle about her it was so long at the back that it dragged on the ground, while in front and to one side it hung most crookedly.

Both the lady and Sir Gawain were put out by this, though the latter made light of it, seeing that his own reputation was far from un-spotted. However, Kay would not let matters rest, but exclaimed that he was glad that he was not alone in feeling disgraced on this day. 'Shall I send you to join my lady?' he asked of Gawain's love, but she only hung her head and answered nothing.

Then King Arthur turned to the lovely daughter of King Uriens, a powerful lord and ally who often rode to the hunt with him. 'I have heard only good things of you my lady,' he said. 'Will you not try the mantle next?'

This she did – but as with the rest it proved ill-fitting, being both over long on one side and too short on the other. Then one of the knights, who was named Geres the Little and who was known to have no good opinion of women, said loudly: 'Now we see how foolish it is to put trust in any woman! They are all too quick to discard a husband or a lover once they tire of him. Indeed they love novelty so much we can never trust them. It seems clear to me that the mantle is long on one side because the lady will not hesitate to lie upon that side; while it is short on the other because she does not care if her skirt is lifted!'

At this many people murmured aloud their agreement or disagreement. The maiden herself looked furiously at Geres, while Gawain stared at him so hard that it seemed he would consume him with the look.

Then the king sighed heavily and called forth the beloved of Sir Paternus. 'My dear,' he said. 'Will you be next? For surely you are the kindest and most true among us.'

But Griflet, the king's fool, spoke up: 'Sire,' he said, 'don't be so quick to judge before you know the truth. The day may well be praised, but such praise is best left till evening!'

Sir Paternus' love, though she trembled to do so, did as the king bade her; but before she could even arrange the mantle about her the ties which held it at the neck broke off and it fell rustling to the floor. At which the lady began to weep and to curse the mantle and he who had brought it. And indeed there were

✦ *The enchanted mantle* ✦

others who looked upon the stranger in their midst with less than friendly mien.

He, however, with scarcely a look at any of them, took up the mantle from where it had fallen and attached fresh ties. Then he turned to King Arthur and held up the mantle again. Suddenly now the king was angry. 'Why are we fasting for so long,' he demanded. 'What is the matter with you all – let us get this matter over with as quickly as maybe, so that we may eat!'

But Griflet the fool spoke up again: 'My lord, I love a joke as well as the next man, but surely this has gone far enough. It seems to me that every lady here might as well admit her faults to her husband or love and have done with it.'

To this Arthur would have gladly assented, but the youth who had brought the mantle spoke up: 'My lord, this is scarcely in keeping with our agreement. Besides, what would all those whose ladies have not been tested think of those who have? Do you want to divide your court!'

Then Yder turned to his lady, who stood close by his side. 'My love, will you try the mantle next, for only this morning I boasted of your loyalty to me in front of Sir Kay here, and now I am wondering if I was right to do so.'

The lady obeyed, and on her the mantle covered her at the front, but at the back it rose almost to her waist, at which Griflet was heard to murmur that he thought this must mean she liked to be taken from behind!

His face dark with anger Yder tore the mantle from the lady's back and flung it on the floor in front of the king. Kay meanwhile led the lady to sit with those who had already tried the fateful garment, muttering that there would soon be a large gathering there.

Now it became clear that there was nothing more to do but to have every woman there, young or old, maiden or wife, try the mantle as soon as might be. But there were none that it fitted, and pretty soon the circle of ladies who had failed grew large indeed, while their husbands or lovers stood by with ever more crestfallen faces.

Then Sir Kay said: 'Do not be put out, friends, for at least we are not alone in our disgrace.'

To which Sir Gawain answered: 'Nor should we forget the ladies themselves, for it seems we are too concerned with our feelings at the expense of theirs.'

At this the youth with the mantle spoke up, addressing the king. 'Sire, it seems I shall have to depart without bestowing the mantle upon anyone here, though I must say that I find it astonishing that not one lady in all of this great court can be found whom it will fit. Are you certain there is no one else that has been forgotten?'

'He is right,' said Gawain. 'Let every room be searched to make certain there is no lady missing from our gathering.'

King Arthur ordered the castle to be searched, and Griflet the fool, who had been glancing around all the while, went at once to the chamber of a certain lady whose name was Guindoel, who he had noticed was absent. There he found her abed, for she was unwell that day. But Griflet said to her: 'Ah, lady, you must rise and come into the court, for there is such an adventure as ought not to be missed!'

Then the lady rose and dressed herself in her finest clothes and went into the court, and the brave knight Sir Caradoc, whose love she was, grew pale when he saw her, for he had secretly been glad that she was not present, since he loved her greatly and was ill-disposed to see her humiliated before all. At once he called out to her: 'My love, do not go near this evil garment, for I care nothing for any misdeed you might have performed, save only that our love is stronger than any such thing.'

'Ha!' said Kay. 'Why do you speak thus? No man wants an unfaithful woman. It's better to know the worst and be done with it.'

But the lady herself spoke out: 'I am not afraid to try the mantle, so long as my love does not care about the outcome.'

'I believe that you are true to me in all things,' said Sir Caradoc 'And I care nothing for this paltry test.'

At this the Lady Guindoel took up the cloak and put it on – and behold it fitted her perfectly both back, front and sides. Very well she looked in it too, for it had the property also that it made even the fairest of women seem more lovely than before.

Then the youth said: 'Now I think that here is a lady fitted to wear the mantle, and I ask that she keep it. As for you, Sir Knight,' he added, turning to where Caradoc stood smiling with joy, 'I dare say you are the most fortunate man in this world. More than seven courts have I visited and in not one of them have I found a lady who was so true and gentle that the mantle fit her so well. Truly has she earned the right to wear it.'

'Madam,' said the king, 'you have upheld the honour of my court where no one else could so do. I gladly give you the right to wear the mantle.' Then he turned to the rest of the court and said: 'And now let us go in to eat, for we have been kept waiting a long time today.'

Thus the court went in to dine, and the young man who had brought the mantle took his leave and hurried away back to his mistress to tell her of the events at Camelot the Golden. Some have said that it was the king's own half-sister Morgana, who bore great ill-will towards her half-brother, that sent the mantle, but if it was not she, and if the one who sent it was not of this earth, I should not be surprised, for women of the Faery race love to play such tricks upon mortal folk. But this I will say: from that day came much sorrow and unrest, for many of the knights forswore their loves that they no longer believed in, and those who had loved a long time were filled with unease about their loves. But Caradoc and his lady were most happy, and when they left the court they placed the magic mantle in a monastery for safe keeping. I have heard it said that it is still there, and that the one who owns it now will soon be setting forth with it to test the faithfulness of women everywhere. Perhaps he will come here one day – who can say? For now, gentle lords and ladies, my tale is ended.

‡ ✠ ‡

So SPOKE THE teller of this tale. Many may choose to see it as a story of unfaithfulness, or indeed of the wiles of the Faery race who sought ever to challenge the qualities of the royal court. As to whether the king himself ever asked of the queen the reason why the mantle did not fit her, I cannot say, and perhaps these things are better left unsaid.

————— ✠ —————

EXPLICIT THE TALE OF THE MANTLE.

INCIPIT THE AVENGING OF RAGUIDEL.

6: THE AVENGING OF RAGUIDEL

---✢---

THE ADVENTURES OF SIR GAWAIN ARE RIGHTLY HELD TO BE THE VERY HEART OF THESE TALES OF CAMELOT THE GOLDEN, AND I HAVE HEARD IT SAID THAT HE WAS THE VERY FLOWER OF CHIVALRY, WHOSE LIGHT, LIKE THAT OF THE SUN, SHONE ITS GLORY UPON THE FELLOWSHIP OF THE ROUND TABLE. AND YET, AS WE HAVE SEEN IN OTHERS OF THE TALES I HAVE RELATED HERE, THERE WAS ANOTHER SIDE TO THE KING'S NEPHEW. IT HAS OFTEN BEEN REMARKED UPON THAT SIR GAWAIN WAS THE SUBJECT OF MANY FAIR LADIES' LOVE, AND THAT MORE THAN ONE, AS I HAVE TOLD ELSEWHERE, FELL DEEPLY IN LOVE WITH HIM – SOME WHO HAD NOT EVEN MET HIM, BUT LONGED FOR HIM WITH SUCH FERVOUR THAT THEY WENT TO GREAT LENGTHS TO CAPTURE HIM AND WERE DRIVEN TO THE POINT OF MADNESS. IT SEEMS FITTING THAT THIS TALE, WHICH CONCERNS ONE WHO HAS BEEN CALLED 'A FOOL OF LOVE', SHOULD SPEAK OF THE TERRIBLE DEEDS THAT MAY COME OF THAT SOMETIMES FATAL SICKNESS. IT IS, IN TRUTH, A DARK TALE THAT OPENS THE WAY TO PART OF THAT TIME OF WHICH MANY WILL KNOW NOTHING. ALSO, MORE THAN ONE VERSION OF THIS TALE EXISTS, ONE OF WHICH I TOLD PREVIOUSLY.* BUT IN MORE RECENT TIMES I HAVE DISCOVERED A VERSION THAT ADDS MUCH TO THE STORY I TOLD BEFORE, AND IS IN MANY WAYS QUITE DIFFERENT. THEREFORE, IN THE HOPE THAT THOSE WHO READ THESE TALES WILL FORGIVE ME, I SHALL GIVE IT AS IT IS TOLD BY MASTER RAOUL DE HOUDENC, A MOST EXCELLENT TELLER OF TALES, WHO ALSO WROTE THE ADVENTURES OF SIR MERAUGIS DE LA PORTLESQUEZ,† WHICH YOU MAY ALSO READ IN THESE PAGES. I WILL LEAVE IT TO THOSE

---

* 'Guingamore and Gaheries' in *The Great Book of King Arthur and His Knights of the Round Table*.
† 'Meraugis and the Wounds of Love', pp. 132–146.

THE AVENGING OF RAGUIDEL

WHO READ THIS STORY – BOTH MEN AND WOMEN – TO MAKE UP
THEIR OWN MINDS CONCERNING SIR GAWAIN AND ALL THAT CAME
OF HIS BEING AN OBJECT OF LOVE.

IN THE STRANGE sad days that followed the achieving of the Grail, the death of Sir Galahad and Sir Perceval's withdrawal into the timeless realm, a silence settled over the land of Logres.* But despite the many knights who were lost in the quest, and who were seen no more after that, still the Fellowship of the Round Table served King Arthur in his task of caring for the kingdom over which he ruled.

So it was that with the ending of spring and the coming in of summer, King Arthur decided that the court should move to Caerleon, where feasting would be held and tournaments ordained, and where the finest of the knights should attend. And, as was the custom at that time, the king declared that he would not dine until some wonder or adventure was brought before him.

On this occasion, no such thing occurred, and thus the king ordered the court to go in to supper, but he himself remained in his chamber alone, doubtless recalling the many adventures on which he had sent forth his knights. And, as I have told before in that other tale, sleep did not come to King Arthur, so that he arose and went forth into the night, and came to the shore of the sea. There he sighted a small ship without sails or oars that nevertheless came to land. And King Arthur went on board and found the body of a knight lying upon a bed, and saw how the tip of a great spear was left in his body.

Filled with wonder, the king examined the

body and found that a richly decorated purse hung from its belt, and that on the dead knight's hand were five rings. Seeing this, King Arthur tried to remove them in case they could help identify the slain man. But he found that they would not come off, no matter how he tried.

Next, he examined the purse and found a letter within it. This he read:

'Here lies the body of a brave and honourable man, slain by an evil coward. He comes to the court of the great King Arthur in the hope that one of the Knights of the Round Table will avenge him. Know this, that two knights shall together avenge him: the one who can withdraw this spear tip from his body, and he who can remove the rings from his hand. Until then his name shall be withheld, as will the way to the place where he was slain. Let those who have chosen to follow this adventure beware of those who shall oppose them.'

Having read this letter, King Arthur summoned servants to carry the body into the great Church of Caerleon, and to lay it in splendour before the high altar. Then he let it be known that any man who wished to answer the call of the letter, should first withdraw the spearpoint and thereafter the five rings on the dead knight's hand.

As word of this spread through the court, several knights were eager to attempt the adventure. First and foremost was Sir Kay, who as ever pressed forward and begged the king to let him try. To this King Arthur agreed, but

---

* An early name for King Arthur's Britain

when the seneschal attempted to pull forth the spear tip he could do nothing but tug and pull until fresh blood flowed from the dead knight's wound.

To Sir Kay's great shame, King Arthur commanded him to cease and others followed him. But though some of the greatest knights tried, even Sir Lancelot, they failed to move either the spearpoint or the rings. The last of all to arrive was Sir Gawain, and though he barely touched the remains of the spear, it sprang forth from the body into his hand! Then, as all there looked on, the king's nephew tried to remove the rings. Alas, in this he failed, and the court retired to eat and await what would follow.

In the morning it was discovered that the vessel that had brought the body had vanished away in the night, and also that the rings had been taken from the dead knight's hand; but none had seen who took them, or where he might have gone. Sir Gawain determined, as ever, to proceed with the adventure as swiftly as might be, begged leave of King Arthur to set forth – though both the king and the knights wondered how he would find his way to the place of the knight's death, since he had neither name nor directions to follow.

S O IT WAS that Sir Gawain followed the road from Caerleon for many leagues, threading his way through the wards of the Great Wood. More than one adventure he had at this time beyond doubt, but it was his meeting with a powerful knight named Maduc the Black of which the story tells. This man was known far and wide as both a mighty opponent and one of great cruelty, who never granted mercy to those he defeated. Each opponent

was beheaded and their heads set upon spikes around the walls of his castle.

When he heard of this, Sir Gawain determined to turn aside from his appointed task and to end the Black Knight's reign of terror. Finding his way to Maduc's castle, he challenged the knight to battle, and there followed such a fight as was seldom seen in those days, despite the many encounters of the Round Table Fellowship. I shall not hold up the telling of this tale with an account of this, for Master Raoul de Houdenc has done so far more elegantly than I, but I will say that not since the battle between Sir Lancelot and Sir Turquine, as described by Master Thomas himself, had such a battle been seen.*

Despite his unquestioned strength and skill, it took Gawain many long hours to defeat his opponent, but in the end he did so and prepared to slay his adversary. When the knight begged for mercy, Gawain asked him why he should be granted this when he had refused so many. At this, Sir Maduc expressed his sorrow for the deaths he had caused, and begged to be allowed to tell Gawain the reason for his unyielding failure to spare those he had defeated.

It was, he said, because of a lady, the ruler of the castle Gaut Desert, who was famed both for her beauty and her strength of will. Some time before, she had declared a tournament to which many knights had come, and in which he had proved the strongest, thus winning the lady's favour. Then, on the last day of the games, a knight had entered the lists who not only defeated all-comers but at length brought down Maduc himself.

'All that I had achieved was destroyed in that moment,' said the knight. 'I lost the love of

---

* See *Le Morte D'Arthur*. Book VI, Ch. viii.

my lady, who declared that she could love only he who had fought so bravely that day. That knight's name was Sir Gawain of Orkney, King Arthur's nephew, and since that day I have hated him more than anyone living. All those who I have slain, and whose heads decorate the walls of my castle, are there because I believed that one day Sir Gawain himself would come to avenge them, and thus allow me to take revenge upon him.'

When he heard this, Sir Gawain was silent, and held his own name hidden. For he remembered the events described by Sir Maduc, whom he had indeed defeated, and how the lady of Gaut Desert had pursued him with pleas to become her champion and her lover. At that time – and perhaps it was one of the very few times that Gawain spurned a beautiful woman – he had declined her advances, and left the tournament as victor. Now that he heard of the many deaths his actions had brought about, he thought to avenge these deaths by killing the Black Knight. Yet something of the story caused him to hold his hand, and instead he demanded that Sir Maduc do penance for those he had slain, to cease his wanton killing of any who came against him, and to swear allegiance to King Arthur.

To this, Maduc swore most readily, and thus was granted his life. Yet Sir Gawain could not forget that he had, though inadvertently, caused the Black Knight to follow a path of hatred from which came the deaths of many brave men, and so it was that he commanded Sir Maduc to show him the way to the castle of Gaut Desert, for he felt in his heart that he could not leave the matter unresolved until he had spoken of these things with the lady of that place.

At first Maduc was reluctant for, as he said: 'Since that time when Sir Gawain overcame me, the lady has come to hate me as much as I hate the king's nephew. And I have heard it said that she has found another champion who is even more brutal than I, and is yet to be defeated.'

But Gawain, who still kept his identity secret from his recent foe, insisted that Maduc should take him to the castle of Gaut Desert, and so it was that the next day the two men set forth together.

When they came at last in sight of the grim castle, Sir Maduc turned back, fearful of what might occur were the lady to see him. Promising to go to Camelot the Golden and to tell his story to King Arthur, he took his leave, declaring sadly that he never expected to see the knight who had so roundly beaten him again. 'For if the fearsome champion of Gaut Desert does not kill you, and you are somehow enabled to defeat him, I fear that you will never leave that place alive. For the lady has many wiles and many ways to hold in thrall those who defy her.'

So it was that Sir Gawain rode up to the gates of Gaut Desert and prepared to request entry. At that moment there came forth a damsel named Blé de Jaune, who had been handmaiden to the wife of a Round Table knight named Sir Spinagros, and who now served the Lady of Gaut Desert. Having spent much time in Camelot the Golden the damsel recognised Gawain at once.

'You must not come within, my lord!' she cried. 'If my lady learns that you are here, you will be captured and slain – for the love the lady once bore you has turned to hate, and she desires only to punish you for the pain you have caused her.'

'None of this was my doing,' said Sir Gawain. 'It was she who sought my love, which I refused her.'

→ *The arrival of the boat* ←

'Nevertheless,' said Blé de Jaune, 'she will do anything to bring you here, and seeks only to do you harm.'

Then she told Sir Gawain that his own brother, Sir Gaheries, was a prisoner in the grim castle. 'Such is the strength of my lady's determination to capture you, she thus hopes you will come here to rescue him. And that is much needed, for every day he is brought forth in the dungeon and whipped until the blood flows.'

When he heard this Gawain's anger was great, and he at once declared that he would demand his brother be set free and that he would himself face the wrath of the lady and her champion. But the maiden begged him to wait. 'There is yet more that you must know of this matter.'

Then it was that Sir Gawain learned more concerning the perilous things the Lady of Gaut Desert had caused, because of her feelings for him. 'So great was her love for you, Sir Gawain,' said the damosel, 'that she had a fine tomb built within the chapel of Gaut Desert. There is a small window through which the rich carvings upon the mausoleum may be viewed. What few know is that she has caused a shutter to be built into the frame of the window, and at her signal it can be released in such a way that it would behead anyone looking through it! Her plan was that when you were lured to this place, she would invite you to view the beauty of the carved tomb through the window, then set the shutter to drop so that you would be killed. As if this was not enough, she told how she would then take poison, and once she was dead, would be buried next to you with your cold lips touching.'

Sir Gawain heard this in horror. 'Truly this lady suffers from such madness beyond anything I have heard. It is clear that I must get Gaheries away from here, and myself also.'

Then he took further thought and asked concerning the lady's new champion.

'He is named Guengasouain,' the damsel told him. 'He is a powerful knight already, but my lady has caused to have made for him enchanted armour which it seems makes him undefeatable. Now, in addition to this, he has caught and trained a bear to defend him. If he ever meets a knight who succeeds in bringing him to the earth, the bear will attack that man and rend him apart. Be sure you have all of this in mind if you intend to fight with him.'

'That we shall see,' said Gawain grimly.

'He is truly an evil man,' said the damosel. 'I have heard tell of a dreadful act that took place but a year since, let me tell it to you so that you may understand who it is that you face.'

Then the damosel told Sir Gawain of a brave knight named Sir Raguidel, who was loved by a faery woman of great beauty. 'Guengasouain saw this woman and he too fell in love with her. Driven by jealousy he plotted to kill Raguidel. He waited in the depths of the wood until he saw the good man coming and challenged him. Because of his impenetrable armour he was able to defeat Raguidel with ease. In the end he ran him through with a great spear with which he struck so hard that it broke off in his body, leaving the head behind.'

'You say that this good knight died with the spearhead still stuck in his flesh?' demanded Gawain in wonder.

'Indeed that is what happened,' replied the damosel. 'But what happened next is even more strange. The faery who loved Raguidel came there and took away the body. She placed it in a magical craft and set it off I know not where, together with a letter that required one of the knights of the Round Table to avenge his slaying. And now I will tell you also that Gaheries, who lies in the dungeon below this castle, took up that quest, for he was able to remove five rings from Raguidel's hand, and by this token knew that this was his task.'

'Now much is revealed to me,' said Sir Gawain. 'The magical craft came to Caerleon, where the court was meeting. I alone was able to pull the spearhead from the body, and I have been seeking the identity of the dead man ever since. If my brother had but waited a while longer he would have learned that he and I together were destined to avenge the death of Raguidel, but he was ever of a hasty nature,

and must have taken the rings in the night and set forth from Caerleon without thought.'

Greatly astonished by this, the damosel swore to help Gawain gain entrance to the castle. 'I know of a way to ensure that you are not recognised, and that neither my lady nor her champion will be prepared for your coming. I will tell her that you are Sir Kay the Seneschal, and thus no one will ask your name and you can remain unknown.'

To this Gawain agreed, and though indeed he felt that to be thought of as Sir Kay was not what he wished, he accepted it in order to rescue Sir Gaheries, and thus was able to enter the castle, where he was greeted without animosity. When the lady of the castle saw him approaching through a window she asked her handmaiden who he was, and she, as promised, swore that he was Kay the Seneschal.

Hearing this, the Lady of Gaut Desert was glad. 'For thus we may make sure that he returns to Camelot the Golden and tells Sir Gawain that his brother is captive here. Thus he will come and I shall at last hold him in my power and cause him to love me, or kill him if he will not.'

So it was that Gawain was made welcome and seated next to the lady herself at supper. She knew him not, as she had not seen him unhelmed in the great joust that had begun her madness. Gawain remained mostly silent and only acknowledged himself as Sir Kay when he was thus addressed. So, too, he had his first sight of Sir Guengasouain, a powerful, dark browed man who spoke little but studied the guest as one who might wish to encounter him in battle and was assessing his warlike abilities.

Meanwhile, the Lady of Gaut Desert boasted to Sir Gawain that she had in her dungeon a knight of the Round Table and encouraged him to return to Camelot the Golden and there to be sure to tell the king's nephew that his brother was a prisoner there. 'Perhaps Sir Gawain himself will come to set him free,' she added, laughing with glee.

To this, Gawain, in his guise as the king's seneschal, said only that he would see to it that Sir Gaheries' fate was known. But after all had retired for the night he sought out the handmaiden, who told him how he might rescue Sir Gaheries.

'In the morning, he will be brought forth and dragged to the courtyard that you may see from your window. There he will be beaten and kicked before he is taken away back to the dungeon. If you leave the castle before prime*, then turn back to the little postern gate you see below, I will leave that open. Thus you may enter and recapture Sir Gaheries.'

Sir Gawain thanked the damosel and retired to his chamber, though it is my belief that he slept but little that night.

In the morning all fell out as the damosel had planned. Gawain rose early and departed the castle, then turned back and crept in via the postern gate. There he waited in the shade of a group of cherry trees, until he saw Gaheries, thin and wasted, and with his flesh much cut by the daily beatings, dragged out into the courtyard by three brutish guards.

There Gawain fell upon them, beheading one and severing the arm of the second and a hand of the other. Then he helped get Gaheries, who wept with joy, onto his horse and together they left the castle by the postern. There, they were joined by the damosel, who knew all too well how her mistress would deal with her once she discovered the truth about Gawain.

Meanwhile, pandemonium swept through the castle of Gaut Desert as word of the attack and rescue of Gaheries spread. At first bewildered, then enraged, the lady sought out her handmaid – only to find her gone. When one of her men entered to tell her how he had recognised the escaping knight as Sir Gawain, her rage knew no bounds. To think that the object of her desire had been in her very presence, but had escaped, along with Gaheries! At once she summoned Guengasouain and her soldiers, and ordered them to follow the escaping knights and to bring them back to her. 'Do not kill them,' she insisted. 'For I wish to be present when they die.'

Thus Guengasouain and a large body of knights and soldiers set out from Gaut Desert in pursuit of Gawain and Gaheries. Riding full pelt they were soon beginning to overtake them, but at this juncture Sir Maduc the Black appeared, having thought more of leaving Sir Gawain to face the Lady of Gaut Desert alone. Now he came with his own forces and sighting Sir Gawain, begged the escaping knights to accept his hospitality.

To this Gawain agreed and thus he and Gaheries took shelter in the castle of he who had but recently been Gawain's adversary. Soon after, the forces of the Lady of Gaut Desert appeared, and laid siege to the castle, and not long after that the lady herself arrived and demanded that Maduc surrender 'the false knight' Sir Gawain to her.

Maduc and the king's nephew stood together on the walls of the castle and the Black Knight swore that he would never again serve her in any manner, or surrender Sir Gawain to her.

'Then know that I will lay siege to this castle for as long as it takes to reduce its walls to dust. After which not only Gawain and his brother, but you also, Sir Maduc, will suffer cruelly before you die!'

---

* The first of the canonical hours. Roughly 6 a.m.

Thus began the siege of the Black Knight's castle. The Lady of Gaut Desert's forces far outnumbered those of the Sir Maduc, and within a week those within were suffering greatly from the constant attack of the opposing force. So at last Gawain himself climbed to the wall above and called out to Sir Guengasouain, who had daily ridden his prancing steed back and forth, mocking those within and calling them cowards and caitiffs. 'Sir Guengasouain,' cried Gawain. 'Let us end this foolishness. Let you and I meet up on the morrow and settle the matter in single combat, as knight against knight.'

Smiling grimly, Guengasouain agreed to meet Gawain, and so matters stood. But that night Gaheries, who had begun to recover from the effects of his captivity, begged to go with his brother. 'Firstly, Guengasouain has the savage bear at his side, so why should you not have an advantage? Also, it seems to me, that while you have the spear tip that slew Sir Raguidel, I had the rings from his hand until the Lady of Gaut Desert took them from me. Remember the words of the letter that said

two men should avenge him. Surely you are one and I the other.'

Reluctantly Gawain agreed, and next morning he and Gaheries rode out side by side to meet their adversary. There, in a field before the Black Knight's castle, men and women from both sides assembled, eyeing each other with hostility. Guengasouain himself appeared, attended by the great bear, which snarled and threatened everyone there. When they saw this, Sir Gaheries begged Gawain to let him do battle with the beast while the king's nephew engaged with the champion. Then he asked: 'Brother, how will you stand against Guengasouain's enchanted armour?'

'I shall do what I can with strength and skill,' answered Gawain. 'But if this is truly an enchantment, then I will deal with it through the magic of the spear tip.' And he showed Gaheries where he kept the broken spearhead in a bag at his saddlebow.

With that the brothers separated, Gaheries riding full tilt at the savage bear, while Gawain, without hesitation, made for Guengasouain.

Gaheries was the first to reach his opponent.

→ *The avenging of Raguidel* ←

53

The bear reared up on its hind legs and struck out with its razor sharp claws, cleaving Gaheries' shield in two and sinking them deeply into his arm. Crying out in pain, Gaheries struck back, wounding the creature, which simply enraged it, so that it struck at his mount, ripping deeply into the brave beast's flanks so that it fell to the earth. Gaheries, leaping clear of his dying steed, drew back his sword and leapt towards the bear, which opened its jaws wide to consume his flesh – but Gaheries thrust his sword right into its mouth and down its throat until the sword emerged from its back, and with a terrible roar the beast fell in its death throes.*

Gawain meanwhile met Guengasouain at full gallop and the two broke their spears into fragments with the force of their meeting. Gawain's lance cracked through the knight's shield and its point struck him directly in the centre of his breastplate. Such a blow would almost certainly have slain him outright, but because of his enchanted armour, it shattered instead, while the champion's own came close to unhorsing Gawain.

Turning in his saddle, the king's nephew drew forth the broken spear that came from the body of Raguidel and with all his force drove it deeply into his opponent's side.

With a cry Sir Guengasouain threw up his hands and fell backward onto the earth with a mighty crash. Gawain leapt down and stood over him.

'Do you surrender?' demanded the king's nephew.

'That I shall never do!' answered the fallen man. 'No man can beat me save by magic. Who are you that wields so much power?'

---

* For another bear that fights with the hero of the story see 'The Story of Edern, the Son of the Bear', pp. 226–235.

'I am Sir Gawain of Orkney,' answered the hero. 'And I carry the spear that you used to slay Sir Raguidel. Thus is he avenged this day.'

'Then kill me,' cried the fallen champion. 'For I will never surrender to you, nor for any man of Arthur's court!' and he turned his head away.

Then Gawain, with a single blow, cut off Guengasouain's head.

A great cry went up from the forces of the Lady of Gaut Desert, and they began to flee, pursued by Sir Maduc's knights. Gawain and Gaheries embraced on the field and Gawain took up the fallen knight's head to show to the Lady of Gaut Desert.

When she learned that it was Sir Gawain who had slain her champion, she wept long and bitterly, and more sorrowful than any man or woman ever was, flung herself from the walls of her castle and dashed her body onto the stones beneath. Thus the madness of the Lady of Gaut Desert was brought to a sorrowful end, whom may God assoil for her sins.

THUS WAS THE good knight Raguidel avenged, and thus a great wrong righted through strength and honour. Sir Gawain and Sir Gaheries returned to Camelot the Golden and told their story, while preparations were made to inter the body of the dead knight. But before this could be done, the magical craft that had borne him thither was sighted, and aboard it was the faery demoiselle who had loved him. She came ashore and thanked Sir Gawain and Sir Gaheries for their bravery. For this avenging, she said, was a matter for men and not the people of Faery. Then she took back the fragment of the spear which Gawain had kept, but to Sir Gaheries she gave the five rings, as a memorial of all that he had suffered, before taking the body of Raguidel onto the ship, which then sailed away, soon vanishing from sight. Nor was it ever seen in the land of men again, though I doubt not that it remains still in the country of Faery.

And as it fell out, the damosel Blé de Jaune, who had helped Sir Gawain so greatly, returned to Camelot the Golden, and having fallen in love with Sir Gaheries when he was captive in Gaut Desert, and he with her, they were married in the spring amidst great rejoicing.

As to Sir Maduc the Black, he became in time one of the bravest and truest knights of the Round Table, and he and Sir Gawain remained friends until the sorrowful breaking of the Fellowship.

✝ ✝ ✝

THUS I HAVE told the story, as Master Raoul de Houdenc related it, for I believe that in it we may see how Sir Gawain, amongst all the knights of that great Fellowship, was the finest and bravest amongst them, and that he learned from these events how those who love too much may bring great sorrow to others.

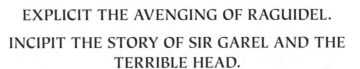

EXPLICIT THE AVENGING OF RAGUIDEL.

INCIPIT THE STORY OF SIR GAREL AND THE TERRIBLE HEAD.

7: SIR GAREL AND THE TERRIBLE HEAD

ONE OF THE KNIGHTS OF THE ROUND TABLE WHO IS LESS OFTEN HEARD ABOUT IN THESE DAYS IS SIR GAREL OF THE BLOSSOMING VALLEY. BORN OF GOOD STOCK, HE WAS AS BRAVE AND CHIVALROUS AS ANY OF KING ARTHUR'S KNIGHTS, AND I CANNOT SAY WHY HE HAS BEEN SO OVERLOOKED IN THE HISTORIES OF THE ROUND TABLE. YET SUCH WAS THE WAY IN THOSE TIMES, WHEN ALL KNEW THE NAMES OF GAWAIN, LANCELOT, AND PERCEVAL, BUT MEN SUCH AS MELERANZ, RAGUIDEL AND GAREL WERE LESS OFTEN REMEMBERED. AS I SHALL SHOW HERE, HOWEVER, THIS KNIGHT WAS A GOOD MAN AND TRUE, AND IN HIS TIME SERVED KING ARTHUR AS WELL AS ANY IN HIS WIDE REALM. ALSO, WE MAY LEARN YET MORE OF THE CREATURES THAT CAME TO THE COURT OF ARTHUR FROM OTHER LANDS, RULED OVER, IT MAY BE, BY THE LORDS OF FAERY.

✠ ✠ ✠

THE STORY BEGINS when Sir Garel set forth in search of adventure. He wandered far until he came to a land that seemed to him both rich and fair, but was strangely deserted. Where fields flourished he saw no one harvesting them, where rivers and lakes seemed filled with fish, no one fished for them, and where game in plenty roamed the woods, no hunters rode there. Several villages through which Sir Garel passed were empty, though he saw no sign of war or pestilence, and no bodies were left to rot in the sun.

Puzzled by this, Sir Garel rode on until he came to where a mighty castle stood upon a high ridge of rock. Only one narrow path wound its way up to the gates. These, when the knight followed the way, he found shut fast, and the drawbridge raised. Yes he smelled the aroma of well cooked meat, and saw where lights shone out into the gathering dark. So he called out to see if he could gain entrance.

Several times he did this before a knight appeared on the wall above the gate and enquired of his purpose.

'Sir,' said Garel. 'I am but a stranger who seeks shelter for the night. May I be admitted?'

The knight hesitated for a time, and all the while looked beyond Sir Garel at the road behind him and the sloping sides of the rock where they fell away below the castle.

At length, the guardian of the gate allowed the knight to enter, and several others came forth to welcome him. Divested of his armour and weapons, his horse led away to the stable, and fresh water brought to him to wash in, Garel soon felt the benefits of this noble household.

Only when he was refreshed did his new hosts lead him into the great hall of the castle, which he learned was called Montrogan and he met the lady who ruled there. Her name was Laudamie, and she had inherited the castle and all the lands around when her father and brother had perished in battle. But this was not the worst of her concerns, as Sir Garel was soon to learn when he was led before the lady, who wore a crown as was her right as the ruler of this kingdom. When he looked upon her Garel thought he had never seen so fair a

→ *The shield of Vulganus* ←

maid; while she, in turn, was much drawn to his manly beauty and stern strength. When she learned that he was one of the Round Table Fellowship, she was even more enamoured, and welcomed him warmly.

So it was that Sir Garel enjoyed a splendid meal, seated beside the beautiful Lady Laudamie, and spoke with her late into the night. There he learned the reason for the empty lands and deserted villages as well as for the caution of those within before letting him into the castle.

A dreadful monster haunted the place – part man and part horse like the centaurs of the ancient world, but with the addition of a fish-like head that allowed it to breathe underwater. Its name was Vulganus, and it lived in a sea cave that was open to land and water. It gave no quarter but killed every man, woman and child it could capture. But it was not just its strength and savagery that made this the most terrifying opponent. The Vulganus also possessed a magical shield, which bore the face of a hideous creature. Anyone who looked upon it at once fell dead and the monster was able to consume them, both flesh and bones together, having first drunken their blood.

Although the story does not speak of this, I am moved to wonder if the face upon this shield was not similar to the dreadful Medusa, which in the tales of the Greeks turned all who saw it to stone? It is said that it possessed hair comprised of serpents, that writhed constantly, and only when the great hero Perseus tricked the creature, was the Medusa slain and its head carried off. What became of that head I have not heard, but I cannot help recall this when the story speaks of something so like it.

Sir Garel learned all that the Lady Laudamie could tell him, including that the beast came each day to the castle gate and emitted a terrible scream, that made all who heard it fall into madness for a time. Some had been known to run outside the walls of the castle in terror, only to be stricken by the monster and consumed.

All of this Sir Garel heard, and while he listened he found that he could not take his eyes off the Queen of Montrogan, and as the evening progressed so he fell ever more deeply under her spell, while Laudamie herself felt such warmth for the knight that when the time came for all to retire, she was entirely in love with Garel, and he with her.

That night, both lay awake in their beds, and in his heart Garel knew that he had met the only woman he would ever love. So it was that he decided he would first find a way to defeat and destroy the monster Vulganus – though how he could not say. Then the thought came to him to call upon the aid of a friend whom he had helped restore to his kingdom when it was overrun by evil men. This was the Dwarf King Albwin, who possessed a cloak of invisibility which gave him the means to go where he wished without being seen or captured.

Garel sent a message to him, and soon Albwin came, eager to help repay the debt of honour owing to his friend. To him Garel explained the presence of the monster and how the shield it possessed made it invulnerable to attack. Albwin thought deeply on this and promised to do all that he could to help.

Donning his magical cloak, he made his way to the monster's home, a dark, dank cave by the sea's edge, filled with the reek of death. There, he watched until he saw the creature emerge. Truly terrifying it was, but the dwarf king remained watching until he saw the Vulganus depart into the sea in search of prey.

Before it left, he saw that it set aside the death-dealing shield, covering it with a sheet of curious fish-skin that gleamed and glittered in colours far brighter than anything he had seen before.

As soon as the monster vanished beneath the waves, Albwin hastened to where it had left the shield and, since it was covered, lifted it and carried it off. Reaching Montrogan castle, he buried it close to the gates, well hidden from even the most curious eyes.

Seeking out Garel, he told the knight all that he had seen, and what he had done. For without the shield, he believed, the odds against the Vulganus were better in favour of his friend.

'Then I shall take my chance against the strength of the creature,' Garel said, and promised Albwin that he would be well rewarded once the matter was settled.

'I seek no reward other than your safe return,' answered the dwarf king.

At that moment there came a terrible howl from the direction of the sea. So loud and terrible was it, that the very air shook and birds flew up in great clouds from the trees. Thus they knew the Vulganus had found its way home and discovered that the shield was missing.

So it was that, despite the desperate pleas of the Lady Laudamie, who feared above all things for his life, Sir Garel set forth next morning. Soon he reached the shore and there caught his first glimpse of the Vulganus, which as he had been told bore the forward half in the shape of a man, with the hindquarters of a horse, and with a head that seemed more fish than man-flesh. It seemed to him the most hideous thing he had ever seen, and he saw too that it seemed clad in mail made of a strange luminous fish-skin such as that described by Albwin.

When it saw him approach, it screamed so loudly that Garel almost turned away in fear, but thoughts of his duty to the Round Table, and above all to the Lady Laudamie, spurred him onward, and there, on the shore in the

PLATE 3: *'Soon he reached the shore and there caught his first glimpse of the Vulganus'*

shadow of grim cliffs, he set his spear in rest and he charged full tilt at the creature.

His spear struck right in the centre of the Vulganus' breast, but the skin that covered its body like armour was so tough that it shattered the lance into a hundred pieces. Again, the creature screamed and laid about it with a great iron mace which broke Garel's shield and dinted his armour. He, in turn, hacked at the monster with his sword, only to see it glance off the fish-skin mail, and so do no damage.

Again and again the knight struck at his adversary, all the while twisting and turning to avoid further blows from the iron mace. Then the Vulganus struck a blow which brought Sir Garel's mount to its knees, so that he was forced to jump clear. Now fighting on foot, the knight realised how tall and powerful the creature was. Then he noted that the Vulganus' arms were bare to the elbow, and quick as thought, he struck, severing the creature's left hand which held the mace.

Though blood spurted, the Vulganus screamed hideously and renewed its attack. It seemed scarcely troubled by its wound, and now it wielded a razor-edged blade in its other hand. Almost overwhelmed by the ferocity of its attack, Garel struck again, this time severing the creature's right hand.

Despite these terrible wounds, the Vulganus came on, now turning so that it could kick out at Garel with its hind legs. Narrowly avoiding this, the knight struck with all his might, severing the knee joints of the monster, which were not covered by the fish-skin mail.

With a final scream the creature fell, and in that moment Garel struck off its head. Then he too fell to the ground, his strength all but gone from the fury of the battle.

Now the Dwarf King Albwin reappeared, having watched the great struggle from beneath the concealment of his cloak, but not daring to intervene in this fight. Eagerly, he helped Garel to stand and brought him water to drink. Then the two friends examined the body of the dead creature, especially the fish-skin mail that covered much of its body.

'If it is your will, allow me to take this,' said Albwin. 'I believe I may be able to make armour from it that will turn any weapon.'

To this Garel assented willingly.

'May this be some reward for all that you have done for me,' he said to his friend.

And the story tells us that the dwarf king did indeed make himself armour from the skin of the Vulganus, and that he afterwards did a great many deeds, since none could harm him while he wore it.

Meanwhile Garel and the dwarf king returned to Montrogan, where you may be sure they both received a warm welcome – especially when they showed the severed head of the Vulganus. When she learned that it was indeed dead, the Lady Laudamie was filled with both gratitude and wonder.

'Sir Knight,' she said. 'I cannot say how much I and my people owe to you! This monster has terrorised and killed so many that it is almost beyond belief that its shadow is lifted at last. But I cannot believe how you did this, and how you lived. What of the shield that none may look upon?'

Then Garel and Albwin told the lady how the latter had stolen the shield with the terrible head and hidden it beyond the walls of the castle. 'Even now,' said Garel, 'I cannot think that it should be allowed to remain in this world, for who is to say whether evil men may not discover its hiding place and turn upon all who oppose them.'

For that time the matter remained undecided, while the knight and the lady planned a more felicitous event – their wedding! For both had made their vows of love to each other, and such was the gratitude of the people of that land that they more than welcomed Sir Garel as their new king.

So it was that Garel and Laudamie were married amid great rejoicing, and soon after the knight was crowned king of that land. But all the while the thought of the death-dealing shield remained in their minds, until at last, King Albwin came to them and suggested that it should be sealed in a cauldron of molten lead and then taken out to sea and consigned to the depths, where no man would ever discover it.

This King Garel commanded, and when the shield, covered from the eyes of all, was drowned in molten lead, he sought out a sailor whom he paid ten Marks* to take the cauldron far out to sea and consign it to the deep.

---

* Approx. £135 sterling in today's currency. Perhaps less than the sailors deserved!

This the man did. He sailed until he reached a place where four seas met, known as Sattel-ege, and there he threw the dreadful object over the side.

At once a huge storm arose, and the seas became tumultuous as if they boiled from within. To such a degree was this that the ship almost sank, but thanks to the skill of the crew it was able to break free of the churning waters and return to Montrogan, where the men were all well rewarded. But to this day the seas where the shield with the terrible head was consigned remain furious, and Sattelege was renamed Wolfsattelege, so that all know to be wary of that place.

As to Sir Garel, now king of the land and happily married to the Lady Laudamie, he continued to serve King Arthur as a knight of the Round Table, and had many more adven-tures – though the story of the terrible head seems to have faded in the memory of those who tell of the great deeds of the Fellowship.

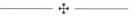

EXPLICIT THE STORY OF SIR GAREL AND THE TERRIBLE HEAD.

INCIPIT THAT OF KING ARTHUR AND KING CORNWALL

8: KING ARTHUR
AND KING CORNWALL

MOST OF THE TALES THAT I HAVE COLLECTED HERE TO FOLLOW THE MIGHTY BOOK OF SIR THOMAS MALORY, CAME FROM THE GREAT COURTS OF EUROPE. BUT THE TALE I TELL HERE IS DIFFERENT – IT COMES FROM ONE OF THE WANDERING SINGERS OF BALLADS WHO ONCE TRAVELLED THE LAND WITH THEIR TALES OF KING ARTHUR AND HIS KNIGHTS. I HAVE HEARD THIS SUNG BY ONE SUCH RAGGED FELLOW ON MORE THAN ONE OCCASION, AND FELT THAT IT HAD NO PART IN THE GREAT EPICS OF CAMELOT THE GOLDEN. YET, ON HEARING IT RENDERED AGAIN THIS SEASON PASSED, I AM MOVED TO INCLUDE IT HERE. THERE ARE THINGS WITHIN THAT I FIND HARD TO TELL, FOR THEY SHOW A VERY DIFFERENT ASPECT OF THE COURT OF KING ARTHUR – YET THERE IS A MOST ANCIENT MAGIC AT WORK HERE, WHICH I CANNOT IGNORE. THE THOUGHT THAT THERE MIGHT ONCE HAVE EXISTED A SECOND ROUND TABLE ALONE FILLS ME WITH WONDER. THUS, WITH RESERVATION, I WILL PROCEED, THOUGH I CANNOT SWEAR THAT ALL HERE IS THE TRUTH. LET IT STAND AS A CURIOUS TALE OF ARTHUR'S REALM, AND LET THOSE WHO READ THESE WORDS DECIDE FOR THEMSELVES WHETHER THEY BELIEVE WHAT IS TRUE AND WHAT IS NOT.

✢ ✤ ✢

MOST WHO KNOW the stories of King Arthur and his knights will have heard how the Round Table, able to seat one hundred and fifty knights, was made by Merlin himself – round in the likeness of the world, where all are equal – and that it was made first for King Arthur's father, Uther Pendragon.

Other tellers have said that it belonged first to King Leodegrance, the father of the Lady Guinevere, and that the table came to Camelot the Golden as part of the bride price when King Arthur married Guinevere. This tale is told by Master Thomas himself. The story I tell now offers a different version of these events.

61

It was on a day in early spring when Arthur thought to call a new convocation of knights to fill all the seats at the Round Table. 'No one possessed of skill and courage, will fail to answer the call,' said the king. But Queen Guinevere, overhearing this, laughed and said: 'This is a great table indeed, my lord. But I have heard of one that is greater still.'

'How is that possible?' demanded King Arthur. 'Is it not true that Merlin made but one?'

'As to that, I cannot say,' answered the queen. 'Only that I have been told, by those whose words I have found to be true, that there is a table far greater than this, seating as many as three hundred knights.'

'And where is this wondrous thing?' asked Arthur.

'Again, I cannot say,' replied the queen. 'Only that it is said to be far from here in the great forest of Broceliande.'

'Then in God's name,' said King Arthur, ' I shall go in search of it. Nor shall I stop seeking until I find it! For if there is truly a table greater than mine, I would see it with my own eyes and if possible bring it here to Camelot the Golden.'

That very day the king summoned the greatest knights of the Round Table Fellowship to go with him in search of the second table. He chose his nephew, Sir Gawain, Sir Tristan, Sir Bredbeddle and Sir Marramiles (of whom little is known, but who was assuredly a mighty knight) to go with him. King Arthur himself chose to carry a plain shield so that he might not be recognised.

The ballad singer reports that King Arthur and his knights 'rode east and west, in many a strange country', in their search for word of the second Round Table. Many castles they visited and many shrines of the old saints also, so that it seemed to those who saw them that they were on pilgrimage. But in truth it was the words of Queen Guinevere that spurred on

the king – for his pride forbade him to believe that a greater table than that at which so many great knights sat could truly exist.

At length the party arrived at a most splendid castle, where they were met by a porter who was clad in the most magnificent regalia. At first he was haughty towards the king and his knights, demanding to know their purpose in coming to his master's gate. King Arthur told him, as he had to each and every noble house they had visited, that he and his companions were knights on pilgrimage, seeking wonders and adventures, as did many in that time.

Then the king took a golden ring from his hand and offered it to the porter if he would but tell him the name of the lord whose castle this was, and beg of him the favour of a bed for the night, two meals and a safe departure in the morning.

'My lord is named King Cornwall,' answered the porter. 'As to your request he will, I am certain, be glad to offer it in return for whatever stories you can tell of your journey.'

To this King Arthur and the knights agreed, and were admitted into the most splendid hall that rivalled even that of Camelot the Golden. The richness of their host was to be seen upon every side – from the golden plates and goblets set out upon the tables, to the richly coloured tapestries that adorned every wall.

There they met King Cornwall, who was both fair of face and manner, and welcomed the knights. So it was that they were seated at the high table for supper, and much talk there was of the adventures the king and his fellows had encountered on their journey. As the evening wore on and wine flowed into the golden cups, talk came around to the mightiest lords in the realm of Logres, and at last King Cornwall asked if they had heard of 'A king named Arthur, who by all accounts has as great a Fellowship of knights as any man may have?'

King Arthur, smiling to himself, replied that he did indeed know of such a king. Whereat King Cornwall laughed and said that he had fathered a daughter upon this king's wife some years before.

Now let it be known at once that this evil statement was later shown to be false – an empty boast by a man without honour or principle. But in that moment, though King Arthur doubted not the faithfulness of his queen, he yet fell silent and did not ask the question he had intended concerning the Round Table.

King Cornwall then proceeded to boast of other things. He brought forth a wonderful horn that, he said, when blown, could summon the people of Faery; a sword that was so sharp it could cut the wind itself; and a mighty axe that if required could cut down all the trees of the Great Wood. Then he spoke of a horse he owned, that could run further and faster than any other. All of these things, he declared, were more powerful than anything possessed by the famous King Arthur.

In time, having heard enough of King Cornwall's boasts, the knights retired, finding they were all housed together in a large chamber with beds for all, each covered with splendid counterpanes and sheets of the finest silk. Once they were alone, they spoke together in hushed tones of the boasts uttered by King Cornwall. All were certain that there was no truth in the accusation against Queen Guinevere, and as for the other things they had been shown, none there believed them to be all they seemed.

Only Sir Gawain, who in his cups was prone to speaking wildly, said that in answer to the King Cornwall's empty boasts he would steal away the most beautiful woman in the castle and take her back to Camelot the Golden to have his way with her.

King Arthur spoke sternly to his nephew then, reminding him of his pledge upon becoming a knight of the Round Table, that he would serve and protect all women.

But Gawain's boast, like that of King Cornwall's, encouraged the others to make similar claims. Sir Tristan said that he would steal the

→ *Berlo-Beanie* ←

63

magic horn; Sir Marramiles then said that he would capture the great axe. Only Arthur failed to speak in this manner, determining that all there were behaving in a way unsuited to his Fellowship and that they should cease these idle boasts at once.

As they argued, the knight named Sir Bredbeddle heard a sound coming from a splendid armoire that stood in the room, and drawing his sword, he opened it and set free a strange and hideous creature. Dark and hairy, its eyes glowed red and both its long arms and legs were armoured with long curved claws.

The story says that this was a fearsome demon baring the strange name of Berlo-Beanie, that served King Cornwall and had been set to keep watch over the knights and to report to his master all that was said.

The knights then drew their swords and attacked the creature, which easily defeated them all. None can say what dreadful end might have been the fate of King Arthur and the knights, were it not for a most powerful relic that Sir Bredbeddle carried upon his person. This was a small metal book, chased with many strange designs, that he had found long since cast upon the shore of the sea. A wise man had told him that it contained many secrets, even unto that of Our Lord himself – but of this I may not comment for it is beyond my knowledge. Suffice it that this relic gave Sir Bredbeddle the power to overcome the demon, whom he conjured into a wall of the room so that its head and hands alone stuck out into the chamber.

There followed the most strange series of events. As if they were all bespelled, as it may be they were, each of the knights called upon Berlo-Beanie to enable them to carry out their boasts. Sir Gawain demanded that the most beautiful woman in the castle be brought to him and that they should both be conveyed by magic to Camelot the Golden.

This the demon accomplished with but a few murmured words, and both the lady and Sir Gawain vanished in the blink of an eye. Then Sir Tristan asked to be brought the magic horn, which again the demon caused to happen. However, when the knight tried to blow the horn and summon the people of Faery, not a single note could be drawn from it. The same thing happened when Sir Marramiles demanded the great axe, for when it appeared before them all, the knight could not even lift it from the ground, so huge and heavy was it.

At this point King Arthur called again for an end to the attempts of his knights to fulfil their foolish boasts. But at this Sir Bredbeddle asked if the king had any wish of his own that the demon could be commanded to bring about. And after taking thought Arthur said that he wished to hold the magical sword that could cut the wind and to be given the strength to wield it.

This the demon Berlo-Beanie did, thanks to the power of Sir Bredbeddle's relic. And when he held the sword at last, King Arthur demanded to know if there was truly a great Round Table in the castle. Snarling and spitting, the demon answered that there was indeed, at which King Arthur demanded to be shown it, and was at once transported to a room hidden in the heart of the castle. There, indeed, was a table more than twice the size of that at which Arthur's knights sat, and there too was King Cornwall himself, who had gone there to admire his greatest possession.

When he saw King Arthur, he fell into a great rage and rushed at him, but with scarcely a thought King Arthur drew forth the magical sword and with a single blow sent King Cornwall's head flying from his shoulders.

As the boastful king fell, so the Round Table

began to crack and fall to dust. Soon nothing remained of it, save a few splinters of wood. Then King Arthur was glad and took the sword back to the chamber where his men awaited him.

'It is,' said King Arthur, 'unwise that these treasures should be allowed to exist, for others will seek them and may use them to do harm.' Therefore he commanded Sir Bredbeddle to instruct the demon to destroy them all.

To this Berlo-Beanie responded that these were ancient and powerful objects that could not be destroyed by him, but that he could place them somewhere where they would not be found in that time. And he did, all the time cursing the name of King Arthur and all those present, especially Sir Bredbeddle, the power of whose little book had bested him.

Then the demon begged to be set free, since his master was no longer living he had no wish to spend all his days imprisoned in the wall. And Bredbeddle, with King Arthur's agreement, set the demon free, and it vanished with a long cry of despair into the bright air above the castle.

By this time, day had dawned, the adventures of King Arthur and his knights having taken a whole night to accomplish. The people of the castle were at first dismayed to learn of the death of their master, and indeed the castle itself had begun to crack and fall into ruin now that King Cornwall no longer lived. And from this we may guess that he was no mortal man or that he possessed powers beyond those of humankind.

King Arthur now revealed to the people of the castle his true identity and that of his knights, and all there who wished were pardoned as long as they swore fealty to him.

Thus was the strange adventure complete for that time – though it is said that Sir Gawain, who had stolen away the most beautiful woman from the castle, went not to Camelot the Golden, but by the demon's power was sent to another place, where he spent many moons in delight with the lady, who must indeed, as it seemed, have had faery blood, so that for ever after Sir Gawain hungered for the love of such magical women.

For the rest, King Arthur returned to Camelot the Golden and was content with the table made for him by Merlin, and if he thought again of the boast made by King Cornwall regarding the queen, he never spoke of it, and the queen, when she learned the whole story of the great table, bowed her head and showed only her love for her noble lord.

✢ ✚ ✢

OF THIS TALE I can say no more than that it is among the strangest I have found in my long search for the stories of the great king and his knights. What happened to the secret relic, I cannot say, for Sir Bredbeddle is seldom mentioned in the other tales I have found. But I give thanks to him for helping to defeat King Cornwall and his demon.

———— ✢ ————

EXPLICIT THE STRANGE TALE OF THE SECOND ROUND TABLE.

INCIPIT THE TALE OF THE MARVELS OF RIGOMER.

9: THE MARVELS OF RIGOMER

MANY AND STRANGE WERE THE MARVELS EXPERIENCED BY THE KNIGHTS OF THE ROUND TABLE – BUT PERHAPS NONE MORE SO THAN IN THE TALE UPON WHICH I EMBARK HERE. IT WAS TOLD BY ONE WHO CALLED HIMSELF JEHAN, OF WHOM I KNOW NOTHING MORE THAN HIS NAME, YET IT SEEMS TO ME THAT IN HIS TIME HE WAS ALMOST AS GREAT A TELLER OF TALES AS WAS MASTER THOMAS HIMSELF. MUCH MAY SEEM ALMOST COMICAL HERE, AND YET BELOW THE SURFACE LIES A DEEPER AND DARKER TALE – ONE THAT SHOWS THAT NOT ALL WAS WELL IN KING ARTHUR'S REALM AND BEYOND. OF THIS I SHALL WRITE NO MORE HERE, BUT LEAVE IT TO THE READERS OF THIS TALE TO DECIDE FOR THEMSELVES. FOR IS IT NOT SAID, THAT WITHIN THE WARDS OF THE GREAT WOOD, NOTHING IS AS IT SEEMS? AND DOES THE LADY NOT DANCE UPON THE GREENSWARD?

✠ ✠ ✠

AS IS SO often told in the stories of King Arthur and his Knights, this story begins with the arrival of a lady. She came as the company awaited a sign that would permit them to eat – for at that time it was still the custom of the Round Table that no meal could commence until some adventure had been begun. I dare say that even in that time there must have been days when all went hungry to their beds, even though there was no shortage of adventures in which the knights took part; for such was the renown of the Fellowship, that all who sought help or desired one of the heroes of Camelot the Golden to undertake the righting of a wrong, knew they had but to come before King Arthur.

On this occasion, the lady who came was, as so often, most beautiful to look upon, and spoke words unlike any that had been heard there since the Round Table was founded. For when the damosel had been made welcome, she looked around at those gathered there and declared: 'Never have I seen such a band of lazy, fat and ignorant fools! How is it possible that this Fellowship has gained such a great reputation when all they can do is loll here

66

in this splendid court and do nothing but talk about their past deeds!'

So shocked were all present that no one answered. Even King Arthur and Queen Guinevere were so astonished they too were silent, looking at the damosel in wonder.

'I see that no one here is worthy of the message I bring,' she said. 'Shame upon you all!' Then, before anyone could stop her, the damosel turned about and left the hall.

Almost before she had passed from sight, Sir Owein, who was known as the Knight of the Lion, sprang to his feet. 'Are we to sit here and let the damosel's words become true?' he cried. 'With my lord's permission I will follow her and discover what challenge she has brought to us.'

King Arthur at once gave his assent, and Owein left the hall, calling for his armour and his horse. Behind him the court was all a-buzz as knight after knight declared that their reputation had been slandered by the lady. But it was only a brief time before Sir Owein returned, bruised and battered, from an encounter with a giant knight who had awaited his coming and who seemed to be the damosel's protector. So powerful was this warrior that he had defeated Owein easily – something which rarely happened unto that brave and powerful man – and sent him home without delay. When last seen they had been following the road to the west.

When he heard this, Sir Sagramore, who was a close friend of Owein's, begged to be allowed to follow the stranger knight and deal with him. Again the king granted him permission and again the knight left, determined to bring Sir Owein's adversary to heel. But he too returned after only a short time, beaten and wounded from his encounter with the mighty knight. 'Rarely have I felt such a powerful opponent,' he said. 'I fear he has been sent here to make us all look foolish and weak.'

At this, Sir Lancelot who, as all who read this must know, was the greatest of the Round Table Fellowship, spoke up. 'It seems to me that we must humble this man before the reputation of our company is damaged yet further.'

To this both the king and queen agreed, and so it was that Sir Lancelot set forth in pursuit of the damosel and her champion. Little did he know that this adventure would take almost two years of his life.

For much of the day he followed the way described to him by Sir Owein and Sir Sagramore, which led through the dark trees of the Great Wood; but as darkness began to fall he had still seen no sign of his quarry. That night he rested in the cell of a friendly hermit and next day set forth again, having been blessed by the man of God. But though he rode swiftly through the forest he saw no sign of the lady or her protector.

So it was that Sir Lancelot arrived at the shore of the sea, and there he learned that the damosel who had spoken so cruelly to the Fellowship, and the powerful knight who had beaten some of the strongest of the company, had indeed passed this way. It seemed that they had taken ship but two days earlier, heading for Ireland.

Now at that time this country was known as a place of strange and wondrous things. Monsters were known to haunt the lands and word had even been heard of a dragon in the high mountains. Sir Lancelot at once prepared to take ship to this savage country, and within a day he set foot upon its shore in the place called Galway. There he heard word that his quarry had been sighted, and set off once again to follow them.

✠ ✠ ✠

NOW I MUST tell you that Sir Lancelot achieved several adventures in the days that followed. These must be told another time if I am to relate all that occurred in the land of Ireland. No matter where he went, or to whose aid he came, one name he heard again and again. That name was Rigomer – a place of such fearful reputation that it was spoken of in hushed tones. All the reports he received of the discourteous maiden and her companion seemed to point to this place. It was, he heard, surrounded on two sides by a swift river, and on the rest overlooked the sea. Within this protected space stood a citadel of great splendour. A single bridge, made of iron, gave admittance to it, but this was guarded by a dragon – perhaps the last of its kind in that land. So fierce was this creature that few survived who came into its presence.

But mostly Lancelot heard of the marvels of that place, of which few could tell in any detail, since those who succeeded in entering either did not return, or became struck with a kind of madness that caused them to behave in a foolish manner. They would laugh and weep and speak of the many games and jests that took place within, but more than this they could not say. Some told of a room full of cats, fierce as they could be, that guarded a great treasure – but to the nature of this they could not speak. All agreed that Rigomer was a place full of enchantment, necromancy and witchcraft, from which no knight who entered ever escaped, or else they were so altered by what they experienced that they were never the same again.

Hearing this only encouraged Lancelot's determination to reach the fabled Rigomer, so that he might experience for himself the marvels of which he had heard so much. So he pressed on until, many weeks after he had stepped ashore in Ireland, he came into a part of the land that was known as Kerry, and there he found himself in a wide meadow, rich in flowers and sweet grass.

Seeking to rest, he dismounted and let his horse go free to feed upon the grass. Then he sat for a while, contemplating all that he believed must lie before him. After a while there came in sight a handsome, well-dressed nobleman who, seeing Lancelot, rode up to him and saluted him.

'What has brought you to this place today, Sir Knight?' he asked.

'I seek a place named Rigomer,' answered Lancelot.

'Ah, you are indeed close,' said the nobleman. 'But let me advise you now, turn back. Only death, or worse, awaits those who go to that place.'

'I give you thanks for your words,' Lancelot said. 'But they only serve to make me long to attempt the marvels of Rigomer as soon as I can.'

'Let me tell you this,' the nobleman said. 'I have seen many knights who came here and were as determined as you to overcome the evils of the place. None have succeeded, and those who returned have been driven mad by what they saw within.'

'Nevertheless,' said Sir Lancelot, 'I must do what I can.'

The nobleman was silent for a moment, then he said: 'May I know your name?'

'I am Sir Lancelot of the Lake.'

'That is a name I have heard often before,' replied the nobleman. 'You have great fame indeed. Perhaps you are the one foretold, who is of such nobility and courage that he can finally break the enchantments of Rigomer.'

'That is my hope, indeed,' replied Lancelot. 'What more can you tell me of this fearsome place?'

'Of what lies beyond the bridge that crosses the river I can say but little,' replied the nobleman. 'But I can tell you that the enchantments of this place extend further than the citadel or the river. Even to this very meadow.'

He gestured to the area around where they sat. 'You see that shady tree over there? If you were to sit there and to remove your armour and set aside your weapons you would at once see marvellous things. For in this meadow there are many people who are invisible to you at this moment. Courteous men and fair women who would entertain you, feed and care for your every need, for as long as you chose to stay.'

Lancelot gazed across the broad meadow, shading his eyes; but in truth he could see nothing.

'I shall not lay aside my arms for anything,' he said to the nobleman. 'But tell me, how is it that you know of these things?'

'My name is Sir Yonés le Noveliers. My family have lived here for many generations. It is our curse that we are neighbours to this place of fear and enchantment. Many such as yourself we have seen, and can bear witness to their loss and destruction. We do not even know who dwells here or who has created the marvels and trials that lie within.' He paused for a moment then said: 'If you will not stay and experience the wonders of this meadow, or indeed, as I would advise you, turn back and return whence you came – then all I can say is, may God watch over you today, and every day that you suffer the marvels of Rigomer.'

Sir Yonés then promised to wait until either Lancelot returned or was struck down, and with this the knight took leave of the good man and followed the way across the meadow to the river and the iron bridge that crossed it. There he saw the dragon, a serpentine creature whose scales, red and green, flashed in the sunlight. Lancelot saw that it was chained in such a way that it could reach either end of the bridge; beyond it, lay Rigomer itself – a vast and sprawling edifice of bell-towers, chimneys and battlements, with walls so thick that they would withstand even the most furious assault.

As he looked upon this place of marvels, Lancelot became aware of a bright pavilion pitched to one side of the bridge near to him. As he looked he saw emerging a giant knight, one of the tallest he had ever seen. So powerful was he that he wore three layers of armour, carried three swords, and had three helmets covering his skull. For this reason he was known as the Knight of the Triple Arms, or sometimes simply the Triple Knight, though his true name was Jorans. He was one of the strongest and most savage fighters in all that land of Ireland, and though he had only the descriptions of Sir Owein and Sir Sagramore to go on, Lancelot knew that this was indeed the knight he had been seeking.

When he saw Sir Lancelot, the giant man gave a great roar and spurred his mighty horse, which was strong enough to carry even so weighty a warrior as he, towards him. Lancelot swiftly set his spear in rest and swung his shield before him. Without any exchange of words the two men met head on. Even Lancelot, who was beyond question the strongest fighter of his time, was knocked from his horse, but so too was the huge knight, who struck the ground with such force that he remained unmoving for several moments. Lancelot gained his feet and swiftly drew his sword, but as any man of honour must, he waited for his opponent to recover. Then the two of them went at it so furiously and with such energy that the whole meadow and the area around rang with the noise of their battle.

Within the castle heads appeared along the walls, as those who dwelled within came to see the contest. Never had the giant knight being so equally matched, and never had Sir Lancelot encountered an adversary as powerful as Sir Jorans.

All that day they fought until, as dusk began to fall, Lancelot dealt his opponent such a blow that it split parts of his armour and cut through to the flesh within. The Triple Knight howled with rage and pain and struck back, beating Sir Lancelot to the ground several times. But each time the great knight sprang up and fought on, and finally the weight of Joran's armour began to tire him. Then Lancelot struck a series of blows that felled the huge man and left him wounded and beaten on the ground.

Now the giant knight cried out for mercy, having never come so close to death before, despite the many heroes he had felled or taken prisoner. Lancelot, as was ever his way, granted the huge man clemency, commanding him to travel to Britain and thence to Camelot the Golden, there to pledge his service to the queen herself and to make amends for his attacks upon the Fellowship. This Sir Jorans promised to do, and withdrew to his pavilion to rest and treat his wounds, while those within the castle were heard crying out at the fall of their great champion.

As night was falling, Lancelot returned to the place where Sir Yonés had made camp, and there he remained for several days while he recovered from his battle and once again determined to engage the dragon and whatever challenges lay beyond in the castle of Rigomer.

As he prepared to depart, he noticed a huge club hanging from the wall of the pavilion. 'May I ask for the use of that weapon?' he said.

The nobleman smiled and handed it to him.

❖ *Sir Gawain approaches the narrow bridge* ❖

70

'Go with God,' he said. 'And may you triumph where all before you have failed.'

Eagerly, Sir Lancelot mounted his horse and rode to the iron bridge. When he arrived at the entrance the dragon saw him and paced towards him, roaring as it came. The dragon was at least seventeen feet long, with wings like a bat and eyes as big as serving plates. Its tail was long and barbed and its skin shone with a metallic gleam. Lancelot dismounted from his steed, which shied in fright at the sight of the oncoming creature. The dragon leapt towards him but was restrained by its chain. Seeing his chance, Lancelot climbed to the rampart of the bridge and holding the great club in both hands brought it down on the dragon's snout. Roaring, the beast retreated, and Lancelot followed up, striking it again and again until it lay unconscious.

Then Sir Lancelot hastened across the bridge with drawn sword and shield at the ready. Just to the left of the gates was the entrance to a cave. Normally it was hidden by the spells surrounding Rigomer, but as Lancelot approached, the veil fell from it and he saw where a trail of smoke emerged from it. Perhaps at one time it had been the dragon's lair, but now it led to the depths of the castle, where the captured knights were held.

Expecting to be attacked, Lancelot approached with care. He was surprised when he saw coming from the cave mouth a most beautiful damosel, who welcomed him gladly, calling out to him: 'Sir Knight, you have done well to drive our guardian down. My Lady Dionise, the ruler of this castle, has watched you from afar and saw how you defeated the Knight of the Triple Arms and then the dragon. She has nothing but admiration for you and offers you her hospitality. She also sends this' – and here she held up a fabulous golden and enamelled ring – 'if you accept it with her blessing, you shall be permitted to enter the castle and all will be well treated.'

Looking at the damosel Lancelot recognised her as she who had come before the king and queen at Camelot the Golden and had spoken so harshly to all who were gathered there. Despite this, Lancelot gave no sign that he knew her and said rather: 'Maiden, I thank you. But I would prefer not to accept this gift until I have spoken with your lady.'

The damosel frowned. 'If you do not take my lady's gift you will be taken and thrown into a pit, there to remain until you are dead. But if you accept this peaceful gesture, you shall be made welcome.'

Sir Lancelot hesitated. He thought that whichever course he chose he could not be sure of the outcome, but of the two at least accepting the gift of the ring would gain him entry to Rigomer. Therefore he bowed his head and having sheathed his sword as a sign of peace, he took the ring and slipped it onto his finger.

Alas! At once he forgot his name and status, and all memory of his appointed task was wiped from his mind. Instead he began to laugh and prance like a beast, and then started singing very loudly.

The damosel smiled when she saw this and called out to the guards who had watched all that passed between her and the great knight. At once they fell upon Sir Lancelot, and while he continued to laugh and sing, they took away his sword and dagger, stripped him of his armour and threw him into a pit where several other knights joined him in dancing and playing, as though they were all as happy as it was possible to be.

Thus was Sir Lancelot, the greatest of the Round Table Fellowship, captured without a blow being struck, and cast into prison. There I shall leave him for this time, as the story turns to the nobleman, Sir Yonés, who had watched everything from the other side of the river and saw how Lancelot was tricked and taken away. Sadly, he returned to his pavilion and there wrote a letter to King Arthur, which he entrusted to a squire to take to Camelot the Golden.

It took many weeks for the message to arrive in Britain, but when the squire reached the great city, he was made welcome. When King Arthur read the letter from Sir Yonés, he at once called his knights together. As soon as they were assembled he read the message aloud. There was great consternation when the court heard how Lancelot was taken and imprisoned. Many of the knights begged to be allowed to set forth with the intention of setting free their comrade.

At this moment, a huge knight appeared at the court. It was none other than Jorans, the Knight of the Triple Arms who had, as he had promised, made his way to Camelot the Golden. Sir Owein, Sir Sagramore and Sir Kay at once recognised him as the opponent they had faced when they followed the proud damosel following their appearance at the feast the previous year. At first they were inclined to attack him, but when the knight bowed his head and spoke humbly of his battle with Lancelot and how he had been spared by the great knight, the Fellowship gathered about him to hear what more he could tell them of Rigomer.

The giant knight replied: 'Long ago a faery lived in that land. She created a paradise on earth and filled it with magic and wonder. Then came men who wanted to drive her away, and they built the castle that you see, and filled it with treasures of their own. Finally they made one of their own kind queen – my Lady Dionise – and at this the faery grew more angry than ever before. So it was that she wove spells and enchantments around Rigomer and made it so that those who lived within the citadel had all that they desired – but could never leave. And to the Lady Dionise, she made it that she could never marry or know true love until there came a knight whose goodness and courage would undo the faery's spells and set free all who had come there and been imprisoned and made to forget who they were.

'Thus,' said Jorans, 'all the enchantments are still in place and only one man may break them. It is my belief that Sir Lancelot may do this, but while he is imprisoned he is as helpless as a child.'

Then Sir Gawain spoke up, declaring that he would lead those who wished to go to Rigomer. 'There, if need be, we shall break down the walls to set Sir Lancelot free!'

'That may not be,' said Jorans. 'For the walls will withstand any and all-comers. But it may be that if God smiles upon you, you may find a way to achieve your goal.'

At this the giant knight was given thanks and invited to remain at the court, which he did – though what happened to him thereafter I know not. But Sir Gawain begged leave to go to Ireland. King Arthur gave permission to fifty of the Round Table knights to go. These included Sir Gawain himself, Sir Owein, Sir Sagramore, Sir Brandelis and Sir Kay, as well many others, all of whom swore they would not rest until they had set Sir Lancelot free and returned with him to Camelot the Golden. And that very day they left and began the journey to Rigomer.

✠ ✠ ✠

THE SIGHT OF the fifty Knights of the Round Table riding together was unlike anything seen in Ireland at that time. Some believed them to be angels or demons, while others swore they were an invading army. They encountered more than one hostile response, but always Sir Gawain explained that they were journeying to Rigomer, and always the response was a shaking of heads and many warnings to turn back.

However, they kept on towards their goal, and at length arrived at the wide meadow from which they could see the palaces, chimneys and bell towers that rose above the mighty walls of the castle.

There they were met by Yonés le Noveliers, who had sent the message to King Arthur, and who told them how Sir Lancelot was captured and made to forget his name. Just as he had before, the nobleman warned the Knights of the Round Table to turn back, since even their might was not great enough to withstand the enchantments of Rigomer.

All of the company refused to turn back and, as if in response, a sudden storm blew up. The waters of the river overwhelmed its banks as dark clouds filled the sky. Rain lashed down, then hail, soon turning to snow, so that the knights and their horses were soon blanketed in white. The waters of the sea rose also, and waves crashed upon the rocks with a sound like the footsteps of giants.

Just as the knights began to get used to this fearsome weather, the clouds withdrew, and bright sun rose in the sky and the heat became such that several fainted in their armour or tore off their helmets to breathe.

'See now what you face,' said Yonés. 'This is nothing to the opposition you will encounter if you continue.'

As he spoke the weather became calm again and the temperature returned to normal. But now across the sea came a ship bearing a strange crew. They seemed like monks, dressed in robes with cowls that hid their faces, but beneath they were clad in black armour and carried long swords. They came ashore quickly and it was clear that they intended to attack.

Sir Kay who, as seneschal, led those who had journeyed to Rigomer, said that to him they looked like demons, and that they would be better off striking hammers in Hell than fighting King Arthur's knights. So saying, he closed his visor and spurred his horse towards the first of the cowled men. He soon regretted his action as the dark knight struck him down. At this, Sir Gawain drew his sword and he and all the other knights charged upon their opponents.

At first they found themselves hard pressed, such was the terrible strength of the cowled knights. Then Sir Cligés, who was riding with them, struck down one of the attackers and in so doing ripped the hooded robe from him. At once the black clad knight fell to the earth and remained unmoving. Realising that their robes imbued them with supernatural strength, the Round Table knights used their weapons in such a way that the cowls were stripped away. Each time this caused the black knights to fall unmoving on the ground, and soon after this, their bodies melted away like smoke.

Scarcely had King Arthur's knights drawn breath than a fresh attack came, this time from a band of creatures with bodies like men, but covered in matted hair and bearing the heads of dogs. They could run as fast as any horse and their unpleasant way of fighting was to attack the knights' steeds and gut them, before dispatching the riders as they fell from their wounded horses. But this time they were prevented from this by the armour covering the sides and chests of each noble steed. Once the knights realised this, they began to use their swords, striking down from their saddles and stabbing or beheading the dog-heads with ease. In only a short time these savage creatures were slain, and as had been the case with the cowled knights, their bodies vanished away. Scarcely a dozen of the Round Table knights were injured in this battle, and after this no more savage beings came against them.

Sir Gawain, who had, as ever, fought in the forefront of the battle, now approached the nobleman.

'Are there more trials to come? Or may we proceed to enter the castle?'

Sir Yonés answered: 'Never have I seen such mighty knights or witnessed so great a struggle against the enchantments! I cannot speak for what tests may lie within the castle, but first of all you must cross the Iron bridge and face the dragon that guards it.'

'Very well,' said Sir Gawain, and spoke with the other knights. 'Will you permit me to essay this alone?' he asked. 'I wish to release Sir Lancelot from this dire prison, and if I fail and am myself captured or defeated, then you shall be free to follow as I have.'

To this the Round Table knights agreed, and Gawain set off for the bridge. He approached with care, his shield held before him and his sword drawn. As had Lancelot before him, he dismounted and tethered his steed to a post at the head of the bridge, then he walked towards the dragon.

It, to the wonder of all who saw it, bowed its head and made no attempt to attack Sir Gawain. Though he could find no reason for this, the knight gratefully passed by the mighty beast and continued towards the gate of the castle. There he met the damosel who greeted him as she had every other knight who came there, and offered him a ring

which would allow him to enter Rigomer. But Gawain, who perhaps knew the wiles of Faery better than most, refused, and when she saw the naked sword in his hand the damosel turned and fled.

As she did so, the entrance, which had been invisible before, came onto view, and without pause Sir Gawain entered there. Inside, all was dark and still, and Gawain felt the presence of powerful enchantments, But as he advanced fearlessly, the destiny long foreseen by the faery of old began to work. The marvels began to unwind and the darkest spells were broken.

Gawain pressed forward until he came, by way of a narrow passage, into the kitchens that lay beneath the castle. There, to his mingled dismay and delight, he saw Lancelot. Dressed in rough and greasy clothes and with a blank look in his eyes, he more resembled a wild beast than a man. In the time that had passed since he was captured he had become the chief cook to the castle and had eaten so well that he had become quite fat, and his hair was long and matted. He hung his head and scarcely looked about him.

'Do you not know me?' asked Sir Gawain.

'Why should I know someone I have never seen before?' growled Lancelot. 'You look to me like you are a demon from Hell. Are you made of metal or is that a skin that peels off?' he added, pointing at Gawain's armour

When he heard this Gawain did not know whether to laugh or cry. Indeed, tears fell down his cheeks as he looked upon the once mighty figure of his friend, reduced to little more than an ape.

'My Lord Lancelot, do you truly not know me?' he asked.

'What is that you called me?' grunted Lancelot, and it seemed for a moment that his eyes cleared. Then he seized a poker from the kitchen fireplace and waved it at Gawain. 'If you don't leave here at once I will call out for help and you will be thrown into this fire and cooked until you are roasted. Then your body will be thrown into the river and you will dissolve and never be seen again!'

Gawain, though sickened by this tirade, simply gave his name.

Again, for a moment, Lancelot seemed to remember something. He lowered the poker. 'Gawain. . .' he mumbled. 'I thought I once knew a man called that.'

'Indeed, that is so,' cried Gawain. 'If you wish you can come with me and return to the world outside this place.'

'There is no world outside,' said Lancelot. 'Besides, if there was and I left here it would upset my lady, who gave me this ring only yesterday.'

He held up the hand on which was the ring the damosel had given him. When he saw this, Gawain remembered the ring the haughty damosel had offered him. He realised that his old friend had no idea that a year had passed since he came to Rigomer, and guessed that the ring was the cause of Lancelot's sickness.

Quick as lightning he seized the ring and pulled it so harshly that it broke in two pieces which fell to the earth.

At once Lancelot stood tall and it seemed that the weight he had gained fell from him in that moment. His eyes were clear at last and he looked at Gawain with recognition. 'Tell me, how long have I been here?' he cried, aware of his greasy clothing and uncombed hair.

'More than a year,' answered Gawain. 'I and others of the Fellowship have been seeking you all this time.'

Then he told Lancelot all that had occurred in the meadow beyond the walls and the assaults the Round Table knights had endured.

'Ah, if only I had my armour and weapons!' cried Sir Lancelot.

'Let us see if we can find them,' said Gawain, and together the two men left the kitchen and passed into a great hall beyond. There were tables, at each one of which a knight worked at some humble task. Some mended pots, others shoes, or repaired saddles and bridles. All were employed at menial tasks such as no knight had ever undertaken.

Shocked as they were, Gawain and Lancelot continued further into the castle until they found an armoury where the great knight was able to find arms that fit him. And just as he was, unwashed and looking like an ill-bred man, he armed himself and caught up a sword.

'Let us cleanse this place of these enchantments,' he said fiercely.

The two knights made their way back to the hall and there they broke or pulled off the rings from each of the knights there, and as they did so the brave men, each of whom had survived the attack of the dragon only to fall victim to the damosel with the rings, remembered themselves and awoke as if from a deep sleep.

At once they sought out armour and weapons and slowly became again the fine warriors they had been. Then Sir Gawain and Sir Lancelot led the newly rescued knights through that part of the castle and out into the streets beyond. At first those who saw them fled, fearing they were about to be slain, but the knights made no such attempt, and gradually fear subsided as word spread through the whole of Rigomer until it reached the ears of the Lady Dionise herself.

At first she, like her citizens, was fearful, but one of her knights quickly reassured her. 'The one has come who was foretold, and he has broken the enchantments and set free those who were imprisoned. It is certain that he will marry you, just as the faery who designed all of these things promised.'

When she heard this Dionise was filled with hope, and donning her finest gown, she went down to greet her rescuers.

There, in the great hall of the castle, they met, and when she looked upon the face of Sir Gawain, the lady at once fell in love with him. And as the company gathered they all heard music unlike any that had been heard there before. It came from instruments that played of their own accord – or by players invisible to all – and encouraged the mood of rejoicing.

So all there fell to making merry, and amongst those who celebrated most was the good nobleman, Sir Yonés le Noveliers, who had helped both Lancelot and the Round Table knights, and who joined them with great delight. He reported that there was no sign of the dragon that had guarded the bridge, and it was understood that it, like all the marvels of Rigomer, had vanished when the enchantments were broken. Very glad was he to see that the evils he had so long observed were finally ended; and you may be sure that he received many rewards from King Arthur himself when word of his part in the adventure became known.

So, through the honour and courage of Sir Gawain, who broke the enchantments by entering the castle, the marvels of Rigomer were ended. All the knights who had been imprisoned were set free and those who had been injured were miraculously healed. Those who had been of the Round Table Fellowship now joined their brothers and there was much renewing of friendships and tales told of deeds done and victories accomplished, while Sir Lancelot and Sir Gawain spoke of the events of the past year and shared the story of the faery who had set all the marvels in motion.

Only the Lady Dionise was sad, because Gawain quite quickly informed her that he could not marry her, and that Lancelot also was unable to grant her wish. But he promised that if she returned with them to Camelot the Golden a suitable knight would surely be found. And thus it was, for the Lady Dionise fell in love with a knight named Blioberis, who had been one of those captured in Rigomer, and he returned her love, so that they were married in the great church in King Arthur's city soon after.

MANY THERE WERE in the wild lands of Ireland who rejoiced at the ending of the necromancy and dark spells at Rigomer, though it is said that the faery who had made the enchantments determined to bring about the ruin of the Round Table, and especially of Sir Gawain. But if she was part of the doom of that company or not, the story does not tell.

EXPLICIT THE TALE OF RIGOMER.

INCIPIT THAT OF KING ARTHUR AND GORLAGON.

10: KING ARTHUR AND GORLAGON

✛

IHAVE LONG PONDERED WHETHER OR NOT THIS TALE SHOULD BE INCLUDED HERE, FOR NOT ONLY IS IT A CRUEL NARRATIVE, BUT IT ALSO SUGGESTS MANY THINGS CONCERNING KING ARTHUR AND HIS QUEEN THAT MAY BE BEST FORGOTTEN. YET, FOR ALL THIS, I BELIEVE IT IS A TALE THAT ALL SHOULD HEAR. THEREFORE, I INCLUDE IT WITH A WORD OF CAUTION TO THOSE WHO LOVE WOMEN AND SEEK EVER TO UNDERSTAND THEM. TO THOSE WHO ARE ANGERED BY IT, I BID YOU REMEMBER THAT THIS TALE WAS TOLD LONG AGO, WHEN TIMES WERE NOT AS THEY ARE NOW.

✛ ✛ ✛

AT PENTECOST ONE year King Arthur kept the festival at the City of the Legions. He invited nobles and knights from all over the land to meet there and celebrate in fine style, with a great banquet to which all were bidden. Courses too numerous to name were served, and wines in abundance. As the evening wore on, Arthur suddenly turned to the queen, and in an excess of joy, embraced and kissed her in front of all the court.

Guinevere blushed furiously and asked the king why he chose this place and time to show such affection.

Arthur replied: 'Because among all the riches and delights of this place I have nothing as sweet as you.'

To which the queen answered: 'Then, if you love me so much, you must feel that you know my heart and mind as well or better than any other?'

'Indeed so!' said Arthur.

'Then you are wrong, my lord. For if you truly knew me you would not make such a claim. Indeed, I would say that you know nothing of women's nature.'

King Arthur looked askance, for this had been said in the hearing of everyone present. But he smiled gently enough and said: 'My love and my queen. If it is true that I know nothing of your heart and mind, then I take heaven as my witness that I shall not rest until I do so!'

When the banquet was ended and the guests were all departed, Arthur summoned his seneschal, Sir Kay, and said: 'I command you and Sir Gawain to fetch your horses, and a third for myself. We are going on a mission. But it is to be kept secret from everyone. We three alone shall know where we are bound.'

Only when the three men were well on the road did Arthur tell them that, because of his dispute with Guinevere, he intended visiting a certain lord named Gargol, whom he had heard was wise in many ways, and to try to discover something of the nature of womankind. 'For though I doubt I am the first to try, yet I believe it is possible to discover some truth about them!'

The three rode on together for a day and a night – for Arthur would not rest – until they came in sight of a castle built into the side of a wooded mountain. Arthur sent Kay ahead to discover to whom this belonged, and the seneschal soon returned with news that it was the chief castle of the very lord of whom they were in search.

Bidding his fellows to make haste, Arthur spurred his mount right up to the castle, and seeing the doors set wide and hearing the sound of feasting coming from within, he rode right into the hall, where the Lord Gargol sat at dinner.

The nobleman looked up at where Arthur sat on his horse and demanded to know who he was that entered in such urgency.

'I am Arthur, King of all Britain. I come in search of an answer to a question that concerns me deeply.'

'And what is that?'

'I seek to know concerning the heart, the nature, and the general ways of women, for I have heard that you are well versed in such matters.'

'This is a very weighty question,' said Gargol. 'Come, my lord, eat with us, and rest here this night, for I see that you are tired from your journey. Give me a while to think upon your question, and I will try to answer you in the morning.'

Denying that he was fatigued, Arthur consented to eat and placed himself opposite Gargol, while Kay and Gawain, who soon joined them, were seated upon either side.

That night they rested and were royally entertained. But next morning when Arthur reminded Gargol of his promise the lord shook his head. 'Sire. If I may say so, you show your lack of wisdom by asking this question. I believe that no man can answer it.'

'Yet I must have an answer,' Arthur insisted.

'Well, if you will not give it up, then I suggest you go a little further, into the next country, and visit my brother, Torleil. He is older than I, and wiser. Perhaps he can help you find an answer.'

With this the king had to be content, and with Kay and Gawain at his side, rode for the rest of the day until they came to the city of Torleil, who welcomed them. When he heard who his guests were the lord invited them to sit down and eat with him, and once again, when Arthur at first refused, then explained his reasons, persuaded him to wait until morning for an answer to his question.

Yet, when morning came, Torleil confessed himself as unable to answer as his brother had been. 'Though, if you must seek further, I recommend that you visit my eldest brother, Gorlagon, who lives in the next valley. He is far wiser than I and I believe he may be able to assist you.'

With this Arthur had to be content, though by now his patience was all but worn away. The three men set out at once, and after a day's ride arrived at Gorlagon's castle where, as in both previous times, they found the lord at supper. When he learned the identity of his guests, and the nature of the king's question, he shook his head.

'This is indeed a weighty question my lord.

Sit with us, take food and drink. On the morrow I will attempt an answer.'

This time Arthur would not be swayed. He swore that not a morsel of food or drink would pass his lips until he had heard what Gorlagon had to say on the matter.

The old lord sighed. 'Well, since you drive me so hard, I will give you an answer, though I doubt it will serve you well. But at least sit down, you and your men, and eat while you listen. But let me say this,' he added, 'that when I have told you my story you may feel you are none the wiser.'

'Say on,' Arthur said. 'But speak no more of eating.'

'Very well, but at least let your companions eat.'

Arthur nodded, and allowed himself to be conducted to a seat at the table. Then, as Kay and Gawain satisfied their hunger and thirst, Gorlagon told the tale that I will tell now.

✛ ✛ ✛

'THERE WAS ONCE a king, famed for his truth and justice. He had built for him a garden of surpassing beauty and richness, and there he planted all kinds of trees and shrubs, fruits and spices which grew in abundance. Among the other trees which grew there, was a slender sapling which had sprung from the ground on the day of the king's birth and was exactly the same height as he.

'Now it was said of this tree that if anyone were to cut it down and striking his head with the slenderest part of it, say: "Be a wolf and have the understanding of a wolf," he would at once take on the form of that animal. For this reason, the king set a guard around the tree, and had a wall built around the garden. No one was permitted to enter there save the

king himself, and a trusted guardian who was his close friend. Every day he used to visit the tree at least three times – nor would he eat so much as a morsel of food before he had done so. He alone knew the reason for this but kept a close mouth about it.

'Now this king had a very beautiful wife, and it chanced that her love for him was less than he believed, for she had a young lover. Such was her passion for him, that she determined to arrange some way that he might lawfully enjoy her favours. Observing how the king entered his garden every day alone, and spent some time there, she became curious.

'One night the king returned home late from hunting, but before he would eat or rest, he went into the garden, as was his wont. And when at last they sat down to eat supper together, the queen smiled a false smile and asked why her lord always went alone to his garden, even though he was tired.

'Quietly, the king answered that he had nothing to say to her on the matter, which did not concern her, and at this the queen cried out that he must be going there to meet with a mistress. Then she said that she would eat no food until he had told her. Saying which she went into her bed and feigned sickness for three days and nights – though in truth her servant brought her food and drink in secret.

'At the end of this time the king grew fearful for her life and began to beg her to get up and take some food, saying that the thing she asked was a secret he dared not share with anyone, but that he was as faithful to her now as he had ever been. "Then," cried she, "you ought to have no secrets from me, not if you love me as much as you say you do!"

'In a great turmoil and feeling the depth of his love for his queen, the king at last gave in and told her the truth about the sapling, having first extracted from her an oath that she would tell no one.

'Of course, she had no intention of honouring this promise, since she saw this as a means to bring about a crime she had long contemplated. As soon as the king went out next day, she went immediately to the garden, and taking an axe, cut down the tree and concealed the topmost branch in the long sleeve of her gown. Then, when her husband returned home, she made a point of going to meet him.

'On the threshold she made as if to throw her arms about him, and then, before he could do anything to prevent it, she struck him about the head with the sapling and cried "Be a wolf!" But when she came to say, "And have the understanding of a wolf," in her excitement she said: "And have the understanding of a man!"

'And so it was. The king fled in the shape of a wolf, pursued by hounds which the evil queen set upon him. But his humanity remained unimpaired.'

Gorlagon stopped and looked at King Arthur, who was totally engrossed in the story, and said: 'My lord, I ask again that you take some food. For this is a long tale, and even though you will be little the wiser for hearing it, still you should not starve in the hearing.'

But Arthur shook his head. 'Continue. I will eat later.'

So Gorlagon, shaking his head the while, began again.

'The queen, having chased away her rightful lord, now invited her lover to take his place, relinquishing all authority to him. Shortly thereafter she married the younger man and in due course had by him two sons. The wolf meanwhile wandered in the woods, and during this time allied himself with a she-wolf, who bore him two cubs. And all this time he thought about the treachery of his queen and how he might be revenged upon her.

'Nearby, at the periphery of the woods, there was a fortified house where the queen and her new lord used often to repair from the business of the world. One day the two wolves and their cubs came there. It happened that the two young boys who were the offspring of the queen and her lover were left unattended, playing in the courtyard of the house. When he saw them, the wolf knew only anger and bitterness, and in his fury, he rushed upon them and tore them to pieces.

'When the queen's servants heard this, they came and chased away the wolves, though by then it was too late to save the children. The queen was overcome with sorrow and gave orders for a close watch to be kept in case the beasts should ever return. And return they did, sneaking into the region of the house some months later. There the man-wolf saw two of the queen's young cousins, who had been left playing unattended, and once again he rushed in upon the unsuspecting children and disembowelled them, leaving them to die a dreadful death.

'Hearing the screams, the servants assembled, and this time succeeded in capturing the two young wolves, whom they hanged at once. But the man-wolf, being more cunning in the ways of men, slipped away and escaped.'

Again, Gorlagon paused and looked at King Arthur. 'Do you wish me to continue?' he asked. The king simply nodded, leaning forward in his chair to listen intently to every word the old lord uttered.

'The man-wolf, maddened by the death of his cubs, began to wreak vengeance against the local flocks and herds, so that his name soon became a by-word of fear, and the people of that land mounted a great hunt to capture and kill him. The wolf, fearful for his safety, fled to the neighbouring land. But there, too, he was hunted, since word of his deeds had gone before him. Finally, he fled yet further from his homeland, into the country ruled by a young king whose nature was gentle and whose fame for wisdom had spread far and wide. There he wrought such havoc, not only against sheep and cattle but against human life also, that the king announced a day in which he would set out and hunt the beast down once and for all.

'It happened that the wolf was out hunting that night. Lurking beneath the window of a certain house, he overheard someone within speaking of the great hunt and of the kindness and wisdom of the king. The wolf, hearing this, fled back to the cave where he had his den and fell to wondering what he should do.

'In the morning the great hunt assembled, and advanced into the woods with a mighty pack of hounds. The wolf, using his human skills, evaded discovery and lay in wait for the king himself.

'Soon he saw the young monarch walking near, accompanied only by two close friends, the wolf ran out of the bushes where he had been hiding, and approaching the king, knelt at his feet, and fawned upon him as would a human supplicant. The two young noblemen, fearing for the king's life, for they had never seen such a large wolf before, cried out: "Master! See, here is the very animal we seek. Let us slay him at once!"

'But the king, moved by the actions of the beast, held his hand. "There is something strange about this creature," he said. "I swear it is almost human."

'The wolf at once pawed and whined loudly, licking the king's hands like a great dog.

'Despite the doubts of his companions, the king blew his horn to recall the rest of the hunt and instructed them to return home. Not without many fearful glances at the wolf, they obeyed, and the king and his companions set out to return to the castle, accompanied by the beast. As they passed through the forest, suddenly a huge stag appeared in the way before them, and the king looked to the wolf and said: "Let us see what you can do, my fine fellow," and commanded him to bring down the stag.

'The wolf, who knew well the ways of such beasts, at once sprang after the stag, and in a short time had captured and killed it. Then he dragged the body back to the king and laid it at his feet.

'"I swear you are a noble creature and ought not to be killed," said the king. "It is clear to me that you understand the nature of service, and that you mean me no harm. Therefore, let us go home and you shall live with me in my house."'

Gorlagon ceased his recital again and looked at Arthur, but the king only signalled brusquely that he should continue.

'The wolf remained with the king, accompanying him everywhere, sharing his food and sleeping at night next to his bed. Then the day came when the king was forced to go on a journey to visit a neighbouring monarch, and since the journey was to take ten days, he asked his queen to take care of the wolf in his absence. But the queen had grown to hate the wolf, being jealous of the bond between the beast and its master, and she begged him not to ask this of her, since she was afraid that the wolf would turn on her once the king was gone. This he denied, for he had seen nothing but gentleness in the creature since its coming. But he promised to have a golden chain forged with which the wolf would be fastened to his bed.

'This was done, and the king departed, leaving the wolf in the queen's care. As soon as he was gone, she fastened the chain to the bed and kept the beast prisoner both day and night, even though the king had given instructions that it was only to be chained at night.

'Worse was to come. The queen, like the man-wolf's own faithless wife, loved another, a servant of the king's, and once her husband was gone from the court, she arranged to meet with him in the royal bedroom. There, they fell to kissing and fondling each other, until the wolf, angered beyond bearing by this betrayal of his master and the memory it stirred within him of his own story, grew beside himself and began to howl and rage against the chain. Eventually the chain gave way, and the wolf fell upon the faithless servant and savaged him thoroughly. But the queen he did not attack, merely glaring at her with reddened eyes.

'Alerted by the noise the queen's women came running, and she, terrified lest the king should learn of her perfidy, invented a story. She said that the wolf had attacked her young son and killed him, and dragged his body away, and that when her servant had come running to protect them it had then attacked him also. Then, as the servant was taken away to have his wounds dressed, and fearful of the king's imminent return, and of his discovery of the truth, the queen took the little prince, together with his nurse, and locked them in a room deep in the foundations of the castle.

'At that moment the king was heard returning. He was met by his wife, with her hair shorn, her cheeks scratched and blood all over her clothing. "Alas!" she cried. "See what that evil beast you call friend has done!" And she told the tale of the wolf's attack upon their son, her servant, and then herself.

'The king was both astonished and in agony over the death of his son, but at that moment the wolf, hearing his voice, rushed out from the corner in which it had been hiding, and

→ *Gorlagon's tree* ←

fell upon him with such evident joy and peacefulness that the poor king was even more bewildered.

'Then the wolf, taking the corner of his cloak in its teeth, began to pull him, at the same time growling and rolling its eyes in such a manner that the king, who was used to its ways, had not doubt that it wanted him to follow.

'Despite the queen's cries that it would turn on him and kill him, the king followed the beast into the depths of the castle, and there, before a small door, the wolf stopped and scrabbled against the timbers. Curious, the king ordered the door to be opened, but even as his servants searched for the key, the wolf drew back, and with great force flung himself against the door, breaking it open. Within was the king's little son, and his nurse.

'"Something is amiss here," said the king, and went at once to the room where the wounded servant was lying. When the wolf saw him, it was all the king could do to prevent him attacking the man again, but when questioned the servant would only repeat the story told by the queen.

'"But you are wrong," said the king, "for my son is alive and well. Therefore, you are lying, and I would know the truth." Then he let loose his grip upon the wolf's collar, and the beast leapt upon the wounded man and threatened to tear out his throat, until the man screamed and began babbling the truth.

'Well, what more need be said? The man confessed all, and both he and the queen were impeached and imprisoned. The king, his anger growing greater as he learned the truth, called his lords, and demanded them to make a judgement. Both the queen and the servant who had been her lover were condemned, she to be torn apart by horses, he to be flayed and hanged.

'After these events the king gave much thought to the extraordinary qualities displayed by the wolf. He even summoned several wisemen from within his realm and discussed it with them. "For I do not believe," he insisted, "that any ordinary creature could display such rare intelligence. It is almost as if he were a man who had somehow been given the semblance of a wolf."

'At this, the wolf displayed such great joy and recognition of the king's words that all were amazed. Then the monarch declared that he would do all that he might to discover the truth of this matter, and decreed that the wolf should lead a party, of which the king himself would be one, until such time as they might reach the lands from which the wolf came.

'All this came to pass as the king wished. He set out with a small party of his noblest followers, led by the wolf itself, who took the way eagerly until he reached the shore of the sea – for by this route he could more quickly return to his own land than by the longer way he had come to the king's country before. And when the king saw this, he gave orders that his fleet be made ready.'

Gorlagon paused and looked at Arthur. 'Will you still not take some food or wine with us?' he asked.

King Arthur shook his head. 'The wolf is waiting to cross the sea. I am afraid he may drown before this story continues!'

Gorlagon sighed and continued:

'The king ordered his fleet prepared and gathered a small but powerful force of soldiers to man it. Then he set sail and in less than a day they made landfall in the wolf's original country. He was the first to leap to the shore, where he stood waiting eagerly for the king to disembark.

'The king led a small party inland to a nearby town where, under cover of darkness, they listened to the talk of the people. It did not take long to discover the truth: how the old king had been turned into a wolf by his evil queen, who had swiftly re-married. The new king also had turned out to be an evil and overweening monarch, so that the whole land groaned under the yoke of his oppressive reign.

'The king had heard enough. Returning to his ships he swiftly mustered his soldiers and marched against the man-wolf's rival. In a series of swift and unexpected forays, he decimated the army of the harsh king and captured both him and the queen.'

Again, Gorlagon paused. Before he could speak Arthur said: 'You are like a harper who constantly interposes extra phrases before the conclusion of a song! Go on, I beg you.'

Gorlagon continued.

'The king quickly called an assembly of the nobles of the wolf-lord's land and had the queen brought before them. "Now see where your evil ways have brought you!" he cried, and there before the assembled company he told the story that I have just told you, omitting nothing. Then he said: "Now, I will ask you this question only once, and I expect you to answer: where is the sapling with which you turned your good and noble lord into a wolf?"

'The queen made no response at first, but

under threat of torture said that she believed it to have been destroyed in a fire. The king refused to believe this and ordered her put to the question. A few days later she confessed to the hiding place of the sapling, and the king ordered it brought to him. Then he struck the wolf lightly on the head, saying: "Be a man and have the understanding of a man."

'There, in the sight of everyone, the wolf was transformed back into his true shape. People said that he was even more regal and handsome than before, for his ordeal had transformed him in many ways. The two kings embraced, laughing and crying together, then the king who had been a wolf reclaimed his sovereignty and prepared to give his judgement upon those who had wronged him.

'The evil king he ordered to be put to death, but the queen he spared, only divorcing her. The young king who had helped him regain his place and his human form he rewarded with all the richness in his power, and they swore undying fellowship before the young king returned to his own land.'

Gorlagon looked at King Arthur. 'There, my lord, you have heard all my story. Thus is my answer concerning the heart and mind and ways of women. Think and then ask yourself if you are any the wiser for it.' Then he smiled and said: 'Now I ask you again to eat and sup with us, for we both deserve something – you for hearing the tale, and I for telling it!'

'There is yet one more thing I would ask,' said Arthur. 'Who is the woman who sits opposite you, and who has before her a dish containing a human head, which she kisses every time you smile, and who weeps whenever you have kissed your wife during the telling of this tale?'

'I would refuse to answer that if it was not known to everyone at this table,' answered Gorlagon. 'This woman is indeed the very same one who wrought such evil against her lord – that is to say against myself, for I it was who was the wolf, and it was my two brothers, the very same whom you visited, to whose lands I travelled in search of help. And the youngest of them is Torleil, who is the same as he who took me in and who helped me find my true self again.'

Gorlagon paused and sighed heavily. 'As for the head in the dish, that is the embalmed remains of this woman's lover, who became king in my place for a time, and died for it. In sparing her life, I decreed that she should have it always before her, and that when I kissed the wife I married after her, she should kiss the remains in token of her evil acts.'

Then King Arthur turned his attention to the food and wine that were set before him, and he ate in silence, speaking no more, and refraining from looking again at the woman whose terrible fate was displayed before him.

Next morning King Arthur, Sir Gawain, and Sir Kay set off back home, and in nine days were in Camelot the Golden. What Arthur told the queen concerning his journey this story does not tell, nor what truth or wisdom, if any, he saw in the tale told by Gorlagon. But now it is told again, and I must bear the weight of that.

EXPLICIT THE TALE OF KING ARTHUR AND GORLAGON.
INCIPIT THE STORY OF SIR CLEGES AND THE CHRISTMAS COURT.

11: SIR CLEGES AND THE CHRISTMAS COURT

✠

MANY THERE ARE WHO TELL TALES OF CHRISTMASTIDE, BUT ONE THAT I HAVE NOT HEARD TOLD SO OFTEN IS THE ONE I TELL HERE. I KNOW NOT WHY SIR THOMAS DID NOT INCLUDE IT IN HIS GREAT BOOK, FOR SURELY IT IS ONE THAT MUST WARM THE HEART UPON A COLD WINTER EVE. ALSO, IT MAKES KNOWN TO US HOW THE COURT OF KING ARTHUR'S MIGHTY FATHER, UTHER PENDRAGON, HAD ITS OWN SHARE OF ADVENTURE, LONG BEFORE THE ROUND TABLE WAS FORGED AND THE KNIGHTS THEREOF BROUGHT TOGETHER IN CAMELOT THE GOLDEN.

✠ ✠ ✠

THE CHRISTMAS COURT at Camelot the Golden was famed far and wide in the lands of Britain in those far off times. Even before that, in the time of King Arthur's father, Uther Pendragon, the season was celebrated with much splendour and in the presence of the greatest in the land.

Now in those days there lived a knight named Sir Cleges, a fair and noble man indeed: open of hand, fair of face, and courteous to all men. And this knight had a wife, whose name was Clarys, who was as good and true a lady as ever lived, joyful of heart and generous to all who came to their house seeking succour. No man, rich or poor, was ever turned away from their door, and thus they were well liked by all who knew them. In time the good knight's

lady gave him two children, who were both fair and merry, and who loved their parents as much as any child could.

Every Christmastide Sir Cleges held a great feast in honour of the day. Everyone was welcome who cared to come. There were minstrels to entertain, food for all, and a warm bed for those who required it. Nor, when the feast was ended, did any guest go away without a gift, be it a horse, a robe, a rich ring, or a silver goblet. Whatever they could afford – was given by Sir Cleges and his lady.

But after ten years of this generous gifting and hospitality to all, the knight's coffers were almost empty. Still, nothing would dissuade Sir Cleges from holding his usual Christmas feast, and thereto he pledged his manor houses in the belief that he would soon redeem them. Thus, the feast that year was as generous as ever, but when it was over and the new year dawned, Sir Cleges and his lady found that all their money was spent and that they had but few goods left. Indeed, they were soon reduced to living on one single estate, which was too poor to support a large household, and thereby Sir Cleges' men began to desert him upon every side, seeking employment elsewhere with other noble lords.

Thus, the year passed in less happy state until it came round to Christmas Eve, and then Sir Cleges heard that King Uther was to hold court that year at Cardiff, which was close by his own lands. Every high-born man and woman in that part of Britain were invited, save Cleges himself, who in truth the king believed dead, so many years had passed since he had heard from him. This sorely grieved the knight, since for the first time in many a year he was not able to celebrate the birthday of Our Lord as he was wont. As he stood at the door of his house, he heard the sounds of revelry come drifting along on the wind, songs and carols and the tuneful sounds of pipe and harp, lute and psaltery. Then was Sir Cleges utterly cast down and prayed aloud to God to forgive him for failing to celebrate the birthday of His Son in a fitting manner.

Then came his good wife Clarys and embraced him and told him to weep no more. 'For this is no day upon which to grieve, husband. Come you in and eat the meat which the Good Lord has provided and let us be blithe and joyful as best we may.'

'That will I,' said Cleges, and did all that he could to be cheerful. They went inside and washed and sat down to eat what fare they could find and spent the rest of the day in joyful mien, playing with their children and making

good sport until night fell. And if Sir Cleges continued to feel sorrow within, he hid it well, and showed the best face that he might.

Next morning, they betook themselves to church, and there Sir Cleges kneeled down and prayed that whatever befell him, his wife and children might be spared from strife. And likewise Dame Clarys prayed that her husband should find peace and contentment and put aside the sorrow that darkened his life.

When Mass was ended they went home again, and Sir Cleges went apart into a little garden where he loved to sit on sunny days, and there he prayed again most devoutly, thanking God for his wife and children, and for the poverty that had been sent them, 'For truth to tell, I believe that it was pride that led me to hold such splendid feasts, and thus to spend all that I had good fortune to possess.'

Now Cleges knelt beneath a cherry tree to pray, and as he stayed there, a bough broke off and struck him on the head. He sprang up and took the branch in his hands and saw that there were green leaves and fruit upon it, fresh as in the season of summer, and when he looked at the tree, he saw that it bore a heavy crop of fruit, which glowed in the dim light of the day like a torch. Then Cleges was astounded.

'What manner of tree is it that bears fruit at Christmas?' he cried. Then he took one of the cherries and ate it, and it tasted better than any fruit he had ever eaten.

Sir Cleges hurried inside and showed the branch to his wife. 'See what a marvel I have found in our garden!' he cried, and the lady was as astonished as he. Then she said: 'Husband, let us gather more of this wondrous fruit and take it with us to Cardiff as a gift for the king. It may be that we shall have better fortune from this moment.'

So on the morrow Sir Cleges set forth with

→ *The cherry tree* ←

his eldest son on the road to Cardiff. They must needs go afoot as the knight no longer had a horse to ride but took instead a sturdy staff to be his support. They took with them a basket filled with cherries from the miraculous tree.

They went their way until they reached the gates of the city, which was full of people come for the feasting, which would continue until the Twelfth Night. There, at the entrance to the hall where King Uther held court, the porter looked at the poor knight, clad in rough clothes and carrying only a staff, and bade him join the line of beggars who awaited the king's largesse.

But Sir Cleges held his ground and spoke firmly. 'See,' he said, 'I have brought the king a gift such as only God himself could send.' And he showed the porter the basket. He, looking within, saw that this was indeed a rare gift, and being a greedy man said: 'I shall let you pass, but you must promise me a third of whatever the king gives you.'

To this Sir Cleges agreed and was allowed into the hall. There he met the royal usher, who raised his staff and threatened to strike him if he did not leave. But again, Sir Cleges held his ground, and opening the basket, allowed the man to look within.

Then it was as it had been with the porter. The usher saw the sparkle of the fruit and agreed to admit the poor knight if he promised a third of whatever reward the king gave him. And again, Cleges agreed, and was allowed to pass.

Now he met a third man, who was the king's steward, and all followed on as it had twice before. The man was about to throw Sir Cleges out, but when he saw what the basket contained, he at once agreed to let the knight and his son pass if they agreed to give a third of whatever bounty the king might give. Then Sir Cleges sighed, for he saw that whatever good might come from his gift he had lost all of it between the three men. But he nodded all the same, and was allowed to go forward.

He knelt before King Uther and uncovered the basket. 'Sire,' he said, 'I bring you this gift which is surely from heaven itself.'

The king took the basket and looked upon its contents with wonder.

'This is indeed a marvellous gift,' he said, and bade Sir Cleges and his son sit down at one of the long tables at one side of the room, meaning to speak with him later.

Then the feast began, and the king was very glad to be able to send some of the cherries to a certain lady of Cornwall whom he much wished to impress. (And it is said that much came of this gift, but that is another story entirely!)*

When the feast was ended, the king called to Sir Cleges to come before him again and asked him what his will was. 'For such a fine gift as that which you brought deserves a rich reward.'

Sir Cleges bowed low before the king and said: 'Sire, I ask only that you give me twelve

---

* Clearly a reference to Ingraine, who became the mother of King Arthur.

strokes with a whip, and that I may be allowed to distribute them as I think fit.'

'What is this,' demanded Uther, frowning. 'I never heard of such a request. If you are jesting, it is a poor jest I think.'

But Sir Cleges held his ground and with a shake of his head the king assented to his request.

Then Sir Cleges went through the hall seeking out the three men who had challenged him the right to enter, and to each of them he administered such strokes that they remembered them long after. And you may be sure that none of them behaved thus again to anyone who craved admittance to the king!

Meanwhile Uther had withdrawn to his parlour, and there held court with much mirth. And it happened that a minstrel sang a song in praise of Sir Cleges. When he heard this, the king took to musing what had happened to the good knight, who in the past had been much wont to visit his court but whom he had not seen for many a year. When the minstrel fell silent Uther asked if he knew ought of the man about whom he sang.

'Nay, sire,' replied the singer. 'He is sorely missed by all who make mirth and joy at Christmastide, yet I hear that he has departed from this land.'

'That is a pity,' said King Uther. 'For he was a good man and true, and I wish that I might see him again.'

Sir Cleges, who had been standing near and heard this, came forward and knelt again before the king and thanked him for the gifts he had received.

Uther looked at him in some wonder and asked him how he intended to use the gifts. Then Cleges told him all that had occurred and how he had doled out the twelve strokes. When he heard this the king and all those present began to laugh heartily. 'Now by my faith,' said the king, wiping his eyes. 'Tell me your name, fellow, for I like you right well.'

Sir Cleges looked at the king and smiled. 'Sire, I am Sir Cleges, that was formerly your knight.'

Then the king was astonished and bade him sit down. And when he heard how the good knight's circumstances had changed because of his generosity to all men, he ordered his coffers to be opened and gave back all that the good knight had lost and restored to him his lands and more. 'For,' said he, 'if I had a hundred knights such as you, Sir Cleges, I should be a rich man indeed.'

Then Cleges and his son returned home, riding on fine new horses and dressed in good clothes and told the Lady Clarys all that had befallen them. And you may be sure that she was glad indeed, and that thereafter they lived a joyful life, and that every Christmas Sir Cleges held as brave and splendid a feast as might be seen anywhere in all the land of Britain.

EXPLICIT THE TALE OF SIR CLEGES UPON CHRISTMASTIDE.

INCIPIT THE TURK AND SIR GAWAIN.

12: THE TURK AND SIR GAWAIN

WITHIN THE TALES OF SIR GAWAIN THERE ARE MANY THAT SPEAK OF A CONTEST BETWEEN HIM AND A BEING FROM THE OTHERWORLD WHICH INVOLVED AN EXCHANGE OF BLOWS. SOME NAME THIS THE BEHEADING GAME, FOR IT OFTEN MEANT THAT THE BRAVE KNIGHT MUST UNDERGO A TEST OF HIS COURAGE WHICH THREATENED HIS OWN HEAD. IT IS POSSIBLE THAT ALL OF THESE STORIES ARE A MEMORY OF JUST ONE, BUT OF THIS I CANNOT BE CERTAIN. OF THE MANY, ONE SUCH STORY I WILL TELL NOW, BECAUSE IT IS FULL OF STRANGE AND WONDROUS DETAILS SUCH AS I BELIEVE WILL BE GREATLY ENJOYED BY THE READERS OF THIS BOOK.

✠ ✠ ✠

ONE DAY NEAR Michaelmas, as King Arthur and his knights were seated at supper, into the hall strode a warrior clad in mail and wielding a sword of great strength. Many there looked at him askance, for he was clearly a Turk, but as ever King Arthur made him welcome and asked what brought him hither.

'I am come,' said the Turk, 'to offer a contest to any man here. I ask him to give me a blow, on the understanding that he will get one in return from me.'

All were astonished by this request, and Sir Kay at once said that he would undertake to teach the pagan a lesson for this insult. At this Sir Gawain, who had looked upon the man and thought him a brave champion, rose to his feet and rebuked the king's seneschal.

'Never shall it be said that one who comes with an honest request should be refused an answer,' said he. 'I will accept your challenge, sir.'

'Gladly will I receive a blow from your hands,' replied the Turk. 'Let it be without swords, but with naked fists.'

Smiling, Sir Gawain advanced and as the Turk proclaimed himself ready dealt him a blow that would have felled a lesser man. The Turk, however, scarcely moved at all, and all the while smiled upon Sir Gawain.

'I thank you, good knight,' he said. 'That blow I shall remember, and so shall I return it as agreed. But not on this day, for first I must test you further. Do you dare come with me on an adventure?'

At this Gawain looked at King Arthur, who nodded his head – though many others shook theirs, for it seemed to them that the Turk bore only ill-will towards them all. But Sir Gawain said to the Turk that he would gladly go with him, and called for his weapons and armour and his brave steed. Then the two men set out at once upon the road.

For the rest of that day they went steadily onwards, the Turk speaking little, until at last Sir Gawain confessed that he was hungry.

'Ha!' said the Turk. 'Only this morning you had all that you could wish for – you and all your companions. Yet no food was offered to me.'

'Sir,' answered Gawain. 'Had you but waited, you may be sure you would have been well fed, but since you seemed in haste to leave, none prevented you.'

'If it is food you require,' answered the Turk, 'you must first endure certain tests.'

As he spoke the sky darkened and there came several great bursts of thunder and flashes of lightning. Rain hurled upon them from the sky and hail rattled upon their armour.

None of this seemed to concern the Turk, who led the way into a narrow valley at the head of which was a great mound. As they approached, a door opened in the hillside, and the two knights entered a strange place, that seemed to Sir Gawain filled with the secret glamour of magic. And at once the gate closed with a great groan, leaving them in a twilight place that seemed so vast neither wall nor roof could be seen.

'I like not this place,' said Sir Gawain. 'Why have you brought me here?'

The Turk said nothing but strode ahead. Sir Gawain was forced to follow, and soon they came to a place where several tables were laid with generous amounts of food. Ever polite,

though hunger gnawed at him, Gawain waited to be invited to eat. The Turk looked upon him and laughed: 'Eat then, Sir Knight.' And Gawain fell to, though his companion ate nothing.

When he had eaten his fill, Gawain asked if he might now receive the blow the Turk had promised. 'For I would as soon leave this place and conclude our business.'

'Not yet,' said the Turk. 'There are more adventures before us. Will you be true to your promise?'

'Indeed,' said Sir Gawain, though in his heart he wished not to remain in this strange knight's company.

Then the Turk led the way to the place where they had entered, and once again the hill opened with a groan and allowed them to return to the outside world. There, the storm had abated, and as the sun shone Gawain saw that they were close to the shore of the sea.

'This way we must go to the next place of adventure,' said the Turk, and putting two fingers to his lips blew a shrill blast.

At once a small craft with a single sail appeared and came to the shore.

'Here you must leave your horse,' said the Turk. 'Tether him to that ring and I promise he will be cared for until your return.'

Despite his doubts, Sir Gawain did as he was bid, and the two men went onto the craft, which turned about and sailed across the water towards an island that appeared upon the horizon.

'Here on this island lives one named the King of Man,' said the Turk. 'An evil man he is, indeed, who commands a band of giants such as few may withstand. Are you ready to undertake the adventure?'

'Indeed I am,' said Sir Gawain.

'Then be sure that I shall help you and fight at your side,' the Turk replied.

So the two knights went ashore and there they saw a strong, dark castle, whose gate stood open. Into that place Gawain and the Turk entered, and there in its hall they saw the King of Man, seated on a great chair and surrounded by his giant servants. Hideous indeed were these giants, tough of skin and tufted with spikes of blackest hair, their teeth broken and grim, their eyes huge and glittering, their bodies wide as haystacks and their hands the size of serving plates.

When he saw the newcomers the King of Man mocked them both, and cursed them for daring to enter his kingdom. He railed also against King Arthur, having seen that Sir Gawain served the King of Logres, who had troubled him greatly. Also he named Bishop Baldwin, that mighty knight, and many of the Round Table Fellowship, who he claimed had done him great harm.

'But I am forgetting the courtesies due such great and noble guests,' said the king, changing his evil look to one of merriment. He called for wine and food and then, when they had eaten, challenged Gawain and the Turk to a game.

Swiftly the Turk agreed and Sir Gawain also gave his assent, though he feared that no game in this place would be ought but savage and cruel.

Tables were cleared away and one of the giants brought forth a huge iron ball which fit his hands but was too large for either the Turk or Sir Gawain.

'Let us play!' cried the King of Man. At which the giant let fly the ball towards the knights. Together they were able to seize it and toss it back, much to the annoyance of the king.

Thus the ball was tossed several times, until at last the Turk, using strength that seemed greater than that of ordinary men, threw it in such a way that it struck one of the giants, felling him to the ground.

'Enough!' cried the King of Man. 'Let us play another game.'

→ *The giant prepares to throw* ←

At his call a giant bore into the hall a brazier full of burning coals, and placed it in front of Sir Gawain, who looked to the Turk.

Now the story says of him that there was no sign, that he had melted away like smoke. But in his ears Sir Gawain still heard his ally's voice.

'Lift the brazier high,' said the Turk's voice, 'and place it close to hand. I shall see to it that you do not feel the heat or are burned by its fiery content.'

Sir Gawain stepped forward and laid his naked hands upon the brazier and lifted it high. After a moment he placed it again to one side and stood back.

In rage the King of Man cried out that this was the Turk's magic, and cursed him for a coward for hiding himself from all.

When the Turk stayed silent, and hid himself yet from all, the king called out that a third and final test awaited them.

At his signal two giants brought forth a mighty cauldron of brass and set it before Sir Gawain, who saw that it was filled with molten lead. Once again he heard the Turk's voice: 'Beware, Sir Gawain, for these evil creatures will try to destroy you by putting you into the cauldron, and since you are not of the Cauldron Born,* you will not survive. But I am with you even though you cannot see me, and I give you my word that all shall be well.'

Then Gawain, his patience exhausted, drew his sword and, striking swiftly, slew one of the two giants. Then, embodied it seemed with strength that must come from the Turk, he lifted the second huge fellow and flung him head first into the cauldron, where he quickly perished.

---

* The Cauldron Born is a Celtic title for those initiated into the Cauldron of Ceridwen, which made them poets.

Now was the King of Man truly maddened with anger, and called out to all his followers to kill Sir Gawain and to find the accursed Turk. At this the Turk himself threw off his cloak of concealment and with a cry lifted the king and threw him into the cauldron.

Despite the death of their leader, the battle commenced and the two knights fought side by side until all of the giants lay dead and the king's other servants had fled.

Then, when they had recovered from their labours, Sir Gawain again requested that he receive the blow from the Turk upon which they had sworn their oaths. And with a laugh the Turk gave to Gawain such a gentle buffet that he scarcely felt it. Then he declared their contest at an end, but asked the king's nephew if he would do him one last service.

'What will you have me do?' demanded Gawain, wondering at the Turk's unchancy ways.

'By your leave, I ask that you cut off my head,' said the Turk.

'That I may not do, by my honour as a knight,' answered Gawain.

'You have my word that I shall feel no pain,' replied the Turk. 'All I ask is that you catch my blood in this golden basin.'

And though the king's nephew begged him to say more, the Turk would not, but gave into Gawain's hands a vessel of gold. Then he bowed his head, and with great anguish the king's nephew struck with his sword.

When the Turk's head fell, blood spurted forth, and Gawain did his best to catch it all. When he had done this, the Turk's body, and his severed head, melted away like smoke, and in their place stood a tall and handsome knight.

In wonder, Gawain asked his name and how he came to be thus enchanted.

'My name is Gromer Somer Jour,' said he

who had been the Turk. 'A faery laid this curse upon me until I found a knight noble enough to undertake my challenge and to set me free. This you have done, and I thank you for it.'

Then Sir Gawain and Sir Gromer embraced and the two men went through the castle, setting free all of those the King of Man had held captive. Many were chained with magic and Gromer once again showed his skill in such matters by setting them free.

After this they returned to the magical craft and were carried again to the shores of Logres. From there they made their way to Camelot the Golden and came before King Arthur and told him all that had befallen. At which point Sir Gromer fell upon one knee and asked that Sir Gawain be made the King of Man by way of reward for his courage and kindness. But though King Arthur was more than willing to do so, Gawain begged in turn that Sir Gromer should be granted this gift.

And so it was, and the story tells that Sir Gromer was as good and gentle a king as any might wish for, and that in time he became a knight of the Round Table and served King Arthur and his Fellowship well with courage and chivalry.

✚ ✚ ✚

So HAVE I told this curious tale of Sir Gawain. Some may recall that Sir Gromer Somer Jour, whose name I believe was also 'Man of the Summer's Day', later became King Arthur's adversary, and demanded of Sir Gawain a challenge which led in time to his marriage to Gromer's own sister, the Lady Ragnall. But this story I have told previously[*] and so shall not comment upon this here, yet I believe this shows that he who had been known as the Turk was blessed with faery blood. But of this I will say no more.

---

[*] 'The Wedding of Sir Gawain and the Lady Ragnall' chronicled in *The Great Book of King Arthur and His Knights of the Round Table*, pp. 352–9.

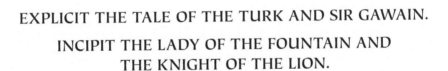

EXPLICIT THE TALE OF THE TURK AND SIR GAWAIN.

INCIPIT THE LADY OF THE FOUNTAIN AND THE KNIGHT OF THE LION.

13: THE LADY OF THE FOUNTAIN AND THE KNIGHT OF THE LION

✛

IT HAS BEEN LONG KNOWN, BY THOSE WHO READ THE TALES OF KING ARTHUR'S SACRED REALM, THAT A CERTAIN FOUNTAIN EXISTED AT THE HEART OF LOGRES. THE PURPOSE OF THIS SPRING IS UNCERTAIN, YES IT WAS DEEMED IMPORTANT ENOUGH THAT IT SHOULD BE GUARDED BOTH BY BEAUTIFUL AND SACRED MAIDENS AND MIGHTY CHAMPIONS. LITTLE IS KNOWN OF THIS, SAVE WHAT I HAVE TOLD IN THE STORY CALLED THE *ELUCIDATION*,* WHICH SPEAKS OF THE GUARDING OF THE GRAIL. ALSO I HAVE HEARD THAT A MIGHTY TREE GREW BESIDE THE FOUNTAIN, WHICH WAS PART OF THE PROTECTION OF THE REALM OF ARTHUR. THAT IT DREW UPON THE POWER OF THE GREAT WOOD, AS WELL AS THAT OF MERLIN, IS ALSO TOLD. HERE I WILL TELL ANOTHER STORY CONCERNING, IT MAY BE, THIS VERY PLACE. AS EVER, I CANNOT BE CERTAIN OF THESE THINGS, BUT MY HEART TELLS ME IT IS SO.

✛ ✛ ✛

ONE DAY WHEN King Arthur and many of his knights were gathered at Caerleon, the king was in the great hall, seated upon a chair of woven rushes, spread with a cloth of finest silk. With him were Guinevere the queen and her handmaidens, engaged on embroidering a new banner for the Round Table Fellowship, and there too were the knights Sir Owein son of Urien, Sir Cynon son of Clydno and Sir Kay son of Ector.

The day was warm and the king was inclined to sleep. 'Forgive me if I rest a while until supper,' he said. 'Send for wine and meats and entertain yourselves as you will.' Then he went into his chamber to rest, leaving the knights to talk.

---

* 'The Elucidation of the Grail' in *The Great Book of King Arthur and His Knights of the Round Table*, pp. 309–325.

As was often the way, whenever those who were part of the Fellowship came together, they fell to talking of their most recent exploits. As ever, Sir Kay mocked the knights for what he termed their 'boastful ways'. To this Sir Cynon answered that the story he had to tell was one of the most wondrous anyone would be likely to hear. At which, the other knights asked him to share his tale with them.

Sir Cynon began: 'I thought that I had seen and achieved as many wonders as I might, but this story shows that there are ever more adventures to be found. This took place not far from here, in that part of the Great Wood that lies to the north. All day I rode, by ways known only to a few, until I came to a most beautiful valley, through which a bright river ran, and this I followed until I came to where a castle loomed above the trees. There I saw where two youths were shooting bows at targets in the meadow below the walls.

'I could tell that they were not like other men from their look and their dress. Both had golden hair and were extremely handsome. They wore clothes of yellow silk, belted with gold, and there were diadems on their heads of the finest design. Their bows seemed to be made of ivory, while their arrows were fletched with peacock feathers and their tips were of gold. The daggers of each were also of gold.

'As I looked in wonder at these two, I saw where a man in the prime of life, with freshly barbered hair and beard, clad in robes of yellow satin, stood watching. On his feet were shoes of several kinds of leather most cunningly woven, with fastenings of gold.

'The man greeted me with a smile and invited me to take my ease in the castle. I followed him within and found myself in a great arched hall with many fine items of furniture and hangings. And there too were twelve of the most beautiful maidens I have ever seen. Other than this, the place seemed empty.

'The maidens at once stopped their tasks and saw to my needs as well as any squire I have ever had. They brought me water to wash and fine wine to drink, helped me to remove my armour and gave me a fine cloak to wear. Then they spread a table with cloth of linen and laid out dishes of gold and glasses of finest crystal. From these I ate and drank as well as I have ever done, even in this hall, or in Camelot the Golden. And all the time neither they nor the lord of the place, nor the two youths, who soon joined us, spoke a word to me, though they were as courteous as anyone could wish.

'When we had all eaten and drunk our fill, the nobleman asked me who I was and what had brought me there that day. He truly was the most well-spoken and handsome man, and his eyes shone with great power.

'I told him that I was in search of adventure – something that would challenge me to the utmost, since I had so easily overcome all who stood against me until then.

'When he heard this, my host smiled. "If you truly wish to test yourself beyond anything you have encountered before, you have come to the right place. Rest here tonight and in the morning follow the path that leads up through the woods. Soon you will come to a place where the road divides. Follow the way to the right until you reach a quiet glade. There you will see a mound at the centre, on which sits one such as you have not seen in all of your adventuring. From there what will be, shall be."

'Greatly intrigued by this I allowed myself to be escorted to a most fair chamber where I would sleep, and indeed I believe I have never slept as well as I did that night, though I was troubled with strange dreams that I cannot now recall. In the morning I rose early and found that my armour and weapons were cleaned and polished, and my horse saddled and bridled. Food was also set ready for me, but of the lord of the castle and the youths and maidens there was no sign.

'So it was that I set forth, following the path my host had spoken of, and soon I came to the place he had described. Trees surrounded the clearing and in the centre rose a low mound. Sitting atop this was the strangest and most fearsome being I have ever seen. He had but one leg, and a single great eye in the centre of his forehead, and he was as tall as two men. In one hand he carried an iron club that I swear would need at least two men to lift. This was not all – for on all sides were great numbers of wild creatures, who seemed to worship him as one might a god.

'In truth I felt almost as if I should bow to him. Instead, I asked how he came to have such power over the animals. For answer, he raised his club and struck a glancing blow upon the flank of a mighty stag. This creature bellowed loudly, and as if at a summons, came hundreds of creatures; some from the sky, others from the earth itself, and countless more from amongst the trees. Amongst them

→ *The Lord of Beasts* ←

were creatures I deemed not to exist: dragons, unicorns, basilisks and their like.

'"These are my children," said the one-eyed being. "I am, and always shall be, the Lord of the Beasts."

'Then he fell silent and I wondered if I could speak to him again. At last I plucked up my courage and said that I had come there in search of an adventure like no other. At this he who called himself the Lord of the Beasts turned his great eye upon me. "Little man," he said. "If you truly wish to encounter such an adventure, follow the path that you see, that leads further into the valley. At its head you will find the way rises to a level meadow. In that meadow you will find a single tree, its leaves greener than any other and its branches wide. At its foot a fountain rises, and next to that is a marble slab. Attached to that is a bowl of silver on a silver chain. Fill it with water from the spring and cast it over the stone. You will see then as great a wonder and adventure as you may ever seek."

'Having spoken thus, the giant turned his attention to the animals around it, and from his lips came the notes of a song – such a one as I have never heard before, but which stirred the very depths of my soul. I found that I could not listen or remain there for another moment, deeming that the song was for the animals alone, so I set out upon the path the Lord of the Beasts had indicated.'

Cynon ceased from his story here, and saw how the other knights, even Sir Kay, were looking on in wonder, and that the queen and all her ladies were as if spellbound, and had ceased from their needlework. At this he smiled, and having drunk deep of his cup of wine, continued:

'Everything fell out as the one-eyed giant had said. I followed the way and came to the flat place where the tree grew. It was, indeed, the most extraordinary tree I have ever seen, so broad was its trunk that at least six men could have stretched their arms around it, while the colour of its leaves was a deeper green than any I have seen, before or since.

'There, beside the tree, a fountain rose and as I had been told, there was a marble stone with a basin of silver chained to it. All was silence then; even the birds had ceased to sing. So, as I had been instructed, I filled the basin from the spring and poured it over the stone.

'At once the sky darkened as if it were midnight, and thunder rolled around the valley. Then came rain, more intense than I had ever known, followed by hail so large I swear it would have killed both myself and my horse had I not placed my shield over its head and mine. And let me tell you that after, when both rain and hail had ceased, my shield was much dented and broken, but my steed and I survived.

'When I lifted my head to look around, I saw that the tree had been stripped of all its leaves, and that its branches were as bare as they could be. Then, as I watched, a cloud of birds descended from the sky and settled upon the tree. And when they were all present they began to sing – so sweetly that I could not stay myself from weeping.

'Then, they too fell silent, and I heard a voice that seemed to come from all sides. "Why have you done this?" it asked. "Because of you, many of the people and beasts in my lands lie dead or wounded, smitten by the storm you summoned by your action!"

'At this a knight clad in sable armour came in sight, riding a horse as dark as midnight. He levelled a spear at me and came towards me at full pelt. I scarcely had time to mount my steed and set my own spear in rest before he struck me. Never have I felt so powerful a blow! I fell from my steed's back and lay breathless upon the ground. Without so much as a glance in my direction, the black clad knight hooked his spear into the reins of my horse and rode off with it.

'I will tell you now,' said Cynon to the company, 'never did I feel such shame – not only that I had been beaten, but that my opponent considered me so worthless that he could not even speak to me. On the morrow I returned to the castle where I had first heard of the one-eyed giant, and though I was once again given every courtesy, no one spoke to me of what had occurred. And in the morning I found a fresh steed prepared for me so that I was able to return here.

'So it is that I tell you this story, though it is about my own failure, for never have I heard another man speak of this place, or of the giant with one eye, or of what had occurred.'

All were silent for a moment, then Sir Kay smiled and spoke: 'How easily do those who claim their might, fall from grace.'

Sir Owein, who had remained silent until now, said: 'It takes great courage to speak of things that have gone against us. I believe that we should go to this place and see for ourselves what might be achieved.'

At this, Sir Kay fell silent, and Queen Guinevere, looking with anger at the seneschal, said to Cynon: 'This story is full of wonder, Sir Knight. I for one would wish to know more.'

At this King Arthur woke from his sleep and declared that it must be time to eat. So all of the company went in to dine and nothing more was said of Sir Cynon's story. But next morning, at the very break of day, Sir Owein prepared his mount and donned his armour and weapons and left Caerleon, following the way Cynon had described.

✠ ✠ ✠

ALL WAS AS Owein had been told. He reached the castle and saw the yellow haired youths outside; the host came to meet him and welcomed him at once. Within the castle Owein saw the beautiful maidens spinning. Just as Cynon had described the host was kind, and made the knight comfortable and spoke of the adventure which waited at the foot of the Fountain. In the morning Owein's horse and armour were ready and waiting, together with fresh food and when he had eaten he rode off at once towards the mound and its occupant.

First, he encountered the one-eyed giant, who gave him instructions to reach the Fountain. There, the knight poured the water onto the stone and endured the storms which followed. Then came the Sable Knight, and the two men met together with a mighty crash and shattered their spears. They continued to fight with swords, until Sir Owein delivered a blow which pierced the Sable Knight's helm and brainpan, so that he knew he had received a mortal blow.

Feeling his death upon him, the Sable Knight turned his horse's head and galloped away. Owein followed him to the gates of a citadel of obvious strength and splendour. There, the Sable Knight entered, but when Owein followed, the portcullis fell behind him, all but killing his horse, while the inner gates were closed against him, leaving him trapped between the two.

Uncertain what to do, Sir Owein peered through a grille in the inner doors. He could see a street beyond with houses on either side, and there, coming towards him, a most beautiful maiden. Her hair was yellow and held in place by a golden circlet, and her gown was of yellow silk. This reminded Owein of those in the castle where he had spent the night, so

that he wondered if she was part of the kindly host's family.

Up to the gate came the lovely maiden and looked at Sir Owein.

'Can you open the gate for me?' she asked.

'Alas, I can no more let you out than I believe you can let me in,' answered Owein.

'Nevertheless,' replied the maiden, 'let me see what I can do.'

She reached through the grille and offered Sir Owein a curious ring set with green chrysolite. 'Wear this turned inward to your palm and as long as you do not show the stone, you will be invisible. Soon men will come from the castle to take you away in chains, but all they will find is your horse. Meanwhile, I shall wait for you next to the horseblock you see beyond the gate. When you are able to get in, come and touch me upon the shoulder, so that I may know you are there.'

Owein gave thanks to the maiden and put on the ring, and just as she had said, soldiers came to carry him off but saw only his horse. While they argued amongst themselves as to where the stranger knight might have gone, he slipped through the gate and hastened to the horseblock where the maiden awaited him. Instructing him to remain invisible, she led the way to a most splendid house, and then to a chamber most richly decorated with paintings and tapestries of the finest kind.

There the maiden, whose name was Luned, brought water and towels and helped Owein wash and set before him the finest food he had ever tasted, and the best wine he had ever had to drink. And all of this time Luned spoke but little, but waited upon the knight as if she had been his squire.

As they finished eating, they heard a great commotion in the streets. When Owein asked what this was concerning, Luned told him that

98

the lord of the city had but lately returned with a wound from which he was like to die, and that the people of the city were disturbed by this, for without their champion the place might fall. Then she led Owein to a couch and encouraged him to rest. And, whether it was from the food and drink, or perhaps a gentle magic from the maiden, he fell into a deep sleep.

In the morning he awoke to the smell of food and once again dined as only a noble lord might. And while he ate, there came again a great noise from outside. When he asked the reason for this, the maiden told him that the people were mourning the death of their lord, which had indeed befallen as expected. Then once again she made him rest and again Sir Owein slept deeply, even though the sun had but lately risen.

When he awoke again it was evening, and fresh food and wine were set before him, after which Owein again slept. In the morning when he again ate heartily, there came again the sound of many people mourning the passing of their lord, and Owein went to the window to see them.

There he saw a procession following a bier upon which was laid the body of a man. Following it was a lady of such beauty that even as he looked at her Sir Owein fell deeply in love with her.

'Who is that noblewoman?' he asked.

'That is the countess who rules over this city,' said Luned. 'She is called the Lady of the Fountain, for the sole means by which all that you see here is maintained is through the power of that spring. And where you, Sir Owein, slew its protector – he whose body you see below us now.'

Then Owein knew that the maiden Luned must be possessed of magic, for there was no other way she could have known all that had occurred. But all he had eyes for was the countess herself, and he admitted to the maiden that he loved her as no other woman he had ever seen.

'Yet I cannot believe she could ever love the man who slew her husband,' he said with great sorrow.

'That may not be so,' replied Luned. 'Though it is but hours since the passing of the Sable Knight, yet I know for certain that the countess did not love him. Also, she must seek a new defender of the Fountain, or else this realm and city may perish. If you were to become that guardian then I believe she would look upon you with favour.'

Then Luned bade Sir Owein to remain inside the house, while she visited the Lady of the Fountain herself, who was most glad to see her, and requested her wisdom as to what action should follow the death of the Sable Knight.

To this Luned answered: 'My lady, first you must find a new champion. I do not believe that any man here is strong enough to undertake this task. May I suggest therefore that I journey to the court of King Arthur to seek a guardian for you? It is said that there is no other place in all of the land where such great knights gather. Surely one of them will take upon himself the task of protecting the Fountain.'

When she heard this, the countess gave Luned her permission to go for, as the maiden had told Sir Owein, she had but little love for the Sable Knight, and the thought of a new champion pleased her greatly and assuaged her fears for the city.

Thus Luned returned to her house and woke Sir Owein and told him all that had passed between herself and the countess. Then she said: 'Now we must wait for as long as it would take me to go to Camelot the Golden and return. Then I shall introduce you to my lady so that she may see for herself what a fine man and the noble knight you are.'

Owein remained hidden in the house of Luned for several weeks, more often than not sleeping, which it seemed the maiden was able easily to induce in him. You may be sure that he dined in such a manner that he grew stronger daily, until one morning Luned brought forth towels and water and a razor with a handle of gold, and washed the knight's hair and shaved him. Then she found fresh garments for him and led him before the countess. And it must be said that when she saw the handsome man and learned that he was the son of King Uriens of Gore and one of the best of the Round Table Fellowship, she was glad indeed to welcome him.

So it was that she offered him the guardianship of the Fountain, which he gladly accepted, and in the months that followed she came to know him well and, in time, to return his love. Nor was it long before she knew with certainty that it was he who had slain the Sable Knight; but this was no let or hindrance to her feelings for him, so that within a year she and Owein were married, much to the delight of the people of the city.

✠ ✠ ✠

SO PASSED THREE years, during which time Sir Owein encountered many knights who came to the Fountain in search of adventure. All of them he overcame, and the story of his prowess spread throughout the land until it reached the court of King Arthur.

Now in all the time since he had departed in pursuit of Sir Cynon's adventure, no word had come of Sir Owein, and many began to mourn him, fearing he must be dead. But in truth, the magic of the Fountain caused him to forget his former life, so that he knew only of the task he had undertaken and his love for the countess.

One day Sir Gawain was attending upon King Arthur and noticed how downcast he was. When he enquired for the king's sorrow, Arthur told him that he was bemoaning the loss of Sir Owein. 'In my heart,' he said, 'it is my belief that he went in search of the adventure described by Sir Cynon. For it was on the next day after he told the story that Owein departed, telling no one where he went.'

'Sire,' said Sir Gawain. 'Let me go forth and seek him. He is my cousin after all, and I too feel his loss.'

'Very well,' said King Arthur. 'But I will come with you. Indeed, let us bring a company of knights, and let Cynon be our guide.'

Next day King Arthur, accompanied by Sir Gawain, Sir Cynon, Sir Kay, and a dozen of the best knights set forth from Camelot the Golden and journeyed north to the country where the adventure of the Fountain had taken place. And everything was as it had been before, first for Sir Cynon himself, and then for Sir Owein. They reached the castle and saw where the youths shot arrows and threw knives; once again the lord of the castle welcomed them and brought them into his home; and as before the maidens ceased their work and served the king and the knights as squires, ensuring their every comfort was met.

Next day the company set forth and visited the one-eyed giant, who had no words for them but pointed the way onward. Then all was as it had been with both Sir Owein and Sir Cynon. When they arrived at the Tree, which had renewed itself and was once again in full leaf, Sir Kay asked to be allowed to carry out the pouring of the water upon the marble stone.

To this King Arthur agreed and all prepared for the storms to come.

This time they were of such violence that several of the king's company were wounded by the force of the hail; but at length the clouds passed over and the Tree, once again stripped of its leaves, received the flock of birds. These sang to the delight of all.

Then there came a knight clad in sable armour, and again Sir Kay was quick to ask if he might try this adventure first. King Arthur agreed, but the seneschal came to regret this soon enough, when the knight easily unhorsed him and rode off without speaking. Kay, angered by this slight, begged to be allowed to attempt the battle one more time, and once again King Arthur agreed for the sake of the love he had for his foster-brother.

The company camped beside the spring that night and on the morrow the Sable Knight returned. When he saw this, Sir Kay prepared to meet him again, thus hoping to recover his pride. But again he was swiftly struck down, as were each of the Round Table knights who, over the next five days, turn and turn about encountered the Sable Knight and were defeated.

Finally, Sir Gawain took his turn and this time the two knights broke several spears and afterwards continued fighting with swords. Neither could get the advantage of the other however, and their battle continued over two more days, until a blow from Gawain's sword knocked the helm from the head of the Sable Knight, revealing his face as that of Sir Owein.

Sir Gawain knew his cousin at once, and at this the spell that had prevented Owein from recognising the king and his companions was broken. The two knights threw down their swords and embraced, and thereafter the company retired to the city, where Sir Owein told King Arthur everything that had occurred.

→ *The wondrous fountain* ←

The countess came forth to meet the company and all were welcomed there and a great feast prepared.

⊹ ☩ ⊹

THUS PASSED A pleasant time, at the end of which King Arthur prepared to return to Camelot the Golden. Before they departed, the king spoke with the Lady of the Fountain and asked that Sir Owein might return with them for a brief time, so that all who knew him might know that he was safe and well.

At first the countess was reluctant, since this would leave the Fountain and the Tree unprotected, but at last she gave her consent and Owein left with the king and his company and journeyed with them. But as they went further from the Fountain, all memory of his adventure, and his love for the countess, went from Owein, and once he returned to the court, the weeks turned to months and the months to years until almost three summers passed by without him once thinking of the countess or the city he had called home.

At the end of this the damosel Luned came to Camelot the Golden, but Owein knew her not, for the spell of forgetting remained upon him. The maiden entered the court and, in front of all there, stripped two rings from Sir Owein's hand. One was that which she had given him long since, that could make him invisible when he wished (though this too he had forgotten and wore the stone facing outward rather than hidden in his palm, as he had been told). The second ring was the wedding band that signified his union with the Lady of the Fountain, whom he had quite forgotten.

'Thus is the faithless man, the traitor, disgraced!' cried Luned. 'Do not seek to return

when you are no longer wanted!' Then she departed before anyone could prevent her.

With her going, Sir Owein remembered all that had occurred, and his sorrow knew no bounds. And there came a madness upon him, so that he departed from Camelot the Golden and wandered far from the court.

Soon he forgot even his name, and wandered in the wilderness until his fine raiment fell from him and he was left with only rags to wear. He had but little to eat and thus became but a shadow of his former self. Wasted, wild and hairy he was, so that none could have recognised him even had they encountered him.

But one day his wandering took him once again into the lands ruled by the Lady of the Fountain – though he did not know it. So starved was he that he found a sheltered hollow in the earth, and there laid down, too weak to move. It seemed then that he must perish, but it fell out that the maiden Luned came that way. At first she was fearful of the desolate, starving man, but then she saw that it was Owein.

Her anger towards him was such that at first she determined to leave him there; then she thought of the times when they had been friends, and instead brought him water to drink. Then, leaving him where he lay, she returned to her mistress and told her what had occurred.

At first the countess too was embittered and declined to help him, but in that moment a messenger came who spoke of a huge knight, almost a giant, who had arrived at the Fountain and, having slain the champion who had been appointed after Sir Owein departed, made himself master of that place.

'It seems you may need the strength of King Arthur's knight once again,' said Luned.

The countess considered this for a time, then took a flask containing a rare drink that had powerful healing properties and instructed Luned to take it to the wasted man. This Luned did, and when she gave it to Sir Owein he at once began to recover, though it seemed that he still did not remember his name or anything concerning the Fountain or its Lady.

Meanwhile, Luned brought water and scissors and having washed the knight's beard and hair, trimmed them – just as she had long since. Then she laid out fresh clothing and also a sword and some armour, as well as plentiful food for him. But always he looked wildly at her, and spoke no words, but rather growled like a beast. So Luned retired a short distance to watch what he would do.

At first the knight looked at all of these gifts as though he did not know what to do with them. Then his mind began to clear and he dressed himself in fresh clothes and ate the food he had been brought. But the armour and weapons he set to one side until his strength returned.

For several days Luned returned with fresh food and water and slowly Sir Owein was restored, though he had perhaps less strength than before. But at last the day came when he put on the armour the wise handmaid had brought, and took up the sword. When she saw this Luned returned to the city and fetched him a fine steed.

In all of this time she spoke few words to the knight, who still had not recognised her or the land where he found himself. When he saw the horse he mounted it and rode away from there, letting the beast choose which way it would go.

So it was that he came to a rocky place and there Sir Owein saw a serpent that lived inside a crevice. There also was a wild black lion that constantly tried to capture the creature, but every time it drew near, the serpent withdrew into the safety of its nest. When he saw this,

Sir Owein drew his sword and when next the snake appeared he struck it in two. Then he rode upon his way, but now the black lion followed him, running at the heels of his horse, or weaving from one side to the other in a playful manner. Nor, thereafter, would the beast leave his side for long, but accompanied Owein wherever he went, and brought him freshly killed food which it shared with him. In time the knight came to accept the lion as his friend and even the knight's horse did the same.

✠ ✠ ✠

AFTER THIS, SIR Owein met with further adventures on his way, and each time the lion assisted him, using its savage strength to help him overcome his opponents. But despite the return of his former strength, still he did not remember his true name, or anything of his former life, either as a knight of the Round Table, or as a guardian of the Fountain.

Thus for a time he was lost again to the world, but one day he arrived at the meadow where the one-eyed giant dwelt. At once the lion went and knelt before him, and in a while the Lord of the Beasts turned towards Owein and looked at him with his single great eye, told him to follow the path to the Fountain and the Tree.

This he did, and there he once again threw water upon the stone, and braved the storms, and saw the Tree stripped of its leaves. Then he heard the song of the birds, and with this his memory returned fully once again, and he remembered his life as a knight of the Round Table and later as the Knight of the Fountain.

Soon after this came the giant knight who had become the new champion of the countess by strength of arms – though to her he was a fearsome enemy who took many of her lands for his own and refused to bow to her.

Sir Owein fought against this huge opponent, and thanks to the lion, which savaged him greatly, succeeded in striking him down. No sooner had he done so than the maiden Luned came there, and he knew her at last and they embraced.

So it was that Sir Owein returned to the city where he was welcomed by the people. A great celebration followed, and when she saw her former love again the countess forgave him his long absence. Indeed, she well knew the power of the Fountain, which had caused him to forget her.

Thus Owein became the Champion of the Fountain once more, helped now by the black lion, which remained with him for many years until its death.

So he became known throughout the land as the Knight of the Lion, and by the dispensation of the countess he was able to visit Camelot the Golden whenever he so desired, while yet remembering who he was.

THUS IS THE story of the Fountain completed. Of the maiden Luned the story tells us no more, but it is my belief that the wise handmaid loved Sir Owein every bit as much as her mistress – though of this she never spoke. Nor can I say whether another champion came to protect the Fountain after Sir Owein, or if the Tree yet grows beside the spring. Yet surely such a wondrous thing must exist in the world, even though many such magics are long since forgotten? At least, so I pray.

EXPLICIT THE STORY OF THE FOUNTAIN.

INCIPIT THE TALE OF GERAINT AND ENID.

14: THE STORY OF GERAINT AND ENID

⁜

OFTEN HAVE I HEARD IT SAID THAT THE LIVES OF THE ROUND TABLE KNIGHTS MADE IT HARD FOR THEM TO FIND LOVE THAT LASTED MORE THAN A BRIEF TIME. THEIR CONSTANT SEARCH FOR ADVENTURE, OR WRONGS TO RIGHT, MEANT THEY WERE ALL TOO OFTEN FAR AWAY FROM THEIR LADIES, AND THAT NOT ALL HAD THE PATIENCE TO AWAIT FOR THEIR RETURN. THE TALE I WILL TELL HERE CONCERNS WHAT OCCURRED WHEN A KNIGHT SOUGHT TO REMAIN AT HOME FOR LONGER THAN WAS USUAL IN THAT TIME, AND HOW WORDS SPOKEN WITHOUT THOUGHT WERE MISUNDERSTOOD AND LED TO MUCH PAIN FOR BOTH. IN THE CASE OF THE GREAT KNIGHT SIR GERAINT AND HIS LADY ENID, BOTH, IT SEEMS TO ME, LEARNED VALUABLE LESSONS FROM ALL THAT FOLLOWS HERE, BUT I AM NOT ABLE TO SPEAK WITH AUTHORITY ON SUCH MATTERS. THEREFORE I LEAVE IT TO MY READERS TO DECIDE THE RIGHTS AND WRONGS OF THIS ADVENTURE.

⁜ ✠ ⁜

ON A DAY when King Arthur held court at Caerleon at the holy feast of Whitsuntide, there came a youth riding a high-spirited horse, dressed in the most splendid garments and wearing a golden sword at his side. He came before the king and bowed to him.

'What news do you bring?' asked King Arthur.

'Sire, I am one of your foresters,' answered the youth, 'and on this day I saw a most remarkable stag, all white, and with antlers taller than any I have seen.'

'I shall go forth tomorrow and hunt this mighty beast,' said the king. 'Since it is white, it may even be a creature of Faery. It is bound to bring great sport.'

So preparations were made for the hunt, and when she heard of this, Queen Guinevere asked if she might accompany them. 'For I have never seen such a quarry as that you seek,' she said.

'You are most welcome to come, my dear,' said King Arthur.

But when dawn came, and the king and his courtiers were mounted and ready to depart, the queen had yet to arise.

'Let us depart,' said the king. 'Clearly my lady prefers to sleep than follow the hunt.'

So the king and the knights set forth, led by the young forester, to the place where he had sighted the stag.

Meanwhile, the queen awoke and summoned her maidservant to ready her mount. 'It seems my lord and all of the court have left already, but I still wish to catch sight of the white beast.'

Thus the queen and her handmaiden set forth. They had not gone far when they saw a young knight approaching. He was clearly not prepared for any adventure, as he wore no armour and carried only a sword at his side. Guinevere at once recognised him as Geraint, son of Erbin, one of the most recent to join the Round Table Fellowship, and still young and untried. When he saw the queen he dismounted and bowed low to her, and Guinevere smiled upon him and welcomed him.

'I am following the king, who is gone in search of a white stag,' she said. 'If you wish, you may attend upon us.'

To this Geraint most willingly agreed, for like many of the knights he acknowledged the beauty and grace of the queen with wonder.

So the small party rode on until they met with an armoured knight whose helmet was closed and who bore a covered shield so that none might recognise him. With him was a dwarf, who when he saw the queen and her companions rode towards them swiftly.

'Ask this fellow the name of his master,' said the queen, and her handmaid rode to meet the dwarf. But when she asked him the name of the knight, the small man refused her.

'Then I shall ask him myself,' said the maiden.

'You shall not!' cried the dwarf. 'You are not worthy to speak to him!' Then he struck the maiden across the face with his whip, drawing blood.

When he saw this Geraint asked permission to approach the dwarf and the knight, and Queen Guinevere, angered at the striking of her maidservant, gave him leave.

Geraint rode to where the dwarf sat his mule and demanded to know what he meant by striking the maiden.

The dwarf laughed at him. 'She had the audacity to request the name of my master. I told her that she was not noble enough to even hear his name. I say the same to you.'

'Then I will ask him myself,' said Geraint. But as he made to ride off the dwarf raised his whip and struck at the young knight, causing a wound upon his face.

At this Sir Geraint's hand went to the hilt of his sword, but then he considered that to kill the dwarf would be an unknightly action, and that since he was himself unarmed he might be easily beaten by the knight – who all this time sat his horse, unmoving, looking neither to right or left and seeming to have no interest in what occurred. Thus Geraint considered that the queen herself might be in danger, so he turned away and made his way back to Guinevere, who was comforting her handmaid.

'You did right, Sir Geraint,' said Guinevere when she saw this. 'For you were not fully armed and could have been slain if the knight chose to ignore the rules of chivalry.'

Geraint bowed his head at this, but still he looked towards the knight and the dwarf. They, no longer concerned with either the queen, her handmaid or Geraint, rode away.

'If only I could find some armour to enable me to fight that proud villain,' said Geraint.

At that moment there came the noise of hounds and hunting horns, and at this the young knight said to the queen: 'May I have your leave to try what I may do against the proud knight? You no longer need my protection now that the hunt is near.'

'By all means,' answered the queen. 'But I beg you to take care, for the knight is clearly a powerful opponent. I shall feel only concern for you until I hear that you have been successful.'

'If I am still alive five days from now, you shall hear from me, my lady,' said Geraint. Then he urged his horse forward and followed the direction taken by the knight and the dwarf.

Soon he came in sight of a fair citadel with strong and well defended walls. There he saw how, on all sides, lay a scattering of tents set up in the fields surrounding the castle, and there were many knights and squires busy sharpening swords and polishing armour.

As he approached, Geraint saw the proud knight and the dwarf entering the citadel ahead of him, to the accompaniment of much cheering. The young knight made to follow but found the gates closed against him. Its guards told him that no one else could enter there that day, but that if he returned on the morrow, he might be permitted to enter – if he had good reason.

Much downcast, Geraint turned away and made his way through the collection of tents. At each one he asked if they had armour to spare, but each one told him the same: 'We are preparing for a great tournament that will begin tomorrow. We have nothing to spare for an unarmed man.'

At last Geraint came to where a once fine manor stood close to the walls. It had the look of neglect, and had clearly been attacked at some time, such were the scars upon its walls. Finding the door open, Geraint entered and found himself in a hall with broken walls and windows. There he saw a man who bore the weight of many years upon him, and whose once fine clothes were old and worn. Clearly, he was a man of some station, who had fallen upon hard times, but he greeted Geraint kindly enough and asked what he wished for.

'I would ask to lay my head here for the night,' he said.

'That you shall do, and most welcome you are,' replied the old lord kindly.

He bade Geraint leave his horse and follow him. He led the way through rooms that must once have been as fine as any in the land, but which were now ruined and broken. Geraint followed his host to the upper floor which, though it too bore the signs of neglect, was comfortable. There sat a lady with as many years upon her as the old lord, but despite this Geraint saw that she must once have been of great beauty. Sitting with her was a maiden whose face and form were also most striking, and when she smiled at Geraint he felt his heart warming towards her.

'Sir, we have no one to attend you, but my daughter Enid will care for your horse and any other needs you have,' said the old lord. Then to the maiden he said: 'This youth is our honoured guest, child. Look after him and his mount and then go to the city and find the best food and wine that you can.'

The maiden rose and hastened away, returning with fresh water and towels for Geraint to wash himself and then bringing his horse inside and seeing that it was comfortable and well fed. Then she departed, soon returning with food and wine which she began to prepare.

Thus, in a while, Geraint and his hosts

dined simply but pleasantly, and the old lord enquired the young knight's purpose in coming. 'I expect you will be taking part in the great tournament tomorrow. Yet I see that you have no armour and only a sword.'

'In truth, sir, I am not prepared for any jousting,' said Geraint. Then he told the couple the story of his encounter and the insult to both himself, the queen and her handmaid.

'Alas that you have encountered the proud knight,' said the old lord. 'He is Edern, son of Nudd – a most powerful man. He has won the prize at the tournament every time for the last three years.'

'What more can you tell me of the tournament that has brought so many knights to this place?' asked Geraint.

'Ah,' said the old lord, 'the contest is for the prize of a most fierce and proud sparrowhawk. On the morrow, in the midst of the meadow that lies beneath the walls of the citadel, will be set up two forked poles, and on them a rod of silver, and on the rod will sit the sparrowhawk. My nephew, the earl, who commands the city, has made it known that each knight who attends must bring with him the lady who is his dearest love, and whose right to be named the most beautiful of all will be given to whoever wins the contest. To her will be given the sparrowhawk and he shall be known as the Knight of the Sparrowhawk for the next year. Three times now Sir Edern has won the tourney, and this year expects to win again.'

'If only I had armour and weapons,' said Sir Geraint, 'I would be glad to challenge this man to answer for the insult to my lady the queen.'

'As to that,' replied his host. 'In truth I have what you need, and will gladly give them to you – though my arms are old and somewhat rusted.'

'For that I give you my thanks,' said Geraint.

'May I know how you came to be living in this sad state?'

'It is a sorrowful tale indeed,' answered his host. 'My name is Yniol, and once the castle and the citadel that you see were mine. But my nephew, my brother's son, took it from me and drove me and my wife to this manor. After that he attacked us again and made a ruin of the house. Now we must live out our lives at his mercy.'

'That is a sad thing,' said Sir Geraint. 'Perhaps I might defend your honour if I may first win the contest of the sparrowhawk. But I would ask a second boon of you. Since I have no lady to go with me to the games, may I ask that your daughter does so?'

The old lord smiled at this, as did both his wife and their daughter. All three gave their assent, and Enid looked with delight upon Geraint.

So it was, that on the morrow Geraint left the manor clad in his host's old armour, which was indeed much rusted and weighed more than the young knight was used to. Also, he carried the old lord's shield. But he bore his own sword and rode his own mount, and went proudly with his host's daughter at his side, for indeed, when the maiden put on her only good gown, she outshone many who were gathered for the tournament.

With them, came the old lord Yniol and his wife, and many there were attending who bowed to them, for the young earl was less popular than his uncle.

As the old lord had told Geraint, when they reached the meadow where the tournament was to be held, they saw the proud knight, Edern, accompanied by a most beautiful lady, waiting by the stand upon which sat the sparrowhawk. And as was the custom, the proud knight announced to all that he was the champion of the contest, and that the hawk belonged to his lady by right of arms – lest anyone dared to challenge him.

Before anyone could answer, Sir Geraint announced that he would accept the challenge in the name of the old lord and his lady and their daughter, the Lady Enid, whom he proclaimed the most beautiful there.

The proud knight looked at Geraint and the old lord's rusted mail, and laughed. 'I am glad to accept your challenge,' he said. 'Though I think it will not delay me long.'

Then the two knights withdrew to the ends of the lists and prepared themselves. The old lord had promised five spears for Sir Geraint, who took up the first of these and set it in rest. The two then charged towards each other and to the wonder of all, both broke their spears upon each other's shields without hurt to either.

To the even greater astonishment of the onlookers, the two broke another four sets of spears, and neither was hurt or unhorsed. Sir Edern himself was shaken by the strength of his opponent, and his anger grew quickly as he failed, again and again, to defeat him.

A brief respite was given to the knights and at this the old lord himself came to Geraint. In his arms he carried a mighty spear.

'Sir,' he said. 'This was my own lance that I fought with in many tournaments in my youth. Not once did it shatter in all that time. Therefore I wish you to carry it for me on this day.' And Geraint declared that he would be proud to do so, and taking up the spear, prepared for a further tilt.

This time when the two knights clashed, the old lord's spear did not break, but the power of Geraint's blow was so fierce that it broke the girths of Edern's mount so that he fell to the ground.

Swiftly Geraint dismounted and helped his opponent to stand. Then the two fell to again with their swords.

How the lists rang to the sound of their weapons striking sparks from each other! The onlookers watched as though entranced, as the two knights fought each other through midday and beyond. At times Sir Edern would gain ground and the watchers would cheer; at others Sir Geraint would beat his opponent back and then there were groans from the crowd.

Both men were by this time close to exhaustion and Geraint began to fall back before Edern's repeated blows. Then the old lord called out from the stands: 'Remember the insult to the queen and her maiden!' and at this, Geraint renewed his efforts and at last struck his opponent such a blow that his helm was broken and his skull so hurt that he fell to the earth. Then Geraint stood over him and the proud knight, no longer proud, begged for mercy.

Sir Geraint granted it on the condition that Edern made his way to Camelot the Golden and swore allegiance to King Arthur, and also made amends to the queen for the insult upon her and her handmaid by his dwarf.

→ *The knight's opponents* ←

To this the fallen man swore, and as the company cheered, Geraint mounted his steed and made his way to where the sparrowhawk sat upon its perch. He took it and bore it to where the old lord and his lady watched and gave it into the keeping of Enid. And she looked upon the young knight with great favour, while his host praised him for his courage and chivalrous ways.

Thereafter the knights who had come from far and near to take part in the tournament, contested with each other and with Geraint for the right to bear the sparrowhawk and wear its name. But of all there, Geraint showed himself to be the best, and after five days he was declared the champion of the lists and given the title Knight of the Sparrowhawk. And all this while Enid looked upon Sir Geraint, and he upon her, until the spark of love burned bright within them both.

With his name and praises upon everyone's lips, Geraint sought out the young earl and asked that all the goods and titles taken from Yniol and his wife be restored to them, and that the manor be restored and made a fitting place for the old lord to live with his family.

And though at first the young earl protested, in To this the young Earl agreed, and promised that he and the old earl would rule jointly over the citadel until the death of Yniol.

When news of this came to him, the old lord and his lady wept and declared their unending gratitude to the young knight for all that he had brought about. Then he made it clear that if, as he believed, Geraint and Enid wished to marry, he would raise no opposition to this, but indeed do all that he could to ensure that the couple were wed as soon as possible.

Both Geraint and Enid were content with this, and according to the young knight's wish prepared to make their way to Camelot the Golden and to King Arthur's court, where they wished to be married. Geraint was mindful of his promise to the queen that she would hear from him in five days, and that more days than this had passed, and also wished to ensure that Edern had fulfilled his promise to attend upon King Arthur and the queen and to make amends for his unchivalrous behaviour.

Indeed, the once proud knight had already reached the royal court, and had spoken with the king concerning his defeat and the promise he had made to Sir Geraint. Then he knelt before Queen Guinevere and declared his sorrow that his dwarf had spoken and behaved in so violent fashion to both the queen and her handmaid.

Queen Guinevere and King Arthur both accepted Edern's apology, and he was permitted to rest and recover from his wounds. Thereafter he became a Knight of the Round Table and remained a good and true man from that time forward – though there were times, as I have told elsewhere, when he was less content with the ways of the Round Table.[*]

Soon after this, Sir Geraint returned to the court, accompanied by the Lady Enid. Both were made welcome, and the whole story of Geraint's adventure was told. Queen Guinevere received the Lady Enid kindly and gave her many fine clothes to wear, since, despite the restitution of her father's lands and goods, she still lacked dresses fine enough for the royal court. The queen also made it clear that if she wished, Enid could become one of her handmaids, and this the old lord's daughter accepted with great delight.

Thus preparations began for the wedding of Geraint and Enid, and soon Earl Yniol and his

---

* See 'The Story of Edern, the Son of the Bear', pp. 226–235.

lady came too. The ceremony was celebrated with much splendour, and even Edern, now recovered from his wounds, attended.

✠ ✠ ✠

NOW THE STORY tells how Sir Geraint became one of the most lauded knights of the Round Table. Many adventures followed and took him throughout the realms of Arthur, but always he most loved to return to Enid. Over time, indeed, he longed more and more to remain at home, preferring the company of Enid and the comforts of their home to those of the open road and the challenges of errantry. At first Enid was more than happy to spend time with Geraint, for their love was most deep and lasting, then one day she overheard two knights talking about Geraint and how he had forgotten his duties and had become soft in his ways. For this they blamed Enid, whose fascination was clearly greater than that of adventure.

At first the lady thought nothing of this, but as time passed and Geraint spent more time in her company, she began to hear more rumours that he no longer sought adventure or took part in tournaments, and in her heart she felt much discomfort.

One day as they were in their chamber, Geraint fell asleep, and as she looked upon him Enid was saddened to see his strength and skill seeming lost. As she did so, tears fell from her eyes onto his sleeping breast, and he awoke in time to hear her say: 'Alas that I am the cause of such regret and the avoidance of knightly duties.'

When he heard this, Geraint believed that his beloved was speaking of another man, and he rose in anger and began to call for his arms and for his steed to be prepared. To Enid he said: 'Prepare yourself for a journey. Wear your oldest riding dress and bring nothing with you!'

Though she understood nothing of Geraint's sudden change of demeanour, Enid did as he bade her. As soon as they reached the road the great knight said to her: 'Ride a little way ahead of me. Do not speak to me or approach me for any reason.'

Enid, without understanding, did as he asked, while Geraint remained silent and rode behind her and watched all that she did.

In a little while they came to a part of the Great Wood and Geraint chose a path that was known to be the haunt of robbers and villains. Soon enough, two men appeared and made their way towards them.

'See,' said one to the other, 'here is a chance to get two fine horses and some armour, as well as a woman to do with as we wish!'

As the two men advanced, Enid turned her mount and rode quickly back to Geraint. 'My love,' she said. 'Here are two ruffians who I believe wish to rob us.'

'Did I not say that you should not speak to me?' said Geraint roughly. Just the same he spurred his mount on and set his spear in rest.

The first man he struck fell dead with the head of the lance in his breast, the other soon followed and Geraint drew his sword and struck him down easily. Then, as Enid watched, he took their horses and tied their reins together. Then, leaving the robbers where they had fallen, he gave the knotted reins into Enid's hands. 'Take charge of these,' he said. 'And do not speak to me again.'

'I shall do my best,' answered Enid sadly, and the pair rode on.

Twice more, robbers came against them, first three, and then four, and each time Geraint made short work of them, sparing no one and seizing their horses.

Now Enid had nine mounts tugging at the reins, but though Geraint saw that this was no easy task, he spoke nothing to her except when she tried to warn him of each new attack, only to be told each time to remain silent.

Soon after this they came to a citadel where they were welcomed by its earl, whose name was Dwnn, who offered them food, comfort, and a chamber in the house of a goodman in the city. This Geraint accepted and he and Enid dined well and then retired for the night to their room. Within, were two beds, and Geraint pushed one of them to the wall, well away from his own. Then he commanded Enid to sleep there, on the far side of the room.

In the morning the earl himself came to wake them, and noticed how they slept apart. Having seen how they did not speak to each other the night before, he began to look upon Enid with lustful thoughts, believing that the knight with whom she rode had no interest in her.

Thankful of the soft bed and time to rest from his battles with the nine robbers, Geraint took his ease. Later the earl returned and spoke with him: 'Do I have your leave to speak with the maiden who travels with you, since it seems to me that you are not close?'

'Indeed you may,' said Geraint and turned away, leaving Enid and the earl to talk.

'Surely it can be no pleasure to journey with this man?' said the earl. 'You have no one to serve you and I can see that he has little care for you.'

'Sir,' answered Enid. 'I would as surely travel with this knight than I would with any number of servants.'

'But I can offer you much more,' said the earl.

'I have no such wish,' replied Enid.

'Then I shall have to take what I want,' the earl told her. 'I will return tonight and kill this man while he sleeps. And if you agree to be mine I shall treat you well, but if you withhold what I seek I shall take it anyway, with or without your consent.'

When Enid heard this, she felt great fear, but thinking quickly she said: 'It is true that this man treats me harshly. But it will not be easy to capture me. Therefore I bid you return tonight and seemingly take me away by force. It should be as if these words were never spoken between us.'

To this, Dwnn agreed. Once he had departed Enid told Geraint all that had passed between herself and the earl.

'Still, it seems, you cannot keep silent,' Geraint said. 'But it is well to be prepared, so I will forgive you.' Then he called upon the host of their lodgings and asked him to prepare their steeds and to instruct him how they might leave the citadel by a different way to that by which they had entered. As a reward he gave the nine horses they had captured to their host.

The good man did as he was asked, and soon Geraint and Enid left the citadel behind them. When, at midnight, Earl Dwnn came there with ten of his best knights, expecting to find Geraint asleep, he was angered and struck the landlord across the face.

He, knowing nothing of what had occurred, told the earl which way the couple had left, and Dwnn at once summoned his men and set off in pursuit.

Meanwhile, as before, Enid rode ahead of Geraint and spoke to him not a word until she saw a cloud of dust on the horizon behind them and then declared that she was certain it was the earl. As ever, Geraint was grim in his desire for silence, but he turned at once and waited for the first knight to emerge from the dust cloud. This man was swiftly dispatched, and the same end was meted out to each one as they followed. Such were Geraint's great strength and skill that none could withstand him.

At the last came Earl Dwnn himself, and seeing his knights fallen, he attacked with fury. Despite the weakness that resulted from his encounter with the knights, Geraint was able to hold his own, and having unhorsed his opponent himself dismounted and fought on foot. Soon he brought the earl to his knees and inflicted a deep wound in his side. Then the earl begged for his life and Geraint spared him on condition that he made his way to King Arthur's court and told the story of his treachery.

‡ ✠ ‡

NOW GERAINT AND Enid took to the road again, and as before the Lady Enid rode a little way ahead while Geraint observed her. In a while they arrived at the head of a valley through which a broad river ran. Beyond it lay a splendid castle whose only entrance was across a narrow bridge. There they met a knight upon the road, who saluted them as he approached and made no attempt to challenge Geraint.

'Tell me, sir, whose castle is that?' enquired Geraint.

'That is the castle of one they call the Little King,' replied the other. 'But let me advise you not to approach it, for you will be assuredly attacked and imprisoned if you do.'

'I give thanks for your warning,' said Geraint. 'But I am mindful to attempt it anyway.'

'Then may God have mercy upon you,' said the knight, and rode upon his way.

So Geraint, with Enid this time following behind, rode on until he arrived at the bridge and there made to cross it. But at that moment there came a knight riding upon a high-stepping horse, who rode into the centre of the bridge and blocked the way. He was so short that he was almost a dwarf, but wore fine armour and weapons such as a king might indeed wear.

'Who are you that dares to enter my kingdom without permission?' demanded the Little King, for it was he.

'I know not why that should be a requirement to enter here,' answered Geraint.

'It is my custom!' cried the other. 'He who ignores it must face me.'

'Then face you I shall!' cried Geraint, and while Enid watched the two knights flung themselves at each other and broke their spears, and the Little King was almost unhorsed.

Then he and Geraint drew their swords and continued to fight. And the Little King, despite his size, fought bravely and with great strength until at last Geraint struck him several blows of such power that he fell to the earth and lay still.

Geraint came and stood over him, and the small man cried out for mercy.

'You shall have it,' replied Geraint, 'providing that you promise to serve me in any way I wish.'

'I shall do as you command,' replied the Little King.

Then Geraint helped him to stand and the king invited him and the Lady Enid to return to his castle and take their ease there while Geraint recovered from his wounds. But Geraint refused, declaring that he wished to continue upon the road.

So Geraint and Enid left the Little King and made their way through the valley and into the rich lands beyond. The wounds that Geraint had suffered in the many battles since he had departed from Caerleon, now began to tell on him. Enid too was exhausted from her long journey and many adventures, but still in her heart she loved Geraint, though she was unable to understand his actions toward her.

As the heat of the day advanced, the young knight became steadily weaker. At length they reached a place where trees grew thickly and there he dismounted and lay down in their shade.

Soon after this there came a clamour of hunting horns and the barking of hounds, and they saw where a party of knights and ladies pursued a mighty stag. So weak was Sir Geraint by this time that he could not stand, but to them came a knight whom he knew well. It was indeed Sir Kay, King Arthur's seneschal, but so bruised and bloody was Geraint that Kay knew him not, and instead demanded to know what he did there in the king's hunting runs without permission.

At this, Geraint found the strength to rise to his feet, and told Sir Kay that he required no such permission.

The seneschal drew his sword and, despite the fact that the young knight was seriously wounded, made to attack him. But Geraint in turn drew his own sword, and weak though he was, quickly disarmed Sir Kay.

Alarmed by the strength of his opponent, Kay mounted his horse and returned to the hunting party, which at that time was setting up camp. Kay went in search of Sir Gawain and told him about the 'fierce and ignoble knight' who had insulted him. 'It is my belief he means no good and that it behoves you to deal with him.'

Gawain, smiling at Kay's avoidance of his knightly duties, mounted his steed and rode through the Great Wood until he came to where Geraint and Enid were. He saw at once that the knight was sorely wounded and made to greet him and his lady. But Geraint, so weakened by his wounds that he could scarcely think clearly, drew his sword and prepared to attack the king's nephew. Then Gawain looked more closely at the wounded man and cried: 'Geraint! Is that you?'

'I am not Geraint,' replied the other, with a wild look in his eyes.

'I know you for him,' said Gawain, sheathing his sword. 'I see also that you are sorely wounded. Will you not come with me? King Arthur is close by and there are healers with us who can help mend your wounds.'

'I shall not,' said Sir Geraint. 'When I am rested I must follow the road.' Then Gawain appealed to the Lady Enid, whom he also recognised. 'Can you not persuade him to come with me?'

But Enid shook her head: 'He will not listen to any word of mine,' she said.

At that moment Geraint finally could no longer withstand the pain and distress of his wounds and the loss of blood, and fell to the earth and lay still. And at once Sir Gawain hastened back to the camp and brought squires with a litter, who placed the wounded knight

❖ *The call to the hunters* ❖

114

within and so brought him back to King Arthur's camp.

Once it was known who he was, the king himself came to look at him, and commanded that every effort be made to care for him. And all this time the Lady Enid watched over him.

For several days Geraint lay unspeaking and barely alive, but at the end of that time he awoke and was able to move, though he was still not strong enough to stand or walk. Nor would he speak to Enid, or even acknowledge her. As to the rest of the company, he seemed not to know them at all.

Thus it was that the rest of the hunting party returned to Caerleon, and Geraint was carried in the litter with Enid walking at his side. There he was cared for by the best physicians and slowly began to recover from his wounds.

Enid, meanwhile, was taken into the care of the queen and her ladies and given fresh clothes to wear, and cared for until the signs of her long and painful journey began to ebb.

For several weeks Geraint was tended by the royal physicians, until he was strong enough to ride and could once again hold a sword. King Arthur himself came to speak with the knight, but though he was grateful for the work of the royal physicians, Geraint had little to say beyond his wish to continue on his way. And though he seemed healed in his body, yet his mind seemed to wander, so that he said almost nothing and remembered none of his old comrades. Enid, however, he did remember, and was, as before, cold towards her and commanded her to answer his every request and to keep silent.

All the court did their best to persuade Geraint to remain with them, at least until he was fully recovered, but he insisted that he and Enid must continue on the way as they had begun. So Enid once more put on her old riding dress and followed her lord, as she had done previously.

✛ ✛ ✛

ONCE AGAIN GERAINT and Enid entered the Great Wood, and they had not gone far before they saw where a thick mist cloaked the air. As they rode forward they came to where a tall hedge stretched across the way. All along the lengths of the hedge there were stakes of wood embedded, and on each stake was the severed head of a man. When she saw this, Enid was greatly troubled, but Geraint insisted they ride along the length of the hedge until they found an entrance.

As they went, they heard the sound of horses approaching, and Geraint drew his sword and prepared to defend himself and Enid. But when the mist parted somewhat it was a familiar figure who appeared – none other than the Little King, followed by several of his knights.

'Sir,' he cried. 'I have followed you here to warn you, as is my duty since I am sworn to be your ally. This is a place of enchantment, and though this mist, which never ceases, hides all that lies behind the hedge, I have heard that within lies a meadow and there a scarlet tent. Inside is the most beautiful lady, who is protected by a knight that no man has fought and lived. You see the heads of those he slew on these stakes – and be sure there is one empty that is meant for you!'

When he heard this, Geraint eagerly declared that he would seek to enter the place. Nor would any pleas made by the Little King or Enid dissuade him. So the company rode another league until they came to where a gap in the hedge appeared. And all around them the mist grew thicker.

Geraint drew his sword and placed his

shield before him and went through the hedge, while Enid and the Little King and his knights remained outside, fearing that they would not see him alive again.

Beyond the hedge, all was as the Little King had described. There the mist did not follow and in the midst of the meadow stood a single apple tree, on the lowest branch of which hung a mighty horn. Next to this was the scarlet tent, and seeing no one in sight, Geraint dismounted and made his way inside. Within, all was hung with silks, and a carpet sewn with golden thread covered the floor. In the centre of this stood two chairs, facing each other, and in one of these sat a lady of such beauty that Geraint at once knew her to be of Faery origin. The chair facing her was empty, and without thought, Geraint sat upon it.

'That is something you should not have done,' said the lady. 'He whose seat that is will have your life for it.'

Before he could respond to this there came into the tent a knight who wore the most splendid armour. He was taller and mightier than anyone Geraint had seen before, and he did not wait to challenge him but drew a long sword and came at the young knight with great fury.

The fight that followed was fearful to see. The two knights quickly drove each other outside onto the meadow and there they continued to rain blows upon each other until their shields were broken and their armour dinted. Soon Geraint's recently healed wounds broke open again and began to bleed profusely, while the huge knight seemed to suffer no such hurt.

As Geraint was driven steadily back, he found himself thinking of Enid, and of all that had happened in the months that had passed. Somehow this gave him renewed strength and he struck the tall knight such a blow that he fell to earth and did not move again.

At once the lady of the tent began to weep, and to beg for her own life.

'I mean you no harm, my lady,' said Geraint. 'I wish only that the enchantments of the mist should end.'

'You have but to blow the horn that hangs upon the apple tree,' answered she, and though each step was heavy and cost him dear, Geraint made his way to the apple tree and took down the horn. Then he blew loudly upon it and at once the mist vanished and the sun shone out. When he saw this, Geraint fell to the earth and lay as one dead.

Now came Enid with the Little King and his men, having heard the horn call, and when she saw where Geraint lay upon the earth, Enid began to lament.

'Ah! Here lies the only man I have ever loved or will love, and now I may never tell him how I feel!'

With great sorrow the Little King saw to it that Geraint was lifted up and placed upon a shield and then carried beyond the shadow of the hedge. Then he made sure that the tall knight was indeed dead, but though they looked for the Lady of the Tent, she was quite gone from there – nor was she seen again, which made all believe she, and all the enchantments of that place, were of no mortal origin.

Thus the Little King had the body of the tall knight buried and that of Geraint carried back to his castle, where it lay in the hall with Enid watching over it until night fell.

Then it was that the Little King came and offered his protection to Enid for as long as she wished, and spoke of the great affection he felt for her. To this Enid responded with gratitude, but made it clear that no other man would ever attend upon her again.

At this the Little King became heated, and raised a hand as if to strike Enid, who cried out.

There, before all present, Geraint stirred upon his bed and sat up, drawing his dagger from its sheath. Though he could scarcely stand, he made to attack the Little King, who fell back before him shamefaced and begged his forgiveness.

'I meant no harm to your lady, but thought only to protect her.'

Geraint dropped his dagger and would have fallen had not Enid hastened to his side, all the time weeping with joy that he lived. Then the Little King sent for surgeons who were able to begin the work of restoring the young knight to health.

And as soon as he could, and they were alone, Geraint spoke to Enid and confessed that he had treated her shamefully. 'As I lay in the meadow beyond the hedge,' he said, 'I heard your words that I alone was your love. Though I believed I would soon die, within me all the anger I felt when I thought you loved another fell away. I ask that you forgive me, if you can.'

Enid wept for joy. 'I have never ceased to love you, and in my heart I always believe that you acted from a place of madness'.

Then she and Geraint embraced and set aside the events of the past. After this they never felt anything but love for each other, and were happy together. Geraint once again journeyed forth in search of adventure and came to be recognised as one of the greatest of the Round Table heroes. But always he was happiest when he came home to the Lady Enid.

✠ ✠ ✠

THUS I HAVE told this difficult story, knowing that many who read it will find Geraint's actions both strange and unlikeable. Yet, the story tells us that the Lady Enid remained unshaken in her love for the young knight, and as one far wiser than I has said: 'This is a story of perfect love.'

———— ✠ ————

EXPLICIT THE STORY OF GERAINT AND ENID.

INCIPIT THE BOOK OF THE TALES OF LOVE AND HONOUR.

BOOK TWO

⧓

TALES OF LOVE
AND HONOUR

Gawain

15: FERGUS OF GALLOWAY

✜

MANY AMONGST THESE TALES THAT I HAVE GATHERED HERE TELL OF LOVE FOUND, THEN LOST AND FOUND AGAIN. THIS IS ONE SUCH, AND IT INTRODUCES A KNIGHT NOT OFTEN SPOKEN OF AMONGST THE ROUND TABLE FELLOWSHIP. YET THIS FERGUS WAS CERTAINLY A HERO OF GREAT STRENGTH AND CHIVALROUS DEMEANOUR, WHO WAS ABLE TO OVERCOME BOTH SIR LANCELOT AND SIR SAGRAMORE AMONG OTHERS. I HAVE FOUND NOTHING MORE OF HIS ADVENTURES OTHER THAN THIS THAT I SHALL TELL HERE – YET THIS SEEMS STRANGE TO ME, AND I AM LED TO WONDER IF THE SILENCE OF OTHER AUTHORS, SAVE ONE GUILLAUME LE CLERK, WHOSE NAME IS UPON THIS MANUSCRIPT, OR OF THE ANONYMOUS POET OF THE VERSION I HAVE READ IN THE LANGUAGE OF THE FRISIANS, AND WHICH DIFFERS IN PART FROM THE FRENCH, MAY NOT BE FOR SOME OTHER REASON. PERHAPS THERE IS SOMETHING MORE THAT IS NOT TOLD OF THIS EXCELLENT KNIGHT, BUT IF SO I HAVE NOT YET DISCOVERED IT. THUS, HERE FOLLOWS THE STORY OF FERGUS, HIS LOVE FOR THE LADY GALLIENNE, AND SOME OF THE MANY ADVENTURES HE UNDERTOOK, BOTH IN HER NAME AND THAT OF THE ROUND TABLE.

✜ ✜ ✜

THE STORY BEGINS, as do so many, with a feast at Camelot the Golden. And with a hunt for a white stag believed to be of Faery origin, such as that observed in the tale of Geraint and Enid.* It had been seen in that part of the Great Wood that lay closest to King Arthur's citadel, and so it was that the great knights came together and, with King Arthur at their head, rode out in pursuit of the stag.

Soon it was sighted upon a hilltop, and at once sped away. Such a chase it was indeed, with the knights driving their steeds through the wood, their hounds racing and baying as though their very lives depended upon it!

---

* See pp. 105–117.

But though they rode as best they might, and hunted through the morning and past noon, the stag was always ahead of them, a flash of white in the gloomy depths of the wood. In the end only Sir Perceval, along with his finest hound, were close to the great beast, whose proud heart beat fast, but which hesitated not as it raced on.

At last they came to where a wide, fast flowing river threaded its way between hills, and there the stag threw itself into the water and swam as fast as it might for the further shore. But even this mighty beast had begun to tire, and it swallowed much water as it went. Perceval's wise and determined hound dived into the river and swam evermore strongly after its prey, until it was able to sink its teeth into the white beast's flank, causing it such pain that it bellowed and in this way took in yet more water. At last its heart gave out, and as Sir Perceval reined in his horse on the riverbank, from where he had followed the chase, the brave and faithful hound dragged the body of the stag to the shore, where its master was able to pull it onto the land.

Perceval blew a long note upon his horn to let all who could hear that the quarry was caught and killed. When King Arthur heard the call he shouted aloud: 'Hear how the stag has been caught! I will swear that it is Sir Perceval's horn that announces it. Let us follow the call and see for ourselves.'

Soon the king and his knights arrived at the river and saw where Perceval had drawn the stag ashore. He sat close by, stroking the head of his faithful hound in thanks for its great skill and determination.

Since night was drawing in, the king and the whole party called upon their attendants to pitch tents beside the river, and passed the night there; and in the morning they prepared to return to Camelot the Golden, proudly displaying the body of the white stag for all to see.

Now it happened that they passed the home of a rich man whose name was Somerled, who, despite being of peasant stock, had married a noble woman, and thus inherited wide tracts of land and a great manor house that lay in an unfrequented part of the country. Near there, several men were ploughing a wide field, amongst them the eldest son of the rich man, whose name was Fergus. When he saw the royal party ride by, talking and laughing with each other, their armour sparkling in the sun, their steeds trotting splendidly in the dawn light, he was so overwhelmed that he ceased ploughing and ran to catch up with one of the squires, whose horse had gone lame and had thus fallen behind.

'Sir,' cried Fergus. 'Forgive me for asking you – but who is that great man who leads you, and who are they that follow him?'

'That is King Arthur himself,' answered the squire proudly. 'The greatest lord in all of these wide realms.'

'And the rest?' asked the boy.

'Why, they are some of the Knights of the Round Table,' answered the squire. 'Can it be that you have never heard of or seen them until now?'

'I have heard many tales of their adventures,' said Fergus. ' Such that I almost did not believe them to be true. But until this moment I have never seen them.'

As the squire prepared to ride on, Fergus called after him: 'Where are you all going?'

'Why to Camelot the Golden, the greatest city in all of this fair land of Logres!' shouted the squire.

'Then I shall follow,' said Fergus quietly. 'For I know it is my destiny that I must join this great company.'

So it was that Fergus made his way home and declared his intention of becoming a knight of the Round Table. At first his father laughed at him, then he became angry when the boy insisted he was determined to follow his dream.

'You are needed here!' cried Somerled. 'If you leave you will get no blessing from me.'

Then the noble lady, who was Fergus's mother, intervened.

'Husband, let him go and try what he can,' she said. 'He is strong and well-spoken and handsome enough. Why should he not have the same chance as any wellborn lad?'

Reluctantly, Somerled agreed, and at his wife's behest, had a suit of armour that had belonged to her father brought forth. It was red with rust and somewhat dinted, but Fergus was delighted to see it. He was helped to put it on, finding that it fitted him as well as any could wish. Then he begged for a sword and a shield, which were also given to him, and last of all, a horse. Somerled, by this time beginning to feel pride for his son, gave him his own mount, a high-stepping steed that was, in truth, as fine a beast as any knight could wish for.

Thus Fergus took his leave of his parents, not without much weeping on the part of his mother, who knew that, though she encouraged her son to seek his fate, that she might not see him again for many days. In the end even his father wished him well, though somewhat grimly, for in truth he feared that Fergus would be forced to endure much laughter and ill humour from those he would encounter at King Arthur's court.

Nevertheless, Fergus set forth, following the high road that led, many days after, to Camelot the Golden. There he made his way through the streets until he came to the great hall where the Round Table Fellowship met, and made bold to enter.

He was met, as had been so many young men intent upon joining the Fellowship, by Sir Kay the Seneschal, who demanded to know the youth's name and origin.

Fergus responded with his name and that of his father, and asked if he might enter and speak with the king.

At this, Sir Kay laughed. 'What makes you think you have the right to trouble His Majesty with your presence?' he demanded. 'Are you some great champion of whom we have not heard? I see that you carry a plain shield – are you in fact a knight?'

'That I am not,' replied Fergus. 'But I hope to be one soon, perhaps from the hand of King Arthur himself.'

At this Sir Kay laughed even more loudly. Others had begun to gather, hearing their voices. 'Enough, Sir Kay,' said Sir Gawain, and smiled at the youth. 'Come inside, and be welcomed.'

'Ha!' cried Sir Kay. 'Do you think he is come to fulfil the prophecy that Merlin made, how a youth would come here and seek the Nou-quetran, that place in the forest where Merlin long dwelled? According to the Enchanter, he will find the lion from whose neck are hung a horn and a wimple, which he shall take, and blow the horn to summon the Black Knight who dwells there? Will he do all of that and slay the knight also?'

'If I am given the right to do so, I shall willingly try,' said Fergus eagerly.

Once again Sir Gawain ordered Sir Kay to be silent as he prepared to mock the youth still further, and at that moment King Arthur himself arrived, demanding to know what all the noise was about. Gawain told him quietly and the king looked at Fergus kindly and asked his name.

'Sire, I am called Fergus, and I am the son

of Somerled, whose lands lie to the north of here. I saw where you passed with your shining knights, carrying the body of a white stag, and I longed to be part of your company.'

'You are not the first to wish that,' said the king gently. 'But it has ever been the way of my court, that any man may join so long as they show themselves worthy.'

In answer, Fergus knelt before the king. 'Then let me prove myself, sire. This man has told me of a quest to be undertaken for a place called the Nouquetran, there to do battle against a Black Knight. Perhaps I may undertake this?'

When he heard this Sir Kay began to laugh again, until King Arthur silenced him. 'Any man with the courage to undertake the adventure – one that the great Merlin foretold – may do so,' said King Arthur. 'If that is your wish, Fergus – then you may go with my blessing.'

At this Sir Kay looked abashed, whilst Sir Gawain and others, who had joined them, looked on and smiled. Fergus, filled with excitement, begged leave to seek lodging in the city, and set off at once.

Having no idea where to go, he wandered the streets until darkness fell and rain started to fall. Thus he was seen by a maiden from the window of her house, and taking pity on the handsome youth, she invited him to come in from the rain, to rest and warm himself by the fire. This kindly damsel was no less than the daughter of the royal chamberlain, who on his return to his house was surprised to find his daughter sitting with a strange youth. But when she explained, the nobleman made him welcome and that evening they heard the story of their young guest. Seeing what poor clothing he had, and what old and rusty armour, the chamberlain took it upon himself to give fresh linen to Fergus and to promise him as good a suit of armour as any knight could have.

At first Fergus was hesitant, wishing to keep the armour given him by his parents, but as he recognised the generosity of the chamberlain and his daughter, he agreed, promising to honour them always and to serve them if ever they required it.

Thus it was, that after a good night in a comfortable bed, Fergus donned the fresh clothes laid out for him, and with the help of the maiden and her retinue dressed himself in the magnificent armour. And before he departed the chamberlain offered to make him a knight. 'For no one, even as brave a youth as yourself, should go upon such a quest without the honour of knighthood.'

At first Fergus declined this offer, saying that he had yet to win his spurs. But the chamberlain told him that he recognised the young man's qualities and that this was simply to honour them.

So it was that Fergus knelt before King Arthur's chamberlain and was dubbed a knight. When at last he set forth from the great city, no one would have recognised him as the poorly clad youth who had come there the previous day.

✠ ✠ ✠

So FERGUS MADE his way, following the route that he believed would lead him to the Nouquetran. For several days and nights he saw no living soul, but instead listened to the whispers of the Great Wood. Then at last he came to the fair castle known as Liddel Mount, and saw a white-haired nobleman flying a hawk from his hand in the meadow below the walls. With him was a maiden of surpassing beauty whose name, the story tells us, was

Gallienne, the nobleman's niece. With helmet off and spear in rest, Sir Fergus rode towards the castle where the elder nobleman greeted him kindly. Gallienne stared in wonder at the youthful knight, as she had never seen his like before, and in that moment she fell hopelessly in love with him.

As the laws of hospitality demanded, the nobleman and his niece escorted Fergus into their home, where squires rushed to un-arm him and take his mount to be fed and watered. Thus they sat down together to eat, Gallienne was on one side of their guest and her uncle upon the other.

As the evening progressed, Fergus spoke of his quest for the Nouquetran and his mission to do battle with the Black Knight.

'The place you seek is not far from here,' said the nobleman. 'But let me advise you if you will, young man, not to go there. I have heard it said many times that knights older and more experienced than you have attempted this task – but none have ever returned, and I believe their heads decorate the walls of the Black Knight's castle.'

'Nevertheless, I have sworn to undertake this task,' answered Fergus. 'If I do not I shall suffer the shame for the rest of my life, and may never return to Camelot the Golden.'

Though both the old nobleman and his niece did all they could to dissuade him, Fergus remained adamant. Soon all retired for the night, but Gallienne found herself unable to sleep. She tossed and turned, all the while thinking of Fergus.

At last she rose from her bed, and flinging a mantle over her shift, crept out of her chamber and made her way to that where Fergus slept. He, woken suddenly, found the maiden kneeling on his bed, tears falling from her eyes upon him.

Surprised, he asked what was amiss.

'Sir,' said Gallienne. 'Though I know it is wrong to speak to you in this way, I must tell you that I am in love with you, and that my heart cries out for you, and beats evermore quickly when I so much as think of you. I cannot bear to see you go to certain death without begging you to remain here as my love and my knight!'

Now Fergus, being young and inexperienced in matters of the heart, felt only dismay at this. He sat up in the bed and took the maiden's hands in his, feeling how she trembled at his touch.

'My lady,' he said. 'Your feelings do me naught but honour – but I have sworn to complete the task appointed to me. If it pleases God to allow me to win the battle with the Black Knight, then I promise you I will return here. If I do so, then you shall certainly have my love.'

Although Gallienne wept and pleaded with him, Fergus would not be swayed, and in the end the maiden returned to her chamber, where she slept but little for the rest of the night. Fergus also lay awake, thinking of the beauty of the maiden and wondering if he would live to return to her. In the innermost chambers of his heart a spark of love ignited in that time, and though he did not yet feel bound to her by love's bonds, he knew that he would never forget her.

In the morning, Fergus prepared to set out again, watched by a tearful Gallienne and her uncle, who felt only sadness to see so young and untried a knight set forth to do battle with one so fierce and powerful that none had ever beaten him.

✠ ✠ ✠

ERGUS'S ROAD LED ever deeper into the Great Wood, following the path described to him by the nobleman until, several weeks later, he came to a place where the land rose towards a high peak. Since there was no means to ride any further, he tethered his mount to a tree and set off to climb the hill towards the summit. There, he found the most beautiful building, decorated by rich carvings and sculptures. Directly in front of the entrance stood a great figure, cast from bronze. It looked like a giant, and in his hand was a great hammer, capable of movement by some means unknown. As Fergus drew near the automaton, it swivelled in its place and the hammer rose and fell, striking the earth, which shook with the power of the blows.

→ *The bronze automaton* ←

At first Fergus knew not what to do. He looked upon the carved figure with wonder, and knew that if he came too close he might never leave that place alive. He remembered also that the Nouquetran, for such he believed the building to be, was once the home of Merlin and therefore doubtless full of enchantment. Then there came to his mind a thought of how he might defeat the automaton. He searched and found a great stone, and with all his might tossed it at the statue. The stone struck the giant full on and shattered both its arms, so that the hammer fell to the earth. The machine continued to twist and turn and its eyes glowed red, but now it was powerless to harm Fergus, who passed it by and entered the Nouquetran with drawn sword.

Inside, all was still. The walls were decorated with many paintings of strange creatures. On all sides stood carvings made of ivory and other precious substances. Fergus looked in wonder at the place, which seemed to him more filled with magic than anywhere he had ever been. At first he looked for the lion, expecting to see

a creature of flesh and bone. Instead he found the most beautiful carving of the beast, crafted from marble. Around its neck hung the wimple and the horn, which he took at once. Then he departed that strange place, and made his way back down to where he had left his horse.

There, he put the horn to his lips and blew a long blast.

He did not have to wait long for a response, for soon there came sounds that seemed as though a whole party of men had come in search of a boar or a deer or some other quarry. Then, in sight, came one who could only be the Black Knight, for his armour was as dark as midnight, and he rode a steed of the same colour, as was his shield and even the spear he levelled at Fergus. As he approached, the knight was already shouting loudly.

'Ha! What brings you here, and how dare you hold those things that are mine! Are you one of those fools who serves that coward King Arthur, who dare not face me alone? Where are those other great knights of his that he sends an untried youth to face me?'

'Insults will not win you any match,' said Fergus, anger raging through him as he prepared to fight.

The two came together with a mighty crash. Both shattered their spears and smashed through their shields and tore their hauberks. Though the Black Knight missed inflicting a wound to Fergus, the latter struck his spear deeply into his opponent's side. As though he felt no pain the Black Knight leapt from his horse and drew a long-bladed sword from its sheath. Fergus too descended and the two went at it like great beasts, swinging their weapons and beating each other like smiths with an anvil.

All the time the Black Knight taunted Fergus, who said nothing until he saw how the bright blood stained his opponent's armour. Then he called for a rest, since he believed his adversary was deeply wounded. The Black Knight refused to stop however, though his breath came ragged from his lips and the blows he struck were less weighty than before.

Finally, Fergus was able to deliver a blow which laid his adversary stark upon the ground, from where he begged for his life.

At first the youth seemed as if he would grant no mercy, then he recalled all that King Arthur and his knights stood for, and stepped back. 'I will spare you if you promise to renounce your evil ways and go to Camelot the Golden, there to swear allegiance to my king. And let it be known that it was I, Fergus of Galloway, who beat you. Remember this also: it is the law of those you named weak and foolish, that has saved your life.'

✛ ✛ ✛

WITH HIS MISSION completed, Fergus gave thoughts to his promise to return to Gallienne. Despite his uncertainty regarding her declaration of love, he found himself thinking of her more and more, and once the Black Knight had departed for Camelot the Golden, he set off back to Liddel Mount. There, he was met by the kindly nobleman who told him, with great sorrow, that Gallienne had left the castle some weeks before, under cover of night. He had no notion where she had gone or why – though he knew something of her deep and lasting feelings for Fergus and wondered if that had played a part.

When he heard of this, the youth found himself struck through the heart with love for Gallienne. He declared at once that he would not rest until he found her and brought her home to her uncle.

To this end, he set out the next day, with the nobleman's blessing. But with no idea where the fair Gallienne had gone, and no guidance in his new quest, Fergus was to wander far through the wards of the Great Wood. On the way he had adventures enough to fill a great book, but none brought him any joy. All he could do was think of the maiden who had offered him her love – which he, in his ignorance, had refused! How could he have been so blind? Day and night he journeyed on, all the time asking anyone he met if they knew anything of the Lady Gallienne of Liddel Mount. Not one, however, neither those he met along the way, nor those he subdued in battle, could help him, and slowly he fell into a state of madness, forgetting both his name and origin, forgetting the knightly life he had undertaken, forgetting even Camelot the Golden and the knights who served King Arthur.

So for a year he wandered, until he was emaciated, hairy as a wildman, and without memory or purpose. But at last he came to a spring that bubbled out of the ground in a clearing of the Great Wood. Though he knew it not, this was a place of great magic, where Merlin in his madness had once dwelled and where he had regained his sanity by drinking from its waters.* So it was with Fergus also, for when he knelt by the water and drank from his hands, the madness that had possessed him for so long, fell away, and he remembered all that had befallen him – his name and life and, above all, the name Gallienne.

Then, too, he was aware of his own state of being, for it was long since he had eaten other than berries and nuts fallen from the trees, or the raw flesh of dead creatures discovered among the leaves. His horse, which had some-how journeyed with him and, noble beast that it was, had not left his side in all this time, was shamefully neglected, having being neither combed nor properly fed in almost a year.

With his mind clear for the first time in this long while, Fergus sought lodging in a castle amid the trees and by good fortune it was a place of subtle magics and the home of a wise dwarf who not only helped Fergus recover his strength, but was able to offer him advice concerning his search for Gallienne. The dwarf, whose name the story does not tell us (for all such keep their names hidden because of the power they give over those who possess them) spoke at length to the young knight, as they sat, day by day together, while Fergus slowly recovered from his madness.

'Sir, I know of your search, and your name is not hidden from me,' said the dwarf. 'Also I am aware that the lady you seek has returned to her father's lands in Lothian. He is the king of that place, a good and noble lord, but his lands are

---

* See 'The Life of Merlin' in *The Great Book Of King Arthur and His Knights of the Round Table,* pp. 3–13.

constrained by another, named Galarant, who seeks to overcome him and marry the Lady Gallienne, who has ever refused him because of her love for you, Sir Fergus.'

'Then I must go at once to rescue my lady and her father,' said Fergus.

'You may do so,' answered the dwarf. 'But you have but one chance of winning back your love and saving her and her father from their foe. Galarant is a dangerous man, wise in the ways of magic and very determined. He is so protected by the power he wields that not even you, Sir Knight, would prevail against him. But there is a way that you may succeed. You must travel first to the place known as Dunnotar. There you must cross a river guarded by a savage boatman, until you come to a place where a white shield hangs upon an ancient tree in front of a castle. Such a light radiates from the shield that it is almost blinding. He who carries it is protected in such a way that he cannot be killed – though he must fight as bravely as ever. If you are to defeat Galarant you must take the shield.'

'Tell me the way and I will leave at first light!' cried Fergus.

'I will,' replied the dwarf. 'But there is more that you must know. The tree and the shield are guarded by a monstrous hag, hairy as a moun-tain goat, who wields a terrible iron scythe, sharp enough to cut through anything. Nothing like her was ever seen in this world before and nothing is known of whence she came. But only by beating her can you gain the shining white shield.'

'I swear that I will overcome this hag, for the sake of Gallienne,' said Fergus fiercely.

So it was that Fergus set forth, strengthened by the care of the dwarf, his armour polished, his sword sharp and his spear strong, following the road until he came to Dunnotar castle, a rugged and partly ruined place clinging to the top of craggy cliffs overlooking the sea. There, on a broad meadow before the walls, grew a single tree, to reach which Fergus must first overcome the fearful boatman, who held the ferry across the water with the help of a band of robbers.

These proved no hindrance to Fergus. He beat them all so utterly that those who lived fled from that place. Thus he was able to cross the river and so came at last to where the tree grew. There, on one of its branches, hung the white shield, so bright that it seemed as though the whole sky was lit up by the sun, even as night fell.

But as Fergus drew nearer he saw coming towards him the hag the kindly dwarf had warned him of. She was, if possible, even more hideous than he had been told. Perhaps a quarter of a league tall, her face sprouted so much hair that she was able to plait it. Her eyes were like saucers and several feet apart on her broad face, and her teeth stuck out of her mouth like tusks. It is my view that she was in fact enchanted, as was the Lady Ragnall that Sir Gawain wed and in so doing transformed her into a beautiful woman – but in this instance no such magic was possible!*

When she saw Fergus coming she ran to meet him, carrying the great scythe, and screaming all the while like one of the Sidhe beings that are spoken of in Ireland and who cry out when death is near.

Knowing that he would have little chance to defeat this apparition, Fergus drew back his arm and flung his spear directly at her. So swiftly was she running that she seemed to hurl herself onto the blade, which passed through her side, leaving a gaping wound from which her blood flowed.

Seeming not a whit concerned by this, the hag came on and swept the iron scythe in a circle that, had Fergus not leapt aside, would have deprived him of his head. As it was, it sliced the top from his helmet and sent the rest flying. Leaping again to avoid another blow, Fergus saw that the hag had buried her weapon in the earth and was struggling to draw it out. In that moment he struck with his sword, cutting off both the hag's hands.

At this she screamed even more loudly and tried to spit poisonous venom at him, but she was weakened by loss of blood and Fergus was able to avoid her poison. He struck out at her again with his sword, piercing her below the breast-bone, so that she fell dead upon the earth.

Fergus took time to rest then, for he had used much of his strength to defeat the hag. Then he mounted his steed and rode onward to the ruined castle. None, living or dead, was to be seen there, and so Fergus went to where the solitary tree stood and took down the white shield, which glowed so brightly that he could scarcely look upon it, while it yet restored him and gave him more strength than he had felt before.

Thus armed, he set forth again, following the route described to him by the dwarf to the Kingdom of Lothian.

✛ ✛ ✛

NOW THE STORY turns to Gallienne, who had slipped away from her uncle's castle following the departure of Fergus. She believed she would never see Fergus again, since no one who had faced the Black Knight

---

* See 'The Wedding of Sir Gawain and Dame Ragnall' in *The Great Book of King Arthur and His Knights of the Round Table*, pp. 352–9.

had ever returned alive. Filled with sorrow at the loss of her love, she made her way to her father's kingdom, and for almost a year after she languished there. Nothing her family could do could ease her grief.

At that time the neighbouring Lord, Galarant, of whom the wise dwarf had warned Fergus, laid siege to the castle of Roxburgh, where Gallienne now dwelled, demanding her hand in marriage and rule over the kingdom. Of course her father refused this and so Galarant pressed his attacks with ever greater ferocity.

So it was that, during a foray from the castle against his adversary, Lothian's king fell wounded and, within days of being brought home, died.

Gallienne, overcome with grief, was now the heir to the kingdom, and despite her years she took command, listening to the wise advice of her father's seneschal and his noblest lords. For months the siege continued, neither side gaining any advantage. Constantly Galarant sent messages demanding that the maiden surrender to him and accept his offer of marriage. Ah, how she longed to see or hear from Fergus, her lost love, who would, she knew, have saved her from this sad plight! But, having heard nothing of him since he had set forth to battle the Black Knight, many months before, she believed Fergus to be dead. So it came to her that she should send a message to King Arthur, asking for a champion to represent her, or even a husband chosen by the king himself.

She sent her handmaid, Lunete, to Camelot the Golden, but when the lady arrived she found the court sadly depleted. Many of the knights had but lately undertaken the quest for the Grail, and were far away or lost in the Wastelands. King Arthur heard her mistress's plea and promised to send help as soon as he could.

With this Lunete left the court and set off along the road back to Lothian. So it was that, as fate would have it, she met with Sir Fergus upon the road that led though the country of the wise dwarf. When she saw him, Lunete at once recognised him, having been attending on her mistress at her uncle's castle when he had first come there. With tears in her eyes, she told him of her mistress's fate, of her father's death, and of the siege by Galarant.

At once, Sir Fergus determined to journey to Lothian and to do what he could to break the siege. He and Lunete travelled on together until they reached Roxburgh castle, and by hidden ways were able to gain admittance.

Then was such a joyful meeting as can scarcely be imagined, as the two lovers embraced each other and wept for joy and sorrow in one.

'Never was I as happy as I am to see you, my love,' said Gallienne. 'But alas you see that we are besieged and that there is no way that I know of to defeat Galarant. I fear that you have come to a sorrowful meeting which may come to no good end.'

'That may be so,' replied Fergus. 'But we must see what can be done.' Then he uncovered the White Shield, so that everyone there was forced to shade their eyes. And for the first time, the people of the castle believed that fate had brought them hope.

Fergus now sent a message to Galarant, offering to undertake single combat with any knight of his choosing. When he heard this Galarant laughed aloud, and sent for his strongest warrior.

'Show this puppy what it truly means to be a knight,' he told his champion.

Thus it was that next day Fergus rode forth from the castle and there met with Galarant's man. Trumpets rang out from the battlements, and banners flickered in the air. The Lady Gallienne herself, and many of her father's men, stood proudly upon the walls and watched as the Knight of the White Shield did battle for them.

He soon proved his worth, not only by his own strength, but with the help of the Shield, which, as the wise dwarf had told him, protected him from all blows. Thus it took Fergus no more than an hour to defeat Galarant's champion, after which he returned in triumph to the castle. There Gallienne greeted him in wonder, having seen for herself that her love had become a knight that few could overcome.

Each day following, Fergus came forth and met another of Galarant's knights – and each one he defeated, up to the number of ten, on which day he sent a messenger calling upon the lord himself to meet him in combat.

Angrily, Galarant agreed, and on the next day the two knights met on the meadow outside the castle. The battle was soon over, for though Galarant was a strong knight who was possessed of magic, he could do nothing against the power of the White Shield, and soon lay dead upon the field.

But a handful of days after this, several Knights of the Round Table, including Sir Gawain, arrived, having been summoned by King Arthur to set aside their quest and come to the aid of the Lady Gallienne. At this, with their lord dead and King Arthur's knights present, the attackers fled the place and peace came again to Lothian at that time.

Sir Gawain was most glad to see Fergus again, and listened in wonder to his story. So it was that Fergus and Gallienne set out and returned to Camelot the Golden, escorted by the Round Table knights. There they were warmly met by the king and queen, and soon after were married with the blessing of all. There came both Fergus's parents, astonished to see him so highly respected and possessed of such chivalrous accomplishments. There also were the royal chamberlain and his kindly daughter who, truth to tell, looked with some sorrow upon the handsome youth and his bride. Also to witness the wedding, came Gallienne's uncle, the wise dwarf who had aided him, and others whom he had encountered upon his journey. All agreed that he was the most valiant knight to attend at King Arthur's court for many a day, and in the time of sadness following the Great Quest of the Grail and the loss of so many of the Fellowship, the presence of Sir Fergus gave much relief to the darkened realm.

Thus my story is almost at an end, though it tells also that Sir Fergus, the Knight of the White Shield, fulfilled his life as a hero of the Round Table in many further adventures. He and the Lady Gallienne were happy together and she bore him children who in turn followed in their father's steps as true and noble knights.

EXPLICIT THE TALE OF FERGUS OF GALLOWAY.

INCIPIT THAT OF MERAUGIS AND THE WOUNDS OF LOVE.

16: MERAUGIS AND THE WOUNDS OF LOVE

ISOUGHT HIGH AND LOW FOR MANY MONTHS FOR THIS TALE, AFTER A LADY CAME TO ME WHO HAD HEARD IT TOLD AND THOUGHT IT TO BE ONE OF THE BEST TALES OF KING ARTHUR'S HEROES, WHETHER SHE SPOKE TRULY OR NOT I LEAVE YOU WHO READ THESE WORDS TO JUDGE. ITS AUTHOR – WHO I AM TOLD MAY HAVE BEEN A KNIGHT AND IS THUS A FITTING COMPANION FOR SIR THOMAS – SAYS: 'THERE IS A STORY I WANT TO TELL THAT HAS NOT BEEN TOLD ENOUGH. IT IS THE STORY OF THE KNIGHT MERAUGIS AND HIS LOVE FOR THE LADY LIDOINE, WHICH TOOK HIM UPON MANY ADVENTURES, ON PATHS STRANGE AND WONDROUS. ALL THIS AND MORE I SHALL TELL, FOR ALL THE BEST STORIES DO BUT AWAIT THE BEST STORYTELLER AND TO THIS I, RAOUL DE HOUDENC, LAY CLAIM.

✠ ✠ ✠

DURING THE REIGN of King Arthur, many high lords lived within the borders of Logres and paid service to him. Amongst those whose lands were great indeed was a king named Escavalon, who had a daughter Lidoine, whose beauty was only excelled by her wisdom, for which she was praised throughout the land. Such was the respect apportioned to her, that when her father died without a male heir, Lidoine became the ruler of his kingdom. This task she performed with great excellence, and held sway over her lands and the knights who had served her father with grace and strength.

Now, when word came to her of a great tournament to be held at Camelot the Golden in the spring, she declared her intent to attend this mighty event, and to observe the Round Table knights and all others who came there, and to allow her own knights to take part.

This tournament, ordered by King Arthur himself, was destined to be one of the finest ever seen in Logres. All of the Round Table Fellowship who were present or able to attend would take part, while others came from all parts of the king's realm and beyond in the hope of achieving fame and fortune in the lists.

As was often the case at such events, two prizes were offered: to the knight who won most encounters on the field, both in single combat and in the melée, was granted a magical swan, that carried with it protection against dark magics. It was also allowed that the same knight could require a kiss from the lady judged to be the most beautiful of all those attending, who would herself be accorded the prize of a well-trained sparrowhawk.[*]

When the day came near that the tournament was to take place, the Lady Lidoine journeyed to Camelot the Golden with a splendid entourage of knights and ladies. When she arrived there was no doubt amongst those who saw her that she must surely be awarded the sparrowhawk, for no other lady was there who, though possessed of great beauty, could hold a candle to that of the Lady Lidoine

And so it fell out, for when the great company met together and the ladies were all seated in the stands that overlooked the lists, there was not one person who did not agree that she shone more brightly than all.

I shall not trouble to describe the tournament. It was a splendid affair, and many knights took part who would be judged the finest in the land. Several new seats were filled at the Round Table, amongst them one Gorvin Cadrus, along with his dearest friend Meraugis. These two had been close friends from childhood, and had shared many adventures together.

In the end it was a knight named Caulas who won the gift of the magical swan, but when it came to claim the kiss from the most beautiful lady, Lidoine showed little interest in the knight, despite his skill with lance and sword and his undoubted bravery. Rather, her attention was drawn to Gorvin and Meraugis, and when these two came, with many other

knights, to where she held court beneath a pine tree, both fell instantly in love with her. And the story tells that while Gorvin was enamoured of her beauty, Meraugis admired not only this, but her wit and wisdom also.

Now Gorvin Cadrus knelt to the lady and pledged his service to her at any time, then or in the future, while Meraugis remained conversing with her for longer than his friend, who was so overcome by her beauty that he withdrew to walk alone, nursing his blossoming love.

Following the great tournament, the time came for the lady and her followers to depart, and it is no surprise that many of the Round Table knights escorted them for the first few miles. Meraugis and Cadrus joined the party, which was merry and cheerful as it followed the road from the city towards the Great Wood of Broceliande, where so many adventures had begun and would continue so to do, and which gave access to the realm of Faery.

The two young knights were able to ride closely with Lidoine for a time, but soon Gorvin Cadrus dropped back, so overwhelmed was he with love that he could not bear to look upon the lady. Meraugis, however, rode on at her side. But as he went, his heart became heavier and heavier, for he deemed himself unworthy of so rich and beautiful a woman, and so in time he too turned back and followed the road back to Camelot the Golden.

Soon he met with Gorvin and the two friends rode side by side in companionable silence for some way – until Cadrus at length spoke of a terrible burden he bore. At once Meraugis declared that he would do all that he could to help his dearest friend, and at that Gorvin Cadrus expressed his love for Lidoine, whose beauty outshone the very stars above.

When he heard this Meraugis was filled with anguish, for he too knew a similar passion.

---

[*] See also a similar contest in 'The Story of Geraint and Enid.' pp 126–138.

Even so, he could not prevent himself speaking out that to love just the outward beauty of any lady was not enough. 'Surely it is equally important to love her spirit also?' he said.

'I care little for that,' replied Cadrus. 'She could carry a demon inside her and I would love her just as much.'

The two men fell silent for a time, but at length Meraugis was forced to confess his own love for Lidoine. When he heard this Gorvin Cadrus flew into a rage. 'How can you profess love for the woman *I* love?' he cried.

To which Meraugis responded with equal force: 'I know that I love her more than you – and I believe she returns my affections.'

Within moments the two men were preparing to fight each other, all signs of their former friendship driven away by their passionate longings. But at this moment the knights who had accompanied Lidoine to the edge of the forest, came back along the road. When they saw Gorvin Cadrus and Meraugis raging against each other they demanded to know the cause of their animosity. None could remember the two knights as anything but the best of friends; now they acted like the bitterest foes.

When challenged, the two held off from attacking each other and confessed that they were fighting to prove who had the right to claim the Lady Lidoine. The Round Table knights did their best to dissuade them from fighting, and while they did so sent one of their number to follow the lady and inform her of what had occurred.

When she heard this, Lidoine at once turned back and made what speed she could to where the party had halted. By this time Cadrus and Meraugis, held back no longer by their companions, had begun their battle. Two spears each they had broken, and now, dismounted, they went at each other with swords, hacking and hewing at each other like mad men, while the rest of the company looked on with great sorrow.

When she saw how the two men were battered and wounded, Lidoine cried out to them to cease their foolishness. On hearing her voice the two knights ceased their battle and hung their heads in shame before her.

'For what cause do you fight each other?' demanded Lidoine.

Both men responded that they fought for her love.

'This is madness indeed,' responded Lidoine, her cheeks flushed with anger. 'How may you fight over me when you have not even spoken to me of your feeling! I command you to cease this battle now. Furthermore I say to you that you must go your separate ways until the Christmas court at Camelot the Golden. Until then, you must not be anywhere near each other. At that time, with the permission of King Arthur, you may contest which of you shall have the right to ask for my love according to your adventures. Thus you have time to come to your senses, and remember your pledges as knights.'

Lidoine then looked to the rest of the company. 'I ask that all here bear witness to my words. Let us hear nothing more of this until the court meets for Christmas.'

As the remainder of the party acknowledged the words of Lady Lidoine, Meraugis and Cadrus had the grace to look downcast. Neither smiled at the other, and without further speech they mounted their horses and, despite being exhausted and bleeding from their wounds, rode away in opposite directions.

✠ ✠ ✠

WHAT REMAINED OF the year passed quickly and Meraugis and Cadrus both followed the path of errantry with great success. Both sent back many a troublesome knight to pledge themselves to King Arthur, and each one saved as many innocent maidens as they possibly could.

At the end of this time, as the court came together to celebrate the holy feast of Christmas, so the two knights returned. Neither spoke to the other but only looked with anger. They who had been friends for so much of their lives now bore only animosity for each other.

King Arthur, meanwhile, summoned his lords to meet and make a judgement as to which of the heroes could ask for the Lady Lidoine's love.

Sir Kay, ever ready with a hasty notion, said: 'Surely, sire, she should offer them her favours for every other month – turn and turn about!'

'That is no worthy answer,' said Sir Owein, and the king and many of the knights agreed.

'I saw it only as a peaceful solution,' said Sir Kay, flushing darkly. 'Since it seems to me these two love but half of the lady each.'

Other knights and lords joined in the discussion, while Meraugis and Gorvin Cadrus sat apart and looked only with anger at each other.

The argument went back and forward for some time, until Queen Guinevere entered the hall and demanded that, since this was an affair of the heart, she and her ladies should be the ones to decide to whom the Lady Lidoine should offer her favours.

At first the king was not disposed to permit this, but the queen insisted, and with Arthur's agreement, given reluctantly it must be said, she banished all of the knights and lords, including Gorvin Cadrus and Meraugis from the hall, which then quickly filled with her own ladies

and others who, on hearing how things stood, came to join the discussion. Even the king was not permitted to remain.

As it had with the knights and lords, the debate was no quick matter. There were those who spoke for Gorvin Cadrus and others Meraugis, speaking of their different approaches to love.

'Surely Meraugis, who loves the lady wholly and without reserve, is more fit to be her knight then Gorvin Cadrus, who has said that he cares nothing for her spirit but loves just her beauty,' said one of the queen's ladies. Many agreed, and after some further discussion the women agreed that Meraugis had the most right to win the love of Lady Lidoine.

'Let us not forget,' said Queen Guinevere, 'that this matter remains the right of the lady to choose. These are just recommendations to set against the warlike anger of the knights.'

Thus it was agreed between them, and so the two knights and the lady herself, who had now arrived at the courts, were summoned and King Arthur and the Lords of Logres returned to the hall.

Before all present, the queen gave the opinions of herself and her ladies.

At once Gorvin Cadrus sprang up. 'I do not accept this judgement! I came here to fight this other knight for the right to pay court to the Lady Lidoine. Any other judgement is unknightly and foolish.'

Meraugis then spoke up. 'It is true that I would rather fight for the lady than have things decided for me.'

King Arthur spoke sternly. 'This is not how I wished matters to proceed. We ordained this court to make a decision that would prevent these two knights from fighting. Instead, we are encouraging them.'

At this Gorvin Cadrus rose to his feet. 'Then

I shall depart this court – for I do not recognise its authority over my heart!'

Then he turned away and left the hall without so much as a backward look.

'It seems the matter is resolved,' said the king, and Queen Guinevere agreed. Meraugis then heard it declared that he was free to present his suit to the lady. Lidoine, who had heard all of what passed, now spoke up. 'I am glad that this verdict prevents the two men from fighting over me, since I am no plaything to be fought over. But let me also remind all, that it is my desire that will make the final choice.' She looked to where Meraugis stood, gladness in his eyes at the thought of winning his love.

'Sir Knight. I have heard the words of this great king and his queen, and with these I shall abide. But,' she added, as Meraugis stepped forward, 'I make the following condition. You may speak of your love to me, and you may claim a single kiss – but beyond that I grant no favours for a year. At the end of that time, I will declare my wishes before all present. Until then you may call yourself my knight, act as my champion – but more than that I shall not grant until the year is passed.'

Many there exchanged astonished looks at this. It was so much the custom of King Arthur's court that women chose a knight to serve them from amongst the strongest and most chivalrous, or indeed those who fought most valiantly in the lists and achieved the greatest feats of bravery. To have such a condition was unheard of in that time, and many were troubled by the lady's words.

Meraugis himself looked askance, but such was his love for Lidoine, that he bowed his head in assent.

There was but one further thing to happen. Lidoine had promised to bestow a single kiss to seal her agreement with Meraugis. The knight

stepped forward eagerly to receive his reward and the lady kissed him upon the mouth.

The story tells that in that moment a spark of love passed between them both, and that Lidoine at once regretted her declaration that nothing more could be between them for a year. Meraugis almost fainted with the fire of love that sprang up within him, for he knew that this was true love and none other, and that, if he lived out the year, nothing further would prevent him from being together ever after with the lady he loved.

So it was agreed, and the court prepared to celebrate the feast of Christmas. As you will expect, this was the most magnificent occasion, with lords, knights and ladies coming from all over Logres to Camelot the Golden. So wondrous was it, that many after spoke of the marvels they saw there. Never before had the court been so splendid and so filled with the joys of the season.

Only two were significant by their absence – one was Gorvin Cadrus, who left the city under a cloud of anger and sorrow, swearing that he would prove himself a worthy knight for the Lady Lidoine, so that a year hence she would choose him over Meraugis. The other was Sir Gawain, King Arthur's nephew, and one of the greatest of the Round Table knights. And though it may seem strange, no one had noticed his absence, despite his great fame and nobility, such was the splendour of the Christmas court.

But on the very next morning, as the king and queen and the knights and ladies returned from mass, a dwarf who everyone agreed was the most ugly they had ever seen, rode into the great hall of the city on a piebald horse. He rode right up to the dais where the king and queen sat and called for silence.

'Listen king,' he said rudely, 'how is it that

you are all making merry when you have no reason to do so?'

'It is the time when we celebrate the birth of the Saviour,' answered King Arthur. 'What news could you have that would prevent our celebration?'

'Look around you,' said the dwarf. 'Have you really not noticed that one of your greatest champions is not present?'

King Arthur looked around the hall. 'Of whom do you speak?' he said at last.

'Can it be,' said the dwarf, as disobliging as he could be, 'that you have not noticed the absence of the great Sir Gawain? Do you not remember that last Ascensiontide your nephew left here in search of the Sword of the Strange Hangings?* Why is he not here do you think? If all was well with him, would he not have returned?'

King Arthur looked about him in dismay. 'How can it be that we did not notice the absence of one who is so important to our Fellowship?' he asked.

A hush fell upon the court, as all there looked at each other and wondered how Sir Gawain's absence could have passed without notice. The king frowned upon the dwarf. 'Do you know what has happened to him?'

'As to that,' said the dwarf, ' I'm not saying whether he's alive or dead. I came to say that if there is a knight in this court who is brave enough to go in search of him, he will find what he will find. But I'll say this, whoever goes – if any man dare – let him be prepared to meet the most terrible of adversaries, and to face the greatest hardships a knight of this Round Table ever did.'

Before anyone else could speak, or the king enquire of his knights who might go, Meraugis

stepped forward. 'My lord.' he said. 'I claim this task, if my lady will allow it.' Lidoine hesitated not at all. 'Most assuredly, if it is the will of the king, I will agree. And furthermore I will accompany the knight on this quest. For despite my declared intent to offer no favours to him in the coming year, yet would I wish to see this knight Meraugis show his courage in this perilous quest for myself.'

When he heard these words the dwarf laughed aloud. 'So shall two fools meet their fate,' he said, and departed.

✢ ✤ ✢

So MERAUGIS AND Lidoine followed the road taken by the dwarf. It was a cold day, for that morning it had snowed, and the country lay white beneath its touch. Soon they encountered the dwarf, struggling to escape the clutches of the snow which, being deep and he but short of stature, caused him great discomfort.

'Where is your mount?' demanded Meraugis.

'Stolen. By a wizened crone who lives in this accursed place!' the dwarf responded.

'Then let us see if we can retrieve it,' said Meraugis. 'After all, you cannot lead us to find Sir Gawain if you have no steed.' Then he asked: 'Where did this happen? If we go there we may be able to find your mount.'

'It was but a league or less from here,' responded the dwarf.

Meraugis reached down a hand and hefted him onto the back of his own mount, then he rode off in the direction indicated, with Lidoine following on her most beautiful palfrey.

Soon they reached a patch of open ground, surrounded by trees, and there they saw where a tent had been pitched. Two maidens were there and next to the pavilion a shield, bearing

---

* Gawain's part in the Grail Quest was for this sword, which was later wielded by Sir Galahad.

the device of a black serpent on a scarlet field, hung from a branch.

When he saw this Meraugis asked what it meant.

'Never mind that,' said the dwarf. 'Look over there.'

When Meraugis looked he saw where an elder woman was moving away from the tent, leading the dwarf's piebald horse.

'That is my horse!' cried the dwarf angrily.

Meraugis at once rode after the woman and quickly caught up with her. Though aged, she yet bore herself upright and with noble bearing. She turned to look at Meraugis and he thought for a moment that she knew him. And in that moment too it seemed to him that she was at once both old and young.

'That horse belongs to the dwarf you see over there,' he said.

'Not any longer,' answered the elder woman. 'It is mine now.'

'Not so,' said Meraugis, and snatched the reins from her hands.

The elder woman cried out angrily: 'You shall not keep it for long. One is coming here who shall destroy you as you stand!'

'Be that as it may,' said Meraugis. 'This mount is not yours. I shall return it to its rightful owner.'

Then he turned and led the piebald horse back to where the dwarf waited with the Lady Lidoine. Grudgingly, the dwarf thanked Meraugis for returning his mount, but the knight's attention was once again caught by the shield hanging from the tree.

'What is this place?' he asked. 'And why is that shield there?'

'It is nothing to do with you,' answered the dwarf. 'Take my advice and do not even touch it. Let us continue on our way.'

But Meraugis was hardly listening. He rode over to the shield and took it from the tree. At once the two maidens emerged from the tent, crying and screaming that he had doomed them all.

'How so?' asked Meraugis.

'He who owns the shield is known as the Dread Knight,' the women told him. 'He is the most fearful and strongest opponent you could ever meet. Many knights have tried to overwhelm him, but all have failed – just as you will – simply from touching the shield.'

Carelessly Meraugis flung the shield aside. 'I am not afraid,' he said. 'Where is this Dread Knight?'

'He will be coming as fast as he may,' answered one of the women. 'I would tell you to flee, but it would do you no good for the Dread Knight would soon catch you. You are dead already. And he will most certainly kill us too.'

The two women now wept bitterly, and Lidoine went to comfort them.

'Who is this man – if man he is? Meraugis asked the dwarf.

'He is a terrible creature,' the dwarf answered. 'Always he has behaved in an evil manner, killing any knight he meets, and raping any women who might have accompanied them. And all because of love.'

'How may that be?' asked Meraugis.

'The Dread Knight had a lady whom he loved greatly. At first she returned his love, but when she learned of his evil ways she made him swear two oaths: one, that he would never kill a man unless he had injured him in some way. This angered him greatly and he hung the shield in the tree to test any knight who came this way, deeming offence if it was touched and thus believing this gave him the right to strike down any who did so.'

Meraugis shook his head. 'What a strange

creature he must be. Tell me: what was the second oath he was forced to take?'

'That he would never again leave this place nor wander far from it unless it was to avenge some shame. Again, he chooses to see the flaunting of his shield by another to be shameful. Thus, by striking it down, you have given him leave to go from here and begin ravaging the country again. After he has killed you of course.'

'That is an evil custom indeed,' said Meraugis. 'I much regret my action, though to be fair I knew nothing of this that you have told me.'

'It is too late for that now,' said the dwarf. 'The dark and dreaded knight is coming, and you'll soon be dead, as will your lady and the two damosels who have served him until now. For I know that he will spare no one.'

'As to that, we shall see,' said Meraugis.

Then he turned his mind to what course of action he should follow, and said to the dwarf: 'I must draw the Dread Knight away from here. When he comes, tell him I hold him in great despite and that I long to fight with him. That will anger him greatly I believe. Meanwhile my lady and I will go from here so that he is forced to follow us.'

With a great show of reluctance, the dwarf agreed. And Meraugis and Lidoine set off at once and made what speed they could until they came in sight of a most glorious castle which lay by the edge of the ocean. In later times Meraugis would call this place 'The Lost Castle' or 'The Castle Without a Name', for after the events that followed he could never find his way there again.

This may suggest that it lay within the boundaries of Faery – though no man may say this for certain. Indeed Meraugis and Lidoine should have realised that this was no ordinary place, for twice as they rode nearer they passed by two young girls and later a boy, who were heard to mutter: 'You have crossed the border.'

Even more strangely, as they drew nearer to the walls of the castle, they saw where a party of knights and ladies emerged onto the meadows before the gates. All were singing at

✦ *The dwarf upon his piebald horse* ✦

the tops of their voices – a sweet sound indeed – and evidently filled with joy at the sight of the knight and the lady.

Lidoine expressed her fear at this, but Meraugis merely shrugged.

Surrounded by people who continued to sing, Meraugis and Lidoine were escorted into the great hall of the castle, where the seneschal of the place greeted them warmly. 'We are glad indeed that you have come, for now at last perhaps you may lift the curse laid upon us.'

'Tell me of this,' Meraugis demanded.

'Follow me,' the seneschal said. He led the way to the walls of the castle and pointed out to sea, where a small, solitary island lay.

'Do you see that tower at the centre of the isle?' asked the seneschal. 'A knight lives there with the lady of this castle and a handful of servants. Every noble knight who comes here must cross to the island and do battle with he who is the guardian of the place. If you win, the island belongs to you. If you lose then you are our prisoner and we may do with you what we like.'

'That is hardly an honourable custom,' said Meraugis.

'Nevertheless, you must undertake this challenge or face death,' said the seneschal firmly.

Meraugis turned to Lidoine. 'My lady, forgive me for bringing you into such danger.' To the seneschal he said: 'May I count upon you to protect my lady until I return, and promise that no harm will come to her if I do not?'

To this the seneschal agreed. Lidoine was fearful for the life of her knight, but Meraugis assured her he would soon return. Then he followed the seneschal and his men to the shore, where a small craft awaited them.

Once Meraugis and his horse were aboard, the craft made a good pace across to the shore of the island, despite the fact that the water was rough and uncertain. As soon as Meraugis disembarked, the craft withdrew, heading back to the mainland. If Meraugis thought this strange, he had no time to consider it, for scarcely had he mounted his horse than he saw the Knight of the Tower approaching. His armour shone like the sun and the trappings of his mount were as rich as anything Meraugis had ever seen – yet his shield was plain, and the visor on his helmet prevented any sight of his face.

The knight waited cautiously while Meraugis settled his horse and readied himself for battle. Neither man spoke but proceeded grimly to their encounter.

Now let me say that the battle between Sir Meraugis and the Knight of the Tower was one of the most astounding ever seen in that time. Not even Sir Lancelot or Sir Tristan, who were considered the greatest to sit at the Round Table, could have equalled the strength of the two knights. Both were well versed in the art of war, and were evenly matched. Having quickly broken their spears and delivered each to the earth, they drew their swords and began to hammer each other with such blows that it is a wonder they did not either break their blades or shatter their armour. Indeed, so many dints they struck each other that by midday both were exhausted and without a word spoken agreed to rest.

But when they set to again, as the sun climbed to the height of the heavens, the Knight of the Tower seemed to grow even stronger, delivering such powerful blows that at last Meraugis drew back: 'Sir Knight!' he cried. 'I must ask your name. For never have I felt such a mighty opponent – not even amongst my fellow Knights of the Round Table.'

The Knight of the Tower lowered his sword. 'You are of King Arthur's court?'

'I am. My name is Meraugis de la Port-lesguez.'

'Then in God's name I salute you!' cried the knight and pulled off his helmet. 'I am Sir Gawain!'

Leaving aside their swords, the two men embraced with joy. 'By my faith, I am glad to see you, Sir Gawain,' said Meraugis. 'I have been sent from Camelot the Golden to find you. Many there believe you are dead.'

'Well, as you see, I am not,' said Sir Gawain. 'But I might as well be.'

'What do you mean?' asked Meraugis. 'Let us summon the ship and return to the castle. Together we can put an end to this evil custom.'

'I wish it could be so,' answered Gawain. 'But no man may leave this island alive.'

'How can that be?' Meraugis said.

'I will tell you,' said Gawain. 'The castle on the shoreline is owned by a lady of great power and strength. Once she was happy, and she met a handsome knight whom she married. But after a time she became so jealous of him that she built this keep and imprisoned him within. Then she declared that no man should be permitted to depart until he had fought against her husband, and that all those he overcame he should slay. So great a fighter was he, that he killed many until I fought and slew him myself – for he refused to ask for mercy. Now, according to the command of the lady, I must remain here until I am beaten and slain. No one may leave this place otherwise, for she who owns it is possessed of great power.'

'Surely the craft which bore me here must return? How else would you get food?'

'The craft does indeed bring supplies, and takes away the bodies of the slain knights whenever it is needed. The Lady of the Tower goes to the shore and signals the boat to come. But if I were to go with her it would at once turn away. Without it no one can come or go for the waters are too harsh to swim. There is no way from here unless one of us slays the other. The Lady of the Tower watches me at all times to be sure I do not escape. I would as soon die than live like this. Perhaps I should throw myself into the sea!'

Meraugis looked towards the tower and saw a pale face at a window. He grew thoughtful at this. Then he said: 'I believe I may know a way that we can save both our lives and end this madness.' Then he explained his plan.

'We must seem to continue our fight and make sure we can be seen clearly from the tower and the castle on the shore. Then, when enough time has passed, I will fall to the earth. You may seem to strike me down. Tear off my helm and throw it into the sea so that it appears you have beheaded me. Then, as soon as it is dark, I will make my way to the tower. We shall see what happens then.'

'That is a fine plan,' said Sir Gawain.

So the two knights fell to battling again, though this time both avoided striking any damaging blows. At last, as the light began to dim, Gawain struck what appeared to be a mighty blow and Meraugis fell to the ground.

From there, everything went as planned. Gawain returned to the tower and was welcomed and praised by the lady. But her delight was short-lived, when Meraugis marched into the hall with drawn sword.

The lady screamed in terror – believing him a ghost, and called upon Sir Gawain to save her. But he did nothing, hiding himself in an antechamber, while Meraugis meanwhile forced the lady and her serving women into a small room, barring the door fast behind them. And though they cried and pled to be released, neither knight listened to them but instead ate a splendid supper.

Meraugis then outlined the next part of his plan. First, he produced a gown belonging to the Lady of the Tower and preceded to don it. 'Thus will I make those on land believe I am she who made this place, and I will call upon them to bring food and remove the remains of the slain knight.'

Sir Gawain laughed aloud at the sight of Meraugis dressed as a woman – though in fact with his slender form and handsome visage he seemed, from a distance, in truth a fair damsel!

✛ ✛ ✛

THAT NIGHT THE two men slept well, tired from their long battle. In the morning Meraugis proceeded as he had planned, dressing in the lady's gown and covering his head with a wimple. Making his way to the shore of the island, he signalled to the castle that fresh supplies were needed.

Soon the small craft arrived at the island and before they had time to do more than drop anchor, Meraugis and Gawain both leapt aboard. The sailors retreated in fear from the knights, believing they would be slain. But Meraugis ordered them to set sail at once away from that place and further along the coast.

Soon the island faded from sight. I cannot say what happened to the women who Meraugis and Gawain had locked up. Perhaps men came from the land and set them free, or perhaps they perished from starvation. Be that as it may, the small ship sailed on until they came to a harbour somewhere along the coast. There, in their eagerness to let the two knights disembark, the sailors failed to notice rocks beneath the surface of the sea and damaged the craft beyond repair. Gawain and Meraugis went ashore and called to the sailors to join them.

'Our quarrel is not with you,' said Meraugis. 'We will see that you are cared for.'

Then the knights made their way inland to where a castle loomed over the land. It belonged to a lord named Glodoain, who was a vassal of King Arthur and knew both men. They received a warm welcome there and were treated as honoured guests. Even the sailors were made comfortable and Meraugis asked that they be looked after and given work, to which the Lord Glodoain agreed.

Thus they rested until at last Sir Gawain declared that he must depart to continue his quest for the Sword of the Strange Hangings. And let me tell you now, that he was successful in this quest, as the story tells elsewhere.*

Before they parted, each swore that whoever returned to Camelot the Golden first, if the other did not appear soon, they would search for him. Then Sir Gawain left and Meraugis, watching him depart, suddenly remembered that Lidoine was still in the castle opposite the island. The thought that he had forgotten her weighed upon him greatly, and so desperate was he that he wanted to set off to rescue her at once. This he soon did, taking his leave of the Lord Glodoain, and driven to the point of madness, rode aimlessly throughout the lands, searching for any word of her.

✛ ✛ ✛

MEANWHILE, SPEAKING OF the fair Lidoine, I must tell you that she observed the seeming death of Meraugis and had fallen to the ground in a swoon. No one

---

* This is part of the story of the Grail Quest as told in the Lancelot-Grail Cycle. There is some disagreement as to whether it was Perceval, Gawain or Galahad who successfully found it.

could console her, but one of the ladies of the castle, a lady named Amice, who had discovered a liking for Lidoine, took her back to her own castle, which lay but a few leagues from the shoreline, and there cared for her and helped her to accept the fact that Meraugis must be dead.

Now it happened that an ill-favoured lord name Bergis, whose lands were adjacent to those of the Lady Amice, and who had designs upon her and her estate, came to the gates of the castle and was admitted. He spoke gently and easily with her at first – though in truth she had no liking for him – but when he learned that the Lady Lidoine was in the care of Amice, and that she mourned for Meraugis, he at once thought that she would make a fitting wife for his son Espinogre, who would thus, through marriage, become King of Escavalon.

It was scarcely surprising that when he requested to meet the sorrowful lady, and at once pressed his suit on behalf of his son, Bergis met with only coldness from Lidoine. At first he pretended sadness that she would not even consider his son, but having left, within weeks of this he returned to the castle at the head of a large force of men who made camp outside the walls. Bergis remained polite and made no outward threats to either lady, but his intent was clear. He brought with him supplies enough to withstand a long siege, knowing that by the time these had been exhausted, all within the castle of the Lady Amice would be forced to give up or face starvation.

Lidoine, having learned of Bergis's reputation as a ruthless, cruel man, with great courage came forth, escorted by only a handful of men, and protested that while she was in mourning, she would consider no man. 'Yet be assured, my lord,' she said, 'that if you wait but a short time I will gladly consider your son as my husband.'

With this Bergis was content, and left to bring the good news to Espinogre, though his army still sat outside the walls of the castle.

Lidoine now begged the Lady Amice to help her.

'My love, Meraugis, is lost to me for ever,' she said. 'But there is another brave knight who loves me also. His name is Gorvin Cadrus and he lives not far from here. Please get word to him that I am in danger from Bergis and beg him to come to my aid.'

Amice sent forth messengers in search of Gorvin, and when he heard of Lidoine's fate, and of the death of Meraugis, he was beside himself with happiness. At once he set about gathering his own forces, calling upon knights with whom he was friendly to join him. He also sent messages to the seneschal of Lidoine's lands, who in turn called her people to assemble and prepare to attack Bergis.

MERAUGIS, MEANWHILE, DESPERATE to learn the fate of his love, came by chance to a castle in one of the deepest and darkest areas of the Great Wood. The place seemed to him to have an unearthly look to it, for it seemed veritably to glow in the shadow of the trees, but he heard music and the sounds of singing coming from within, so he went closer until he saw where a narrow little gate opened in the walls. Within he saw a strange sight. A dozen fair ladies, each one touched with an earthly beauty that proclaimed her of Faery origin, danced in a circle, singing most sweetly. And in their midst, clad in full armour and with his shield hung at his back, was a knight. And though weighed down by his arms, yet he seemed unable to cease from dancing, though

Meraugis could see from the way he moved that he was exhausted.

Then it was that Meraugis noticed the device on the dancing knight's shield: a black serpent on a red ground. It was none other than the Dread Knight! Without a thought, Meraugis drew his sword and sprang through the little gate. No sooner had his feet touched the ground than he was impelled to dance. Struggle though he might, his limbs were forced to follow the rhythm of the song sung by the circling women. At the same time, he saw that the Dread Knight was released from the dance and fled through the narrow gate.

The story tells us that in that place, there must always be twelve ladies singing and dancing, and that any knight who entered there must join them, until another came, at which point the first was released. And indeed, Meraugis might have danced until he fell into a stupor or died from exhaustion, had it not been that another, stranger knight came by, and just as had so many others, heard the music and was drawn to enter the castle.

At once Meraugis was released and took his chance to escape. Outside the walls he paused to recover his breath. Then he saw that the Dread Knight, who had been set free, had not ridden away, but instead waited for him. Just as Meraugis had observed the device on his enemy's shield so had the Dread Knight seen his and awaited his chance.

'You have shamed me greatly and taken down my shield from the tree,' he cried. 'For that you shall die.' Saying which, he spurred his mount towards Meraugis, not even waiting for him to prepare.

But the young knight had fought many battles and withstood greater adversaries. He mounted swiftly, set his shield in place and lowered his lance. Both shattered their spears in the first round, then fell to with naked swords and continued thus for some time, both inflicting deep wounds upon each other. But at the last Meraugis got the better of his foe, and with a great blow felled him dead upon the earth. The young knight's own wounds were such that he had no strength to get back on his horse but lay unmoving on the ground.

There it chanced he was discovered by a lord named Melian de Lis, who was in fact leading a party of knights and soldiers to join Bergis. He, having heard of the imminent arrival of Gorvin Cadrus and the forces of the Lady Lidoine, had summoned whatever help he could.

When he saw that the wounded man had slain the Dread Knight, whose fearsome reputation was known to him as it was to all who dwelled in that place, Melian thought to himself that only the strongest hero could have overcome so terrible an adversary, and that if he could be healed of his wounds he might become an ally to Bergis and turn the tide of war in his favour.

With this in mind, Melian ordered Meraugis to be carried in a litter and summoned surgeons to search his wounds. These were far less perilous than they had appeared, and once Meraugis had rested and his wounds were dressed, he began to recover from his battle with the Dread Knight.

✣ ✣ ✣

So THE THREADS of this story begin to weave themselves together into their final pattern as the year turned towards autumn. Bergis had already begun his siege of the Lady Amice's castle, in which Lidoine was entrapped. There came Gorvin Cadrus with his followers and shortly after that the soldiers of Lidoine, led by her seneschal. So Bergis found himself facing these combined forces, while on his side was only Melian, in whose tent lay Meraugis, wounded but beginning to regain his strength. Thus the three chief players in this game of love and rivalry were brought to within a league of each other, none knowing the whole story; and thus were the peoples of three kingdoms prepared to do battle.

Now I shall tell you what occurred.

Melian, seeing that Meraugis was almost recovered, begged him to fight on the side of Bergis, explaining to him that his lord had been promised the hand of a certain lady, who had then refused him, hence the war that was about to be fought. At first Meraugis hesitated, but in gratitude towards Melian for the care he had lavished on him, agreed to fight alongside him and Bergis.

In the morning the sides were drawn up and battle was prepared. But before they could begin, a commanding fanfare of trumpets announced the arrival of King Arthur himself, with a company of Round Table knights led by Sir Gawain, who had arrived back at Camelot the Golden and told how Meraugis had saved him and all that followed. He then told the king that he had promised to come to Meraugis's help if he came home first, and with King Arthur himself declaring that he would do all in his power to resolve these issues – for it was an ill day when his vassals fought against each other – they set out from Camelot the Golden for the lands of the Lady Amice.

Now King Arthur called for all those involved to attend upon him. Bergis and Melian came from one side; Gorvin Cadrus and the Seneschal of Escavalon from the other, and lastly came the Lady Amice herself, who rode out from the castle accompanied by Lidoine. There, in the midst of the field, Meraugis and she saw each other, and before any could stop them they ran into each other's arms. At this Bergis protested that the lady was affianced to his son, while Gorvin Cadrus again claimed that Lidoine was rightfully his.

So matters stood while each declared their rights in the matter. King Arthur listened to all three claimants for Lidoine's hand, and declared that Bergis had no claim, since the lady herself had never agreed to any such match. To this Lidoine wholeheartedly agreed. The king then commanded both Bergis and Melian to withdraw upon pain of his displeasure.

Next he turned to Gorvin and Meraugis. 'It seems to me that this quarrel has continued far too long. It must be settled in the only way that is right. These knights must do battle for the hand of the Lady Lidoine.'

The two men protested, as did Lidoine herself, proclaiming her love for Meraugis, but King Arthur would brook no refusal. He said: 'Strength and virtue should be present in all men, especially those who sit the Round Table. Meraugis and Gorvin possess both. Let them be tested.'

So it was that the two men, who had been friends until love drove them apart, faced each other in sight of all the warriors gathered there. Meraugis made an effort to persuade his old comrade not to fight, but Gorvin grimly claimed that only thus could he be satisfied. 'Let God decide,' he said.

Thus the battle began. Both knights were well matched and each knew the other's tricks of fighting. Lidoine watched with her face as pale as the moon, praying aloud for the life of her true love. But though they fought for many hours neither could get the better of the other, until Meraugis at last struck a blow which disarmed his opponent, who fell to the ground and prepared himself for death.

Meraugis stood over him and said: 'For the

sake of our friendship I ask that you concede to me. If you do so I will pledge myself to be your friend again, for as long as we are both alive.'

Gorvin looked towards the Lady Lidoine, and on seeing her kneeling in fervent prayer for the sake of her love, at last gave in. 'You have won the lady fairly,' he declared, and he and Meraugis clasped hands together.

All around them the warriors of both sides applauded and cheered, while Lidoine rushed to embrace Meraugis, and Gorvin saluted them with a bow that acknowledged their true love.

King Arthur said: 'Let this be an end to the ill feeling that has arisen here. Love should not drive such a blade between friends.' Then he welcomed Gorvin Cadrus back and reminded both knights of their vows to the Fellowship of the Round Table.

What more is there to tell? Meraugis and Lidoine were married soon after. He and Gorvin resolved their differences and became friends again – though perhaps never quite as they had been. Gawain, too, declared his

undying gratitude to Meraugis for rescuing him from the Tower on the Island. Bergis retreated behind the walls of his castle and though he doubtless remained an ill-favoured fellow, was heard of no more – at least not in this tale.

THUS YOU HAVE heard the story of Meraugis and the wounds of love, and you may judge whether it has found a worthy storyteller. Doubtless such wounds occurred often in those days, as they do still. The loves of Lancelot for Queen Guinevere, and Tristan for the Lady Isolt, are but two that all men know and that Master Thomas chronicled in his Great Book. Though the tale of Meraugis and Lidoine may not be so well known, may it be remembered again, for within it is much to learn of the way fate may play a part in the lives of men and women. For, as Sir Thomas himself wrote in his book: 'Love in those days was not as it is now.'

EXPLICIT THE STORY OF MERAUGIS DE LA PORTLESGUEZ.

**INCIPIT THE TALE OF MELERANZ AND THE
LADY OF THE FOUNTAIN.**

17: MELERANZ AND THE LADY OF THE FOUNTAIN

MOST OF THE STORIES OF THE DAYS OF KING ARTHUR AND HIS KNIGHTS TELL OF HIS SISTER'S SONS – ESPECIALLY SIR GAWAIN, SIR GAHERIES, SIR GARETH AND SIR AGRAVAINE, SONS OF KING LOTH AND THE LADY MORGAUSE, DAUGHTER OF KING UTHER PENDRAGON. YET IN THIS TALE THAT I HAVE FOUND, KING ARTHUR POSSESSED A SISTER, BY NAME OLYMPIA, WHO BORE A SON NAMED MELERANZ, NEPHEW THEREFORE TO THE GREAT ARTHUR HIMSELF. AS THE TALE SHALL TELL, THIS GOOD YOUTH WAS AS GREAT A KNIGHT AS THOSE NAMED ABOVE. AND IN THE ADVENTURES RELATED HERE, WE SHALL SEE A BOLD YOUNG MAN, WHO SOUGHT TO LIVE HONOURABLY AND TO LEARN ALL THAT HE COULD FROM THE EXAMPLE OF THE ROUND TABLE KNIGHTS. AND HOW HE WAS LED INTO THE WARDS OF THE GREAT WOOD WHERE HE MET HIS GREATEST LOVE – AND HIS FATE. WHAT CAME OF THAT, YOU SHALL SEE.

✛ ✛ ✛

IT IS SAID that in the days when King Arthur ruled over the land of Logres, life was not as it is now. Especially, that men and women lived lives dedicated to honour, truth and goodness, which they sought to share with all who came to Camelot the Golden, and which the Fellowship of the Round Table made it their goal to establish throughout the kingdom and beyond. Master Thomas Malory himself told us how, in matters of love, things were not then as they were in his time, and it may well be said, in all honesty, that to this day many things have changed. Indeed, some would say the world is a much darker place than it was.

But in that time, the story tells of a youth named Meleranz, who was indeed a nephew to King Arthur, the royal Lady Olympia having wed the King of France, and given birth to the boy who, as he grew to manhood, showed himself to be serious, gentle, and possessed of all the very best aspects of human character.

Throughout his childhood it was frequently

remarked concerning his resemblance to King Arthur, and he heard often of the kingdom over which that noble king ruled, and of the great Fellowship founded there by Arthur and the wise enchanter Merlin. So it was no surprise then when he was but fifteen years of age – the very same as King Arthur himself had been when he took the Sword from the Stone and was crowned king – that Meleranz decided he would go to Logres and seek out his uncle, but that he would do so in secret, without telling anyone of his intent, and travelling incognito. For thus, he thought, he could see for himself what kind of welcome would be given to a stranger from another land.

So it was that Meleranz set out, telling no one of his destination. He dressed as finely as any young nobleman was expected to do, and chose the finest steed from his father's stable, as well as a splendid sword and shield from the armoury, the latter bearing no symbol of his origin or status.

Thus accoutred, Meleranz crossed the sea between the shores of France and Logres, and rode into the forest that lay beyond. This was indeed part of the Great Wood known as Broceliande. In that time, it was filled with many strange and wondrous creatures, and was a home to those of the faery race.

Meleranz knew nothing of this, but followed a path that, having begun as broad and well paved, became narrower and rougher as he went deeper into the Great Wood. All of that day he rode, until night began to fall when, since there was nowhere else to shelter, he was forced to sleep beneath the stars. Having searched for grass for his steed, he lay down, but he was too restless to sleep for long and woke as the sun climbed into the heavens, to the sound of small bells, that rang sweetly amid the trees.

Filled with curiosity, Meleranz took his way onward, leading his horse rather than riding upon it. As he went the tinkling of the bells grew louder, and at last he emerged into a wide and beautiful meadow, liberally adorned with flowers. In the trees birds sang, and the air had a sweet scent. There, in the centre of the meadow, grew a tall linden tree, its leaves overshadowing a spring that rose from a rocky outcrop and fed into a natural basin.

In the shadow of the tree a rich and brightly coloured pavilion was set up, and there Meleranz saw a group of girls laughing and singing together. All of them were beautiful and Meleranz wished to speak with them. However, as he approached, they espied him and ran off, despite the fact that he called out that he meant no harm, and begged them to remain.

As he approached the pavilion he saw how the water gathered in the fountain as if it were a bath, and that within it was a lady of the most glorious beauty. Quite naked but for her long golden hair, she watched as the youth drew near. She seemed unafraid and made no move to cover herself. Meleranz stared at her in wonder, his cheeks glowing red as he took in the beauty of her skin, her glorious hair, and the fair shape of her body.

'Who are you that disturbs my bathing?' demanded the lady.

Lowering his eyes, Meleranz spoke gently to her, apologising for his presence and hoping that he caused her no distress.

'Most assuredly not,' she replied. 'Indeed, I was told that you would come here on this day.'

Astonished, Meleranz asked how she could have known he would come.

'My godmother, a lady of great wisdom and knowledge, told me,' answered the lady in the bath. 'She is wise in the ways of the stars, and much more besides. She told me a young man named Meleranz would come here, and that I would fall in love with him.'

Meleranz blushed even more than before. 'My lady, let me say with all honesty that I have never before seen anyone as beautiful as you. If there is any way that I may serve you, you have only to ask.'

The lady in the fountain laughed. 'You may indeed. Over there you will see my clothes hanging from the branches of the tree. There are fresh towels and a robe of green silk. I bid you bring them to me, since you have frightened off my ladies.'

Meleranz saw where the clothes were hung from the lowest branches of the linden tree and without hesitation fetched the things the lady had requested.

'Now go a little way off, while I get dressed,' the lady told him.

Meleranz did as she asked, turning away from the sight of the lady until she called him back.

'Now let us go into my pavilion,' she said, and the youth accompanied her into the tent, which was more splendidly decorated than anything he had ever seen. In the centre was a great bed, richly decorated and draped in

✦ *The three bells* ✦

samite and finest silks. The lady sat upon the edge of this and began to comb her hair.

'Since you know my name, may I ask yours?' said Meleranz.

'My name is Tydomie. If you wish to serve me further, you must ring one of the bells that you will find in the branches of the tree. There are three, each one of a different size. Ring the smallest first.'

Meleranz did as he was asked, and as the small bell rang out, the lady's handmaids returned, no longer seeming fearful of Meleranz, and began to prepare a meal.

Then Tydomie called to Meleranz, asking him to ring the second bell. This summoned a bevy of courtiers, all of them richly dressed, who helped the women set up tables and set out a most splendid feast. After this, Meleranz struck the third bell, and this time there came a number of knights, who spoke to the youth most respectfully, as though he was a great lord.

And all the while Meleranz had eyes only for the Lady Tydomie, and within him the first stirrings of love began in his young heart.

Soon after, came the lady's godmother, who was herself of great beauty and looked kindly upon Meleranz, asking him what had brought him to this part of the forest. To this he responded concerning his desire to see the world and attend the court of King Arthur.

'Ah,' said the godmother. 'Your uncle.'

Once again Meleranz marvelled at her knowledge, and confessed that he did not know the way to Camelot the Golden.

'It is not far from here, as those who travel in the Great Wood know,' replied the lady. 'Rest here tonight, and on the morrow I will show you the way.'

So it was that Meleranz spent the evening in great joy, sitting next to Tydomie and listening to her gentle voice, while all the while the flame of love grew within him.

Next morning he awoke to the sounds of music, the source of which he could not see, and found that the company of the night before had vanished as completely as if it had never been. The tables had been removed and the pavilion was empty save for Tydomie, her maidens, and her godmother, who declared that she would set the young man on the right road.

Before that, Meleranz spoke to Tydomie. 'My lady,' he said. 'I am but a youth, untrained in the ways of men. I hope to learn much at my uncle's court and in time become a knight. Dare I ask that when I am able I may visit you again?'

'Indeed you shall,' replied Tydomie gently. 'You will find me here when the time comes.'

And if Meleranz found it strange that the lady of the fountain seemed to live in the pavilion in the shade of the linden tree, he banished such thoughts from his mind as her godmother led him to where his mount awaited, fed and watered and with its coat brushed until it shone. 'If you intend to visit the realm of Arthur,' the lady told him, 'follow that path through the trees. It will take you to the royal city.'

With these words Meleranz left the pavilion and the lady who had stolen his heart, and followed the road that led to Camelot the Golden. As he drew nearer to the royal city, he encountered a huntsman who had been sent to capture a stag. It was intended for a feast that King Arthur had commanded to celebrate the many great deeds of the Round Table Fellowship. When he heard that Meleranz was making his way to meet the king, and seeing the likeness to his lord, the huntsman suggested that the youth should ride with the hunt and help capture the beast which had been sighted nearby.

To this Meleranz agreed, and what happened next surprised everyone. For the youth displayed such fine horsemanship and skill with a spear that he alone out-ran the rest of the hunt and brought down the stag single-handed. The huntsman, astounded by his skill in capturing the beast, insisted that Meleranz present the prey to the king.

This he did, and thus came into the presence of the king whose fame had brought him so many leagues. The story says that King Arthur did not recognise his nephew, though more than one of the courtiers remarked upon Meleranz's likeness to their lord. Nonetheless, the youth was welcomed and his gift of the stag accepted with gladness.

Filled with wonder at the splendour of the royal city, Meleranz made no attempt to identify himself. When asked what had brought him to Camelot the Golden, he spoke of his wish to see for himself the wonders of the Kingdom of Logres and, if the king permitted, to remain there, serving as a squire, until such time as he might be allowed to undertake knightly training.

To this, King Arthur readily agreed, and so it was that Meleranz remained at the court for another two years, learning all that he could and, it must be said, winning the affections of both King Arthur, Queen Guinevere and the knights with whom he began to train. All of the latter spoke well of him, and praised his growing skill.

Soon, the time came for him to take part in his first tournament, a splendid affair to which lords and ladies from throughout Logres and beyond were invited. These included the King of France and King Arthur's sister Olympia, who had lamented the loss and possible death of their son since the day he had left them.

Great indeed was their wonder and delight to see Meleranz amid those who welcomed them, and thus was his true identity revealed.

His parents greeted him with joy, but King Arthur demanded that he tell the court why he had presented himself as an unknown youth in search of adventure.

'My lords,' replied Meleranz. 'Throughout my life I have been called "King Arthur's nephew", and I have heard many tales of the great Round Table Fellowship and its heroes. I sought to come hither and see for myself – and to be acknowledged as someone from a different land who came seeking the training of a knight. This I have received and will be forever grateful for.'

So impressed were the king and queen and the Knights of the Round Table, that they praised the youth for his honourable intentions. Many indeed spoke out for his growing skill and natural ability, which were, they believed, destined to make him a great knight.

At this the King and Queen of France were greatly pleased, and King Arthur himself declared that it would be his honour to be the one to knight Meleranz when he was deemed ready to receive the buffet.

So it was that Meleranz remained at Camelot the Golden and continued to learn the ways of chivalry, until the time came for him to receive the honour of knighthood. Once again the king announced a grand tournament, both to allow his nephew to display his skill in the lists, and to celebrate his becoming a knight.

It was at this time that Meleranz received a letter from the Lady Tydomie, who wrote that her love for him remained as true as ever, and that she honoured his becoming part of the Round Table Fellowship. She enclosed, with the letter, a jewelled belt which she had been wearing on the day the youth found his way to the linden tree, and stated her desire that when he was ready, he return to her, thereafter, never to leave her side. Overjoyed by this, Meleranz

fastened the belt around his waist and wrote a letter to Tydomie, in which he once again declared his love and the hope that he would soon be able to return to her, having proved himself through the winning of an adventure which, he believed, must soon come to him.

In the days that followed, Meleranz displayed such courage, strength and skill in the lists that he was declared the victor over all-comers to the grand tournament. He even engaged in a contest against his own cousin, Sir Gawain, and to the wonder of all present succeeded in unhorsing the great knight, who declared himself fairly defeated and willingly spoke of his love for the youth.

Thus it was that Meleranz was made knight, and all honour awarded to him by King Arthur himself. But still no adventure had come his way, and so he decided to go forth in search of a task that he would worthily undertake.

✛ ✛ ✛

JUST AS HE had once departed from his family home, so Meleranz left quietly from Camelot the Golden. He was attired in fine clothes and magnificent armour, and rode a mighty steed – all gifts of King Arthur. He left before dawn and followed the road that led once again into the depths of Broceliande. There he journeyed for several days, seeing day turn to night, and night to day, as the road wound on before him. And as was the way with the hidden secrets of the forest, he crossed into places where few had ever been before him – the home of faeries and creatures too strange to be described here.

At length he found his way to a valley, where the trees had been cleared on all sides, and many of them used to build a great house of logs. Then Sir Meleranz saw coming towards him a man and woman who were themselves taller than the trees. But these were not the rough and savage giants of which he had heard as a child, but tall and fair of face and form.

When they made no sign of aggression towards him, Meleranz advanced and saluted them. The giants looked down at the young knight and greeted him gently. Though it was clear that they could, if they had wished, do great damage to both the youth and his steed, yet they made no attempt to do so, while Meleranz, in turn, removed his helmet and set aside his shield and weapons in a clear gesture of peace.

Having heard only stories of giants as mortal adversaries to all who came against them, Meleranz was surprised to be invited to enter their huge house. There he heard their story, how these two gentle folk, husband and wife, had been forced out of their own land, far to the east, by a cruel tyrant. The giant, who named himself Pulaz, told their story. 'In this country we have fallen upon a new trial. Not far from here lives a savage and violent lord named Gonodas of Terrandes. He too was driven from the land in which he was born, but unlike us he has sought only to steal and kill from those who come here. His reign of terror extends over many leagues, and none who pass this way may leave again. He has forced us to become his servants and to help him to capture those who we find. Wherever possible we send people away. Therefore we beg that you take shelter here this night, but that when dawn comes you should return whence you came.'

Meleranz thanked the kindly giants and remained to dine and sleep in the huge house that night. But he also sought directions to the place from where Gonodas came forth to pillage the land.

'Surely you are not thinking of going there?'

said the giant's wife. 'He will not spare you, and believe me that no one who has found their way into his clutches has ever escaped alive.'

The giant echoed his wife's words. 'You are our guest, and as such we offer you all the protection that we can. But beyond this valley you will be at the mercy of Lord Gonodas and his men. I do not believe they can be beaten, even with an army of men such as yourself.'

'Nevertheless, I shall try what one knight of the Round Table may accomplish,' answered Meleranz.

'If go you must,' said his host, 'then you have but to follow the road that leads beyond this valley. Stay upon it for another eight leagues and you will come to a wide water. Beyond it you will see a great castle with mighty walls. To get there you will see that a boatman waits to ferry you across the river. Beyond that you will meet with Gonodas's seneschal, a powerful knight who serves as guardian to his lands. I have heard of no man who successfully beat him. If, by some chance, you do overcome him, you should proceed to the castle. There, many fearsome and powerful knights, all who have sworn allegiance to Gonodas, will attack you. Be sure they will have only one desire, and that is to kill or maim you in honour of their lord.'

DESPITE THESE URGENT warnings, Meleranz set off next day for the castle of Gonodas, following the instructions given to him by the giant. Soon he arrived at the river and there he met the ferryman, who spoke no words to him but beckoned him aboard. Meleranz led his horse on board the ferry and they crossed the river in silence. Once they reached the further shore – from which Meleranz could see the walls of the castle, the ferryman spoke

PLATE 4: *'Then Sir Meleranz saw coming towards him a man and woman who were themselves taller than the trees'*

up: 'Sir Knight, I fear I have done you a great disservice by bringing you here. I do but obey my master in doing so, but I am certain that only death awaits you.'

'Sir,' answered Meleranz. 'I thank you for your words, and for helping me to cross the river. Do not fear for me. I have only myself to thank if I meet my end in battle against Gonodas' men.'

The ferryman shrugged at this, and putting a horn to his lips blew three blasts. 'Now you will regret coming here,' he said, and returning to his craft poled the way back across the river.

Grimly, Meleranz mounted his steed and prepared for battle. Soon enough, he saw a mounted man approaching. This he knew must be the seneschal against whom the giants had warned him. Certainly he was both tall and powerful, his armour and weapons of the very best, and his horse a mighty charger. Seeing Meleranz, he saluted, and the two men rode at each other without further ado.

The battle that followed lasted much of the day until at last, Meleranz delivered blows that felled his opponent and left him barely alive. Then the seneschal begged for mercy. 'Never have I encountered such a knight as you, fair sir,' he said. 'If you will spare my life I swear my allegiance to you for as long as you need it.'

Meleranz bowed his head and, sheathing his sword, offered his hand to the fallen man. And, as was the custom of that time, having proved their might upon each other, the two knights spoke together more as friends then enemies. The seneschal, whose name was Corsun, then invited Meleranz to return home with him and to take his rest there. 'For, if you intend to fight with my lord, you will need all the rest you can get,' he said.

Thus the two men went together to the seneschal's castle, where they were welcomed by Corsun's wife and daughter. Together they dined well, and the seneschal told Meleranz more about his master Gonodas, who had held the lands about there for several years, and in all that time had never once been beaten in battle.

'He is a cruel man,' said Corsun. 'Anyone he defeats becomes his prisoner, without possibility of ransom. He treats them harshly, making them serve him with menial tasks. I have been forced to serve him by his threats to my family, and all those I have beaten have been given over to him. There are many who reside in his dungeons. His victories have made him mad, for he does not believe he will ever be beaten.'

'Then I shall hope to prove him wrong,' said Meleranz.

The two men spent a pleasant evening together, so that by the time the young knight was shown to a fine sleeping chamber, they were fast friends. In the morning, Corsun elected to go with his guest to his lord's castle. 'For,' as he said: 'It is my wish to see the combat between you. I have never seen anyone fight as well as you, but my lord also has a terrible strength. I do not know who will win the battle between you.'

The two rode together until they arrived at the walls of Gonodas's castle. There, in the field outside, stood a solitary tree, and from its branches hung an ivory horn, chased with gold. 'This you must blow three times,' Corsun told Meleranz. 'My lord will know you challenge him and he will come forth to fight.'

Meleranz rode to the tree and took down the horn. Setting it to his lips he blew three mighty blasts that echoed out across the meadows and was clearly heard within the castle. Then the youth took the horn and dashed it against a rock, so that it shattered into pieces.

'Why did you do that?' demanded Corsun.

'It will not be needed again after this day,'

replied Meleranz grimly, and fell to preparing himself for the coming contest.

Soon Gonodas himself appeared, mounted upon a great warhorse and clad in magnificent armour. His pride and arrogance were clear to see, and his face was marked with savage strength. He made no salutation, but rode straight at his challenger. Meleranz prepared to meet him and the seneschal withdrew.

Again, the battle between the two men was as great as anything seen in that land, or perhaps even the whole of Logres. Neither gave way, and the blows they exchanged, which rang out across the land, were of equal ferocity.

Meleranz drew strength from the thought of Tydomie, for he could not bear never to see her again, or to cause her pain by his loss. He had indeed come fully into his own strength by now, and fought with a concentration seldom seen.

For several hours the two knights fought, driving each other back turn and turn about. In time both began to tire and Gonodas finally requested that they take a short rest. Meleranz agreed and both men removed their helmets and sat down on the ground to regain their strength.

'Never have I encountered such a powerful opponent!' said Gonodas, glowering at the younger knight. 'Perhaps we may agree that since neither of us can gain the advantage, we agree that our battle is over, with neither one a winner?'

'I should be glad to do so,' said Meleranz. 'But only on the condition that you set free all the knights you have imprisoned, and swear fealty to my lord King Arthur.'

'That I will never do!' roared Gonodas, and jumped to his feet. Then the two knights re-commenced their battle, hacking and hewing at each other until their shields were shattered,

their armour dented, and their breaths came harsh and loud for all to hear.

Meleranz gave ground and avoided his opponent, so that Gonodas was forced to follow him around the field. Exhaustion began to plague the powerful man, and it was then that Meleranz redoubled his attack, finally striking a blow which cut so deep into his adversary's helm that it split the skull beneath and left him dead.

When they saw this, the people in the castle cried aloud in sorrow and anger, so that the young knight believed he would soon be attacked by Gonodas's followers.

At this, the seneschal Corsun came to him, and bowing his head in tribute to the young knight, begged him to return to his own castle. 'Give my lord's followers a night to recover, and those who wish to, time to grieve. In the morning we shall return and you may accept the surrender of all and the release of the prisoners.'

To this Meleranz agreed, for in truth he was weary. Together the two men rode back to Corsun's castle and there the young knight was at last able to rest from the second great battle he had fought in as many days.

In the morning he returned to Gonodas's castle, accompanied by the seneschal, and there, despite some of the dead lord's followers wishing to attack him, Meleranz accepted the capitulation of the knights who were in favour of accepting him as their new lord. Many recalled, indeed, that such was Gonodas's confidence in his own strength, he had made all who followed him swear that if any knight succeeded in vanquishing him, they should bow the knee to him.

So it was agreed, and when the company heard that their new master was the son of the King of France and nephew to King Arthur, they were more than ready to welcome him.

The prisoners were now set free, many but shadows of their former selves. Their treatment had been harsh indeed, chained in groups of twelve, whipped and beaten and made to labour at whatever task Gonodas had demanded of them, so that they were glad indeed to be freed. More than grateful to their rescuer, they praised Meleranz greatly on that day, and thereafter acknowledged him as one of the finest knights in the world.

Also Meleranz discovered, hidden away in the castle's vaults, a huge treasure, acquired though Gonodas's savage reign of terror. All of this Meleranz distributed to the poor and gave back what had been theirs to the prisoners to help them re-establish themselves in the world.

To the seneschal Corsun, Meleranz granted freedom from the allegiance he had sworn to him, and to the giant Pulaz he sent word that the savage lord was dead, and that they who had served him were now released. Further, he invited them to attend upon King Arthur at Camelot the Golden.

For these things alone, Meleranz, now styled Lord of Terrandes in his absence from that place, was judged one of the finest and most generous men of that time, and word of his ability and courage spread throughout the land until it reached not only the ears of King Arthur, but also of the Lady Tydomie.

⚜ ⚜ ⚜

NOW YOU MAY hear what all who have read my tale thus far have doubtless waited to hear – how Meleranz and his love were able to fulfil their vows to each other.

It is soon told. While he was still celebrating his victory word reached Meleranz from his beloved. Not long after their meeting at the secret fountain, Tydomie's father had perished in battle and she had come under the guardianship of her uncle, Malloas. Now he was preparing to marry her to a knight who was offering to combat his right with any man who sought him out at the linden tree in the Great Wood.

Meleranz was so overcome by this news that he was unable to sleep or think of anything other than the fate of his love, and he prepared to depart next day, determined to rescue Tydomie from her unwanted suitor. But Corsun the Seneschal spoke to him, advising him to wait another day. 'For,' he said, 'you have here many men who would gladly support you. Also there are the giants, who few if any in that country where your lady dwells will have seen. Surely if we go there together, no one will stand against us.'

Meleranz saw the truth of this, and agreed to follow Corsun's advice. He called before him the rescued knights, those who were previously followers of Gonodas, and sent word to Pulaz and his wife. All responded that they would follow Meleranz to the land where Tydomie dwelt, and if need be, force her uncle to submit.

So it was, that on a day not long after this, the people of Terrandes saw what seemed to them a great army, with two mighty giants in their midst, led by Meleranz and the seneschal, surrounded by many knights. When Malloas saw this he came forth to meet them and argued that, as the guardian of Tydomie, he had the right to assign whoever he wished to be his niece's husband. At the same time, the knight who claimed her came forward and demanded the right of combat with Meleranz.

Both men were soon forced to capitulate: the uncle when he saw the two giants and the forces who had accompanied the young knight; the would-be suitor after Meleranz unhorsed and beat him to his knees following a brief combat.

Then it was revealed to all that Meler-anz was the son of the French king and the nephew of King Arthur, and at this Malloas began to sing his praises and to encourage Tydomie to accept his offer of marriage. This, of course, she was more than willing to do, and so it was that a great cavalcade made its way from Terrandes to Camelot the Golden, and in the spring, the most unequalled wedding seen in the royal city was celebrated. King Arthur himself blessed the couple, and everyone who was present, including the young knight's parents, who had journeyed from France with a great company, agreed that they had never seen a more handsome couple than the two lovers.

It may well be asked if there was magic afoot in this tale, for the appearance of the lady of the fountain recalls many others I have heard that speak of her as a faery woman. It may be that Tydomie's godmother had a hand in all that followed, but the story is silent about these things, so I will say no more.

But I have heard it said that the giant Pulaz and his wife were made welcome at Camelot the Golden, and remained there for some time – a cause of much wonder and amazement amongst all who saw them. Whether this is true or not, I cannot say, but there were many wonders in that time, and though I have never seen a giant, I find no reason why they should not exist. Of the future of Meleranz there is little to tell, save that he became one of the finest of the Round Table Fellowship, and that he and Tydomie had several children – but of them the story says no more.

EXPLICIT THE TALE OF MELERANZ, WHO WAS NEPHEW TO KING ARTHUR.

INCIPIT THE STORY OF TRYSTAN'S MADNESS.

18: THE MADNESS OF SIR TRYSTAN

THOUGH MORE HAS BEEN WRITTEN ABOUT THE LOVE OF SIR LANCELOT FOR KING ARTHUR'S QUEEN, YET THERE IS ANOTHER STORY OF LOVE, BETRAYAL, AND SORROW, THAT SIR THOMAS WROTE MUCH OF IN HIS GREAT BOOK. THESE ARE THE STORIES OF SIR TRYSTAN DE LYONESSE AND OF HIS LOVE FOR QUEEN ISOLT OF IRELAND – SHE THAT WAS MARRIED TO KING MARK OF CORNWALL, OF WHOM MANY SPOKE ILL BECAUSE OF THE HIDDEN ILLS HE CAUSED, NOT ONLY TO HIS WIFE, BUT TO OTHERS IN LANDS OVER WHICH HE RULED. AND INDEED, ISOLT LOVED SIR TRYSTAN ALWAYS, AND THOUGH HE WAS FORCED TO FLEE FROM KING MARK'S VENGEANCE, YET SHE NEVER CEASED TO THINK OF HIM. ONE STORY OF THIS SAD AFFAIR IS NOT INCLUDED IN THE MORTE D'ARTHUR, SO I PLACE IT HERE, IF NO MORE THAN AS A WARNING TO THOSE WHO LET LOVE TRIUMPH OVER ALL, UNTIL THEY BECOME MAD.

✢ ✢ ✢

TRYSTAN WAS ALONE in Brittany. Parted from his love, wedded to another whom he did not love, his passion for Queen Isolt was as great as ever, and threatened to overwhelm him. What point was there in living when he was separated by so many miles from the place where his heart longed to be? Daily he walked about the palace of King Hoel, avoiding Isolt White Hands, his wife, doing his best to hide his true feelings from his friend Kaherdin, all the while longing to journey back to Britain and re-join his love.

Remembering his wounding by the terrible Morholt, and his healing at the hands of the fair Isolt, now there seemed no cure for his ills, except to be in her arms again. Thus he began to scheme to find a way that he might fulfil his need. He was too well known in Britain, his fame as a warrior having spread wide throughout the realms ruled by King Arthur. Therefore, he decided to go incognito on foot rather than on his great warhorse, and without armour or weapons save only a dagger.

Once he had made up his mind, Trystan wasted no time. He rose early one morning, stole out of the palace and made his way to a nearby port. There he took ship on a stout merchanter bound for Britain. None recognised the poorly dressed man who paid in gold for his passage and spoke little to anyone during the voyage.

It chanced that they made landfall in Cornwall, indeed at Tintagel itself, where King Mark held court with Queen Isolt. Trystan looked upon the castle where his heart dwelled and sighed deeply. It was a mighty building indeed, having been built by giants long ago. Its walls were of marble blocks, coloured red and blue, set so finely that there was scarcely a join. It was said, by the local people, that this was an enchanted place, and that the castle disappeared twice every year, once at midwinter and again at midsummer. All around stretched meadows and woodlands full of game, and a bright stream coursed by the walls and fell cascading down to the sea. It was indeed a most powerful place, virtually impregnable by either land or sea, its gates well-guarded by soldiers.

Trystan walked into the town and asked for news of the king and queen. Indeed they were there, he heard, and a great court with them. People spoke well of King Mark but commented that Queen Isolt looked sad. When he heard her name Trystan sighed again and began to think of ways that he might gain entrance to both the castle and its royal folk. He knew that neither prowess nor knowledge, skill nor intelligence would gain him admittance to Isolt. Mark, he also knew, hated him above all men and, if he ever succeeded in capturing him, would surely order his death.

'Yet,' he murmured, 'what matters it if I am killed. As well be dead and at peace than alive and in torment. I am more than half mad with this love.' As he spoke Trystan began to think. Why not pretend to be mad indeed, play the fool and trick everyone? 'Who will suspect me?' he wondered. 'Not even Isolt herself shall recognise me. I shall walk into the castle as free as a bird!'

So saying, he set about his plan at once. Waiting until he saw a poor fisherman coming along the road, Trystan offered to exchange his own plain but well-made clothes for the other's ragged hose and stained tunic and hood. The man was well pleased with the exchange and ran off before the stranger could change his mind. Then Trystan stained his face dark with the juice of a certain herb and taking out a little pair of golden scissors, which he always carried since he had been given them by Isolt, cut a strange tonsure in the shape of a cross on the top of his head. Then, having completed his disguise, he set a rough wooden club on his shoulder, adopted a shambling gait, and set off for the castle.

The porter saw him coming and strode out to meet him. 'Who and what are you?' he demanded.

'I am called Urgan the Hairy,' replied Trystan, choosing the name of a giant he had killed long ago. 'I have just been to the wedding of the abbot of Mont St. Michel. He wedded the abbess, who was a very fat nun. Every priest and cleric and monk from all around was there. After the wedding they all went down to the pastures below Bel Encumbre and began jumping and playing in the shade. But I had to leave them, because today I am destined to serve the king.'

The porter laughed, deeming this a mad but innocent fool. 'Well then, Urgan the Hairy, you'd better come inside. I'm sure you'll give us all some fun.'

So Trystan the fool walked into Tintagel. At once some young men saw him and began to chase him around the courtyard, throwing stones and clods of earth at his head. Trystan dodged as best he might, making sure that some at least struck him. He danced around until he was near enough to the entrance to the hall and ran inside.

King Mark was seated on a dais at the further end of the room, with Queen Isolt at his side, silent and withdrawn. When King Mark caught sight of the outlandish figure he demanded to know who he was. 'Have him brought here,' he ordered.

When the fool stood before him, King Mark looked him up and down and then asked whence he came and who he was.

'Not hard, lord King,' said Trystan, disguising his voice to sound like a cracked bell. 'My mother was a whale who dwelt in the sea like a siren. I've no idea where or when I was born. But I was nursed by a tigress, who found me under a stone and thought I was her cub. She gave me milk from her teats. As to why I've come. I have a beautiful sister, even cleverer than me, and I thought I'd like to exchange her for your queen. Come, you must be tired of your lady by now – try someone new. It will be a fair exchange, I promise.' He leered at the king out of one eye, closing the other tight and screwing up his face.

King Mark laughed. 'And what would you do with the queen, if I were to give her to you?'

'Ah,' replied the fool, 'I have a castle up in the clouds. It's made of glass, and the sun shines through the walls every day. That's where I'd take her.'

Everyone who heard laughed aloud, and King Mark nodded and smiled. Only Isolt sat still and unsmiling at his side.

'Why so sad, lady,' Trystan cried, and using the name by which he had often disguised himself before, he added, 'I'm still Tantris you know!' He capered and leered at the queen, who looked upon him with anger.

'How dare you speak to me thus!' she cried.

Trystan tried to look abashed. 'But I speak the truth,' he whined. 'Surely you remember me. Did I not fight the Morholt and get a dreadful wound that would not heal? No one in the world could make me better, and I took to sea in a little boat. Then I came to Ireland, and you, sweet lady, healed me. Remember how I used to play my harp for you?' He made strange gestures like a man playing an invisible harp. Everyone laughed, save Isolt, who changed colour.

'Tantris was a fine and noble man,' she said quietly. 'You are misshapen and ugly, and very likely mad. Be off with you and stop saying these foolish things. I do not care for your jokes – or for you.'

Then Trystan began playing the fool for all he was worth, shouting and waving his hands and driving everyone from the dais. 'Leave us, leave us!' he shouted. 'I have come to court the fair Isolt. Leave us alone!'

Smiling, Mark asked: 'Come, admit it, you are her lover are you not?'

'Indeed I am,' replied Trystan, capering madly.

⇸ *Sir Trystan the fool* ⇷

'Liar!' cried the queen. 'Throw this fool out!'

'But, my lady,' said Trystan. 'Don't you remember how this great king sent me to Ireland to fetch you? I was much hated for having killed the Morholt, but I did as I was bid. I was a great knight, famed from Scotland to Rome.'

'You, a knight!' Now Isolt was almost laughing through her anger. 'You are a disgrace to manhood, a congenital idiot! Get out of here.'

'But surely you remember how I slew a dragon in your name? Remember how I cut out its tongue and then how the poison affected me so that I lay half-dead in the road. You came there with your mother the queen and saved me. That was the second time, surely you remember now?'

'These things are common knowledge,' answered Isolt. 'You are no hero!'

'But my lady and my love,' Trystan said, pouting. 'Don't you remember how you nearly killed me in the bath when you found out I had killed the Morholt, the guardian of your land? Isn't that true?'

'It is a lie!' shouted Isolt. 'You went to bed drunk last night and dreamed all this nonsense.'

'It's true I'm drunk,' said Trystan sadly. 'But of this drink I'll never be sober.'

He capered again before Isolt. 'Surely you must remember the drink we supped together on the ship from Ireland? I did my duty, I brought you home to Cornwall and this noble lord.' Here he bowed comically to Mark. 'But on the way we drank a drink that sealed our fate. I've been drunk of it ever since.'

Isolt stood up, drawing her mantle a round her and preparing to depart. Mark stayed her, placing his hand on her arm. 'Wait, my dear, let's hear all this folly.' He turned to the fool. 'You said you wished to serve me. How will you do so?'

'I've served many kings and nobles. I can do all sorts of things.'

'Do you know about dogs? Horses?'

'Oh yes. I teach greyhounds to catch cranes as they fly, I teach leash-hounds to catch swans and geese. I have caught many coots and bitterns.'

The entire court was in uproar with laughter at this. Mark, laughing, said:

'Little brother, what do you catch in the marshes?'

'Why, whatever I can,' answered Trystan. 'With my goshawk I catch wolves. With my gerfalcons, roebuck and fallow-deer. With the sparrowhawk, foxes. With the merlin, hare. With my falcon, wild cats, beavers, and such like. I know everything there is to know about hunting – and I can play the harp and the rote and sing to any tune you like. I can love a queen, or any woman, better than most men, and I know how to cut chips of wood and float them downstream. Today I'll serve you well.' Saying which he took up a staff that was lying nearby, and began to belabour the courtiers, crying: 'Go home! Haven't you eaten enough of the king's food!'

Laughing, Mark rose and began calling for his horse and hounds – it being his intention to go hunting, as was his custom in the afternoon. He bade the fool find a place to rest his head until later, when he was sure to entertain them all some more. Isolt, pleading a headache, retired to her chamber, where she poured out her heart to her confidante Brangane.

'I am filled with misery,' she said. 'A fool has come to court, a monstrous fellow, ugly and misshapen. Yet he seems to know all my life, even things that only you and I and Sir Trystan could know. He even referred to the chips of fresh-cut wood he used to send downstream to warn me that he awaited me in our secret place!'

'How can this be, my lady?' replied Brangane. 'Unless this is really Trystan himself.'

'It could not be!' cried Isolt. 'This man is hideous, filthy. He has a tonsure like a cross on his head. He behaves like a madman. Curse him I say. Cursed be his life and cursed be the ship which brought him here!'

'Now my lady, be at peace!' urged Brangane. 'Have you never heard of disguises? Surely you know that Trystan is clever and resourceful. I believe it could well be he.'

Isolt hesitated. 'Dear Brangane, if only it were true! Go to the fool, I beg you. Try to find out who he really is.'

Brangane hastened into the hall, which she found deserted, save only for the fool. As she approached, he jumped up and welcomed her.

'Fair Brangane, how glad I am to see you!'

'Who are you?' demanded Brangane. 'How do you know me?'

'Before God, I am Trystan. You know me well.'

'Trystan never looked like you.'

'Listen, fairest lady. When I came to Ireland the queen herself entrusted Isolt and you to my keeping. She held you by her left hand, Isolt by her right. To you she gave a little leather flask. It contained a potion designed to make Isolt fall in love with King Mark. Then, on the ship, when I grew thirsty, a boy fetched me a drink. It was from the flask. He poured it into a golden goblet and offered it to me. I drank, then gave some to Isolt. That drink was the sweetest poison ever devised! It brought love and pain to your lady and to me. Brangane, do you still not know me!'

Brangane stared at the fool a moment longer, then she rose and beckoned him to follow her to Isolt's chamber. When they entered the queen backed away from the fool, her face white. Seeing this Trystan himself fell back,

pressing himself against the wall. There he looked at Isolt sorrowfully.

'Alas that you should forget me so soon!'

Isolt was desperate. 'I look at you, but I see nothing of Trystan.'

'My love,' said he, 'what more can I say to help you? Do you remember the seneschal who first denounced us to the king? Or the dwarf who was set to spy on us? He put flour on the floor of your chamber, so that when I came to you, I left marks that showed where I had been. Remember how my wound bled on your sheets? How Mark found blood on my own linen and banished me because of it? And surely you must remember Petit-Cru, the little dog I sent you as a love-gift to remember me by? So many things there are that we have shared. So many that you must remember as well as I.'

But still Isolt looked at the face of the fool and doubt showed in her eyes. 'You could have learned all of these things by magic,' she said. 'You cannot be my Trystan.'

Trystan stared at her. 'Do you remember,' he began, 'the tree in the very garden of this castle where we used to meet? One day King Mark climbed into its branches and hid there, hoping to spy on us. As chance would have it, I saw his shadow on the ground, and when you came spoke loudly, asking you to reconcile me with the king, to beg him to let me go from his service. On that occasion we were saved.'

Desperately he went on: 'There was another occasion when I was disguised. Do you remember? The king ordered you to undergo an ordeal by fire to prove that you were faithful to him. We contrived it that I, disguised as a pilgrim, should help you ashore from the craft that carried you to the testing place. There, as I lifted you, I pretended to stumble. I fell between your legs. Thus, you were able to swear that no man save the old pilgrim and the king himself, had lain between your thighs!'

Isolt, showing the fear and anguish she felt in every look and gesture, shook her head. 'How can I betray the memory of my love, when I cannot believe you are he?'

'Lady,' said Trystan. 'There is but one more proof I can offer, and though I am heart-sick at your disdain, I will speak of it.'

He drew a breath. 'Remember the time when we were banished together, before King Mark's heart turned black with hatred for me. We fled, the two of us, to the Forest of Morois. There we found a beautiful place, a cave hidden behind a rock. The entrance was narrow, but within it was large and dry. There we found rest and shelter and there we lived together as true man and wife. I even trained my dog, Husdent, not to bark so that he could not give us away if someone passed that way. I hunted for us every day with Husdent and my hawk.

'Dear heart, you must remember this and how we were caught, the king's dwarf leading him to our hiding place. But remember that, as we lay, my sword had fallen between us, and so the king believed us innocent. He even laid his glove across your face to shade you as the sun shone down through a crack in the rocks. When we woke, he awaited us, ready to take us back. It was then I gave you Husdent…'

Trystan stopped, then, light dawning in his eyes: 'Lady, send for the dog! Do you still have him? He will know me surely, even if you do not.'

Brangane was sent at once to fetch the dog, and as soon as it saw its old master, it leapt at him, whining and licking him for sheer joy.

Isolt watched in wonder, for the dog permitted no one near him save herself and Brangane.

Trystan held the dog close, stroking him. To Isolt he said: 'See! He remembers me, his master, better than you remember your love!'

Isolt stared and trembled, not daring, even now, to believe.

→ *The castle on the island* ←

Trystan looked at her sadly. 'When last I saw you, you gave me a gold ring as a token.'

'Do you still have it?' asked Isolt eagerly.

Trystan dug into his tunic and produced the ring. Isolt took it and looked at it. 'Now, alas,' she said. 'I know that my love is lost. For only in death would he have been parted from this token!'

Trystan looked long at her, then he spoke for the first time in his normal voice.

'My love?'

Isolt looked up in wonder.

'You are the fairest of all women, and I love you all the better for doubting me,' Trystan said, standing straight. 'Only true faith would keep you so loyal.'

Then Isolt knew him at last and rushed into his arms. Trystan looked at Brangane and asked her to bring him water to wash the colour from his face and arms. The lovers embraced, laughing and weeping in equal measure. That night, while King Mark remained away from the court, they were happy for a time. And when at last the king returned, Trystan fled once more, escaping with his life, renewed for a time by the few sweet hours he had spent with Isolt.

As Master Thomas has told, few more such meetings were to be granted to them before death made them one – but that is told in another tale, while this one is ended!

EXPLICIT THE TALE OF TRYSTAN'S MADNESS.

INCIPIT THAT OF GISMIRANTE AND THE LADY WITH THE HAIR OF GOLD.

19: GISMIRANTE AND THE LADY WITH THE HAIR OF GOLD

THE GOOD MAN WHO WROTE DOWN THIS TALE TELLS US THAT WE SHOULD BE AWARE THAT AT THE TIME OF THE GREAT KING ARTHUR MAGIC WAS A COMMON THING AND CAUSED MANY WONDROUS THINGS TO HAPPEN. WHETHER THIS IS SO OR NOT, YET I FELT THAT THIS TALE WAS WELL WORTHY OF INCLUSION HERE FOR THE WAY IT SHOWS HOW THE BORDER BETWEEN FAERY AND OUR OWN WORLD IS BUT A THIN LINE. WE MAY SEE, ALSO, HOW IT MAY HAVE BEEN THAT THE NAME OF THIS KNIGHT HAS FALLEN OUT OF MEMORY AMONG THE ROLL CALL OF THE ROUND TABLE KNIGHTS. IN TRUTH, I FEEL SOME COMPANIONSHIP BETWEEN MYSELF AND SIGNOR PUCCI, A GENTLEMAN OF ITALY, WHO FIRST TOLD THIS TALE, FOR LIKE ME HE SPEAKS OF SEARCHING THROUGH THE PAGES OF OLD BOOKS TO DISCOVER THE EVENTS HE NARRATES, JUST AS I HAVE DONE FOR THESE GREAT TALES.

✛ ✛ ✛

IN THE DAYS when the strength of the Fellowship of the Round Table was at its height, many knights wandered far in search of adventure, seeking always to right wrongs they found upon their way. One such knight, whose name is not recorded, but who was known as the Courteous Knight, followed his heart to the very gates of Rome, and beyond that into the great city itself. There, he met and fell in love with the most gentle lady, who in time gave birth to a son, whom they named Gismirante. By the time he was fifteen, this boy was widely acknowledged to be one of the strongest and finest youths in the whole of Rome, but it was at this time that his father grew sick and was like to die. He spoke to Gismirante from his deathbed, saying that his greatest wish was that his son should journey to Britain to the court of King Arthur. There, he should seek out the company of Sir Lancelot, Sir Gawain, and Sir Tristan, whom the Courteous Knight remembered as the greatest among the Round Table Fellowship.

After his father died, Gismirante took leave of his mother and began his journey to Britain.

When he arrived there and it was learned whose son he was, he was made welcome. No lesser knight than Sir Gawain took over his instruction in the arts of swordsmanship, archery and jousting, finding Gismirante a ready pupil. Indeed, within the next seven years, Gismirante's fame grew. His nature was kindly and courteous, as his father's had been, and he quickly became a favourite amongst the knights – while more than one fair lady sighed at the beauty of his looks.

Now, in that time, as many who read these words will know, it was the custom of King Arthur that when the Round Table Fellowship met together they were not permitted to eat until some new adventure was proposed and undertaken. So it fell out that, towards the height of summer, a day dawned when the king and his knights assembled, but though they waited through the day, no new adventure or quest was advanced. Indeed, two days passed and still the king refused to let food or wine be served, so that more than one of the company were heard to groan that they could stand their hunger no longer.

At this moment, Gismirante approached the king and begged that he should be made a knight. 'For if I am, my first quest shall be to find a wonder or adventure that will enable the court to dine.'

At this, King Arthur smiled, and for the love he bore the youth and the memory of his father, he granted Gismirante's wish. Then the youth, armed by Sir Gawain himself, riding a powerful steed and clad in splendid armour and with a sword and clutch of spears, set forth from Camelot the Golden in search of wonder.

On that first day he saw no living soul upon the road, and that night he slept beneath the stars. Then in the morning he found himself close to the edge of the great forest of Broceliande where, it is said, there dwell many magical beings, and where Merlin had walked in the days before the coming of Arthur. Also it was said (and indeed this is still so, I am told) the Great Wood was closer to the borders of the Kingdom of Faery than any other place on earth.

So it was that Gismirante found himself face to face with a woman who glowed with such beauty that he knew at once she was of no mortal stock. To her he bowed his head, and greeted her with the greatest courtesy.

To his amazement she addressed him by name: 'Sir Gismirante. I have come far to meet you here, and to bring a gift for your noble king that will most certainly allow both him and his court to eat.'

Saying which, she produced a small box which she gave to the young knight. 'Within this, you shall find a single hair of gold. It comes from the head of the most beautiful woman, daughter to the king of a land far from here. This king hates all men of valour, no matter how noble they are, and he keeps his daughter locked away. No one may see her, and only on one day does she emerge from her confinement. On that day everyone in the king's citadel must remain indoors. Anyone daring to look upon the princess is immediately imprisoned and within days condemned to die. Only I was able to see this most beautiful of creatures, for neither she nor her father's guards could see me unless I chose it. As she walked through the streets to the church where the mass of Saint Martin was to be celebrated, a hair fell from her head. This I have preserved as a wonder for your king, and an invitation to the bravest of his knights to set free the beautiful princess.'

Gismirante listened in amazement to this story. He held the box in both hands but dared not open it himself. In that moment the

Woman out of Faery vanished away, leaving Gismirante filled with joy. At once he turned, and leaving the Great Wood, rode back full pelt for the court, where he stumbled into the hall calling out that he had 'found a wonder!'

King Arthur at once gave the order for food to be served, and all fell to with a will. Then, when supper was ended, Gismirante presented the little box to the king, along with the story as the Woman out of Faery had told it to him. King Arthur opened the box, and there, nestled amid the lining, was a golden hair at least two cubits in length.*

Everyone marvelled as the hair was passed from hand to hand so that all might see it, for it seemed veritably to glow in the torchlight. Several of the knights were determined to go forth in search of she who owned the hair, but loudest of all was Gismirante, who begged King Arthur to give him leave to undertake the adventure.

This Arthur did, and the very next day Gismirante set forth from Camelot the Golden in search of the Lady with the Hair of Gold. For many days he travelled without meeting a single adventure, until he entered the Great Wood, and there he saw a battle taking place between a gryphon and a dragon. So bright and glorious was the gryphon, that Gismirante could not stand by as he saw that the serpent seemed likely to be victorious. Drawing his sword, he leapt upon the dragon's back and with a single blow severed its head from its body.

The gryphon flew up at once into the air and gave a great cry, then it circled Gismirante's head three times before disappearing into the west.

Now, as the young knight continued, he saw how a mighty eagle circled above him, crying

out loudly in hunger, and seeming as if it might attack him. And Gismirante, who loved all good creatures, opened the pack that hung from his saddlebow and from it drew a piece of meat, which he threw into the air. The eagle seized it and, also circling his head three times, flew off, calling loudly.

Soon after this, as Gismirante rode on, a third event occurred. He heard the shrill cries of a sparrowhawk, and came to where the bird was caught in the branches of a tree. Uttering gentle words Gismirante dismounted and climbed to where the sparrowhawk fluttered in an effort to escape, and with care he set the bird free, so that it was able to fly. And once again, as had the gryphon and the eagle, the sparrowhawk flew three times over the knight's head before vanishing amid the trees of the Great Wood.

Thus Gismirante rode on, ever enquiring after the kingdom whose princess was kept hidden away. The forest seemed ever to grow thicker around him, until at last, he reached a clearing, and there, sitting upon a most beautiful red horse, sat the Woman out of Faery who had brought him the golden hair.

She greeted him by name and enquired after his reason for entering this enchanted glade. Gismirante at once told her of his quest, but the faery shook her head. 'What you attempt is impossible,' she said. 'No human may achieve this without finding death.' Then she smiled upon him and said: 'It would be far better if you remained here with me. I promise I will make you happier than you have ever been.'

But Gismirante shook his head: 'I thank you, my lady, but I am determined to achieve the task set me by King Arthur, or die in the attempt.'

Then, blushing red, he added: 'Yet you may be certain of one thing. If I do not succeed, and if I am still living after that, then I shall return

---

* Approximately three feet.

to you – for never did I see a more beautiful lady in all of my life.'

The Woman out of Faery smiled at him. 'Very well. If you are set upon this course, then I shall give you a gift.' And she set up a great call, and from the depths of the trees came a mighty horse, the most proud and powerful that Gismirante had ever seen.

'This noble beast will carry you faster and further than any steed living,' said the faery. 'It will take you to the place you seek in less time than a dozen ordinary horses could do. There is no other way you will find your way to the city you seek.'

Thanking her, Gismirante mounted the mighty steed and scarcely giving him time to say goodbye, it set off at such a pace that the world seemed to become a whirlwind around him, and in what seemed no more than an hour he found himself in sight of the walls of a city. There he sought shelter for himself and the faery horse at an inn, and enquired of the princess. But all he spoke to looked askance and were either silent or warned him of the foolishness of such questions – for none might see the Lady of the Golden Hair save those her father permitted, and these were few and far between.

Despite these warnings, Gismirante determined to await the day when the princess was permitted to walk through the streets to the cathedral where the mass of Saint Martin was celebrated.

Eventually that day arrived, and the king's herald rode through the city, crying out that all must remain inside until the morning. Everywhere people did as they were bid, the innkeeper locking his door so that no man might enter or depart. But Gismirante found a way to leave by a window left unlocked and made his way through the silent streets until he stood before the towers of the House of God. There he entered and hid behind the high altar to await the coming of the princess.

Soon she entered and made her way through the empty building until she stood before the altar and knelt down. When he looked upon the princess, Gismirante at once knew that she was the most beautiful lady he had ever seen – more beautiful even than the Woman out of Faery whose gift had brought him there. And he marvelled at the glory of her hair, of which a single strand was as nothing to the beauty of that which tumbled about her face and fell to her waist. So enchanted was he that he made a sound and at once the beautiful princess looked to where he had hidden himself and called out to know who was there.

Suddenly shy, the young knight emerged from his hiding place and bowed before the princess.

'Who are you?' she demanded, gently enough, for she had noticed what a handsome youth he was. 'You know that it is death to look upon me.'

'My lady,' replied Gismirante. 'Though I may pay for it with my life, yet have I come all

✦ *The great eagle* ✦

the way from King Arthur's court to look upon you – led by the sight of a single hair from your head. And if your face is the last thing I see in this life, it will have been worth my while.'

At this, the princess laughed aloud. 'Never has any man dared to flout my father's wishes,' she said. 'Now I see that you are a knight of many fine qualities.'

Then she smiled, so that the sun seemed to shine out and fill the cathedral with light. 'If you would have me, you must return tonight and watch for a light in my window. Then I will instruct you how you may achieve what you wish.'

Astonished by these words, Gismirante fell to his knees before the princess and pledged to do all that he could to secure her. Then they spoke for a time together and in those moments love blossomed between them. But at last it was time for the princess to return to her father's castle, and so she did, walking alone through the silent streets, while Gismirante returned to the inn and crept in through the unlocked window. There, he prepared as he had been told, and passed the time until Matins,* when he made his way to the castle. There he waited until he saw where a light shone forth from a certain window. Looking out, the princess called to him: 'I am ready, Sir Knight. But how shall I carry all my jewels with me?'

Gismirante replied that such things meant nothing to him as long as he could save her from her father's protection and carry her off to a safe place. Then the princess laughed aloud and promised to join Gismirante if he would wait for her by a certain gate. This he did, and soon the princess joined him, having dressed as a squire and taken a bold and gentle horse from her father's stables.

---

* Midnight.

Together they rode to the main gate, where the guards demanded to know who they were that made such a noise in the middle of the night. Gismirante drew his sword and told them that unless they opened the gates they would all find themselves dead, and such was the strength and fierceness of the young knight that they brought forth a key and unlocked the gate.

Gismirante and the princess galloped away and soon put several miles between themselves and the city. There, meanwhile, the king had discovered his daughter's absence, and filled with rage, gathered a number of knights and soldiers and set off in pursuit.

Soon they spied the two figures on horseback and gave chase. When the princess saw the large troop coming after them she grew fearful, but Gismirante spurred his great steed on, and holding the bridle of the princess's horse, led the way until they came to a river. This was far too broad and deep to cross, but when she saw this the princess produced a curious wand, which she offered to the young knight. 'Use this,' she said. 'One touch of it will cause the river to sink until we may cross it. A second touch of my wand will cause it to overflow its banks.'

This Gismirante did, and it was as the princess had said. When the water sank he told her to cross, but he himself remained behind, touching the magic wand to the water so that it overflowed.

Seeing this, the princess wept and called upon him to cross to her, but Gismirante waved to her and cried that he would join her soon. Then he turned to face the king and his men and drew his sword. Riding on the mighty faery steed he ran against the approaching force and drove all before him. So powerful was this magical beast that it threw many knights to the earth without needing Gismirante to strike them with his sword. At last he drew close to the king himself and struck him a blow which caused him to fall from his horse. When the knights saw this they turned and fled, fearful of Gismirante's strength and power.

Then the young knight stood over the king with his sword and told him his life was forfeit. The king said: 'This I accept, for you are the best and bravest man I have ever seen. I ask only that you care for my child whom you have so successfully stolen away.'

Then Gismirante looked on his fallen foe with kindness and said: 'Sire, I shall spare you in your daughter's name, and I tell you that I am taking her to Camelot the Golden, the court of my lord King Arthur. If you wish you may follow in your own time and wait upon my lord.'

The king bowed his head, and with all his former pride gone from him, said: 'If any man should have my daughter, it is one such as you. I have heard of the great King Arthur and his Fellowship and know them all to be noble and true. Go then, with my blessing, and my thanks for sparing my life.'

Gismirante saluted the king and at once touched the river with the magical wand, causing it to lower until he could cross. There the princess awaited to embrace him, and he caused the waters to rise again. Then the two of them rode together until they entered the Great Wood and so travelled on towards Camelot the Golden.

Lacking the speed and stamina of the faery horse, the princess's steed soon grew tired, and as the pair came to a sheltered valley where there was a fountain, they stopped to rest. And there it was that Gismirante owned his love for the princess, and she for him, and they lay together as man and woman will. And after

that Gismirante fell asleep with his head in the lap of the princess and she slept also.

Now it happened that at this time there lived close by a certain Wildman, whose skin was as green as the grass and the leaves upon the trees, and whose eyes were as red as coals. So it befell that he came that way, and when he saw the beauty of the princess he caused her by magic to fall even more deeply asleep, and thus stole her away, placing a stone beneath the sleeping knight's head, so that when he awoke, only then did he discover that the princess had gone.

So desperate was the young knight that he cried aloud in his despair: 'How may I find she whom I love?' Then he remembered the Woman out of Faery who had helped him, and mounting the magical steed rode faster than the wind to where he had met her before.

Near that place he came upon a river that was deeper even than the one he had enabled to run dry, but when he touched it with the princess's wand, this time it had no effect.

Now Gismirante prepared to cast himself into the water, though with little thought to survive, for this was a fast and cruel water. But while he thought thus, the gryphon that he had helped earlier flew down to him and spoke: 'Sir, for the help you gave me against the dragon, let me help you now!' And he picked up Gismirante in his mighty claws and flew with him across the river, setting him down on the further bank. Then he flew back across the water and picked up the faery steed and brought it there also.

Gismirante gave thanks to the mighty creature, which then flew off, leaving the knight to continue on, until suddenly the Woman out of Faery was before him.

'I see that you have lost what you had found,' said she, and Gismirante, with tears on his face, told her all that had occurred.

'I fear you have lost the princess for ever,' said the faery. Then she said: 'But if you wish to remain here with me, I promise you shall soon forget her.'

Gismirante bowed his head before her and replied that he was more grateful for her kindness than any man before or since, but that he would sooner lose his life than the princess. Then she told him of the Wildman who had stolen the princess, and that he lived in a castle of iron, with twenty-four other women whom he had captured through his magic. 'The entrance to this place is hidden, but there is a way you may gain entrance,' said the Woman out of Faery. And she told Gismirante what he must do.

'The Wildman is a creature of great power and even greater cunning. Once, he was a man like you, but an evil sorcerer enchanted him into the form he now has. There is only one way to kill him, for he has hidden the heart out of his body, and only if you can discover where it is located and destroy it will you succeed. At a certain hour every day the Wildman goes hunting. While he is away you must call your lady to a window. Tell her she must discover where the Wildman has hidden his heart.'

Thanking the Woman out of Faery for her kindness, Gismirante mounted the faery steed and rode to the Iron Castle. There, he remained in hiding until he saw the Wildman depart, striding out with a huge spear in his hand and a grim look on his face. The greenness of his skin and his red eyes made him a truly fearful creature to behold, and despite himself Gismirante shivered as he watched the creature vanish into the forest.

Gathering his courage about him Gismirante left his hiding place and circled the iron walls of the castle until he spied a brightly lit window.

Urgently, he called out to his love, who soon appeared.

'You must flee from here,' she said. 'The creature that holds me is too strong for any mortal to defeat.'

'The faery who helped me before has told me a way that he may be killed,' answered Gismirante. Then he told her what the Woman out of Faery had said. 'Only you can persuade him to tell you the secret of where he has hidden his heart.'

The Lady with the Golden Hair at once agreed to try, though her face grew pale at the idea of attempting to persuade the Wildman to tell her his secret.

'Go now,' she told Gismirante. 'I will do what I can. Watch out for the light in my window when it is safe for you to return. Until then, stay in hiding.'

Gismirante did as she told him, though his own heart quailed at the thought of encountering the Wildman, and he feared greatly for his lady.

She, meanwhile, waited until the Wildman returned from hunting and made a great show of welcoming him home and being overjoyed to see him. He, greatly enamoured of her beauty, banished all but her from his presence and embraced her.

As the Lady with the Golden Hair lay in his arms she beguiled him so much that when she told him that she had learned that he had hidden his heart from all the world, and begged him to tell her where it was kept, so that she might worship it with all her soul, the Wildman smiled at her.

'My love, it is hidden within this very pillar.' And he showed her where a mighty stone upheld the roof. But though he smiled and caressed her golden hair, the lady knew that he lied. Nevertheless she insisted upon kneeling before the pillar for the rest of the night, praying out loud for the well-being of her captor.

When he saw this, the Wildman laughed aloud. 'My dear,' he said, 'do not waste your time. My heart is not within that pillar, it is hidden inside a giant beast, the boar named Torrencino. At this moment he terrorises the city of Rome by watching the roads and capturing and eating anyone foolish enough to come that way.'

Then he smiled at the lady, and added: 'Even if anyone was strong enough to defeat the boar, it would do them little good, for within it lives a hare, which would at once flee away if the boar was killed. And if anyone was foolish enough to catch it, that too would serve him naught, for within the hare lives a sparrow, and it is within that my heart is hidden.'

Then the lady thanked him and remained at his side until the morning, when once again he went hunting.

Gismirante, seeing him stride off into the forest once more, hastened to the Iron Castle and when his love appeared at the window he heard all about the creature's heart. 'But this task is beyond any man to achieve,' said the Lady with the Golden Hair. 'You must leave here and forget me, for I will never escape the Wildman.'

Then Gismirante wept aloud and said: 'I will not fail you, my love. I will go to the faery who has been so generous in helping us both. I am sure she will know how this fearsome creature may be destroyed.'

So Gismirante hastened from the Iron Castle to the place in the Great Wood where he had met the Woman out of Faery. And there she awaited him as before. He told her all that had been revealed about the Wildman's heart and the Great Boar Torrencino.

'I know of this creature,' replied the faery.

'Not even you will be able to overcome him.'

But Gismirante said that he would give his life if needed to save his lady. Then the faery thought for a while and said: 'Your strength and your devotion are great indeed. I wish that you would remain here with me, but I know that you will not. There is but one more way that I can help you. The steed which has carried you so well, and has such great strength, shall help you to overcome the beast, and I shall give you armour and weapons that will add my power and enchantment to your battle. But even so,' she added, 'I cannot promise that you will succeed, for the boar is a terrible opponent and you are but a mortal man.'

'Nevertheless, I must try, for the sake of my lady,' answered Gismirante. Then the Woman Out of Faery gave him armour and weapons that were enchanted with strong spells of protection.

So it was that Gismirante made his way to the great city of Rome, along roads where the great boar ravaged. There he presented himself to the emperor and told him that he intended to destroy the creature that so terrorised his land.

The emperor, filled with amazement, promised not only his greatest knights to accompany him, but also, if he succeeded, the hand of his daughter.

The young knight replied that he needed no help, and no reward, for he did this deed in the name of another. Then he set forth from the city, while the emperor himself and his court followed, and repaired to a hill from where they could watch the battle to come.

Gismirante meanwhile rode on to the great plain that lay beside the main way into the city, where the mighty boar was wont to roam. Soon he saw where the huge creature lay sleeping, surrounded by the bones of those it had killed. Huge it was indeed, perhaps four cubits from

⭢ *The wildman* ⭠

nose to tail, with huge curving tusks stained red with blood. And it happened that snow had fallen that night, and that Gismirante's magical armour shone so brightly that it dazzled the great boar.

Thus the creature lay still, feigning sleep and preparing to leap upon his attacker. Gismirante came close to the mighty creature and when he saw it was unmoving he crept nearer and stabbed it in the belly with his spear.

At once, the boar rose up, screaming in rage and pain, and attacked Gismirante, knocking him to the ground. There, it stood over him, its breath rank on his face, and began to savagely strip the armour from him, as it were flesh from a corpse. Then Gismirante prayed aloud to the faery and in his heart he heard her telling him to be strong and to leap upon the boar's back. As he struggled to rise the boar held him down with a mighty foot, and

thus he might have perished had not the faery steed struck the beast with its hooves, felling it to the ground. Seeing his chance, Gismirante leapt up and drawing his knife leapt upon the creature and struck it again and again in the heart until it lay dead.

With his last strength the knight cut deep into the side of the beast, and there, amid the blood and entrails of the boar, he saw where the hare was concealed. But before he could capture it, the creature leapt away and fled into the forest.

Desperately, Gismirante tried to follow it, but his strength failed and he wept aloud. In that moment there came into his sight the great eagle that he had fed when seeking the Lady with the Golden Hair. Like a feathered sword it fell upon the hare and in a moment let it fall at Gismirante's feet.

'For the help you gave me, I offer this,' said

the eagle, then it flew away, leaving Gismirante to kill the hare. But when he opened it, the sparrow that hid within flew away too fast to catch, and once again Gismirante was in despair. But in that moment he heard the cry of the sparrowhawk and the same creature he had set free from the tree stooped upon the sparrow and bore it to him in its claws.

'My thanks to you for your kindness,' said the bird, letting fall the sparrow. This Gismirante secured, still living, and placed within a leather bag. The knight gave thanks to the creatures who had helped him, then mounting upon his magical steed he rode back to the glade where the Woman Out of Faery awaited him.

'You did well indeed, my brave knight,' said the faery. 'If you had killed the sparrow you would not have been able to enter the Wildman's castle. Now you must call upon your love to help you one more time, and if you succeed in this next task you will win the day.'

Then she told Gismirante that he should disguise himself as a doctor, for she said: 'The one thing the Wildman desires above all things is to be changed in such a way that he is no longer wild and green, but may walk among ordinary people again. Tell your love she must persuade him that you alone can make this happen, and that he must open the door to the castle to allow you in. Once inside, kill the sparrow, and all will be well.'

Then she looked at him and said: 'All that I have done was for love of you, but I know that your heart is given elsewhere, And you should know that the three creatures, gryphon, eagle and sparrowhawk, whom you helped and which have now helped you, are my brothers. So I give you my blessing, for you shall not see me again.' And with these words the Woman Out of Faery vanished away. And though it is

believed that those who are of that Other race have no hearts, yet this seems to me to give the lie to such ideas.

Gismirante hastened now to the castle, and knowing that the Wildman would be hunting in the Great Wood at this time, called out to the Lady with the Golden Hair. She came at once to the window and heard all that he had to say. She praised him for his courage and skill in slaying the great boar and capturing the sparrow, and promised to do all that she could to persuade the Wildman to let Gismirante into the castle.

Soon enough the Wildman returned, and when she had greeted him with kindness and affection, the lady told him that she had learned of a famous doctor who was close by and who, alone of all his kind, could bring about that which the Wildman most longed for.

At first he was suspicious, but as the lady spoke of how much more she would love him if he once again looked like a man, at last he gave her the key which hung about his neck. 'You may allow this doctor to enter. But be warned,' he added, 'if there is trickery here, be sure that both the doctor and you shall die by my hand.'

The Lady with the Golden Hair hastened to the gate, and unlocked it. Gismirante, who was waiting outside, was able to enter at once. No sooner had he set foot in the Iron Castle than he heard the roar of the Wildman, who had sensed the presence of the sparrow in Gismirante's pack.

Then with all speed the knight pulled the bird forth and killed it with a single blow. The Wildman at once stopped where he stood in the doorway of the hall, and without uttering a word, fell dead upon the floor.

The lady then embraced Gismirante and thanked him a thousand times for his courage. And at this all the other women captured by the Wildman appeared and clustered around Gismirante, showering him with their thanks.

But he, though gladness filled him that he had achieved his task, spoke only of the faery who had helped him throughout, and who maybe in his heart he loved also – though not as much as he did his own lady.

On the morning after, Gismirante and the Lady with the Golden Hair, accompanied by all who had been captured by the Wildman, left the Iron Castle and made their way by many roads, coming at last to Camelot the Golden. There, King Arthur and the members of his mighty Fellowship who were present, came forth to greet them, and a great feast was held in celebration of the young knight's deeds. All the stories were told, and all were amazed at what had transpired. And at the end of it all Gismirante and the Lady of the Golden Hair were married, and the others who had been held captive were able to return to their homes.

THUS ENDED THE adventure, and thus have I told the story of Sir Gismirante, as it was chronicled by Signor Pucci. I cannot say how true it may be, since there is much here of magic, and I am not certain whether this be real or not. Indeed, there are those who say that magic is dead, or even that it never was. And yet, while the Lady still dances in the greensward, I cannot say if this is so, only that it seems to me that a world without magic is somehow reduced, and that those who have named it false, or untrue, are themselves made less. In the time of King Arthur it was not so, for thus Sir Thomas Malory and many others have attested.

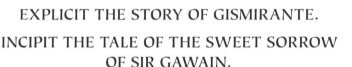

EXPLICIT THE STORY OF GISMIRANTE.

INCIPIT THE TALE OF THE SWEET SORROW OF SIR GAWAIN.

20: THE SWEET SORROW
OF SIR GAWAIN

⁜

THIS TALE CAME TO ME BUT LATE, WHEN I HEARD IT SUNG BY
A BALLAD MAKER. HAVING NOT HEARD OF IT BEFORE, I MADE
ENQUIRIES AND DISCOVERED IT TO BE AN ANCIENT SONG THAT
HAS BEEN SUNG IN THESE LANDS FOR MANY YEARS. IT MAY BE THAT
SIR THOMAS KNEW OF IT, BUT PERHAPS FELT IT UNWORTHY OF HIS
GREAT BOOK. THOUGH I SHOULD NOT SEEK TO DISAGREE WITH MY
MASTER, YET I WILL SAY THAT IT HAS THE RING OF AN ANCIENT
TALE OF THE FAERY KIND. ALSO, IT MIGHT BE THAT SOME MAY SEE
HERE THE REASON FOR SIR GAWAIN'S MANY CONNECTIONS WITH
THE WOMEN OF THAT 'OTHER' PLACE. THUS, I INCLUDE IT, DESPITE
ITS BREVITY, TO SHOW HOW THE BEINGS OF FAERY SO OFTEN SEEK
TO DRAW US IN.

⁜ ✠ ⁜

ONE DAY KING Arthur had a dream, and this was the way of it. He had, as was often his wont, gone hunting in the great forest of Broceliande, and there in the darkness of the wood he heard the silver song of a harp. Following it, he came to a clearing, and there he saw a most beautiful maiden seated on a fallen tree, playing a harp that seemed to shimmer as though made of gold. In the dream the king dismounted from his white steed, Llamrai, and knelt before the girl, entranced by her playing. And after a while, as she smiled upon him so that the sun seemed to come out from behind a cloud, and to shine so brightly that even the trees of the Great Wood could not hold it back, then it was that she sang a song – her voice was as beautiful as a day in May, when the blossoms open, perfuming the air with their scent.

And so it was that King Arthur fell hopelessly in love with this maiden, and begged her to become his wife. But before she could answer, though the king thought he saw delight in her eye, he awoke with a shout and reached for his sword – for he felt that he had been enchanted by the maiden, who must surely be of Faery. But even as the dream faded he found that he could not forget the maiden's face and form, or indeed her music and her song.

All that day, and for days that followed, King Arthur was full of sorrow and seemed as though he still slept, and every night he dreamed the same dream, and every night became ever more enchanted by the maiden.

So it was that Sir Gawain, the king's nephew and the foremost of his knights, saw that his uncle was troubled and begged to help if he could. The king told him of his dream and described the place in the Great Wood where he went every night, and all that occurred there.

'Sir,' said Sir Gawain. 'Let me try to find this lady who troubles your sleep. For surely if you have seen and heard her so often then she must be real.'

So King Arthur gave Gawain leave to go, and the knight rode into the depths of the forest. There he wandered for many days until at last he came to where the sea touched the land, and there he saw a small craft tethered to the shore. It bore a sail of silver cloth on which was the image of a harp, and thus he thought that this was a message meant for him.

So he went aboard with his steed and at once a wind arose and filled the ship's sail, so that it sped across the glittering sea until it came to an island, where it stopped. Above Sir Gawain, the cliffs rose up on all sides, preventing him from entering the island, yet from above he heard the song of birds and smelled the scent of blossoms such as seemed a sign of spring. And in the distance it seemed to him that he heard a faint sound of music on the air.

As he looked, a black chain, made of ancient iron, descended from above and hung over the deck of the ship, and without hesitation Sir Gawain began to climb, and soon found himself stepping onto the earth of the most beautiful place he had ever seen. The very air itself smelled sweet and was a balm to his troubled thoughts. So he made his way inland, through flowering meadows and tall trees, until at last he came to a palace that seemed to him made of glass. From within came the sound of sweet song, and in his heart he knew that this was the very same singing which had so enchanted King Arthur in his dream.

Before him now, Gawain saw a narrow gateway, and he made his way through it into the castle. There he found himself in a great hall, hung with rich tapestries and carpeted in silk. In the centre of the room was a golden chair, much like a throne, and upon it sat the fairest and most wonderful maiden he had ever seen. Just as King Arthur had described her she played upon a golden harp and sang with a voice as pure as the purest water.

In that moment Sir Gawain fell every bit as deeply in love as had the king, and desired nothing so much as to be in the presence of this lady and to know her love.

After a time the maiden ceased her song and looked upon Sir Gawain kindly. 'You are far from your home,' she said. 'Did your lord send you in search of me?'

'That is the truth,' answered Gawain. 'My lord King Arthur bade me to find you and, if it were possible, to bring you to him at Camelot the Golden.'

'That will be a hard thing to do,' said the maiden. 'For I am kept here by a dreadful lord who knows nothing of mercy and cannot be killed.'

'I must try, nonetheless,' said Sir Gawain. 'What more can you tell me of this dread knight?'

'His name is Bleheris, and he is the most powerful faery. So strong is his enchantment that no man – not even you Sir Gawain – for yes, I know your name – can stand against him. There is only one way to kill him, and that is with his own sword.'

'How may I get this weapon?' demanded Sir Gawain. 'Certainly this man will not give it up.'

'Perhaps there is a way,' said the maiden. 'Bleheris cannot resist my playing, so it may be that I can make him weak and thus allow you to slay him.'

At this moment there came a long call upon a hunting horn, and at once the maiden grew pale. 'He comes,' she said. 'You would be advised to depart now.'

But Gawain, as was his wont, refused. He stood by the maiden and drew his sword, and at that moment there entered the hall the faery knight. Tall he was, and slender of build, and his eyes gleamed grey in his face. Yet he was as grim and powerful a figure as Gawain had ever seen. On one foot he wore a spur of gold, and on the other one of silver, and the sword he carried blazed with brilliance so that Gawain could scarcely look at it.

'Who is this that has come to meet his death?' demanded the knight.

'I am Sir Gawain of Orkney – knight of King Arthur,' replied the king's nephew.

'It is from such as you and your king that I guard and protect this lady,' said Bleheris. 'I shall soon kill you. Then I shall own that fine steed I saw on the ship below, and indeed that vessel that carried you here. Your armour too shall be mine, and even your puny sword.'

'Then let it be as it shall be,' said Gawain, and the two knights prepared themselves to do battle.

At that moment the maiden began to play her harp and sing in her most beautiful voice, and as she did so the fire went from the faery knight's eyes and he looked only at her. In a few moments he lay down upon the floor at the maiden's feet and seemed to forget everything around him, including Sir Gawain.

On and on the maiden sang, ever more sweetly, until at last the faery knight fell into a deep sleep and let fall his brilliant sword. Seeing this, Gawain snatched up the shining blade and with a single blow cut off the sleeping man's head. At once the body dissolved in smoke and was blown away by a sudden wind that blew through the castle.

➜ *Sir Gawain climbs the black chain* ✦

As it did so, the walls began to shake and the earth to shiver, and all the while the maiden sang. And now it was Gawain who fell beneath its spell. All the ardour of battle fell away from him and he felt only love and sorrow – for in his heart he knew the maiden was not for him, nor indeed for King Arthur. And while he looked at her again he thought for a moment that he saw a great queen of Faery before him, and knew that she had brought him hither to set her free.

So it was that Sir Gawain left that place, and when he looked back there was no sign of the castle of glass, or the maiden – but still he heard her voice and it seemed to him that she lamented, though for what he could not say.

Thus Sir Gawain made his way back to the ship which had brought him to the strange island, and when he went aboard the sails once again filled and carried him across the ocean to the shores of Logres.

When he came again to Camelot the Golden and sought out the king, he saw that his uncle's eyes were clear once more, not as they had seemed when he sent his nephew forth to search for the maiden. Nor did he seem to feel any of the sorrow that filled Sir Gawain's heart when he heard the adventure of the island and the faery knight.

After that neither the king nor Sir Gawain ever made mention of the matter again – and if either remembered the maiden and the sweet sorrow of her voice, the story does not tell, though it is said that ever after Sir Gawain sought for the love of faery women. But indeed it is true that the song of the adventure is still sung to this day in the realms of King Arthur.

EXPLICIT THE STORY OF SIR GAWAIN AND THE SWEET SORROW.

INCIPIT THE TALE OF SIR GAURIEL AND THE FAERY WIFE.

21: GAURIEL OF MUNTABEL AND THE FAERY WIFE

NOT EVERY KNIGHT WHO SAT AT THE ROUND TABLE IS REMEMBERED, AND NOT EVERYONE WHO JOINED THE FELLOWSHIP REMAINED PART OF IT, OR INDEED RETURNED OFTEN TO CAMELOT THE GOLDEN. ONE SUCH IS THE HERO OF THIS STORY: GAURIEL OF MUNTABEL, WHOSE STORY IS CONCERNED WITH WHAT IT TAKES TO BE A LOVER AND A KNIGHT, AND TO GIVE EQUAL VALUE TO EACH. IT ALSO SPEAKS OF THE FAERY WORLD, AND OF AN AGREEMENT, ONCE BROKEN, THAT TOOK GREAT EFFORT TO RESTORE. FOR IT IS ALSO TOLD, OF THAT FAR OFF TIME, WHEN THE LADY DANCED UPON THE GREENSWARD, THAT THERE WAS FOR MANY YEARS A GREAT ANIMOSITY BETWEEN CAMELOT THE GOLDEN AND THE PEOPLE OF FAERY, WHICH CAUSED MANY VISITS BY THOSE OF THE OTHERWORLD WHOSE INTENT WAS TO CHALLENGE THE COURT OF KING ARTHUR, AND THAT THIS WAS ONLY RESOLVED AT THE TIME OF THE GREAT KING'S DEATH. BUT THAT STORY MUST BE TOLD ANOTHER TIME.

✠ ✠ ✠

THE KNIGHT GAURIEL of Muntabel was married to a faery. Her name was Fatuse, and together they dwelled between that world and this in a place known as the Flowering Throne. They shared a deep and abiding love, and Fatuse asked only one thing of her knight – that he should never speak of her to any other man or woman, unless they too were part of the faery realm. For a long while Gauriel kept his word, and when he returned to the outer world, as he did on occasion, he never once referred to his wife or to the wonderful place in which they lived.

Let me tell you that the land of the Flowering Throne was amongst the most beautiful places in any world. So, too, was the palace where Gauriel and Fatuse lived, which was richer and more elaborately carven and decorated than any of the castles or palaces in King Arthur's realm – even including Camelot

179

the Golden itself, which it is said Merlin the Enchanter created in a single night. As for Fatuse, she was one of the most beautiful of all faery women – in a race famed for their beauty, she outshone them all. Small wonder if, in the end, Gauriel could not resist breaking his word. How it happened is soon told.

One morning early in the month of May, Sir Gauriel crossed from the world of Faery into the lands ruled over by King Arthur. He had done this many times before, and was well known to the people of the forest and those who dwelled close to Camelot the Golden.

On this occasion, Gauriel followed a small seemingly little used track through the Great Wood of Broceliande. After a time, he heard the sound of voices raised in merry song. It seemed to him that the birds in the trees joined in, and the sounds filled him with such joy that he forgot for a time where he was.

The path led to a wide meadow where a most beautiful tent was set up. The music came from within and Sir Gauriel, light of heart, dismounted and entered there. Within he found a group of ladies gathered. Some played music on rote, fiddle, dulcimer and timbrel, while others raised their voices in song. In the centre of the group was a fair queen named Ourel. When she and her companions saw Gauriel enter the pavilion, they all fell silent for a moment, but so handsome and graceful he was that none wished him to depart. Indeed, Queen Ourel bade him welcome and invited him to sit at her side. Then the music was resumed and it may well be that Gauriel himself raised his voice and joined with them in song.

Soon, food was brought to the tent – more splendid viands than you may imagine, served on plates of gold, and with wine in glasses of elegant style such as are best known in the lands of Italy. So it was that the queen spoke

with Gauriel, asking him if he had ever seen such beautiful women as those in her company. And thus it came about that the knight betrayed his promise to Fatuse, for his answer to the queen was that he had truly only ever seen one lady more beautiful than all of them – and that was his own wife.

As he uttered these words, he felt a great ache in his heart, and in that moment heard the voice of his beloved bemoaning his failure to keep silent.

'You have betrayed your promise to me for no better reason than to boast of knowing one more beautiful than those where you are. Know that you are banished from my lands and my presence from this moment.'

When he heard this Gauriel became so cast down that the queen and her ladies begged him to tell them why. But now he knew better than to add to his shame, and left them, retiring to his own castle at Muntabel, fearful that his sorrow would bring him to an early end, so great was his longing to see Fatuse again.

For many days he languished, overwhelmed by sorrow, and because of this he soon grew wasted and lines of woe marked his face – until in time he was almost unrecognisable, and seemed to many to have become ugly. The story says that this was the will of Fatuse, but others say that it was sorrow that marked him thus.

At last Gauriel could no longer bear to lie in the great bed that his love had made for them, carved from the wood of Broceliande and decorated with gold and silver and precious stones and curtained with silk and satin. Instead, Gauriel decided that he would go forth in search of adventure, for thus it might be that he would win enough fame to come to the attention of his lady once again.

Now it happened that Fatuse had gifted him with a most unusual gift – a goat that had such intelligence and strength that it went often on adventures with its master, more than once lending its aid to him in defeating foes ranged against him, including the strange beasts that dwelled in the Great Wood. Because of this Sir Gauriel was sometimes known as the Knight of the Goat, and many had seen how this wondrous creature was enchanted and able to bring about wondrous deeds with his bold master. Thus on his shield Gauriel wrought a goat of gold on a field of green.

✢ ✢ ✢

FOR MORE THAN a year Sir Gauriel wandered, and many knights he encountered he defeated, so that word of his presence reached the ears of King Arthur, who wished greatly to meet this bold knight who seemed no one could beat.

Meanwhile, Gauriel decided that he would make camp in a certain meadow within the forest and there await whoever might come that way. He set up a pavilion there and made a palisade of spears, set around him in a frieze of steel-tipped power. In the tent he had a magical cup that he had brought from the Otherworld, and that shone with a light that made it seem as bright as day even when night fell.

When he had been there but a few days a lady came riding on a red horse. She was one that he knew from the Lady Fatuse's retinue and his heart leapt at the sight. This lady rode up to the knight's tent but would not dismount. Instead, she gave Gauriel a letter from her mistress. Here is what it said: that she could not forgive him for his failure to keep his promise, but that she would consider allowing him back into her kingdom if he could capture enough of the greatest knights of the Round Table to demonstrate that he was himself one of the

greatest warriors of his time. She added that she would know when and how he succeeded, and would make her decision in the light of his skill and strength.

Thus the knight's spirits soared, and he prepared to do as his love had commanded.

In Camelot the Golden meanwhile, word had reached King Arthur of the Knight of the Goat, who lived behind a hedge of spears, and the king desired greatly to meet him. At first Sir Kay wanted to go and bring him back by force, but the king declared that he did not wish this to be the bold knight's first encounter with his court. Then Queen Guinevere herself declared that she would send one of her handmaidens to invite the knight to attend upon them.

So it was that a maiden arrived at Gauriel's tent, accompanied by a page with a message from the king and queen. Having greeted her gently, the knight heard her words. Then he responded: 'Fair Lady, I am come to this land with but one reason – to seek adventure and to prove myself against all-comers. I have heard of your king and his Round Table, and I believe they may well be some of the best knights in

➤ *The mighty goat* ◄

the world. But I do not plan to go there at this time, and will remain here until the month of May is out.'

Then he looked at the maiden. 'You have delivered your message well. But you have also given me an opportunity to bring your king's knights to me. To this end I shall make you my prisoner. Do not fear for your life or your honour, but send your page back to King Arthur with this message.'

'This is a most unwise and unknightly action,' the maiden answered, lowering her gaze from his ravaged face. 'I advise you not to do this, Sir Knight. You do not wish to anger my lord.'

'Nonetheless, I shall do as I have said,' replied Gauriel, at which the maiden swiftly commanded her page to return to Camelot the Golden and to give the king and queen the knight's message.

When they heard this, both King Arthur and Queen Guinevere were angered. 'Who is this man?' asked the king. 'What shield does he carry?'

The page described Gauriel's shield with the image of the goat, and at once one of the knights spoke up. 'I have heard of this man. He is said to be amongst the strongest fighters ever to come into this land. It is said also that he has lived in Faery and that he travels with the very creature displayed upon his shield – so fierce is this goat that it has faced the most terrible of adversaries and beaten them. I for one would not fight this knight without others to help me.'

When they heard this, the Round Table knights began calling for their horses and armour – each one determined to be the first to bring down this arrogant knight. King Arthur gave them his blessing and commanded that they bring the Knight of the Goat to heel, and return with the queen's handmaiden.

However, things did not fall out as the king

wished. Rather, the first knights to reach the clearing where Gauriel had set up his pavilion were all defeated with such ease that the rest turned back and returned to Camelot the Golden with word of their encounter and the great strength displayed by the Knight of the Goat.

When he heard this, and saw how many of the Fellowship were hurt, King Arthur called together the finest of his company, including Sir Owein, Sir Sagramore, Sir Pettipace and others.

'Clearly this knight is stronger than we supposed,' he said. 'Therefore I propose that we make our way to the place where he resides and undertake to overcome him. Also, the queen herself shall accompany us, since it is her handmaid who is held hostage. I swear that I shall not return to this court until we have overcome the Knight of the Goat!'

So it was that next day a crowd of servants, cooks and courtiers, arrived at the clearing where Gauriel remained, and set up a royal pavilion and other tents for the Round Table knights, only a short distance from his own. When he saw this Gauriel smiled. 'I believe that this king is responding to my challenge,' he said, while in his heart he wondered if his former love was indeed watching him through her arts, and knew of the task he had undertaken.

Soon, the king and queen, along with many of the Round Table knights, arrived. When all were present, King Arthur addressed them. 'Remember to be courteous to this knight who challenges us, nor to forget that he may have the strength of magic about him. Also be aware of the goat that attends him, for we have heard that it is a fearsome creature. Lastly, since it is the queen's handmaiden who is held hostage, let each of you ask your lady a blessing before you undertake any battle.'

To this all agreed, and set about preparing

themselves, strengthened by Queen Guinevere's blessing. The first to encounter Gauriel was a knight named Sir Karident. Having challenged the Knight of the Goat, he rode against him, but was swiftly unhorsed and left wounded upon the ground. The second knight was a grim fellow called Brantriver, who was seldom seen to smile, unless it was when a church was set on fire or a man fell dead with blood spurting from his helm. He lasted but two jousts with Gauriel before the latter struck him such a blow that his soul left his body in that moment.

After this, several more knights came against him, each one defeated with little effort. As night began to fall the king called a halt to the encounters and all retired. But though the queen's handmaid asked yet again if Gauriel would release her, he refused. 'Only when one of these knights defeats me, shall you be set free.'

And so the next day dawned and this time some of the greatest knights challenged Gauriel. Amongst them were Sir Palomides, Sir Dodinel le Sauvage, Sir Lanval, and Sir Griflet le Fils le Do. Once again, the ugly knight defeated all-comers, while Gauriel's shield was not even dented, and though he broke many spears he was never once unhorsed. As the day progressed the king and queen watched with ever greater concern, as knight after knight was either defeated or slain, while Gauriel continued unhurt and seemed unconcerned by the attacks of the Round Table heroes. He did not even trouble to capture the knights he overcame, but left them lying where they fell, alive or dead, and returned to his tent. This was seen as a further insult to all of the Round Table Fellowship, as well as to King Arthur and Queen Guinevere.

✛ ✛ ✛

IT HAPPENED THAT several of the greatest knights of the Fellowship were absent from the court at this time, but when three days had passed without any sign of Gauriel tiring, two of them arrived. These were Sir Gawain, the king's nephew and Sir Owein, the Knight of the Lion who, when they heard how things went with the Fellowship, requested of the king that they be allowed to challenge the Knight of the Goat.

Arthur gladly gave them permission, and after some discussion Gawain was the first to meet Gauriel. The battle between them was so powerful that all who witnessed it declared that they had never seen such a contest. Both men fought long and hard, first on horseback and then on foot, until Gawain's sword was struck from his hand – and since his opponent gave him no opportunity to retrieve it, Gawain was forced to surrender himself to the Knight of the Goat. The latter invited him to return with him to his pavilion, and there he received attention to his wounds from the queen's handmaiden, who was skilled in the healing arts.

The two men exchanged words, and Gauriel confessed that he had never met another knight who came so close to besting him. In return, Gawain did his best to persuade the Knight of the Goat to allow the battles to cease. But Gauriel responded only that he had come there with the intent of defeating every Round Table knight who came against him; nor would he consider ending the situation by returning the queen's lady to her.

'Then,' said Gawain, 'I warn you that an even greater fighter than I, Sir Owein by name, shall face you on the morrow, and may God help you then.'

At this moment Sir Owein's page arrived at Gauriel's tent and gave him a message that his master would indeed meet with him and that at his side would be the beast that had earned him the title the Knight of the Lion, and that he wished for the Knight of the Goat to bring the creature that journeyed with him, so that it should be knight upon knight and beast upon beast.

To this Gauriel assented willingly, also requesting the page to tell King Arthur that Sir Gawain lived and was well, but that he remained a prisoner until such time as the Knight of the Goat was beaten, or chose to release the king's nephew out of respect for his prowess.

So it was that on the morrow, Sir Owein, accompanied by his lion, took the field while Gauriel did the same, together with the mighty goat who had been the gift of the Lady Fatuse. Its coat was full and curled around its body, and its horns were covered in gold that shone and glittered in the sunlight.

Now Owein and Gauriel saluted each other and fell to with a will. Owein, rarely beaten in any battle, held his own, but eventually began to tire, while next to the men the two creatures fought against each other.

The roaring and bellowing of the two beasts was such that it almost drowned out the clash of sword on sword as the two knights battled. The lion's claws wrought dreadful damage to the goat, while the goat's horns opened up deep wounds in the lion. To this day men recall the battle between them – so unlike anything seen in those lands in that far-off time. But mighty as the lion was, it had little chance against the goat, which being of Faery was imbued with unearthly strength. After a time the lion let forth a terrible cry and fell dead. Hearing this, Sir Owein faltered in his own battle, overwhelmed by the death of his friend. But anger quickly replaced sorrow, and with a roar of rage he leapt away from Gauriel and delivered such a blow to the goat that it too fell dead.

Now both men were driven to fury at the deaths of their companions. They fell to with renewed ferocity, and Sir Owein began to gain ground. Then, as he struck blow after blow upon his opponent, suddenly his sword shattered, so that he was left unarmed. Just as he had with Sir Gawain, Gauriel demanded that Owein surrender to him. This the great knight was forced to do, and as King Arthur and the court looked on, he was led away to the Knight of the Goat's pavilion.

Now King Arthur himself could restrain himself no longer, but called for his armour and weapons and his great warhorse. Despite the wishes of the queen and the courtiers, the king rode out into the meadow, ready to challenge the Knight of the Goat to combat. But when he saw that it was King Arthur himself who came, Gauriel took off his armour and laid his weapons aside. Then he rode out bareheaded and unarmed to meet the king.

'Sire, I cannot and will not fight with you,' he said. 'I have tested the bravery of your knights and though I have been victorious I can only praise their worth and their chivalry. To you, my lord, I give praise, for in all my life I have never heard of a king so worthy of honour.'

King Arthur looked askance at the ravaged face of his adversary. 'You have done me great disservice,' he answered. 'Not only have you slain several of my knights and now hold others captive, you have refused to grant freedom to the maiden you hold hostage.'

'I deny nothing that you say,' replied Gauriel. 'And I ask your forgiveness. All that I have done is in service of one I cannot name, or otherwise make mention of. For this I make no excuse, but I swear that I will release these great knights and also the queen's handmaiden at once. All I ask is that you forgive me and allow me to be a service to you.'

At this King Arthur spoke more gently. 'I will do as you ask, for in truth I have never seen such strength in battle as you have displayed, nor have you failed to uphold the qualities of chivalry. Therefore, if you do as you have said, and providing that the queen forgives you, then there shall be peace between us.'

To this Gauriel agreed and, accompanied by the king, Sir Gawain, and Sir Owein, as well as the handmaiden, they returned to where the rest of the court awaited. There, Gauriel begged forgiveness from the queen who, once she had heard from her lady that no harm or dishonour had come to her, also forgave the Knight of the Goat.

So it was that after the two mighty beasts had been laid to rest, and suitably mourned, the whole party returned to Camelot the Golden, and Gauriel went with them.

Once they had returned to the city King Arthur invited the Knight of the Goat to become a member of the Round Table. But to the wonder of everyone, he refused. 'Sire, I am greatly honoured by this, and were I able to do so I would gladly accept your invitation. But I am duty-bound to another, and until I have earned her forgiveness I may do nothing else but seek to prove myself, even as I have done here against your knights.'

Nor would he alter his decision to go in search of further adventures, agreeing only with reluctance to remain at Camelot the Golden for a week, so that his wounds could be searched and healed. For in truth, as the story tells, he had received many such in his great battles with the Round Table knights, though nothing compared to those he had given them!

✠ ✠ ✠

AT THE END of this time, King Arthur again asked Gauriel if he would join the Round Table Fellowship, to which the knight replied that he must first of all seek further trials but, that if he received again the blessing of she in whose service he lived, he would return and stay at King Arthur's court for a year.

With this the king and queen had to be content, and soon after, Gauriel departed. With him went, with the king's permission, Sir Owein, for he and Gauriel, each mourning the loss of the lion and the goat, had become friends.

So they set off together, and the story tells that they undertook many adventures together, until at last Gauriel received a message from Fatuse requesting him to meet with her at the border of her kingdom. This he did, and was welcomed with great joy.

'You have more than proved yourself worthy of my love,' said the faery. 'You have my leave to return to my land and to dwell with me once more.'

At this Gauriel knew such joy that it seemed his heart would burst, but then he spoke to the Lady Fatuse gently and told her of the promise he had made to King Arthur, to return to Camelot the Golden and remain there as part of the Fellowship for a year. When she heard this the faery gave him her consent. 'For,' she said, 'you have learned that the life of a chivalrous knight must find a balance between love and service, and that the giving of a word is not to be broken. And thus all disagreements between us are ended, and I give you freedom to come and go from my lands and my person as you wish.'

Then she called her women and instructed them to care for Gauriel before he set forth for King Arthur's court. And especially she asked that he be bathed and given healing potions, and that he should be treated with a certain salve which, when applied to his face, smoothed out the lines and disfigurements that had made him appear ugly, so that he once again recovered his looks and took upon himself the likeness of a handsome man.

After this, he took leave of Fatuse and the faery court and made his way to Camelot the Golden, where all welcomed him gladly and praised him for his prowess. Thereafter, for a year, he became part of the Round Table Fellowship and rode with them in search of adventure and wrongs to right. In all that time all agreed that save for Sir Lancelot, Sir Gawain and Sir Tristan, there had never been such a brave and powerful knight in all that company.

At the year's end, despite all the regrets, both of King Arthur, Queen Guinevere, and all of the knights, especially Sir Owein, Gauriel declared that he must return home to the land of the Flowering Throne and his faery wife.

But before he could depart there came word of the approach of a most wonderful company.

There, led by the faery Fatuse at the head of her own most honoured people, the Court of Faery came to the Court of Men in peace and harmony, despite the many years of strife between them. And there the knight Gauriel renewed his vows to the Lady Fatuse and the most splendid celebration took place. Not even the court of Camelot the Golden could match the splendour of the Flowering Throne, for with its lady came, at her command, a company of the People of the Sea, who came ashore from the ocean and set before all the most glorious feast ever seen, even in that place of richness and plenty.

Amongst the Lady Fatuse's retinue were many who came from Faery. Some had horns, others were part beast, while the merfolk themselves were clad in scales. Beings with eyes like cats were there, and even one that was so tall it could only be counted as a giant. Another had bones that glowed with a fierce light so that they shone through its skin; while there were

✦ *Retinue of the Lady Fatuse* ✦

others that had several sets of eyes, or teeth that were more like tusks. All of these and more came to the meadows below the walls of Camelot the Golden, and a most wondrous camp grew up there throughout the time of the celebration.

There were many old quarrels forgotten, and the two courts came together in friendship. And if there were times when the people of Camelot the Golden were amazed at the appearance of their guests, they quickly hid their wonderment and greeted all with grace and kindness.

So the great celebration continued, and then Gauriel and the Lady Fatuse pledged themselves to each other once again, amid much rejoicing. After which the great company of Faery departed, and he who had been called the Knight of the Goat went with them. But ever after, he returned to the realm of King Arthur whenever he felt the desire for adventure, and the border between the worlds remained open for many years – though it is said in other tales that this was not always so, and that there was still much animosity between King Arthur and those of the faery realm. Of that I shall speak no more at this time, but ask only that the name of Sir Gauriel should not be forgotten, nor his time in the world of men cease to be celebrated. And thus I end my tale.

———— ✝ ————

EXPLICIT THE TALE OF GAURIEL AND THE FAERY.

INCIPIT THAT OF WIGAMUR, KNIGHT OF THE EAGLE.

22: WIGAMUR, KNIGHT OF THE EAGLE

OF ALL THE MANY TALES OF THE ROUND TABLE THAT I HAVE READ AND TOLD HERE, FEW SPEAK OF THE CREATURES THAT DWELL BENEATH THE SEA. THOUGH MANY CHRONICLE THE WAY THE PEOPLE OF FAERY CAME OFTEN INTO THE REALM OF KING ARTHUR, WHEN THE LADY DANCED UPON THE GREENSWARD, FEW MENTION THOSE WHO CAME OUT OF THE SEA AND PLAYED THEIR PARTS IN THE WONDERS SURROUNDING THE COURT OF CAMELOT THE GOLDEN. IT IS MY BELIEF THAT, HAD MASTER THOMAS MALORY FOUND THIS STORY, THAT HE WOULD HAVE INCLUDED IT IN HIS MASTERLY BOOK OF KING ARTHUR – BUT IT SEEMS, AS I HAVE DISCOVERED IN MY SEARCH FOR MORE OF THESE TALES, THAT MANY COMING OUT OF THE GERMAN LANDS DID NOT FIND THEIR WAY TO BRITAIN. SUCH IS THE TALE I NOW TELL, WHICH SPEAKS OF A KNIGHT OF PEERLESS COURAGE AND GENTLENESS, A WORTHY HERO OF THE ROUND TABLE FELLOWSHIP, WHOSE NAME IS LESS OFTEN SPOKEN THAN THAT OF PERCEVAL, GAWAIN, OR LANCELOT, BUT WHOSE WORTHINESS IS BEYOND DOUBT.

✣ ✣ ✣

IN THE TIME of King Arthur, many kings were invited to come to Camelot the Golden, or to Carduil, as well as other great cities that flourished in this time. Amongst these to whom the king sent letters asking them to attend upon him, was one named Paltriot, who, together with his wife, a fair and lovely woman, ruled over the Kingdom of Landry, which lay far to the west of Britain. When he received the letter

from King Arthur this lord at once set out with a company of his best knights, and with his lady the queen at his side. Their son, recently born and named Wigamur, was left behind in the care of the queen's ladies.

So it came about that the child's fate was sealed, for at this time there lived in a cave by the shore of the great sea a Wildwoman whom many called a mermaid. Fair was she,

↣ *The mermaid Lespia* ↤

but her body was covered in scales and her fingers webbed. Also she was able to breathe beneath the water.

Her story was a sad one. Her husband had been killed by a terrible Sea-Wight, more fish than man, that also lived beneath the waters. This left the mermaid, whose name was Lespia, alone with two children, girls, who did not share her scaled appearance and whom she longed to raise so that they could take their place in the world of men. Yet she knew that their origin would work against them, since to most of humankind she was known as 'The Sea Devil'! So it was that she thought of a means by which she could accomplish her dream – by stealing a human child she could marry to one of her daughters when all three were fully grown.

By evil fortune this brought great sorrow upon King Paltriot and his wife, for Lespia's attention fell upon the baby Wigamur, and seeing her opportunity while the royal party were in far distant Camelot the Golden, she crept at night into the castle where the king's family dwelled, and stole the baby away. Only one woman in the castle saw what she did, happening to look out of a window in time to see the Wildwoman hastening away with the babe.

So it was, that when King Paltriot and the queen returned at last from King Arthur's feast, they were met by weeping women who told them how their child was taken. Enraged, King Paltriot, who was himself a doughty warrior, at once ordered a search to be made. But though his knights and soldiers sought for long weeks far across the realm, especially along the shoreline where the Sea Devil was believed to live, they found no sign of either the stolen infant or his captor.

In the end the king and queen came to believe they had lost their son for ever, and as the years passed and the queen gave birth to no more children, the royal couple grew to accept that they would never see their son again.

Meanwhile, the Wildwoman from the sea cared for the infant Wigamur with all the love and gentleness she lavished upon her daughters, so that the boy grew towards manhood believing himself Lespia's child, and the two girls his sisters. Together they lived in a series of great caves that overlooked the sea, hidden from the eyes of men. There, whenever Lespia left them alone, she rolled a stone across the entrance, so that none could enter or depart, for always she feared the presence of the Sea-Wight.

So matters might have stood, and no one may say what path Wigamur's life might have taken, but a day came when everything changed. Always the mermaid sought to avenge herself upon the Sea-Wight, and kept watch for him daily. And it happened that one day, as she swam out to sea, she caught sight of the creature, and using an enchanted rope, caught and contained him. She brought him back to the caves and bound him fast in a cavern from which she made sure he could not escape, binding him with spells and enchantments. Then, warning the frightened children to be alert and on no account to leave their own cave, she set off for the Great Wood. There, her two wild brothers lived among the trees, and with their help she planned to destroy the Sea-Wight.

Now it happened that King Paltriot himself went hunting on that day, and as he rode through the forest in search of prey, he caught sight of the Wildwoman, her scales glinting in the sun, hastening in search of her brothers. At once the king and his companions gave chase and, fleet-footed though the mermaid was, the hunters' steeds were faster, and soon one of them loosed an arrow that pierced their quarry's leg, so that she fell to the earth unable to run further.

Triumphantly, the king ordered her held and brought back to the castle, where she was questioned regarding the missing child. At first the mermaid would say nothing, but the king ordered her to be whipped and showed her the gallows upon which she would soon be hung.

'If you have cared for my son all this time, and if you tell me where to find him, you shall be set free,' said the king. 'But if you have harmed him in any way, or keep silent as to his whereabouts, then you shall suffer death upon the scaffold.'

Lespia, fearful not so much for her own life but those of her daughters and Wigamur, fell at the king's feet and told him the whole story – how she had sought to bring her own children into the world of men by marrying one to the king's own son. Then she told him where the caves in which she had lived all her life were, and where Wigamur and her daughters were to be found.

At once the king and his men set forth, bringing Lespia with them, bound in shackles of steel. Soon enough they reached the secret cave and the mermaid opened the way for them. But a terrible sight awaited them within, for the mermaid's two daughters lay dead in their own blood and of the king's son there was no sign.

When she saw this Lespia knew at once that the Sea-Wight had somehow broken his bonds and escaped the spells she had placed upon him, and when she looked upon her dead children a terrible cry escaped her and before any of the king's men could stop her, she ran from the cave and seizing a piece of rock from the shore, dashed it against her own head so that she fell dead.

Then the king wept, believing the Sea-Wight had either killed his son or taken him beyond the reach of any human. But though the sea creature had indeed carried off Wigamur to the place beneath the sea where he dwelled, he had not killed him. Instead, by his arts, he caused the youth to be able to breathe under water, and so made him a new home on the floor of the sea.

✠ ✠ ✠

TIME PASSED AND Wigamur grew to manhood. Very beautiful he was, and fair of face. The Sea-Wight cared well for him and during their time on land trained him in archery and as far as he was able the ways of men. But the creature's knowledge of the world above was not as great as he believed, so that while Wigamur could throw a spear and shoot an arrow he did not learn how to ride a horse or to converse with others.

At length the day came when the Sea-Wight knew that he must return the human youth to the world above, for with every day that passed he grew more restless and sorrowful. He asked Wigamur if he remembered the mermaid and what he felt about her. The youth responded that he had always believed her to be his mother, and her children his sisters. Then the Sea-Wight told him the truth – that he was of human stock, and had been stolen away by Lespia, from where he knew not. 'Thus I saved you from her wiles,' said the Sea-Wight. 'Now it is time for you to go above the water and make your own way in the world. Maybe you will discover your true parentage and be reunited with those from whom you were stolen away.'

Wigamur had no memory of his father or mother or of the kingdom they ruled over. But once he had heard the story from his foster-father he longed to go in search of his true lineage. Thus he set forth from the Sea-Wight's dwelling and walked upon the land for the first time. In his hand he carried a bow, and at his back a quiver of arrows, while his clothing was made entirely of fish skin, which gleamed in the light of day so that he seemed as though clad in a rainbow.

For several days he walked, looking with wonder at all he saw, until he came upon an army of knights who were about to lay siege to a castle. Knowing nothing of such ways, and having never seen mortal men before, Wigamur approached them. As he drew near, they stared in wonder at the beautiful youth, clad in strange rainbow clothing. Then they ignored him, having other work to be about.

Wigamur followed behind the company, speaking to no one. Soon they reached the walls of the castle and began their attack. Those within fought back bravely, and many men died on both sides. So much blood was spilled that Wigamur marvelled at the way the earth turned red. He watched as the two sides fought and died, until at last the attacking force breached the gate of the castle and pushed inside. Then began an even greater slaughter, and soon the attackers set fire to the castle, which began to burn. Then, content with their spoils and filled with the harsh joy of battle and victory, they rode away.

Wigamur watched them depart and wondered greatly. 'If these are men,' he said, 'I wonder if they always behave in this way.'

Then he went inside the castle and saw many dead knights and broken walls from which bitter smoke arose. There Wigamur found a horse, ready saddled and bridled, which had somehow escaped death, and seeing this he turned to where the body of a knight lay who was similar to himself in height. With difficulty, he removed his blood-stained armour and clumsily dressed himself in it. Then he sought out a sword amongst the wreckage of the battle, and was thus fully armed. Next he climbed onto the back of the stallion, though he had little idea how to ride, and let the beast find its own way. And both were relieved to escape from the smoke-laden air and the walls of the ruined castle.

Without guidance the steed took its own way, and gradually Wigamur began to sit straighter in the saddle and to understand how he could urge the beast on with his heels and steer it with the reins.

So it was that a knight of that country, named Glakoteles de Loir, spied the strange figure riding clumsily and clad in bloodied armour. Puzzled, he galloped closer, until Wigamur's mount, being trained in all matters of war, itself began to charge towards what it saw as an opponent.

Wigamur was almost thrown by the fury of his mount's charge, and had to hold on to the saddlebow with both hands. When Glakoteles saw that he could scarcely ride, he reined in his own steed and dismounted, drawing his sword.

'You there, come down from your horse and fight me!'

Wigamur stared at him in puzzlement. 'Why should I wish to do that?'

'Because it is what knights do,' thundered Glakoteles.

'But I am no knight,' answered Wigamur. 'I took this armour from a dead man in the castle I saw attacked, and the horse was standing by, so I climbed on its back. Alas,' he added, 'I have no knowledge of how to ride as you do.'

Astounded by all of this, Glakoteles nonetheless repeated his demand for battle, and Wigamur dismounted and drew his sword. Then they rushed together, and for a time the air rang with the sound of sword striking sword.

At length, despite knowing little of the art of swordplay, Wigamur struck his opponent such a blow upon the helm that he fell to the earth. Wigamur stood over his foe and it seemed that he would give him his death. But Glakoteles cried mercy and said: 'Sir, if you allow me to live I shall be your liegeman for ever.'

'What is a liegeman?' asked Wigamur, sheathing his sword and standing back.

'It means one who promises to serve another hereafter. In return for granting me my life, I offer this to you.'

'I shall spare you,' said Wigamur. 'But I need no man to be my servant.' Then he asked: 'Just

→ *The Sea-Wight* ←

now I saw many men attacking the castle that lies over that hill. Despite the efforts of the defenders, the castle fell and was burned to the ground. Can you tell me why this should be?'

Glakoteles stood up, helped by Wigamur.

'The castle belonged to the Lord of Pontrafort. He plagued these lands for many years, attacking those who live about here and despoiling them of life and goods. It is welcome that the King of Doloyer, whose men you saw, decided to rid the country of this evil man, and as you saw, he was successful.'

Wigamur gave thanks to the knight and the two men clasped hands and went their separate ways. Wigamur, however, felt a compulsion to return to the ruined castle. He could not say what it was that took him there, but when he arrived he saw again the bodies left for the crows and wild animals and smelled the bitter reek of burning that hung over all. He noticed that the gatehouse was more or less intact, and having explored it found there was sufficient shelter for both himself and his horse. He then set out to explore what remained of the castle.

Scarcely had he begun to do so than he found a maiden sitting alone amid the ruins. She seemed unhurt but tears ran down her cheeks and her clothing was stained with soot from the fire.

'Who are you?' asked Wigamur.

The maiden started with fear as she raised her eyes and saw the armed man. But Wigamur removed his helmet and looked gently at her, so that her fear left her.

'I am called Pioles,' she answered.

'Why are you so sad?' asked Wigamur.

'Can you not see?' asked the maiden, raising her hands towards the ruins. 'This was my home until yesterday. Now all is lost. The man I was destined to marry lies dead, and I have nowhere to go.'

'I am sorry to hear this,' answered Wigamur. 'Perhaps we may help each other? I cannot get out of this armour or take the saddle from my horse, for both are strange to me.'

The maiden named Pioles looked at him in wonder. Despite her sorrow, she smiled at the handsome youth and lent her fingers to unfastening his armour and helping him to unsaddle his horse and remove its bridle. Then the two of them went into the gatehouse together, stabling the horse there, before climbing the stairs to where there was a small room in which they could take their rest. They even found food and drink and were able to satisfy their hunger.

After this, they talked for a while into the night, exchanging stories of their lives. Pioles listened in wonder at Wigamur's tale of his life beneath the sea, and why he knew so little of the ways of men, such as how to put on armour or ride a noble steed.

At length they fell asleep beside each other, and in the morning Wigamur declared his intention of seeking help for the maiden. With her assistance he dressed again in his borrowed mail and saddled and bridled the horse. Then he set off quickly into the forest, leaving Pioles standing sadly at the entrance to the ruined castle – believing in her heart that she would never see him again.

In this she was proved wrong. For after riding for several hours without meeting anyone, the youth spied a pheasant, which he shot with his bow. Then he returned to the castle again and that evening the youth and the maiden ate well of the bird, along with bread Pioles had found in the ruins, washed down with water for wine. Despite all that had occurred, they were merry enough that night, and once again slept close to each other in the room above the gatehouse.

Next morning Wigamur set forth again and

having begun to understand better how to ride, made good speed. He continued on until he came to where an ancient, moss-grown castle stood. As he approached the entrance to the place he saw coming towards him a dwarf, dressed in magnificent livery, who greeted him pleasantly and asked to know why he came there. Wigamur explained the story of the siege and his discovery of the maiden Pioles, whose champion he had become. Then he begged the dwarf to find food both for himself and the maiden.

At first the dwarf hesitated, then, having recognised the honesty and gentleness of the young man, bade him wait outside the castle walls while he fetched victuals. Soon he returned with cold chicken, bread and wine, which he willingly gave to Wigamur. Then he told the youth his own story. His master, who lived within the castle, was an evil lord named Lespurant, who had forced himself on the lady of the castle, Dame Ligronite, following the death of her husband. Taking over the castle, he had made himself lord of that country, imprisoned the lady and her children, and from there onwards showed himself a tyrant, leading his men out to raid and pillage the surrounding lands.

'Now he is the most feared lord in the region,' said the dwarf mournfully. 'My lady is filled with sorrow but dares do nothing to oppose Lespurant for fear of her children's lives.'

When he heard this, Wigamur was filled with anger towards this lawless lord, and pledged to return and set right the wrong done by Lespurant as soon as he had taken food and drink to the maiden Pioles.

Leaving the dwarf full of hope that the noble youth would fulfil his promise, Wigamur returned to the burned-out castle and told the maiden all that he had learned. When she heard the tale of the Lady Ligronite, Pioles grew pale.

'But she is my sister!' she cried, and told Wigamur that Lespurant had himself been a close ally of the Lord of Pontrafort, and that together they had exerted a reign of terror over the surrounding lands. When he heard this Wigamur grew silent. Then he told the maiden of his promise to the dwarf that he would return and do all in his power to defeat Lespurant. 'It seems this is my destiny,' he said. 'Let us go together to your sister's castle, so that I may deal with this evil lord.'

So the two set off next day and soon arrived at the castle, where the dwarf came out to meet them. When he saw the maiden Pioles he wept, recognising her as the sister of his mistress.

'It is my intention to make an end to this Lespurant,' Wigamur declared. 'How can I gain entrance to the castle without alerting the guards?'

'That is easy,' replied the dwarf. 'I know a secret way within. Do but follow me and I will show you the way.'

Thus it fell out that when darkness fell Wigamur gained entrance to the castle and followed the dwarf to the very chamber where Lespurant slept. There Wigamur crept inside and taking out his sword slew the evil lord as he slept.

(You may think this was an unchivalrous thing to do, but I would answer that in those days the custom was not as it is now, and I would bid you remember that Wigamur had been raised in ignorance of the ways of men, so that to him the deed was no cause for shame, but was rather a fitting end to the tyrant.)

So it was that in the morning the evil lord's followers learned of the death of their master, and found Wigamur seated in the central hall of the castle, with his drawn sword resting upon his knees. The grimness of his look caused them to acknowledge him as their new master. Indeed, many were loyal still to the Lady Ligronite, who now came forth with her sons, filled with joy at the ending of her imprisonment and declaring herself forever grateful to Wigamur. When she saw her sister the two women embraced and wept with joy to be reunited and freed from the possession of both tyrannical lords.

The Lady Ligronite, indeed, begged Wigamur to remain there and become the lord of her lands. She had seen how Pioles was drawn to the youth and thought that they might be wed and rule over the two kingdoms together.

But Wigamur shook his head. 'My lady,' he said. 'I am but a poor unknown man, without lands or title. It would be unworthy of me to lay claim to either of your lands – or indeed,' he added, smiling at the maiden Pioles, 'to venture to become the husband of this gentle lady. I have far to go in search of my heritage and, if fortune favours me, to discover my family.'

Despite the pleading of both women Wigamur took his leave soon after, promising to return when he had discovered his true identity. So he set forth again upon the road and soon after experienced another adventure which was destined to bring him closer to achieving his wish to know his true lineage.

⊹ ⊹ ⊹

WHEN HE HAD been upon the road but a few days Wigamur came to a place that was of such beauty that he marvelled at it. Lush green meadows spread out upon every side, trees with leaves that seemed made of pure gold cast patterns of light upon the earth, streams of pure water threading gentle hills, and everywhere there was the song of birds. Filled with wonder, and thinking that perhaps he had strayed into the land of Faery, he rode on until he saw where a mighty castle stood, many pennants fluttering from its towers. As he approached, a company rode out to meet him. At its head was a man of great strength and beauty, his hair curling about his shoulders and his complexion that of an ageless man. He bade Wigamur welcome with great kindness and invited him to attend him within the castle. This Wigamur did and his host made him welcome and asked him where he came from and what he sought.

'I am come from the sea,' answered the youth.

'What brings you here?' asked the noble man.

'I am in search of my heritage, and my family.'

Then he found himself telling his host all of his story – of the Wildwoman Lespia and the Sea-Wight, and all that had occurred since he stepped onto the land. He spoke of his need to discover his true parentage and all that went with it. But most of all that he might learn how to live among men and perhaps, in time, become a knight.

His host smiled. 'Stay here for as long as you wish. And if it please you to learn more of our way of life, it would be my pleasure to teach you. Once, many years since, I was host to King Arthur himself. I am his uncle, brother to his father King Uther, and after the youth became king by pulling the Sword from the Stone, it became my task to teach him as I will now teach you. For there is that about you that I feel is of noble origin and deserves to be brought forth.'

Thus Wigamur came to dwell in the castle of Lord Ettra, who declared himself uncle to King Arthur himself. This I find to be of utmost interest, for nowhere in Sir Thomas Malory's book is there mention of this man, though I have often wondered how, once he was no longer in the household of Sir Ector de Maris, the young king learned to be such a skilful warrior.

So it was that Wigamur began to be trained in the arts of war, chivalry and of courtly life. Those who came to know him found him courteous, gentle, and wise beyond his years, and soon learned that he was a strong and able fighter, who quickly learned to wield both sword and lance better than many of the young men training to be knights. He also learned how to ride and hunt with the best of the Lord Ettra's men. Nor did his host neglect the arts of music, dancing, and how to behave in the company of women, so that Wigamur soon lost his shyness and learned to converse with the maidens and ladies of the castle as well as any man there. Indeed, so handsome was he that many sought his company, but always he thought only of discovering his true family, and refused all advances made to him, ever protesting that he was unworthy of anything until he knew his rightful name.

Time passed and Wigamur grew stronger and proficient in the ways of courtly life. But always he felt the need to prove himself, and to discover the secret of his birth. At last he declared his desire to go forth in search of adventure, and while the Lord Ettra felt keenly that the youth he had grown to regard almost as his own son was still untried in the ways of the world, yet he knew also that it was wrong to hold him back from his quest.

So, on a day in the spring, Wigamur was made a knight, and at that time Ettra said to him: 'One thing you must promise me. When you are ready, journey to Camelot the Golden and present yourself to King Arthur. For if ever I saw a knight who should sit at the Round Table, it is you.'

And though his modesty prevented Wigamur from believing his host's words, yet there grew within him from that day a longing to see the High King's city.

✠ ✠ ✠

SO IT CAME about, as the newly knighted Wigamur rode in search of adventure, that he came to a wide valley, and heard a mighty clamour that echoed from all sides. Before him he saw a scene which caused him great sorrow. A vulture had fallen like a dark cloud upon an eagle's nest, and while the eagle was hunting had torn apart her three chicks. Too late to save them, the mighty bird attacked the dark vulture, her golden feathers bright against the shadowy plumes of the larger bird. Wigamur came upon them as they fought and he saw at once that the eagle, powerful though it was, was being driven down by the vulture. At once he unslung his bow, nocked an arrow to the string and shot the vulture through the heart. The dead bird struck the ground nearby and the eagle, screaming her defiance, flew back to her nest, sending forth terrible cries of sorrow at the broken bodies of her chicks.

Then a strange thing happened. The eagle flew back up into the sky and began to circle the young knight. Closer and closer the great bird came until he could see her golden eye staring at him. For a moment he believed she would attack, but instead the bird came to rest in a nearby tree and remained looking at him intently. Several times she cried, but gently, not like the furious screams of anguish and fury over the death of her offspring and her attack on the vulture.

Now, when Wigamur urged his mount forward, the eagle took off and continued to keep pace with the knight, never approaching too close but always keeping him in sight. All that day the golden bird followed him, and when night began to fall and Wigamur prepared to sleep beneath the stars, the eagle roosted in a grove of trees, while the knight took shelter under their canopy through the hours of darkness.

And so it was from there onwards. Wherever Wigamur went the eagle accompanied him. Soon he began to share his food with it. Even his horse, though nervous at first, grew used to the bird's presence.

So, as Wigamur began to encounter adventures along the way, the bird was always with him. Sometimes it flew down and attacked his adversaries, at others it simply stayed near him, watching as he fought other knights he encountered, or joined in tournaments, where he quickly proved his growing skill with sword and lance. So it was that in time people began to call him the Knight of the Eagle.

The story tells how he went about in the wildlands, seeking wrongs to right and helping those in need. And in this time he learned more of the ways of men, and proved himself a mighty warrior, while yet being a gentle and noble man. His reputation began to spread throughout Britain, until it came to the ears of King Arthur himself. The king sent forth messengers in search of the young knight, inviting him to come to Camelot the Golden. For a long time there was no response, but then on a day in spring Wigamur arrived in the great city and came before Arthur. All stared in wonder as the young knight entered the hall, accompanied by the faithful eagle, which flew to perch on the back of a seat and stared fiercely at those gathered there.

King Arthur welcomed the knight and said: 'We have heard your name spoken in many places, and have learned of your deeds. Surely, you should have a place at our Round Table.'

But to the wonder of all who were present, the young knight shook his head. 'My lord King. You do me the greatest honour, but I cannot accept your offer. Though I long to join your Fellowship, I am unworthy to do so. I know nothing of my history or even of my family. Now I am made knight by the kindness of the noble Lord Ettra, yet it may be that I am unworthy of this. Until I know what I am and from where I come, I do not dare join the great company I see here.'

Then the king looked on him kindly.

'Never have I heard such words from any knight who has come to this court,' he said. 'Whatever your origin may be, I cannot believe you are other than of noble lineage. For such is your gentleness and your honourable nature, it seems to me that you are more than fit to be seated here. And if my uncle has indeed chosen you to train as he once trained me, then I know that you are well prepared for whatever may transpire. And even more do I believe you shall one day sit at the Round Table.'

Wigamur bowed his head. 'Great lord, if you have a task that I may undertake in your name, then I beg you to give it to me. Perhaps in this way I may earn a place in this court.'

King Arthur nodded. 'It shall be as you wish, Sir Knight,' he said. 'Take your place at one of the lower tables and whoever comes in search of help next, that task shall be yours.'

✛ ✛ ✛

THAT EVENING, AS the court was preparing to dine, a large party of knights and ladies was seen approaching the gates of

Camelot the Golden. So splendid were they that more than half the court and many of the Round Table knights hastened to the walls to observe them.

Foremost came a lady of imperious beauty, whom many recognised as Isopi, the Queen of Holdrafluos, famed for her generosity to all and for the splendour of her court. Accompanying her were a dozen fair ladies, dressed in the most wonderful silks, their horses decked out in coats of samite threaded with gold and hung with tiny silver bells that rang sweetly as they rode. All were peerless beauties, and more than one young knight sighed at the sight of them. Also in the rich company were two dozen knights, their armour reflecting the sun and their mounts armed with chest plates and face pieces that glittered in the light.

Together this wondrous party arrived before the gates and were at once admitted and made welcome. The Queen of Holdrafluos entered first and was greeted warmly by Queen Guinevere and King Arthur himself. Tables were set ready and many of the visiting knights and ladies joined the company of the Round Table and were served with the finest food on plates of gold and wine in crystal goblets.

Never, the story says, did a fairer and more splendid company sit down together. Queen Isopi was seated next to King Arthur and once the feast was done she spoke of her reason for coming.

'A wild and heathen king, whose name is Marroch, King of Sarazein, is threatening to invade my lands. He has already attacked and burned several castles on the borders of my country. Now he moves closer to my chief city. He seeks to force me to marry him so that he may become Lord of Holdrafluos, but I would rather die than agree to this. His army is larger than my knights and soldiers can defeat,

therefore I am come here to beg that you, my lord, send out your finest knights to help me defeat this evil king.'

At once King Arthur declared that he would indeed send his greatest knights to aid the Queen of Holdrafluos. Already Sir Gawain, Sir Eric and others cried aloud that they would do all in their power to defend her honour. Now Wigamur came forward and spoke to the king. 'My lord, though I am but a newly made knight, I beg that I may accompany those of the Round Table Fellowship on this task.'

Mindful of his promise, the king gave his consent, and the young knight retired to prepare himself. As ever the eagle was present and both the Queen of Holdrafluos and her ladies looked in astonishment at the great bird, while many also admired the beauty of the young man.

King Arthur himself determined to lead his company against the attacking army. News arrived at this time that told how the forces of King Marroch had arrived at the city of Podogar, which lay in that part of Queen Isopi's kingdom that was bounded by the sea. King Arthur bade Sir Gawain to scout ahead and judge the size of the opposing force. Wigamur accompanied him, along with Duke Unarck, a most powerful knight who was justly famed for his strength and skill on the tournament field.

Together the three knights rode ahead of the king's army, and reaching a hill, observed the camp of the King of Sarazein. Many warriors were there, and many knights bearing shields with unfamiliar devices.

As they watched they saw where three of the opposing force had ridden out and were crossing the flat plain that lay between them.

'These must be scouts,' Sir Gawain said. 'Let us go to meet them.'

The six knights met in the centre of the

plain. The three from the opposing force looked at King Arthur's knights and greeted them arrogantly.

'Do you see that mighty force behind us?' said the leader of the enemy scouts.

'Indeed we do,' answered Sir Gawain courteously. 'We would know why you are here in King Arthur's lands?'

'We are come,' said the knight of Sarazein, who was a prince in his own country, 'to destroy the country ruled over by Queen Isopi. She has refused our master King Marroch, and so we shall burn her castles to the ground and lay waste to all her lands, before taking her by force.'

'You would be advised to turn back,' Sir Gawain answered. 'My lord King Arthur is coming with a great host, and I promise you that soon you and your king will be in flight from our swords.'

In answer, the three nights of King Marroch drew their own weapons and advanced in warlike fashion. Gawain, Wigamur and Unarck did likewise, and the three pairs fell to. Gawain fought the Prince of Sarazein, Wigamur his fellow, and Unarck attacked the last of the three.

None of these were insignificant fighters, but they were no match for the Round Table knights. Gawain swiftly defeated the prince, and Wigamur felled his opponent with ease, while the eagle flew above them screaming out his victory. Duke Unarck, meanwhile, dealt his opponent with such fury that soon he lay on the ground and was like to die.

Then the three knights of Sarazein begged for mercy and this Sir Gawain granted them. 'Return to your king,' he told them. 'Say to him that you are prisoners of King Arthur and that you are bound upon your honour to attend him tomorrow. And say to him, that if he does not wish all his knights to be struck down as you were, he had best return to his own lands – for we are the champions of Queen Isopi.'

So the three beaten knights returned to their camp and told the King of Sarazein all that had occurred. Marroch reacted with fury. 'Our force is powerful enough to overcome this king's knights!' he cried. 'Let us teach these foolish men a lesson!'

Gawain, Wigamur and Unarck meanwhile returned to King Arthur and told him the extent of Marroch's army.

'They must be told that they are not welcome,' said the king, and he commanded a letter to be written which told the Lord of the Sarazein that he should know how a king was expected to behave, and that to force a lady and then to attack her lands was a barbarous act which could not be permitted to go unpunished. 'Go now,' the letter read, 'or expect to feel the wrath of myself and my knights.'

When the letter was brought to Marroch his anger was great. 'Let us show this king and his men what our warriors can do!' he cried.

The following morning the two great forces came against each other and for a while no other sound was heard but the clamour of sword upon sword and the cries of the wounded and dying. The army of Sarazein was strong and its warriors skilled in battle, but against the chivalry of the Round Table they were as nothing. On each side doughty heroes fought against one another. King Arthur himself fought as bravely as any man, despite receiving wounds, while Sir Gawain did many brave deeds, and Sir Wigamur cut a swathe through his adversaries, leaving many dead or wounded behind him. With him flew the eagle, employing talons and beak to savage effect.

The enemy fell back before him, until at last he faced a single figure – none other than King Marroch himself. The young knight attacked and was soon victorious. In the end he seized the bridle of the king's horse and led him from the field.

Thus was the invading force beaten, and King Marroch captured. When he stood at last before King Arthur, chained and broken, he agreed not only to pay a great sum of gold to Queen Isopi in reparation for the sorrow and death he had brought to her people, but also swore an oath that he would never enter her lands again, or offer harm to anyone from her court. Lastly he was forced to swear allegiance to King Arthur.

Thus was the war between the two lands ended and never again did the Sarazein enter Britain. Of all who fought in the battle, Wigamur was singled out by the king for special praise, while Queen Isopi offered him great riches by way of reward, even offering him the crown of her kingdom together with her hand in marriage if he so desired.

Once again the Knight of the Eagle protested that he was but a humble stranger without a name, lands, or family, and that only if he could discover these would he accept any reward for his accomplishments. Then he declared his wish, with King Arthur's permission, to continue his quest.

✟ ✟ ✟

THUS MATTERS STOOD, and perhaps Sir Wigamur might have lived out his life in a different way, had not fate decreed otherwise.

Throughout the next year the Knight of the Eagle journeyed far in search of his heritage, but though he fought many battles and overcame powerful adversaries, he found no word of his origin. Then, one day, he arrived at the borders of the Kingdom of Delferant, which

bore all the signs of having fought a long and bitter war. Wigamur came first to the city of Leidisar, where he was offered hospitality, since even here the deeds of the Knight of the Eagle were known.

Wigamur asked what was the cause of the war, and was told that the old King of Delferant had died without heirs, and that now two kings, Altroglat and Paltriot, fought to become rulers of that land.

When he heard this, Wigamur asked what claims each of the kings had over the country. Both, it seemed, were uncles of the dead king, so they believed they had equal rights to the kingdom, but neither was willing to share with the other. Even now, Wigamur learned, King Paltriot had assembled an army which was moving upon Delferant. King Altroglat had already fortified the city of Leidisar, where Wigamur found himself, claiming the right of possession.

Now it happened that on one of his many adventures Wigamur had been of service to a lady named Dulciflur, who was the daughter of King Altroglat, and that the two had shared feelings of love for each other. When she heard that the Knight of the Eagle had entered the city, she at once sent messages to bring him before her. Having welcomed him, she begged him to fight on her father's side.

As the story tells, though Wigamur had declared as ever that his ignorance of his lineage forbade him from declaring his affections, now he elected to fight for King Altroglat, much to the delight of all who were preparing to face the invading army.

Thus, in ignorance of the fact that this king was his own father, Wigamur prepared to do battle against him.

Within a week, the army of Landrieu arrived at the border of Delferant, and King Altroglat led his own force out to meet them. At his side rode the Knight of the Eagle, with the great bird circling overhead, uttering its most warlike cries.

Following the usual exchange of threat and counter-threat, the two forces met in battle. Many brave knights and soldiers fell upon both sides, and both kings fought bravely and with determination. At the end of the first day, neither side obtained any advantage, despite the presence of Wigamur, who accounted for so many slain enemies and more with wounds that would prevent them from fighting again for many days. But always he looked with sorrow upon the field of war, and wished that he might prevent further bloodshed.

To this end, Wigamur sought out King Altroglat and begged him to suggest that each side should choose a champion to represent them, and that the battle be decided by the winner of this encounter. At first the king was reluctant to follow this suggestion, but when Wigamur himself declared that he would fight for Delferant, he agreed to suggest the idea to King Paltriot. Needless to say, Dulciflur urged him to do this, and cast looks of love towards the Knight of the Eagle.

When he received word from his adversary, King Paltriot quickly agreed to the challenge, and declared that he would fight for his own cause on the morrow. And though many of his best knights begged him to allow them to face the Knight of the Eagle, the king, who despite his years was still a valiant warrior, insisted.

So it was that on the next morning, in the sight of both armies, Wigamur and King Paltriot rode out to face each other. When he understood that his opponent had not offered himself to the fight, Paltriot demanded that king should fight king, since it was they who each claimed the right to rule over Delferant.

To this Wigamur declared that he had been fairly appointed to act as champion, and begged the King of Landrieu to accept this. Then King Paltriot spoke harshly to the Knight of the Eagle, demanding to know what lineage he came from, since only a nobly bred knight should face an anointed king.

Then Wigamur did a most curious thing. He laid aside his shield and doffed his helm. Then, before all, he told how he had been stolen from his parents by the mermaid Lespia, raised first by her then by the Sea-Wight. 'Since then,' he declared, 'I have sought my lineage across many lands. The Lord Ettra, uncle to King Arthur, made me a knight, and I have followed a path of errantry from that day to this. I do not know if I am rightly of a station that permits me to fight with a king – though it seems to me that he is but a man as I am – but I stand ready to defend the right of my Lord Altroglat.'

Then King Paltriot, who had listened with wonder to this story, wept openly and cried aloud: 'Sir Knight, I am your father! It was from myself and my queen, your mother, that you were stolen by the mermaid. Though we sought for you for many years after we were unable to find you and believed you lost to us for ever!'

Then the king and the Knight of the Eagle embraced before the whole company of both armies, and many wept at the sight of their reunion.

Wigamur now returned to King Altroglat and declared that he could not fight against his own father. To this the king assented and then said: 'How may the conflict be settled between our two lands? We must seek another champion, or else the King of Landrieu and I must do battle.'

Then it was that one of King Altroglat's most senior advisors, a duke named Miligagram, spoke up: 'Sire, if I may, there is perhaps another solution to this. I believe it is not the wish of any man here that the battle between our two lands should continue, and to seek champions seems now to be wrong. Today we have witnessed a miracle in the coming together of the Knight of the Eagle with his true father. Let me therefore suggest, if all here are agreed, that Sir Wigamur be married to your daughter, the fair Lady Dulciflur. Thus are the two families who contest for the lordship of Delferant become one, and this animosity may end.'

When they heard this, both kings requested a truce be made between them while these matters were discussed. When Wigamur and Dulciflur learned of Duke Miligagram's suggestion both were happy and assented willingly to be married. Dulciflur had long loved Wigamur, as he had her, and thus were both made glad by this arrangement.

Thus it was that the most glorious wedding was celebrated, and King Arthur himself came, with many of the Round Table Fellowship, to attend. So the Knight of the Eagle was restored to his family, and married to the lady he most desired. And amongst those who attended the wedding and the great tournament which followed – where I promise you the Knight of the Eagle carried off the greatest number of prizes – there came the Lady Pioles, she whom Wigamur had long since rescued from the ruined castle. And it fell out that the knight to whom she had been promised, and whom she had long believed dead, still lived, and came to take part in the tourney – for he had merely been captured in the attack upon the castle and were later ransomed by his family.

Thus a second wedding was celebrated, amid great rejoicing, and in time Wigamur became king of both Landrrieu and Delferant and ruled over them with justice and fairness with the beautiful Dulciflur at his side. And it is said also that he visited the Sea-Wight and forgave him for his part in his early life. Also that the eagle, for the rest of its days, continued as Wigamur's most faithful companion, and to accompany him on further adventures. For, as he had promised, Wigamur returned to Camelot the Golden and claimed a seat at the Round Table, fulfilling many adventures from that time forth.

THUS IS MY telling of this tale over, and it is my hope that the story of the Eagle Knight has pleased you who read it, as it would, had he known of it, have pleased Master Thomas Malory.

EXPLICIT THE TALE OF WIGAMUR.

INCIPIT THE STORY OF SIR GAWAIN IN THE LAND OF WONDER.

23: SIR GAWAIN IN THE LAND OF WONDER

I N ALL OF THE STORIES WHERE SIR GAWAIN IS THE HERO, THE PRESENCE OF FAERY MAGIC IS NEVER FAR AWAY. NONE MORE SO THAN IN THIS TALE THAT I RELATE NOW. HERE THERE IS SO MUCH DETAIL THAT I CANNOT BUT BELIEVE THIS WAS MORE THAN THE IMAGINATION OF THE TWO AUTHORS WHO COMPOSED THIS TALE OF WONDER. INDEED THAT PERHAPS AT LEAST ONE OF THEM MAY HAVE CROSSED FROM THIS WORLD INTO THAT OTHER PLACE. FOR HOW ELSE COULD ANY MAN SO WELL DESCRIBE THE LAND OF WONDER ITSELF, UNLESS IT BE WHEN THE LADY DANCES ON THE GREENSWARD? ONCE AGAIN, I AM LED TO THE QUESTION OF WHETHER SUCH A PLACE TRULY EXISTS. I CANNOT SAY WITH ANY CERTAINTY, BUT IT IS MY PROFOUND WISH – AS PERHAPS WAS THAT OF MASTER THOMAS THAT THE LAND WHERE WONDERS OCCUR IS AS REAL AS OUR OWN.

✛ ✛ ✛

ONE DAY KING Arthur declared the feast for all who could come to Camelot the Golden. And it fell out that, when all were gathered in the great hall that had seen the start of so many wondrous adventures, there came through an open window a curious thing: no less than a most miraculous chessboard, that flew into the hall and hovered in the air for a few moments before settling on the ground. The board was of ivory set into a table with legs chased in gold, while each of the pieces that sat upon it were so finely carved that it seemed they would come to life at any moment.

All who were there looked in wonder at the object, and King Arthur especially coveted it at once. But all believed that it could only come from Faery, so beautiful and uncanny it was, and because of this no one wanted to touch it.

After a moment the chessboard with all its pieces flew back up into the air, and passed out of the window. Several knights rushed to see where it went and saw it vanish from sight into the trees of the Great Wood.

'By my faith, I wish to have that chessboard and its pieces,' declared King Arthur. 'Who will go and fetch it for me?'

At first there was no response. The knights looked at one another, but none wanted to be the first to set forth on what they all knew would be a fearful quest. Even when the king offered whatever reward they sought, they did not respond, so that he declared them to be poor representatives of the Round Table.

At this, Sir Gawain, who was ever willing to undertake any mission, spoke up. 'I will seek out this thing, sire,' he said.

At which Sir Kay, who was as ever filled with resentment against his fellows, said: 'Be sure to take a rope so that you may secure it to your saddlebow!'

While some laughed, others reproved Sir Kay for his unjust comment. But Sir Gawain merely smiled and called for his armour and weapons. Then, while all the court looked on, he mounted his great steed, Gringolet, and with the good wishes of the king and the knights in his ears, set forth, following the road in the direction taken by the floating chess set.

⁜ ⁜ ⁜

SO QUICKLY DID his mighty steed gallop that in a while Sir Gawain caught sight of the chessboard in the air not far ahead. He redoubled his efforts to overtake it, but then suddenly before him saw a mountain rear up. He was sure he had never seen this before, and in truth it blocked his way.

Then the knight saw how his quarry flew towards this implacable place, and how a great crack appeared in its side, which opened up so that the chessboard passed within. Without thought Gawain spurred his steed after it, so that he went directly into the heart of the mountain.

Within, all was lit by a dim glow. Gawain found himself in a cavern the size of which was that of a hundred halls built by men. Its roof glittered with gems, which gave off light like distant stars.

Of the chessboard there was no sign, but as Sir Gawain gazed in wonder at the vastness of the cavern, there came a great rumble and the crack which had opened to let him in, closed. In semi-darkness man and horse were filled with fear, and Gawain drew his sword in preparation for the attack he believed must come. Instead, all was silent and still, and after a time the knight urged Gringolet onward, passing deeper into the mountain.

Time seemed to stand still in that place, and Sir Gawain had no knowledge of how far he had gone before he saw a red glow ahead which slowly grew brighter, until he found himself looking down into a pit where there were four young dragons, who writhed, coiling and uncoiling, in the darkness.

At once they became aware of the knight and rose as one to attack him savagely. Setting his shield before him, Gawain waited until they emerged from the pit, then struck out at them. One he speared to death at once, another he cut off one of its clawed feet. The rest continued to attack him, but he slew them both and then the one he had wounded.

Scarcely had he sheathed his sword than he heard the sound of the mountain opening again, and as he turned towards the light of day, a fully-grown dragon flew in from the outside. In its claws it carried a cow, which it must have caught to feed its young. Flying down to the nest it saw the bodies of the four infant dragons and bellowed in rage.

When it was aware of Sir Gawain it let fall the dead beast and at once attacked him. By good luck he struck his spear deep into its body,

PLATE 5: '. . . he found himself looking down into a pit where there were four young dragons, who writhed, coiling and uncoiling, in the darkness'

but when the spear broke, the dragon came on, knocking the knight from Gringolet's back.

The terrified horse galloped away, leaving Sir Gawain sprawled upon the earth, while the dragon prepared to feast on his flesh and bones.

Only by leaping to one side and raising his shield did Gawain escape being burned to death by the dragon's fiery breath, though he received many wounds despite this. The mighty beast then succeeded in wrapping him in a coil of its tail, and then flew up quickly into the air, where it attempted to carry him to a smaller cavern. But thanks to the spear, which was stuck deeply in its body, the beast could not fit into the tunnel between the two chambers, and became trapped there.

In its fury it began to tighten its grip upon the knight, who groaned aloud and struggled to draw his sword – only to find that it had fallen from its sheath in the struggle.

In desperation, Sir Gawain drew his knife and stuck it deeply into the dragon's harsh skin, again and again. At first this did no more than cause the beast to loosen its grip, but this was enough to enable Gawain to reach out and drive his dagger deeply into the creature's belly, so that it roared in anguish.

Now its hot blood spilled forth and Gawain feared he must die of the poisoned fire. He hacked again at the dragon's tail, until at last he was free and fell to the earth as the mighty beast thrashed itself to death, with a great blast of flame that all but incinerated Sir Gawain.

But at last it was dead, and the knight was able to rest and examine his many wounds. Some were superficial, others deep, but since Gawain had long since learned the healing arts from the hand of a faery, he was able to tend himself until he felt some strength return to him.

At this juncture Gringolet returned, though the horse itself had suffered wounds from the young dragons before Gawain slew them. Together, the knight and his steed rested. Gawain did what he could to treat the horse, then lay next to it, his head resting upon its side, until both slept and were restored sufficiently to go on their way.

Then, to Sir Gawain's delight, he saw daylight coming through a great fissure in the mountainside, which he guessed to be the way that the dragon had come and gone. Wearily, but with ever-lightening heart, he followed the path until it emerged into the open air. Before him lay a wide valley, and in the distance he saw how the sun glanced off a building that shimmered like gold.

Eager now for rest and food, Sir Gawain urged Gringolet onward and within an hour they came in sight of the golden walls and towers of a castle that seemed as if it was also a palace. As he came close, Gawain thought that he could hear voices raised in such sweet song as only angels could make, and he wondered for a moment if he had indeed died from the wounds made by the dragon. But since he still felt the pain of these, he believed he must still be alive, and having tied Gringolet to a tree outside the gates, he entered that wondrous place.

✛ ✛ ✛

THOUGH HE KNEW it not, Sir Gawain had entered the Kingdom of Wonder, the ruler of which was responsible for the fabulous objects which he had created with his own hands and which adorned the castle on all sides. There were statues carved as if from life, some depicting creatures such as Gawain had never seen, and much else besides.

I do not know if the king was of the Faery race, or simply a mortal man who possessed such skills that seemed like magic, but Gawain could only look with amazement upon all that he saw as he made his way slowly across the great courtyard and inside to a fine hall, all decorated by the will of the King of Wonder himself. Tapestries there were, which seemed to move on their own, giving the illusion of life to the figures upon them. Indeed, some depicted stories of the Fellowship of the Round Table, though Sir Gawain was too tired to look upon them at that time. There sat the King of Wonder, as finely dressed as any man Gawain had ever seen – more richly clad even than those who walked the halls of Camelot the Golden. With him was a youth, his son Alesaunder, and together they were playing chess upon the very board that Gawain sought.

As he entered, the king arose and greeted him warmly, asking his name and purpose. Sir Gawain gave his name but said nothing about the chessboard. Instead, he told of his battle with the dragons in the hollow mountain where they lived.

The King of Wonder looked upon the knight and saw how many wounds he had suffered and how broken and spoiled were his armour and his clothing. At once he called his servants and ordered them to do all they could for his guest. This they did, giving fresh water for him to drink, then assisting him to remove his armour and clothes and drawing a bath of heated water in which he could ease his tired limbs and clean his wounds. And when he enquired after his steed, he was told that it would be well cared for, fed and watered.

Then, as if in a dream, as it seemed to him, the king's servants led Gawain to a chamber where he was laid in a magical bed that had this power: that anyone who slept there who was wounded was healed completely by the time they awoke.

So it was with Sir Gawain, who woke in the morning to find his wounds vanished as if they had never been, and much of his old strength returned. Then he came before the King of Wonder and saluted him and offered his thanks for all that had been done for him.

'You are most welcome, Sir Knight,' the king answered. 'Will you now tell us what adventure drew you here?'

'Sire,' replied Gawain. 'I am come in search of the very chessboard that I saw you play upon when I came into your hall.' Then he told all that had happened at Camelot the Golden, and how King Arthur sought the chessboard and had sent him to seek for it.

'May I ask, on behalf of my master, the most noble king, if I may fulfil his longing and take him the thing he desires?'

'I am well aware of your king, and of his famous Round Table of knights,' declared the master of the golden hall. 'Indeed I sent the wondrous chessboard to him in order that his best knight should come in search of it. But I must tell you, Sir Gawain, that only by fulfilling a further quest on my behalf, may you take the chessboard to your lord.'

At this Sir Gawain asked what quest it was that the King of Wonder demanded of him.

'There is a certain sword, known as the Sword with the Two Rings, that I desire greatly,' answered the king. 'Its power is great, but only a knight of great virtue and wisdom may find and wield it. Are you such a one, Sir Gawain?'

'I make no such claim,' replied the king's nephew. 'But I promise to try my hardest to achieve this task. Yet I am afraid that my armour was sadly broken and my sword and spear likewise, in the battle with the dragons, and I have only the clothes your servants allowed me to put upon myself.'

At this the King of Wonder smiled. 'Even now your armour is being repaired by my smiths, and I should be glad to provide you with new clothing and weapons such as you require. Until then, I ask that you rest until you are fully recovered from your wounds.'

So it was that Gawain took his ease within the Castle of Wonders, and saw many strange and delightful things. He dined on the finest food, served on golden plates, seated at a table of marble. And when night came he was taken to a chamber where he slept in a bed that had carved upon its head the story of the world, from the beginning to its end – though afterwards, Gawain could remember nothing that he saw. Anyone who slept in that bed, no matter on what night of the year, they would hear some part of that story; though had they slept a whole year without waking they would still have not exhausted its many wonders. That night, Gawain thought that once again he heard voices as sweet as any ever heard, raised in song. So beautiful were these that he slept all the more deeply and dreamed dreams of such

rare joyfulness that when the day dawned he felt not only rested but more than ready to undertake the task given him by his host.

☩ ☩ ☩

NOW SIR GAWAIN followed new roads – though it seems to me that he never truly left the Land of Wonder until the end of his quest. Always he sought for word or sight of the Sword with the Two Rings, but found nothing. But after several weeks sleeping beneath the stars he came to a place where he saw a fine castle perched high up on a cliff. Only one path led to its gates, through a tunnel and by perilous ways above deep fissures and crevices in the earth. Thanks to the skill and strength of Gringolet, he came at length to the entrance to the castle and saw that its gates stood wide.

He entered at once, and saw many fine knights and ladies playing games – chess, backgammon and others they enjoyed, as well as

➤ *Roger the Fox* ❖

ball games. All seemed most happy and content, and when they saw Sir Gawain they came to greet him and see to his every need.

In a while, freshly clothed, washed and barbered and given good wine to drink, Gawain was led before the master of this noble place, whose name was King Amoraen – a great lord of that land and cousin to the King of Wonder.

He greeted Sir Gawain kindly and asked that he remain there as his guest for as long as he wished.

'My thanks to you, sire,' answered the knight. 'I am grateful for your hospitality, but I may not stay more than one night, for I seek a rare object that I must find for another great lord, and so must depart to continue my search.'

'What is this thing you seek?' asked the king, and when Gawain told him of the Sword with the Two Rings, he fell silent for a time. Then he spoke up: 'If you seek that sword then you must be both a valiant and noble man, for only such a one could hold the weapon without it turning upon him. Tell me your name, Sir Knight.'

'I am Sir Gawain of Orkney, nephew to King Arthur, High King of all the lands of Logres.'

'Then you are doubly welcome, for I have heard much of you and have longed to know you. Only such a man as you can be of help to me.'

'How may that be?' said Sir Gawain.

'I shall tell you,' said King Amoraen. 'But first let me show you the sword you seek.'

The king sent for the sword to be brought to him, and there it was unwrapped and set before the knight. A most glorious weapon it was, made of the best steel and decorated by many jewels and rich designs on its hilts. The two rings were part of its decoration and shone with a deep and magical light.

When Sir Gawain saw the sword he was amazed. 'Sire,' he said. 'I am indeed seeking this very sword for the King of Wonder, who possesses a marvellous chessboard which I must obtain for my uncle, King Arthur. Is there any way that I may get it from you?'

'First, we must test your right to hold the sword,' answered the king. 'It was made for a king who caused two lovers to be cruelly killed, and when they were dead he placed their plighted rings into the hilts of the sword. Since then, once it is drawn from its sheath it cannot be returned there until it has drawn blood. Only he who is destined to wield it, and who is true in love, may do so without suffering its curse.'

So saying, he drew the sword partly from its jewelled sheath. At which the weapon seemed to come alive and of its own accord flew out of the sheath and fell upon the earth at Sir Gawain's feet, burying itself point down. And from the two rings on its hilts came a chime that seemed the sweetest sound ever heard.

'Now I know that you are the one who will bear this blade, for otherwise it would have struck you down,' said King Amoraen. At which the sword flew back into its sheath.

'I swear that you shall have this weapon,' said the king. 'But first I must tell you of a trouble that you may be able to help me overcome.'

'What is this trouble?' asked Sir Gawain.

'For many years I have loved a most beautiful maiden named Ysabeau, who is a princess in her father's kingdom,' said the king. 'She is, I believe, more beautiful than Queen Isolt of Ireland, or maybe even Queen Guinevere, your own king's wife; but her father, Assentijin, has placed her within a great castle that he had created. It has seven circles of walls, and between each runs a deep moat. Many soldiers guard its gates. Assentijin has locked her within so that I may not marry her – though I believe she returns my love. If you are able to find a way to rescue her and bring her to me, then the Sword with the Two Rings shall be yours.'

'It seems to me,' said Gawain, 'that if I am to accomplish this task, then I will need to wield the sword. Will you honour me with its loan until such time as I may prove my worth to bear it?'

To this King Amoraen agreed. 'For,' said he, 'it has shown that it accepts you to be its rightful bearer.'

Thus it was that when Sir Gawain departed the castle next day, the Sword with the Two Rings was belted at his side. And though he had yet to draw it, he felt its power even as he rode.

✠ ✠ ✠

FOR SEVERAL DAYS Gawain followed the way King Amoraen had instructed him, until he came in sight of the castle of King Assentijin, which towered like a threat over the land around it. There Gawain saw how a river ran past it, swift as smoke blown on the wind. It seemed to him far too wild to cross, but he could at first see no bridge. Then he saw where a crossing place lay, and above it a bridge of steel arched. But when he approached this he saw that it was made like a sword, with an edge sharper than the sharpest blade.

When he saw this, the knight thought that he could never cross it unscathed, since it was clearly designed to wound anyone, even one clad in mail as he was, who attempted to cross it. Thus he turned his attention to the river that ran beneath it, and wondered if Gringolet could ford it. Before he attempted this, he decided to test it to see how deep it was. Taking his spear in his hands he thrust the point into the water.

At once the lance burst into flames and was consumed in moments. Then Sir Gawain thought that there was no way to cross the river and reach the castle where the Lady Ysabeau was held. How then, was he to achieve his task and obtain the magical chessboard for King Arthur? Sick at heart he sat upon the bank of the fiery river until the sun began to set. Then, as he had no other place to rest, he looked for shelter. Close by he found a wall overgrown with ivy, and made his way along it until he came to a small gate which opened at his touch. He found himself in a most beautiful garden, richly bedecked with flowers that released the most beautiful scent upon the air. Seeing no one of whom he might ask permission, and having tethered Gringolet to the branch of a tree, Gawain lay down on the soft greensward and rested his head upon his shield, as he had done so often in the past.

Thus he fell into a deep sleep, from which he did not so much as stir when there came into the garden a strange creature that looked like a fox, yet could walk upright at need and possessed the dexterity of a man.

The fox looked down at the sleeping knight, then carefully took the Sword with the Two Rings, along with Gawain's fine helmet and the armour that he had laid aside before he slept. These things the fox carried away and hid in a place where he kept many things of value that he had stolen. Then he returned and, untethering Gringolet, led the mighty steed away to a stable hidden amongst the trees of the garden.

After this he returned to where the knight still slept, and waited until he awoke with the dawn. So it was that Sir Gawain found the sword, his horse and much of his armour had been taken away, and he was sorely angered.

Seeing the fox sitting close by him, Gawain

gave the creature such a blow with his fist that it fell prostrate and unconscious for several minutes. When it opened its eyes again it saw the angry knight standing over it with a dagger and at once cried out – in a most human voice – 'Do not kill me, I beg you!'

Sir Gawain looked at the fox with amazement. 'How is it that you can speak? You look like a fox, yet you sound like a man. What enchantment is this?'

'Enchantment indeed,' answered the fox. 'For ten years I have lived here in this garden which was made for me. Let me tell you my story.'

Sir Gawain sat down and laid aside his dagger, then he listened to the fox. This is its story.

'Once I was human, a child much beloved of its mother and father, who did all they could to educate me in all things. But at last my mother died and in time my father took another wife. At first this woman seemed well disposed to us both, but the day came when I reached manhood, and on that day my stepmother came to me and offered herself to me. When I refused her, she rent her clothing and scratched her body and called for help. When it came she claimed that I had tried to rape her, and went before my father, who became so angry that he declared he would have me killed for this violent crime. Only the protest of his brother, my uncle, who was a wise man, saved my life, though I was still to be banished for ever from my home.

'When she heard this, my stepmother cursed me, and using an old magic she possessed, gave me this form that you see now. When word of this came to my father's ears, he determined to put aside my stepmother, and so it was that my uncle, who was also knowledgeable in the ways of magic, cast upon her the shape of a toad, and made it that she must wait by the gate

of our castle until such time as both she and I could be restored to our true forms.

'Despite his knowledge, my uncle was unable to set me free, so he built this garden where I have lived ever since.'

'That is a most lamentable story,' said Sir Gawain. 'Is there no help for you?'

'There is only one way that I may be restored,' answered the fox. 'Only if I am in the presence of three men may I regain my human form: these are the King of Wonder, his son Alesaunder, and the noble knight Sir Gawain.'

The king's nephew was silent for a time, then he said: 'Where is the sword you took from me? Where are my horse and my armour?'

'Sir. They are nearby and I shall bring them to you at once.'

The fox ran off and swiftly returned with the Sword with the Two Rings and the rest of Gawain's armour. Then he went to the stable and brought forth Gringolet, who had been well cared for and was none the worse for his adventure.

Gawain, meanwhile, took up the sword, careful not to draw it from its sheath, and showed it to the fox.

'Do you see where there is a name carved upon this weapon? It is the name of the King of Wonder. The sword belongs to him until I have completed a task he has set me.'

Then he smiled at the fox and said: 'What is your name, sir fox?'

'My name is Rogier,' answered the creature.

'And mine is Sir Gawain of Orkney,' said the knight.

When he heard this the fox almost fainted. 'You are he who can help me? And you know the King of Wonder?'

'That is so,' answered Gawain. 'Both he and his son await my return. But first I must succeed in rescuing the damsel who is kept prisoner in that castle beyond the burning river. Do you know how I may cross it?'

'Indeed that is a fearsome place,' replied Rogier the fox. 'There are many walls and many gates and all are well protected.'

'Nevertheless, I must attempt it,' said Gawain. 'I believe the Sword with the Two Rings will aid me in this.'

'Then I will do all in my power to help you,' said Rogier the fox. 'I know a way that you may cross the river in safety. But you must leave your horse here since it would not survive the way we must take.'

'How may I know that I can trust you?' said Sir Gawain. 'Is it not well said that no one may trust a fox?'

'But remember that I am no ordinary fox,' replied Rogier. 'I swear that I will help you in return for my life and for the promise of regaining my true shape, if God wills it.'

With this Gawain was content, and the two set off together, having tethered Gringolet close to a spring from which the steed could drink. They reached the bank of the river that looked so ordinary in the light of day, yet Gawain knew that to step into it would mean certain death.

At the bank, the fox stopped and drew aside a bush that hid the entrance to a cave, and beyond it a tunnel which led steeply downward.

'This will take us below the river,' said the fox, and led the way inside.

Warily, Gawain advanced and followed the fox through a dark and narrow tunnel until they emerged on the furthermost bank of the river. Before them now stood the first gate into the castle, and there Gawain saw many guards on its walls.

'How may we gain entrance?' he asked, and the fox replied: 'There is a wicket gate that no one guards and which I know will be open.

This will bring you into the first courtyard and near the gate to the second – but I say to you again, no matter how valiant you may be, or how powerful your sword, you will in all likelihood perish before you reach the heart of the castle.'

'That may be so,' answered Sir Gawain. 'But I must try anyway.'

Then the fox turned away, for he was fearful both for his own life and that of the knight. 'I shall wait here for you,' he said, and ran off as fast as he could to hide in a nearby thicket.

Gawain advanced to the wicket gate, which was unlocked just as the fox had said. He passed within, surprising the guards who were sitting down to eat.

When they saw him they leapt up and drew their swords. 'Who are you and what do you seek here?' they demanded. 'Surely you are looking for death.'

'That is as may be,' answered Sir Gawain, and drew the Sword with the Two Rings, which rang in his hands.

The battle commenced and just as King Amoraen had said, so it proved to be – that the sword could not be sheathed until it had drawn blood and that it gave strength to he who bore it. In the hand of the great knight it did deadly work. In no time at all Gawain stood over a heap of bodies, while the rest fled before him to the second gate of the castle. There they begged to be admitted, though their fellows were reluctant to do so.

As the second gate opened, Sir Gawain rushed forward and attacked the next company of guards. Once again he fought with such skill and strength that he soon slew most of those who dared to stand against him.

So it was at the third gate, and the fourth, and the fifth, and soon word of the terrible opponent who could not be killed began to pass from one to another in the castle – though yet no word of it reached Lord Assentijin.

Soon night began to fall, and the moon rose over the castle. So many of the guards now lay dead or wounded, that when Sir Gawain entered the fifth hall he found it deserted. All who had been set to guard the place had fled, leaving tables laden with food and wine.

Sir Gawain locked and barred the fifth gate behind him and set up a place where he could see the sixth, which remained shut fast, as all within were in such fear of the terrifying knight that they no longer sought to encounter him.

Gawain ate and drank well, though he never ceased watching the gate, nor indeed did he sheath the Sword with the Two Rings. At length, wearied by his long battle, the king's nephew lay down before the fire in the hall where he had eaten, and allowed himself sleep.

No one troubled him that night, but within the castle King Assentijin received a visit from his daughter, she who Gawain had come to set free. She told her father of a dream she had had that night, in which a figure with a sword of fire and a shield with the arms of a lion, entered the castle and felled all who stood before him.

The king, troubled by this, nevertheless dismissed it as no more than the dream of a young girl, and chose to ignore her warning. But with the dawn came word of the fell knight who had penetrated six gates, leaving in his wake so many dead or wounded that none dare face him, and whose sword shone with a magical glow.

In fury, the king ordered all his closest allies and best knights to gather in the main hall and to prepare to encounter the attacker. He also sent men to secure his daughter's chamber and stand guard before it. At length, Gawain came to the seventh and final gate, through which he entered the great hall, driving all before him. There the king's strongest knights

advanced upon him, and even with the power of the Sword with the Two Rings, and his own great strength, Sir Gawain gradually weakened. Finally, the king himself joined in the fray, and came face to face with Gawain. There he struck the knight a blow which caused the enchanted sword to fly from his hand. At which, knowing that he could no longer win, Gawain allowed himself to be captured.

SO IT WAS that Sir Gawain was thrown into a cell in the depths of the castle. There he bemoaned his fate, above all the loss of the sword which had been the only means by which he could obtain the magical chessboard for King Arthur.

Raging against the one who had deprived their lord of so many brave men, all the knights called for his death, but at that moment the king's daughter came and begged to have the keeping of the attacker for that night, during which she promised to make him regret every blow he had struck. She begged that she might be allowed to punish the knight herself. 'Let me visit him in his dungeon and stay for a while with him' she said. 'So that I may drive him insane with the terrible things I promise will come to him!'

Surprised by this, the king could not refuse his child. Indeed, he felt pride in her strength and determination to make the attacker pay for his deeds.

What he did not know, was that the princess, whose name you may remember was Ysabeau, had fallen in love with the knight as she watched from a tower window, while he fought like a lion and slew so many. She knew him from her dream, and became convinced that he was destined to be her love. So, too, she thought of the way her father had locked her away from the world, and how much anguish this had caused her.

So it was that, fuelled by resentment, she planned to help the knight. Later that day she entered the cell where he had been tossed and where he lay rueing his failure to do all that the King of Wonder, King Amoraen and King Arthur, had required of him.

For a time Princess Ysabeau spat and taunted him violently, then she ordered her guards to leave, telling them she intended to deal with the knight in such a way that none should see her do so. Then, once they had left, she at once set Sir Gawain free and told him the truth: that she loved him above all men and would as soon die as be parted from him. 'I will do all that I can to set you free,' she said.

Gawain, amazed and, it must be said, delighted by the beauty and gentle words of the princess, thanked her, but made no mention of his task, which was to take her King Amoraen.

✠ ✠ ✠

NOW LISTEN TO what happened next, as the story tells. First the princess led Sir Gawain secretly out of the dungeon and along a passage that led to the most beautifully decorated chamber – her own private place where even her father was not permitted to come without her leave. There, so the story tells, the pair fell into each other's arms and made love upon a bed of the greatest richness. Then the princess showed Sir Gawain the entrance to a secret passageway which would lead them to freedom. This she had caused to be made in secret, hoping one day to set herself free – but until now being too fearful of leaving the shelter of the castle on her own.

Indeed the pair might have escaped had it not been for a certain knight, who had himself fallen in love with Ysabeau, but whom she had shunned. Having learned of her secret chamber, he had made a spy hole which enabled him to watch her. So it was that he spied upon the couple in their love-play, and in a jealous rage went to find King Assentijin and told him all.

Imagine how angry and distressed the king was to learn, not only of his daughter's betrayal, but also of her love for the knight. He summoned every man he could and together they stormed the princesse's chamber.

Within it, the princess prepared to flee, but Sir Gawain refused. 'There are armour and weapons enough for me here,' he said. 'Let me defend myself and my honour, as well as yours, my lady.'

Reluctantly, Ysabeau agreed, and decided to remain with the knight, despite her fear at what her father might do to them both.

Hastily Sir Gawain armed himself from the mail he found in the chamber, and when the attackers finally broke down the door to the princess's chamber, he stood ready to fight them. More than anything he longed for the Sword with the Two Rings to lend him strength, but even without that, and though still exhausted from his earlier battle, Gawain fought against the knights and soldiers with such ferocity that he killed many who forced their way into the room. Even King Assentijin himself came against him, and Gawain struck him such a blow that he fell unconscious to the earth.

At first the soldiers bemoaned the king's seeming death, but when he revived, Assentijin railed against them and drove them to attack Gawain again. In the end, even Sir Gawain's great strength and bravery were not enough, and he was overwhelmed and made secure again.

Thus he was once again thrown into a bleak cell, while next door the Princess Ysabeau was herself incarcerated. Then, such was the king's fury and distress at the betrayal of his daughter and the savage battles against his knights, that he began to prepare the most cruel torture and death for both.

So it might have been that Sir Gawain's life could have ended on a scaffold, alongside the damsel who had briefly made him her lover. But fate decreed otherwise, for Rogier the fox, having watched and observed how many of the castle guards were slain by the knight, and that every one of the gates now stood open, found the courage to slip unnoticed into the castle, and to seek out his friend.

✠ ✠ ✠

NOT WITHOUT HIS own magics, the fox made his way unseen through the great castle, opening all doors that were locked with his spells, until he found his way to the dungeon where Gawain and Ysabeau were kept. On the way he happened upon the Sword with the Two Rings, that no one had dared to pick up because of its great power. Calling upon every ounce of his strength and courage the fox was able to carry it to the knight.

Thus both Gawain and the princess were set free, and made their way back to the fair Ysabeau's chamber, from where they fled by way of the secret passageway leading them out of the castle. There the fox led them back through the tunnel under the burning river, to the shelter of his secret garden.

Both Gawain and the Lady Ysabeau thanked him, while the fox danced with delight that the means by which he could once again regain human form might at last be in sight.

'For now I have but to stand before the King of Wonder and his son, with you, Sir Gawain, at my side, and I shall be restored.'

So it was that the small company left behind the castle which had been the prison of Princess Ysabeau for all her life, and with Gringolet restored to his master and the princess seated on his saddlebow before him, they set off to the Kingdom of Wonder with the fox trotting at their heels.

That night, as they camped beneath the stars, Sir Gawain finally told the princess the true reason for his coming to her home – to bring her to King Amoraen. At first she was stricken with anger and sorrow for, as she said: 'Once I was in love with the king, but now that I have found you, Sir Gawain, I care nothing for him!'

'Yet I have given my word,' answered the knight. 'How can I break it? Only in this way may I keep the Sword with the Two Rings so that I may bring it to the King of Wonder.'

'Then you must choose,' said Ysabeau, 'between myself and your task.'

This filled Gawain with anguish, for he truly loved the princess, but duty required him to carry out the task he had promised to perform. The fox, meanwhile, overhearing this, remained silent, for to him also the success of Gawain's adventure carried with it his own freedom.

The next day the party continued their way. Neither Gawain nor the Princess Ysabeau spoke to each other, and soon they came in sight of the castle of King Amoraen. There, they saw how the walls and windows were draped in palls of black cloth, and upon reaching the castle, learned that the king had fallen sick and died but two days before. The people in the castle were in mourning for their lost lord, and Gawain was filled with uncertainty as to the proper end to his quest.

Finally, he approached the three lords of the realm whose task it was to prepare the way for the one who would succeed their dead master. When they heard the story of Gawain's adventure, and the freeing of the princess, their leader shook his head.

'Sir Gawain, you have done everything my master asked of you and thus fulfilled your obligation to him. Therefore you should keep the Sword with the Two Rings, for it seems to me that it brings only death and misery to those who carry it. Thus I release you from your task. The new lord of this land already has a wife, so the Princess too is set free.'

When he heard this, Sir Gawain brightened at once and hastened to tell the Princess Ysabeau. At first she said little, since Gawin had chosen to come to the castle, thereby sealing her fate. But when the king's nephew begged her forgiveness and spoke of his duty as a knight of the Round Table, she softened, and from that moment love spoke in her heart as strongly as ever.

Thus it was that Gawain, Ysabeau, and the fox departed the castle and set forth upon the road to the Kingdom of Wonder. Several days it took to cross the land, but in time they came in sight of the golden palace and were greeted by the king's retinue, who had been sent to meet them.

✢ ✚ ✢

W HEN HE SAW Sir Gawain, the king's eyes were alight – for he knew that the knight would not have returned without succeeding in his task.

So it was that Sir Gawain gave the Sword with the Two Rings to the King of Wonder, who received it with great joy. 'Though this is a perilous weapon indeed,' he said, 'it is one that I shall use well to protect my kingdom. For this you have my gratitude, Sir Gawain, and

as I promised you, you shall have the magical chessboard for your king.'

To this Gawain responded with thanks; then he raised the matter of the fox, who had received many strange looks from the people of the Land of Wonder, but had remained silent while Sir Gawain discharged his task.

Now the King of Wonder looked at the creature and smiled. Then he called to his son, Alesaunder, to come into the hall. As soon as the youth came there, so the curse laid upon the fox by his stepmother began to unravel. As he stood in the presence of the King of Wonder, his son, and Sir Gawain, the fox-shape fell from him, and in its place stood a handsome youth whose red hair was the only sign of his previous shape.

➜ *The magic chess set* ✦

At the same time, as the story tells it, his stepmother, who had been cast into the form of a toad, also resumed her true form, and went at once before her husband and begged for her life. She confessed all that she had done and asked to be forgiven, to which the king replied that it was his son's choice so to do, but if so then he would abide by that.

When the youth at last returned, he showed his nobility by forgiving his stepmother, so that in time the family were able to live together in harmony. And in time, the boy who had once been a fox sought out Sir Gawain, and was invited by King Arthur to join the Fellowship of the Round Table, where he accomplished many good and brave deeds. And it may well be that his years as a fox gave him the gift of cleverness that stood him in good stead thereafter, but of that I am not sure.

Sir Gawain and the Princess Ysabeau, meanwhile, now in harmony with each other, set out with the blessings of the King of Wonder, carrying with them the chessboard and all its beautifully carved pieces. Thanks to the magic of the king, the board floated above them all the way to Camelot the Golden, and settled in the great hall for all to see. King Arthur was glad indeed to see it, and in a future time this very chessboard became the means by which a battle was fought and many men slain, but that is a story others have told far better than I.[*]

✣ ✣ ✣

THUS SIR GAWAIN completed his quest and the fox became a man again. As to the Princess Ysabeau, I cannot say whether she remained with her lover, or indeed if they married. Truth to tell, if the king's nephew wed all the women who were said to love him, he would have had many wives, but as to that I cannot say, since the story does not tell of it.

---

[*] The story referred to here is "The Dream of Rhonawby". It is to be found in *The Mabinogion*. The battle is between Arthur and Owein ap Urien, fought between the latter's raven warriors to decide the fate of the land.

EXPLICIT THE STORY OF SIR GAWAIN IN THE LAND OF WONDER.

INCIPIT THE TALE OF TANDEREIS AND FLORDIBEL.

24: THE TALE OF TANDEREIS AND FLORDIBEL

IT IS WELL KNOWN THAT LOVE DOES NOT ALWAYS BRING HAPPINESS, AND THAT THOSE WHO CHOOSE EACH OTHER MAY SOMETIMES CHOOSE WRONGLY. INDEED, THOSE WHO DECIDE IN HASTE THAT THEY LOVE ONE ANOTHER ARE OFTEN SUBJECT TO PAIN AND SUFFERING. HERE I SHALL TELL SUCH A TALE, WHERE THE ARROWS OF LOVE STRUCK DEEPLY INTO THE HEARTS OF TWO GENTLEFOLK, AND HOW A PROMISE GIVEN EASILY CAUSED THOSE NAMED IN THE TITLE OF THIS TALE TO UNDERGO MANY YEARS OF TORMENT. BUT AS THE AUTHOR OF THIS STORY, WHO NAMES HIMSELF PLEIER, DECLARED, 'WISDOM THAT IS NOT ACCOMPANIED BY HAPPINESS, WILL OFTEN CONCEAL GREAT SORROW'. THIS STORY ALSO SHOWS HOW THE CUSTOMS OF CAMELOT THE GOLDEN COULD SOMETIMES BE SEEN TO POSSESS A DARKER SIDE, WHICH EVEN THE MOST CHIVALROUS ACTIONS FOUND HARD TO REDRESS. FOR ALL THAT, IT SEEMS TO ME A FINE STORY OF WHICH MANY WHO READ MAY FIND MUCH TO GIVE THEM REASON TO REFLECT UPON THEIR OWN LIVES.

✢ ✢ ✢

IN THE FIRST years after he became king by the drawing of the sword from the stone, King Arthur and Queen Guinevere accepted into their household a noble youth named Tandereis, the son of King Dulcimer, who ruled over the Kingdom of Tandanas. He became, as was the way in that time, a ward of the royal household, and since Dulcimer was brother to Queen Guinevere's father Leodegrance, the youth was made doubly welcome. Indeed, he soon became greatly loved by all of King Arthur's courtiers, such was his gentle and honest demeanour; and within a year of becoming a page, he came to serve the king himself, doing so with great willingness and caring most deeply for his master.

Thus matters stood until the time when King Arthur held a great feast at Whitsuntide, to which kings and knights and their ladies came from many parts of the kingdom and

217

adjacent lands. So splendid was this feast that it was spoken of for many years after, and on this occasion the company did not have to wait for the coming of a supplicant to ask the king's favour – a custom long practised in the realm of Arthur.

On this day, as the guests foregathered for supper, word came that a most beautiful maiden had been sighted on the road. Soon enough she arrived in the court and among the first to come forward to take her horse was Tandereis. Though still a callow youth, he was enchanted by the beauty of the girl, whose clothing was of the very richest kind and whose horse wore the most wondrous harness. The story tells that on its reins were five golden bells, each of which made a sound like the song of a bird: a lark, a nightingale, a thrush, a blackbird and a finch, and that together they made such a pleasing sound that all who heard them, though they were plunged in sadness, yet were at once made to feel joyful. The story tells us that these remarkable bells were made by a faery smith for a goddess – but of that I cannot speak with any authority, and the story says no more. Nonetheless, wondrous as the horse and its trappings were, the maiden herself was as beautiful as the morning and as radiant as the sun, which seemed to shine all the more brightly where she came.

Pages and squires clustered around her, each one vying with the next to serve the maiden in any way they could. Sir Kay, who in his role of seneschal had been the first to greet her, spoke to the king: 'Be careful of this fair maiden, my lord. Such beauty can be the cause of great distress. Take thought upon what it is she may ask.'

To which King Arthur replied that, so long as any request the damsel made caused harm to no one, or was unworthy of his consideration, he would not refuse her.

So the noble girl was brought before the king and queen, who greeted her gently. 'How may we serve you this day?' asked King Arthur.

'Sire,' answered the girl, 'I have heard only of your courtesy and honour wherever I have travelled, and news of this has reached even the furthest part of the world. I wish to ask two favours of you. First that you allow me to enter your service, and that of the queen.'

'That I should be glad to allow,' said King Arthur. 'Tell us what else we may do – but first tell us your name and of whose kingdom you come.'

'My name is Flordibel,' answered the maiden. 'My father is king of a far-off land, but it was my mother who sent me here so that I might learn the ways of this great court, and see for myself the Fellowship of the Round Table of whom word is spoken even in my land.'

'Then you are welcome indeed,' said the king. 'Tell me then, what is the second thing that you would ask of us?'

For a moment the Lady Flordibel hesitated, then she said: 'For the sake of my honour, and that of this court, I ask that if any man here asks for my hand in marriage, you will either instruct him to depart this place or face death.'

'That too shall I grant,' said King Arthur. 'Though I fear that many here this day will find it hard not to fall in love with you!'

Thus it was that Flordibel entered the queen's service, and soon became amongst the best liked and loved of all her handmaidens. And many looked upon her with more than simple fondness, but kept their thoughts to themselves, remembering King Arthur's promise.

Inevitably, the maiden was often in the company of Tandereis, and fate caused them to fall in love with each other. Both kept their feelings hidden, mindful of the evil fortune that awaited any man who looked upon Flordibel with anything more than friendship. Tandereis, however, though still young, became so deeply infatuated with the maiden that he soon ceased to sleep at night, and often neglected his duties as he struggled not to watch her at every opportunity.

Three years passed in this way, until Tandereis was close to becoming a knight – a gift that all knew would be his from the hand of the king himself, and to which he longed, as did all the young men who came to Camelot the Golden.

One day it happened that Tandereis, following a sleepless night, rose earlier than usual, and having made his way to the royal chamber, waited outside until such time as he was called. There, soon after, came Flordibel, and the two, with much hesitation, seated themselves in a window, side by side. There, for the first time, they spoke openly of their love for each other.

Both confessed that they had felt the stirrings of love for long days before this, but that neither had dared speak out because of the promise made by King Arthur to banish or kill any man who offered love to Flordibel.

'Soon, I shall become a knight,' said Tandereis. 'Then I must undertake an adventure to prove myself worthy of a place at the Round Table. Yet I do not know how I shall be able to go from here without you, my love.'

'Indeed, I too would find it beyond bearing to be unable to see you every day,' answered Flordibel. 'It is my belief that we should flee this place.'

Tandereis agreed. 'Let us journey to my father's kingdom together. I have no doubt that he will offer a shelter until we may be wed.'

So it was that the two pledged their love to each other, and until the royal couple awoke and summoned them to attend upon them, spoke of how they would escape from Camelot the Golden. In the meantime, they did their best to avoid showing anything of their feelings and served the king and queen as they had always done.

Soon after this, it was time again for the great feast at Whitsuntide, and as always came a great number of knights and their ladies. There, amongst those who were come of age, Tandereis received the honour of knighthood from the hand of the king himself. What dark thoughts may have plagued him, knowing that he would soon depart in secret with Flordibel, the story does not say, but it seemed even to the maiden that Tandereis was ill at ease.

Nonetheless, by this time love ruled them both, and amidst the gathering no one noticed when the couple slipped away and departed from Camelot the Golden. Only later that day was their absence noted, nor did it require much thought to guess why they had left.

King Arthur was both disturbed and angered by Tandereis's desertion. 'Not only has he broken the promise he made to me but yesterday, when he received the buffet* from me and swore allegiance to me for all his days, but he has cast a slur upon this court by taking away a lady whom we have undertaken to protect. Her own wish was that any man who dared declare himself in love with her should be banished or accept death. I cannot allow this to pass unpunished.'

Then the king sent a message to the King of Tandanas, demanding that if his son came there in search of protection, he should at once be brought back to Camelot the Golden to face his fate. Meanwhile Tandereis and Flordibel

---

* A friendly blow received from the new knight's master on this occasion.

had indeed arrived, much to the discomfort of King Dulcimer.

'I seek no war with King Arthur,' he said. 'Yet I will not give you up, my son. You shall both be safe here with me, whatever may transpire.'

When he heard this, King Arthur was even more angered than before. 'I cannot be seen to go against my own word,' he declared, and ordered that his knights and soldiers prepare to march upon the Kingdom of Tandanas and lay siege to the citadel where Tandereis and Flordibel had sought shelter.

SO IT WAS that from the granting of what seemed but a slight or transient wish, the Kingdom of Tandanas found itself under attack by King Arthur and his army. Great indeed was the force that came against them, led by the king himself. With him came the greatest knights of the Round Table, including Sir Gawain, Sir Owein, Sir Gommerflanz, Sir Lancelot, and Sir Dodinel le Sauvage, among many others. They brought great engines of war, including battering rams with iron masks that could smash the gates of the city.

When news of their coming reached King Dulcimer, he declared that it would be impossible to meet the attacking force in battle, and that therefore all the castles in his kingdom should be strengthened and victualled to withstand a long siege. He himself, along with Tandereis and his strongest knights, remained within the city and prepared its walls and gates to be guarded by the very finest of warriors.

All this time the king sought for a way to heal the breach between himself and King Arthur, and to find some means of saving the life of his son. Thus he sent a messenger

requesting a truce so that he could meet with King Arthur and discuss how this might be brought about.

To this the king agreed, and Dulcimer came to meet him under a flag of truce. Together the two monarchs spoke, and Dulcimer begged that Tandereis should be forgiven. 'He meant no harm to you, sire. Love alone drove him and the Lady Flordibel to flee from your keeping.'

'Nevertheless,' replied King Arthur. 'I made a pledge to the lady that if any man requested her hand in marriage I would either send him away or take his life. Not only did Tandereis do this, but took the lady away with him without permission. Thus, he has earned my wrath, for I cannot permit anyone to flout my authority in this way.'

'Then what may we do, my lord?'

'There is only one way to avoid this war,' replied King Arthur. 'You must return both your son and the maiden Flordibel to my keeping. And as I have sworn, I will take the life of Tandereis.'

'That I will never do,' answered King Dulcimer.

'Then we will meet again on the field of war,' answered King Arthur.

KING DULCIMER RETURNED to the citadel with a heavy heart and told of his exchange with King Arthur. All there were greatly downcast, but Tandereis stood before them and declared that he would offer single combat to any one of the Knights of the Round Table, so that not only could he prove himself worthy of knighthood, and of his love for Flordibel, but also that he might prevent total warfare between the two kingdoms.

Despite the pleas of Flordibel, that such an action could well rob her of the one she loved, matters came about as Tandereis had suggested. Each morning he rode out from the citadel and challenged any one King Arthur's knights. And thus it was that he showed to both sides that he was a much greater fighter than any had known. On five successive days he defeated Sir Kay, Sir Bleoberis, Sir Gommerflanz, and Sir Dodinel le Sauvage, taking them prisoner and bringing them into the city, where they were required to swear allegiance to Dulcimer and his queen.

When she saw this, Flordibel rejoiced to see her love win such fame that his name began to be on everyone's lips, on both sides of the conflict. But it came to her that it would only be a matter of time before Tandereis became so weakened that he would be unable to continue his battles, or that one of those mighty knights such as Sir Gawain or Sir Lancelot would come against him and beat or slay him. Therefore she came before King Dulcimer and Queen Albiun and begged them to find an advocate who would plead her case.

'For truly neither Tandereis nor I have broken the vows we made. Nor have we disobeyed King Arthur in any way other than by fleeing from the court together.'

When they heard this, the king and queen asked who of all men Flordibel would like to be her advocate.

'I would ask for Sir Gawain,' replied the maiden. 'For of all the Knights of the Round Table he is the most noble and best understands the ways of love.'

So it was agreed, and a message was sent to King Arthur, asking for safe passage for both Tandereis and Flordibel, and whether Sir Gawain would speak for them.

✦ *Tandereis approaches the fair castle* ✦

At first, King Arthur was reluctant to grant this request, but Gawain himself, along with several of the greatest knights, begged the king to do so, since it might well prevent a long war and the deaths of many brave men.

So it was that King Arthur agreed, and Tandereis and Flordibel, escorted by the best of Tandereis's knights, came into the camp, where they met with King Arthur. There, Sir Gawain spoke with the maiden at length, and then put her words to the king.

'Sire, the lady swears that Tandereis has not broken his oath to you, that he would always watch over her but never request her hand in marriage. Indeed, though such a thing would have been a great joy to her, she has never been asked nor agreed to any such bond. Nor have the two lain together, or the maiden with any other, in all this time.'

King Arthur looked from Tandcreis to Flordibel.

'Is this true?'

'It is, my lord,' said the pair.

'Then this is my ruling,' said King Arthur. 'I will spare your life, Sir Tandereis, in memory of your service and the love I have for you. But I will also banish you from my lands for ever for departing with this lady without my permission or that of the queen.'

Then he turned to Flordibel. 'And you, my lady, shall remain at Camelot the Golden as my ward, never to see Tandereis again in this life.'

When she heard this Flordibel wept, both with joy that her great love was to be spared, and with sorrow that she might never see him again. But nevertheless she bowed her head, as did Tandereis, who was equally filled with sorrow, but saw that by this means the war between the two kingdoms could cease.

So it was agreed, and the two kings ended the war between them. Following which the lovers were permitted to take their leave of each other, which they did with the shedding of many tears. To Flordibel, Tandereis said: 'Be certain of this, my love, I shall find a way to return to you and to be with you. My love for you shall see no end.'

So the army of King Arthur returned to Camelot the Golden and the forces assembled by King Dulcimer were able to rest. And, amid much lamenting, Tandereis departed, riding away from both kingdoms in search of adventure. For in his heart he had determined that if he made his name in the world, thus would he be able to return and claim his love.

MANY WERE HIS adventures indeed, but these I shall overleap, so that the ending of this tale of love lost and found may be concluded. Yet I will say that Tandereis displayed not only his strength and courage, but also the honour and chivalric behaviour that had marked him out from the start.

His first adventure involved his routing of a band of robbers, whom he prevented from carrying out their evil ways, and after that he overcame a trio of horrible giants whose names, the story tells, were Durkion, Margon and Ulian. These Tandereis slew only after three great battles, but from them he won a fine castle filled with stolen gold.

Thus Tandereis became rich and owned large areas of land, and at this time also he fought bravely in several tournaments, so that word of his fame spread to Camelot the Golden. King Arthur and his knights heard of it, as did Flordibel, whose joy knew no bounds as she learned how her love continued to make such a powerful way through the world. News of this reached King Dulcimer and his queen also, and their pride at their son's achievements was great. But always King Arthur remained determined that Tandereis should not return to Camelot the Golden. Nor would he speak of these matters to the maiden. But even so came a succession of knights, each one beaten by Tandereis, whom he sent to pledge themselves to King Arthur.

✠ ✠ ✠

DESPITE HIS SUCCESS in overthrowing robbers and giants, or winning every prize in the tournaments, Tandereis was ever restless. Not a day passed that he did not think of Flordibel, and as time passed his passion grew ever greater. So it was that he set forth again in search of adventure, and soon reached a land ruled over by one who was known as the Queen of the Wilderness. This tale I will briefly rehearse, for the manner in which it shows that Tandereis was not only a mighty knight, but noble hearted and generous also.

The land there was especially beautiful, rugged and rich by turn. One day Tandereis came to where a waterfall emptied from a cliff face into a pool. Next to it stood a fair castle, and without hesitation Tandereis entered the gate, which stood wide open as if to invite him inside. There he found everything deserted. Tying his horse to a rail he went into the keep and found that also silent and deserted. Despite this, a table was laid with food and drink and to this Tandereis helped himself until he was satisfied. After which he set out to explore the castle, but however hard he sought, he neither saw nor heard anyone.

After a time, he mounted his steed again and rode out to where he saw a most beautiful meadow, surrounded by trees, its floor covered in wildflowers. Here he saw coming towards him a most glorious group of women, each one dressed in robes so rich that he knew them at once to be of noble stock. At their head rode a most beautiful and stately lady, whose head bore a golden crown.

When he saw this Tandereis noted that no guards accompanied the women, so he dismounted and laid aside his helmet, shield and sword, to show that he offered no threat. The lady, who was indeed none other than the queen of that country, greeted Tandereis warmly. Noting his handsomeness and courtly behaviour, she invited him to return to the castle, which was indeed her own. This he did, and spent the next hours in close and gentle discourse with the queen and her ladies.

From them he learned that a neighbouring knight, a man of great strength and cruelty named Kurion, was tormenting her and her people by constantly attacking them. This man believed, without foundation, that her lands, which had been left to her by her father, were rightly his, and referred to all as 'his' meadows or 'his' waterfall or 'his' castle. Only a day before, he had snatched away one of the queen's ladies and ridden off with her to his manor, which lay nearby.

When he heard this, Tandereis at once declared that he would go there and challenge the knight.

'That is the most noble thing you offer,' said the Queen of the Wilderness. 'But you should know that he is a man of great strength and wickedness, and that I have heard tell he remains unbeaten in war or joust. Also, I hear tell that he keeps two leopards, who protect him against all-comers.'

'Nevertheless, I shall do what I may to defeat this wicked fellow,' said Tandereis. And next day he rode out to where Kurion was to be found.

223

When he saw Tandereis coming, the knight at once mounted his mighty warhorse and came forth, his two leopards running one upon either side. Without any exchange, the two knights clashed together, each breaking a lance and drawing blood. Then they drew their swords and fell to. Tandereis made good his attack and drove back Kurion, who was taller and stronger than anyone he had encountered in the lists. But try as he might he could not get close enough to strike a blow, since the two leopards attacked his horse, tearing at it with their savage teeth and claws.

At length Tandereis succeeded in slaying one of the fearsome creatures, and wounding the other – which only made Kurion renew his own attack. But though his strength was great, Tandereis began to wear him down with the skill and determination of his attack, until at last he landed such a blow on his adversary's helm that he fell from his saddle and lay scarcely moving upon the ground.

Tandereis stood over his adversary, preparing to end his life, but Kurion begged to be spared, and swore that never again would he trouble the Queen of the Wilderness, or her women, and that he would return the lady he had stolen away.

On this assurance, Tandereis spared him but, as he had with every other knight he had beaten, he made Kurion swear to make his way to Camelot the Golden and promise allegiance to King Arthur.

This done, he returned to the castle and received the most rapturous reception by the Queen of the Wilderness and her folk. Showering him with thanks and gifts, she invited him to remain there for as long as he wished. But though he courteously insisted that he must leave, he begged to ask one question.

'In all the days and nights I have remained here, I have never seen a sign of a serving man or woman, yet every day the tables are filled, chambers swept and linens washed. By what magic is this done?'

At this the queen smiled. 'It is no magic,' she told Tandereis. 'My people are of the dwarfish kind, who live in the hills to the east of here. I have protected them as did my father before me, and in return they serve me as part of my household. But they are shy of us, and prefer to be unseen.'

Then the queen summoned her dwarvish people, who came out at once from the shadows and thanked Tandereis for his bravery. There were as many as four hundred, each dressed in the finest livery, and amongst them were those excellent in every skill – blacksmithing, cooking, as well as grooms and armourers, who honoured their queen greatly and served always at her command.

Soon after this Tandereis took his leave of the queen, though both she and her ladies were sad to see him depart and swore that they would be ready to provide him with anything he might need at a future time.

✛ ✛ ✛

SO IT WAS that Tandereis continued to ride in search of adventure, sending many more knights to Camelot the Golden and adding to his growing reputation. And as the stories of the brave knight's exploits came to be heard and spoken of in the royal court, so at last the Lady Flordibel requested an audience with King Arthur and Queen Guinevere, so that she might renew her plea that Tandereis should be forgiven and allowed to return.

Seeing how great was her devotion to the knight, and having heard that she had refused offers of marriage from several suitors, and remembering the good service both he and the queen had received from Tandereis and Flordibel, King Arthur at last relented. To Flordibel's great joy he sent forth none other than Sir Gawain himself to seek out Tandereis and invite him to return.

When he learned that he was pardoned, Tandereis's happiness was glorious to see. He prepared at once to return, and sent messages to his father and mother, as well as to others he had encountered in his wandering ways.

So it was that a very different figure arrived at the great city on a fine day close to midsummer. A long line of knights came with him from those whom he had beaten in the lists or encountered along the way. There also came the peoples of the kingdom once ruled by the three giants, and those whom the robbers had terrorised. Also came King Dulcimer and his queen with many knights, and last of all the Queen of the Wilderness, riding at the head of a hundred of her dwarfish soldiers. Together these thronged the streets of the city and filled the great hall where the Fellowship of the Round Table met. There they swore fealty to

King Arthur and Queen Guinevere and told again many stories of Sir Tandereis's bravery.

And here, at last, Tandereis and Flordibel met again, and expressed their love for each other and asked leave of the king to marry.

King Arthur gave his blessing upon them both, and with the coming of Whitsuntide, when they had long since first met, the pair were married with great splendour and rejoicing.

THIS STORY CANNOT end without telling that they remained in happiness and love for each other until the end of their lives, so that they were ever after named as two of the most true and noble lovers that ever lived. As for Tandereis himself, he joined the Fellowship of the Round Table and thereafter brought only honour to that famed company – as the poet Der Pleier has told so famously and that I have written here, in this book of tales that celebrates the realm of King Arthur, in honour of Sir Thomas Malory, may God keep his soul for ever.

EXPLICIT THE STORY OF TANDEREIS AND FLORDIBEL.

INCIPIT THE STORY OF EDERN, THE SON OF THE BEAR.

25: THE STORY OF EDERN: THE SON OF THE BEAR

✠

WHILE IT IS CLEAR FROM THE MANY ACCOUNTS OF KING ARTHUR'S COURT, AND THE ADVENTURES OF HIS BRAVE AND CHIVALROUS KNIGHTS, THAT THESE WERE MEN WHO OUTSHONE MOST OF THEIR KIND IN TERMS OF STRENGTH AND HONOUR, YET THERE ARE SIGNS THAT ALL WAS NOT WELL IN THE REALM OF THE GREAT KING IN THOSE EARLY DAYS AFTER HE CAME TO POWER. WE HAVE SEEN BEFORE HOW SIR KAY, KING ARTHUR'S FOSTER-BROTHER AND THE SENESCHAL TO HIS COURT, OFTEN FAILED IN HIS EFFORTS TO IMPRESS BOTH HIS LORD AND HIS FELLOW KNIGHTS. IN THIS STORY, HE IS SHOWN TO BE BOTH COWARDLY AND FULL OF SPITE. I CANNOT SAY IF THIS WAS SO – THOUGH MASTER THOMAS'S OWN WORK SEEMS TO CONFIRM IT – BUT I AM MORE CONCERNED BY THE WAY THE KING HIMSELF SEEMED TO GO AGAINST THE VERY VISION HE ESTABLISHED WITH THE ROUND TABLE FELLOWSHIP. PERHAPS IT MAY BE THAT THE AUTHOR OF THIS WORK, WHOSE NAME IS LOST, HAD LESS LIKING FOR KING ARTHUR THAN IS USUAL IN THESE TALES, OR THAT HE KNEW OF ANOTHER TALE THAT I SHALL MAKE MENTION OF LATER. BUT OF ALL THE STORIES OF THAT GREAT FELLOWSHIP THIS IS ONE MARKED NOT ONLY BY BRAVERY, BUT ALSO BY JEALOUSY AND BETRAYAL, SUCH AS IS SELDOM TOLD OF IN THE TIME OF KING ARTHUR. I MUST ASK THOSE WHO READ THESE POOR WORDS OF MINE TO DECIDE FOR THEMSELVES WHAT THE TRUTH MAY BE; FOR THE MOMENT LET US JOIN THE YOUTH NAMED EDERN AT THE BEGINNING OF HIS LONG JOURNEY TO FIND HIS TRUE PLACE OF ORIGIN.

✠ ✠ ✠

IN THE DARK days before the coming of King Arthur and the creation of the Round Table, a child was born to a certain noble lady who loved a man named Nudd, who some say may have possessed faery blood. To him she bore the babe she named Edern, but in that time her lover deserted her, leaving her with part of a ring which he said should be given to their son when he came of age. 'Thus he may be able to seek me out, when the time comes,' said Nudd before he departed.

So it was that Edern lived with his mother and grandmother until he came of age. He had the best of life that they could give him, despite possessing few riches, only sufficient for the poorest way of life.

Then, on his seventeenth birthday, his mother gave him the half ring his father had left with her, and told him the story of his birth. Edern was greatly disturbed by this, and declared that he would leave to go in search of his father and demand that he recognise his son.

Having no one to make him a knight, he set off with little but the clothes on his back and the half ring, carried in an embroidered purse which was never far from his side. Somehow his mother and grandmother found the means to provide him with a horse and armour, though neither of these were of great quality. Despite this, the young man began to show that he had the makings of a warrior, for within days of leaving his home he fought several battles and saved more than one gentle maiden from the cruelty of powerful men.

Thus it was that Edern was led to the land of a certain young queen named Guenloie, for whom he performed a great service when she was attacked by a savage and unchivalrous knight. Edern arrived on the scene at a crucial moment, and seeing how the noble lady cried out against her attacker, drew his sword and challenged the knight to defend himself. In the battle that followed, Edern was wounded, but despite that, and his youth, he succeeded in killing the knight and thus received the gratitude of the young queen, who offered him the hospitality of her home until he recovered from his wounds.

In the weeks that followed, Edern and Queen Guenloie spent many hours together, and in that time began to feel deep love for each other. Guenloie gave Edern many gifts, including armour and weapons and a steed of far greater quality than he had possessed before. But despite her dawning love, she refused his clumsy declaration, telling him that if he truly loved her he should prove it by seeking out more adventures. 'When you have proved your abilities and grown to full manhood, I shall be glad to hear your profession of love,' she said. To Edern, her words seemed harsh, but in truth the lady saw the promise within him and sought only to give him greater independence.

So it was, that when he was fully recovered, Edern took his leave of the queen and set out in search of new adventures. And as chance, or luck, or the turn of Lady Fortune's wheel would have it, he came into the Great Wood that covered much of the land of Logres in that time, and there he heard the sounds of battle.

Emerging into the clearing he saw a knight being attacked by two others, and at once he came to the aid of the single man who, though he fought bravely, was suffering greatly from the onslaught of two knights against him.

Within moments, Edern slew one of the attackers, and thus enabled the lone knight to dispatch the other. The solitary knight then thanked him – though he seemed distracted. He told Edern that he was part of a hunting party, but that he had become separated and lost his way in the Great Wood. 'Those two knights attacked me without cause, only your timely arrival saved me.'

At this moment both men heard the sound of a hunting horn some way off. 'I believe I know that call,' said the knight. He set his own horn to his lips and blew a series of notes that were quickly answered. Soon a great party of lords and ladies, all most splendidly clad, arrived and surrounded the solitary knight. He, clearly much pleased to see his fellow hunters, made much of them – embracing one lady in particular and lifting her onto his saddle to sit before him.

All this Edern watched, forgotten in the throng of servants, squires, pages and knights. When he saw a squire passing near he called out to him: 'Who is this man that is so warmly greeted?'

'Do you truly not know?' answered the squire.

'I do not.'

'That is King Arthur,' replied the other. 'The noblest and finest man in all of this kingdom. He alone pulled the Sword from the Stone, because of which he became king of all this great land of Logres. And that,' he added, 'is the queen, Guinevere herself, the fairest lady in all this land.'

When he heard this Edern was happy indeed. *Surely,* he thought, *this great king will make me a knight, for the service I have done him.* But to his sorrow, not only did the king fail to look for him, but seemed to have forgotten him entirely.

So Edern followed the hunting party, leading the horses belonging to the two dead knights, as it made its slow progress through the forest. Soon they came in sight of the greatest city Edern had ever seen. This, he knew, must be the famed Camelot the Golden – for even in his distant homeland word had reached his ears of the great king and his noble knights, and the city said to have been raised in a single night by Merlin the Enchanter.

Thus, Edern believed that fortune had indeed smiled upon him, and that soon he would be able to return to his love Guenloie, having proved himself worthy of her.

But this was not to be, for though he entered the city with the king and his entourage, he found himself but one youth among many who crowded into the great hall to observe the king and queen, along with the greatest of the knights, seated on a dais, where supper was served from golden dishes and in cups of crystal.

There, Edern saw how a fair damosel arrived who stood before the king and queen and begged them to send aid to her mistress, Queen of the Castle of Maidens.

'Only recently my lady gave allegiance to you, my lord,' she said. 'Now she is under attack by the Black Knight of the Mountain.* She asks that as her liege you send help to her at once.'

King Arthur frowned. 'I would be glad to send help to your mistress,' he said. 'But I have undertaken to ride against Talac of Rougemont, who has refused to offer allegiance to me and must therefore be punished.'

'Can this be true!' cried the damsel. 'Do you not owe my lady your protection?'

'I do indeed, and she shall have it,' replied the king. 'But only when I have settled the matter of Talac.'

'Shame upon you!' cried the maiden. And so saying, she turned away and left the hall.

Edern, who had watched all of this, felt only dismay at what he saw. That the king had still not sought him out, or rewarded him for his services, made him less than happy, and now to see how the request for help was dismissed

---

* Unnamed in the original.

dismayed him greatly. So he resolved to depart from Camelot the Golden and seek his future elsewhere.

He slipped away from the hall and made his way back to where he had stabled not only his own steed but those of the dead knights who had attacked King Arthur. On his way, he encountered a young man whose downcast look was such that he stopped to ask him what was amiss.

'I am a poor man,' replied the youth. 'But I hoped to find a place for me here in this wonderful city, where the greatest knights attend upon the greatest king. But alas all those to whom I have spoken see only my poor clothing and lack of riches.'

When he heard this, Edern once again felt that the stories of Camelot the Golden did not reflect the reality he had observed. To the youth, he said: 'Follow me. I will see to it that you receive a better accounting than you have so far.'

He led the way to where the horses were stabled, and gave the two extra mounts to the boy. In wonder, the youth accepted them, for by this means, since both the horses were warhorses that would fetch a fine price, he was at once made a rich man. Thus encouraged, he returned next day to the great hall, attired now in fine clothes, and was well received. Those who had scarcely acknowledged him before enquired how he had been able to change his fate, and the boy told them how Edern had gifted him with the two warhorses, which had enabled him to ready himself for the splendours of the court.

As he stood talking with several young men, the king himself came past, and hearing them laughing amongst themselves asked what cheered them.

The youth whom Edern had befriended at once told his story. As he listened, King Arthur became stricken with dismay. 'Surely this is the man who helped save me from those attackers! How could I have forgotten him! Tell me quickly, where is he?'

The youth explained that he had last seen Edern departing the city, and that he seemed quite downcast.

At once King Arthur summoned several of his closest allies among the knights and told them the story. 'Go after this youth and bring him to me,' the king said. 'He shall be greatly rewarded for the service he did.'

So the knights set forth, following the descriptions of those they met on the way of Edern's passage. But try as they might, they could not discover where he had gone, and were forced to return to Camelot the Golden without news of the young man. Sadly, King Arthur required that if anyone could discover the young man's name or story, they would be well rewarded. But even this had no success, and so it was that the king had to wait for some time before he again saw Edern.

✢ ✠ ✢

THE YOUTH HIMSELF journeyed to the south of the great city, but on his way it chanced that he met with the king of the lands through which he journeyed, who asked him his name and purpose. Edern told the king, whose name was Ivenant, of his visit to Camelot the Golden, and how, despite having saved the life of King Arthur, he had received no reward and had been quite forgotten.

'I had hoped to be made knight by the king himself,' he said. 'But instead I am forced to seek another liege lord whom I may serve.'

'Perhaps you have found such a one,' replied King Ivenant. 'But first you must pass a test. If you succeed, I will make you a knight and allow you to enter my service.'

'What is the test I must undertake?' enquired Edern.

'Follow this road and you will come to one of my castles,' said the king. 'There you will be welcomed by my wife, who is the fairest lady you will see in all your life. I wish to test her fidelity to me. Be pleasant with her and see if she approaches you with desire. If so, I shall know she is unfaithful – and of course, if you allow her to seduce you in any way, you shall pay for it with your life. If, however, you resist her wiles, or indeed if she behaves in a proper way, then I shall believe her faithful, and I shall reward you with knighthood and many rich gifts.'

To Edern, this seemed a strange game that King Ivenant was asking him to play, but so great was his desire to become a knight, and thus perhaps discover the status of his father, that he agreed. Following the way the king directed he soon came to the splendid castle, where he was warmly made welcome and offered every comfort. Seated at last in a comfortable chair before a hearty fire, he fell asleep.

Meanwhile, elsewhere in the castle, the king's wife called for a bowl of water to wash her feet. Her handmaid hurried to serve her mistress, but as she crossed the hall her eye fell upon Edern, sleeping peacefully before the fire, and such was his beauty that she stopped to admire him for some time – until she heard her mistress calling out to her.

Shaking off her viewing of Edern, the girl hurried back to the queen's chamber, only to realise that she had forgotten to fill the bowl with water. The queen scolded her maid, demanding to know where she had been and what had so distracted her.

'Madam, I am sorry. I saw the most beautiful young man in the hall. I have not seen him before, so I believe he is a guest. I must say that my heart beat faster when I looked at him.'

Intrigued, the queen asked her maid to take her to where the youth slept, and when she saw Edern she acknowledged his manly beauty and at once guessed that her husband had sent him to test her.

She leaned close to him, until her breath on his face woke him with a start. He humbly begged the queen's pardon for falling asleep.

'Do not feel badly,' answered the queen, smiling at him. 'Let me guess that you met my husband the king in the forest and that he sent you to test my fidelity. Speak the truth now!'

Edern hung his head. 'Indeed, what you say is true,' he replied. 'I beg forgiveness for coming here with such an evil intention.'

'Let me tell you,' said the queen, 'you have been tricked. My husband has done this many times. He sends any handsome knight he meets and if he sees anyone of them looking too long and admiringly at me, he throws them into prison and demands a ransom.'

'I fear he would get nothing for me,' said Edern, and told the queen something of his story. She, in turn, was becoming ever more fascinated by him, and sought to sit close to him and smile and to touch his hand or his face.

Edern, who was thinking all this time of Guenloie, drew back and spoke harshly to the queen, telling her that he wanted nothing of her attention since he loved another and would not betray her.

The queen was unhappy at this, but soon after the king arrived and looked around for a sight of Edern. His own men had watched the exchange between the youth and the queen and repeated how he had refused to be tempted by her. At this Ivenant said that he must keep his bargain with the youth, and called him to approach.

→ *The captured bear* ←

'I see that you have behaved with great courtesy towards my lady,' he said. 'Therefore I shall do as I promised and make you a knight and provide you with the best armour and the finest horse that I have.'

So it was, that by this curious path Edern received the rank of knight, and was gifted by the king with a new steed and armour such as he could not have previously hoped to own, better even than that he had received from the Black Knight of the Mountain. That same day he attended mass in the castle's chapel and dedicated his sword to the fulfilment of his knightly vows and to the best service he could give to all those in need.

Next day Edern left the castle of King Ivenant and rode on until he came to a manor hidden amongst the trees of the Great Wood. There he encountered a knight who had lost most of his money and lived there with his son, exiled from the world of courtly life.

The son, whose name was Luguain, was yet only a callow youth, but when he heard of Edern's quest to find his father and to win

favour as an errant knight, begged to follow him and become his squire. To this Edern agreed, and with his father's permission, the boy followed when he left to continue his search.

Soon they became fast friends, and Edern spoke not only of his quest but also of his love for Guenloie. Luguain listened with great attention and afterwards said: 'Sir, you should know that King Arthur lays siege to the one named Talac not far from here. Perhaps you might go to the aid of this knight and thus earn fame as one who fights against the great king. Surely your lady shall hear of this and allow you to offer her your suit.'

'Certainly, I want nothing to do with King Arthur,' answered Edern.

'Then let us go to the castle where Talac is besieged,' said Luguain. 'I know it well, and in truth I have heard no harsh words against Talac. It is only his desire for independence that has brought about this conflict.'

So it was that Edern arrived at the castle of Rougemont and saw the great camp of King Arthur's knights and the fine tent where the king himself resided. That night, under cover of darkness, he was able to gain entrance to the castle and to meet Talac, who greeted him kindly and when he heard that Edern wished to serve him, expressed his happiness.

'So many of my men have deserted me because of the fame of King Arthur and his knights. I fear that I cannot hold out much longer.'

'Let us see what can be done,' replied Edern.

Next morning, clad in the armour given him by King Ivenant, he rode out and challenged any one of the Round Table knights to do battle for the sake of the quarrel. King Arthur, who had no wish for further bloodshed, agreed and sent Sir Calogreant to accept Edern's challenge.

That first encounter was a ferocious event. Calogreant and Edern fought for several hours, neither giving way, but in the end the younger knight achieved a victory and took King Arthur's man prisoner.

On each successive day thereafter, for a week, he did the same, overcoming each of his adversaries with increasing skill. Amongst those who were roundly defeated was Sir Kay, who was allowed to return to King Arthur's camp when his steed failed him, but who felt only hatred for the one who had defeated him.

At length King Arthur was forced to send out Sir Gawain against Talac's champion, and all this while Edern had no knowledge that Guenloie was camped nearby and was watching the battle, for she too knew that in time King Arthur would call upon her to become part of his realm, and she wanted to see how Talac fared. She did not recognise Edern in the splendid harness he had received from King Ivenant, but even seeing how well he fought, day after day, she could not help but admire his courage and prowess.

Thus the morning dawned when Edern was set to meet with Sir Gawain. When courtesies had been exchanged between them, they fell to. Edern broke three spears on his opponent's shield before finally unhorsing him. Those looking on were astonished to see their greatest hero overcome, but Sir Gawain quickly recovered and when Edern dismounted they fought until both their shields were splintered and their swords seemed heavy in their hands.

It was at this point that Sir Kay, who had watched the battle, came up suddenly behind Edern and stabbed him in the back with his sword.

Edern fell to the earth and lay still, and silence spread across the field of battle as all there saw what had occurred. Sir Gawain threw aside his weapons and cried out that Sir Kay brought shame upon all of the Round Table Fellowship and upon the king himself by his actions. The seneschal slunk away at once, whilst Gawain called for surgeons to treat Edern. Thanks to Kay's treacherous blow, he was deemed unlikely to live, and a litter was summoned to carry him back to Talac's castle.

King Arthur himself arrived now, and expressed his sadness to see the brave knight so sorely wounded and in such a treacherous manner. Only his love for his foster-brother prevented him from demanding the ultimate punishment for his unknightly actions. Instead Arthur banished the seneschal from his kingdom for a year.

At this time Luguain arrived and cried aloud when he saw that his master was so sorely wounded. 'He was but recently made a knight and took me as his squire. Surely this is the greatest pity that he should perish in this way!' He, like all who were there, believed that Edern could not long survive the wound.

A slow sad procession made its way to Rougemont Castle, led by Talac and several of his knights, and with Luguain walking by the side of the litter, weeping all the time to see his friend and master so close to death.

So it was that when Guenloie, who had watched the battle from afar, came that way and saw the litter she stopped to honour the brave knight as he passed. When she saw him it seemed that her heart must stop, and she fell in a swoon to the earth, for she recognised Edern at once as her one true love, and so great was her sorrow that she could not speak for some time. But at last she gathered her strength and called upon Luguain to wait while she examined the wound.

It fell out that Guenloie had spent some time visiting a nearby abbey, where she sought to find consolation for the love she felt and for having sent Edern away in her pride. There, a wise physician named Guinard attended the sick and wounded from the battle as well as those poor folk who sought succour at the abbey, and here Edern was taken at Guenloie's behest. There, his wound was searched and it was discovered that part of the weapon used by Sir Kay was lodged within the wound. Together, the lady and the surgeon were able to withdraw this, and the physician dressed the wound with herbs and leaves and gave Edern a draught which caused him to sleep deeply while his wound healed.

Once she was certain that Edern would recover, Guenloie returned to her own lands, leaving word that the young knight should follow her when he was strong enough to do so.

Meanwhile, King Arthur and Sir Talac met and the latter agreed to become the king's liegeman. Thus the war between the two was ended, so deeply shocked were both by the actions of Sir Kay.

✠ ✠ ✠

IN TIME, THROUGH the healing skills of Guinard, Edern regained his strength. But despite receiving the message from Guenloie to go to her, he chose instead to return to Camelot the Golden, where Arthur himself greeted him and spoke of his sorrow at having overlooked the courage of the young knight who had helped save his life. Indeed, so great was the praise heaped upon Edern, that King Arthur himself felt some degree of jealousy – especially when he heard Queen Guinevere speaking words of admiration for him.

Then it happened, on a day of fair weather, that a bear which had been captured for the evil practice of baiting, escaped and found its way to the royal apartments. There it threatened the queen and her ladies, who cried aloud for help.

It fell out that Edern himself was passing, and hearing the cries of the women, entered the chamber and saw the bear. It had been blinded and could see nothing, but it tried to scent those who were present. Then Edern did a brave thing, that ever after earned him the title of 'Bear's Son'. He rushed up behind the great beast and threw his arms around it. Such was his strength, or perhaps because the bear had been starved, as was the way in those times, it was unable to break free, though it did its best to bite the knight's arms. Edern, using every bit of strength he possessed, drove the beast before him to where a large window opened upon the courtyard far below. There he was able to push the savage creature out so that it fell to its death.

When King Arthur heard of this he felt a great conflict. On the one hand gratitude for saving the queen from the savage beast; on the other displeasure that another man had done this and in so doing achieved yet more admiration from the queen, who smiled whenever he came into the room,

So it came to the king's mind to send Edern on a quest from which he was unlikely to return, to find and subdue a knight named Le Chevalier Noir, who was causing great consternation amongst the people of a neighbouring kingdom. Several knights had met their death at his hand, and the king was certain Edern would not survive.

Having thanked the young knight for his courage and resourceful thinking, King Arthur sent him to undertake the task. Edern, who had been about to set forth to the home of his one love, did as he was required – for at last he was truly a knight of the Round Table and at the service of its great king. So he set forth by hill and dale to the place where the Chevalier Noir dwelled, and came at length to a valley where shadows seemed to lie long upon the ground. There he met the grim dark knight.

Their battle was long and gruelling, for neither would give way and they were evenly matched. At last, they drew apart by mutual agreement, to rest from their labours. Both removed their helmets and when Edern looked for the first time on the face of his adversary, something stirred within him. Then it was that the dark knight looked strangely at Edern, then he smiled and drew forth a half circle of gold that matched the one kept by the young knight.

Then the Chevalier Noir said: 'I have waited for this moment long years, my son. Thus have you proved yourself.'

So it was that Edern knew that this was indeed his father, Nudd, for whom he had sought so long, and the two wept and embraced, all thoughts of combat ended.

Father and son spoke together for long hours after that, sharing all that had passed in the years of Edern's coming to manhood. Nudd told how he still felt love for Edern's mother. And the youth spoke at length of his love for Guenloie and how he felt at last that he had earned her respect. Nudd promised to seek out Edern's mother, and swore also to cease marauding the land in that place and to swear allegiance to King Arthur.

Then, for a time, the two men separated, and Nudd went to where the lady he still loved was to be found, while Edern made his way to Queen Guenloie's castle. There, he received a rapturous greeting, and at last the two spoke of their true love and admitted to each other that pride and wilfulness had kept them apart. Then they pledged themselves to each other and soon after made their way to Camelot the Golden, where they were married with the blessing of the king and queen.

And if he felt any shame at sending Edern on a task that he did not believe he would survive, King Arthur kept his own counsel now that he saw the love between and Edern and Guenloie. Soon after this Nudd himself came to the city, accompanied by his lady. They, too, were married, amid much rejoicing.

The story tells that Edern and Guenloie lived long and happy lives, and that Luguain served as Edern's squire until he too was knighted, and showed himself to be as brave as his former master. Edern himself had many adventures after this, but the story does not tell of them, perhaps because the knight's restless ways led him to journey far afield, so that he was less often to be seen at Camelot the Golden.

✢ ✤ ✢

BUT THERE IS another, darker, tale of which I have heard. It will be remembered that Sir Thomas Malory wrote of the abduction of Queen Guinevere by the knight Meleagraunce, and how she was rescued by Sir Lancelot. But there is an older tale that I have found which gives a different name to the queen's abductor: Edern. Perhaps it fell out that the hero never forgot his first encounter with King Arthur, and how later the king sent him on a mission from which it was deemed unlikely he would return. Perhaps he harboured a grudge for many years after, and in the end sought revenge by the stealing away of the queen. Perhaps also, as one in whose veins ran Faery blood (if such we are to believe), he too played a part in the battles between King Arthur and the realm of the Shining Ones. Of these things I cannot say more, since my knowledge of such matters is but slight except, perhaps, when the Lady dances on the greensward. But I mention it here so that my readers may consider for themselves whether Edern was a true hero, or a foe to King Arthur.

———— ✜ ————

EXPLICIT THE STORY OF EDERN AND OF THE LIBRE SECUNDUS OF THIS COLLECTION.

INCIPIT THE BOOK OF THE GUARDIANS OF THE GRAIL.

BOOK THREE

❧❧

GUARDIANS OF THE GRAIL

LANCELOT

26: TITUREL'S DREAM

— ✠ —

THOUGH MASTER THOMAS WROTE AT LENGTH IN 'THE BOOK OF THE SANGREAL' CONCERNING HOW THE FELLOWSHIP OF THE ROUND TABLE LEFT CAMELOT THE GOLDEN IN THE QUEST OF THE GRAIL, YET HE SEEMS TO HAVE KNOWN NOTHING OF THE ACCOUNT WHICH FOLLOWS HERE, WHICH SPEAKS OF THE BUILDING OF THE GRAIL TEMPLE, WHEREIN THE MOST SACRED VESSEL IN CHRISTENDOM WAS TO BE KEPT. NOR DID HE MENTION THE MYSTERIOUS PRIEST-KING, JOHN, WHO I HAVE HEARD BECAME A GUARDIAN OF THE GRAIL IN THE DAYS FOLLOWING THE BREAKING OF THE REALM OF ARTHUR AND THE FELLOWSHIP OF THE ROUND TABLE. ONLY HERE, IN THE STORY TOLD BY ONE WHO NAMES HIMSELF ALBRECHT, HAVE I LEARNED MORE. OF THIS MAN I KNOW NOTHING, BUT THE TALE HE TELLS IS ONE OF SUCH ILLUMINATION THAT I AM CERTAIN MASTER THOMAS WOULD HAVE INCLUDED IT HAD HE KNOWN OF IT. FOR IN TRUTH IT TELLS OF THE GRAIL BOTH BEFORE AND BEYOND THE TIME OF THE ROUND TABLE, AND THAT I BELIEVE TO BE OF INTEREST TO ALL.

✠ ✠ ✠

THE STORY BEGINS long before the time of King Arthur, when there lived a man named Titurel, a wise and noble lord who was well loved by his people, and whose piety was well known beyond the borders of his land. One night he dreamed a most powerful dream, in which an angel appeared to him and told him that he had been chosen for a holy task. 'You shall go forth and build a temple that shall contain a mighty gift from God, which shall be called the Grail.' When Titurel asked how this might be, and where the temple should be built, the angel told him that he must go to the Land of Sarras, beyond the Hidden Sea, and there seek out a mountain called Muntsalvach, and there await further wonders. 'Fear not, Titurel,' the angel told him. 'You shall have all the help you need to complete this task.'

When he awoke, Titurel was greatly troubled, for in his heart he believed that the dream

239

was true but feared that if he spoke of these things openly, he would be thought mad and that no one would help him in this appointed work.

In this he was mistaken, for on that same day there came a great number of people from different parts of the land, who offered to journey with him to Muntsalvach and there to work to build the temple for the sacred vessel. All had dreamed a dream similar to Titurel's, and all had chosen to take up the task.

In the weeks that followed more than a thousand men and women came to the court of Titurel, many from distant lands, offering to help him. As the word spread and more of his own people learned of Titurel's dream, they also wished to join him, and none thought that he was mad or had been led astray by demons, as they might well have done.

So it was that a large company left Titurel's court, and set out for the land of Sarras, which lay many days to the west. They passed through strange landscapes, forests that contained trees that grew nowhere else, and many plants and birds and animals that were unknown to them. In the end, after many weeks of travelling, they arrived at a great valley, and there they saw the mountain they had been told to seek. Around it lay a vast encampment, containing many more hundreds of people – all of whom had been summoned there by mysterious voices that spoke to them by night and day.

When they saw Titurel, they came forth to meet him and said that they were ready to begin work on the temple. And they said that the Grail itself could be seen in the sky at night, hovering above the mountain, and that every day they were miraculously fed from its goodness, so that they never required food or drink.

That night Titurel dreamed again of the angel, and was told that the mountain was invisible to all who came that way who were not pure in heart, and that all those who came there with good intent were protected and would be helped in their task, and that all the materials, including wood, stone and gold, as well as food enough for all, would be provided.

So the work began.

First, Titurel had the plants and grass cleared from the summit of the mountain. There they discovered a block of pure onyx, six feet high and thirty feet long, which Titurel ordered to be polished until it shone like the moon. Then, as he was considering the best design for the temple, he received further guidance from the Grail. For in the morning, he found a plan etched into the polished stone that showed the exact dimensions of the building.

Here Master Albrecht gives the most extraordinary description of the temple, so detailed it is as though he had walked there himself. It was based upon the shape of a rotunda, wide and high, around which were twenty-two octagonal chapels. The entire building was supported on pillars of bronze, while the interior, lined with precious stones, shone forth in a multitude of colours. Arches rose to meet sweeping buttresses, intricately carved with elaborate designs, decorated with pearl and coral. High above, in the dome of the roof, were the forms of two angels, so beautifully carved and cast that anyone who saw them would have believed them to be real,

It is said that the altars were more beautifully adorned than any that had been seen before that time. Curtains of green velvet hung above them and when the priest sang mass, a cord could be pulled that caused a mechanical dove and angel to fly down from the arch above. When they met in the centre of the temple it was as if the angel descended from Paradise and met with the Holy Spirit.

A tree of red gold, covered in elegant foliage, was also created. Ornamental birds were placed upon this, and a bellows sent breath through them, causing them to make sounds like that of their natural songs. The windows were of ornamental glass made from crystal, which focused the light so brightly it could have blinded an unwary viewer. Inlay there was in plenty, designed to diffuse the brightness, so that the lavishness of the Temple and the Grail could be fully appreciated.

Master carvers decorated everything with rich stones of many colours. Sapphire gave the colour of azure, emerald a brilliant green, while other stones gave yellow, red, brown and white. The amethyst gave three shades of colour: purple, violet and rose, bright and clear. Topaz was there also, giving two shades – yellow and golden. Anyone who saw these felt strengthened, for they contained healing energies. Other stones – chalcophanus, ruby, carnelian, chrysoprase – were there also, while as many as sixty shades were attributed to octalamus, karisian, and ardisen – all beyond the ability of the storyteller to praise.

Whatever human mind could imagine was created for the Temple of the Grail. Carved vines curled up around the arches, bending over the seats on either side, each six feet tall. Below them a forest was created, carved from stone and set with gold and silver. There roses bloomed, and bushes and boughs, bearing red and white blossoms on green stems, flourished. Other flowers of many colours, from every conceivable plant, were there also, seeming as real as possible, though created in stone and decorated with veins of pure gold.

The leaves were painted green and decorated with emeralds, and hung thickly, offering shade to those who were seated beneath. They could be heard rustling as if in a real wood, accompanied by the sound of bells, as though a great flock of falcons rose into the air, with their harness chiming. Whatever voice was heard in the temple, the effect of the gems was such that an echo filled the space, giving it a sweet tone, as that made by young birds in Maytime.

As for the roof, it was of red gold, overlaid with niello work. Both the sun and the moon were modelled in silver and gold and placed within the dome for all to see.

Beneath the surface of the onyx floor were hollowed-out shapes, where fish and other wonders of the ocean were carved in exact likeness. Pipes brought air for them from outside, causing them to move beneath the crystals that covered the floor. From some distance outside, windmills provided the power for this illusion of movement. The floor thus appeared like a lake of rippling water, covered in ice. Within it, one could see fish, animals and sea monsters that seemed to fight amongst themselves.

Outside, where the shape of the chapels rose up in great curves around the central rotunda, all was decorated with vines, leaves and curious creatures such as dwarves and sea monsters. Such things caused many who saw them to smile. Between these, all along the walls, were even more wonderful carvings.

A single great tower rose from the centre of the temple, crafted in pure gold, inlaid with thousands of bright stones. These decorated the whole tower, which was twice as tall as the temple. At the very summit of this tower was a huge carbuncle, its radiance bright enough to lighten the darkness. No matter how far the Company of the Grail went from the temple they could see the light, which called out to them to return safely to their home.

The work was carried out with masterly

skill by those who had come from so far to help in the creation of the building; everything was made beautiful in the name of the Grail. Despite this, the work could not have been completed by human hands alone; only through the power of the Grail itself was it done.

As it was, the work took thirty years to complete, but at the end of that time the Grail was established in the heart of the temple, where it rested until the Grail seekers came in search of it.

✠ ✠ ✠

SO IT WAS that the most sacred vessel of the Sangrail remained hidden in the temple built by Titurel, with the help of angels. There, in due time, came the three knights of King Arthur: Sir Galahad, Sir Perceval, and Sir Bors, who awoke the sleeping light of the Grail so that it spread across the realm. And afterwards Sir Galahad journeyed in the spirit to the presence of God, and Sir Bors returned to Camelot the Golden to relate all that had occurred.

This much Sir Thomas told in his mighty book, and he tells us also how, in the end, the Grail was taken up to heaven – *'since when was there never man so hardy as to say that he had seen the Sangreal.'* * Whether this is true or not this tale offers another telling. For what of Sir Perceval? He, as others who tell the story of the Grail will say, returned to its earthly home atop the mountain of Muntsalvach and there the vessel came once again into the realm of King Arthur, and Perceval became its new guardian.

But this is not the end of the story, for in the book by Master Albrecht, we are told that

---

* *Le Morte D'Arthur* ed. J Matthews, Book XVII, Ch. xxii.

in a later time, the descendants of Titurel and Perceval began to quarrel over the possession of the sacred vessel. Also, that they were concerned that others, from beyond the realm of Arthur, might seek to destroy the most holy relic.

Long they debated, and many disagreements were heard and fought over – until at last, Titurel himself, whose life had been extended far beyond that of any other man, spoke out.

'It seems to me,' he said, 'that the Grail must be taken from here and delivered into a place where it will be safe from the darkness of the world. I have prayed and sought for an answer these many nights, and have asked to be shown a place where the Grail may rest in safety until such time as it is needed again, so that others may seek it. To accomplish this we must undertake a journey.'

All agreed to follow Titurel, as they and their predecessors had done for so long. And so began the next great adventure of the Grail. The company of the sacred vessel set forth in search of a new home, guided once again by the angels, who spoke with the ancient king, and also fed them on their journey.

They travelled for many months across lands both strange and familiar, until they came to the edge of the sea. There they took ship for a distant island named Pitimont, where they were welcomed by those who had been told of the coming of a wise man who was the guardian of the Grail.

There the company remained for several days, and in that time the Grail provided food and drink for all upon the island. The leader of the people then came to Titurel and begged him to be their king and to rule over them. But the ancient Grail Lord refused, declaring that their path lay elsewhere.

Sadly, the people wished them well, and

afterwards they renamed their city Grals, and built a temple in the likeness of that on Muntsalvach with twenty-two altars.

Meanwhile, the Company of the Grail sailed across the Hidden Sea. There they encountered savage waters, churned to a maelstrom by a mighty lodestone which lay beneath that part of the ocean. For many days their ship was tossed upon the waves and more than one of the company was swallowed by the sea.

But at last they reached shore in a land that no one recognised. They went ashore and followed the road that led them into a place of great beauty. No words exist to describe this place, so marvellous was it. Soft grasses grew there and flowers blossomed on every side, perfuming the air. Tall trees grew from the earth and birds sang from their branches. Strange beasts followed the company and could be heard calling to each other in the night.

On the third day the company saw before them a most wonderful city, its walls of crystal and its gates of gold. No one of the company had ever seen a fairer place, unless it was the temple of the Grail itself. As they approached, a group of riders came forth to meet them. At their head was the most noble man, and accompanying him came a bevy of lords of great renown.

Titurel himself greeted the nobleman as both priest and king: 'Sire, we ask for shelter and bring you news of a great wonder.'

The priest-king, who was known as Prester John, King of Ind and all the lands to the east, unto the very walls of Paradise, welcomed them all. 'I have dreamed of your coming this past five nights,' he said. 'You are welcome to my lands and free to stay for as long as you wish.'

So it was that the Company of the Grail came to that most wondrous land, of which

→ *The Temple of the Grail* ←

so much has been written, though few have trodden there. It is said that its rivers run full of jewels, and that trees of gold and silver grow on the fertile soil. There also, creatures believed to be fabled roam free, and the priest-king rules over many hundreds of wise and noble people.

Welcomed to this place, the company found themselves led to a mighty palace, at the centre of which was a vast courtyard with twenty-five circular levels. At the centre was a pillar on top of which was a vast ciborium which dispensed incense around the whole palace. Above it, hovering in the air, was a vast mirror which showed within it everything that was taking place in the lands around for many leagues.

All this and many more wonders the company saw, some even greater than those created on the summit of Muntsalvach. Titurel and the priest-king spoke together for many days, and the old Grail Lord told all the history of the sacred vessel. And at length Prester John asked if he might see this great thing. 'For now that I have heard of this wonder, my heart longs to see it for myself.'

So the Grail was brought forth and uncovered and the priest-king looked upon it and then knelt before it and bowed his head. At this Titurel said: 'My lord, you have seen this divine vessel. Will you allow us to give it into your care?' For this was what the angels who guided him had said he must do.

'Of that I shall be the most glad of any man on this earth,' answered the priest-king.

'Then I ask but one thing of you,' Titurel said. 'For five hundred years I have watched over this vessel, and I would be released from its service. The only one way I may be permitted to die is by passing it to you, and being thus no longer able to see it. For those who do so every day cannot die.'

Prester John gave his word that this would be so, and with that he took up the Grail and carried it into the temple that stood at the heart of his palace. There he placed it upon an altar of chalcedony and swore to protect it for as long as he lived.

Only then was Titurel permitted to die. He lay upon a great bed in the palace for one more night, while the members of the Grail Company came to take their leave of him. On the next day he died, and his spirit, so the story tells, was carried to heaven by the angels who had guided him all this time.

As to the Grail, Prester John took it into his care, and so at last it passed out of memory. None can tell how long the priest-king lived beyond that time – but perhaps, like Titurel, his life was extended so that he is living yet. But neither he nor the Grail were seen again in the lands of men, and in time the kingdom of Prester John became a place of mystery, in which few believed.

✛ ✛ ✛

THUS WAS TITUREL'S dream completed, and the story of the Grail was left to be written by many wise storytellers, including he who named himself Albrecht. And this, it seems to me, is a fitting end to the history of the Sangrail as it was begun by Master Thomas and is here concluded.

EXPLICIT THE STORY OF TITUREL'S DREAM AND WHAT CAME AFTER.

INCIPIT THE STORY OF KING ARTHUR'S QUEST.

27: KING ARTHUR'S QUEST

MANY ARE THE TALES TOLD OF THE GREAT QUEST FOR THE HOLY GRAIL, NOT LEAST THOSE WHICH SIR THOMAS INCLUDED IN BOOKS THIRTEEN TO SEVENTEEN OF HIS MIGHTY WORK. IN EACH OF THE TALES THAT I HAVE READ, AND THOSE THAT I HAVE INCLUDED HERE AND ELSEWHERE, IT IS MOST OFTEN OF GALAHAD, PERCEVAL, AND BORS THAT WE HEAR. THESE WERE THE GREATEST KNIGHTS TO ACHIEVE THE MYSTERY IN ALL ITS WONDER AND FEARFUL POWER. BUT THERE IS ANOTHER STORY THAT I HAVE FOUND, WHICH IN SOME MANNER LOOKS FORWARD TO THE QUEST, BUT IN WHICH IT IS KING ARTHUR HIMSELF WHO SETS FORTH ON A JOURNEY THAT TAKES HIM TO THE VERY HEART OF THAT LAND WHICH LIES SOMEWHERE BETWEEN THE GREAT WOOD OF BROCELIANDE AND THE SHINING CITY OF SARRAS. HERE, THE HOLY VESSEL IS SAID TO HAVE BEEN TAKEN BY SIR GALAHAD BEFORE, AS SOME SAY, IT WAS RAISED UP TO HEAVEN. OF THESE THINGS I SHALL NOT SPEAK, FOR OTHERS HAVE DONE SO IN WAYS MORE TRUE THAN MINE, AND INDEED MASTER THOMAS HIMSELF HAS WRITTEN OF THEM DEEPLY AND PROFOUNDLY – BUT I PLACE THIS STORY HERE, AMONGST OTHERS OF THE GRAIL, TO SHOW HOW KING ARTHUR HIMSELF, WHO WAS IN A CERTAIN WAY A WOUNDED KING, SUCH AS WAS THE GUARDIAN OF THE VESSEL, LEARNED OF IT AND THE PART IT WOULD PLAY IN THE HISTORY OF LOGRES.

✠ ✠ ✠

THROUGHOUT THE LONG years of King Arthur's reign, despite the strength of the Round Table knights, there were still times when darkness spilled out across the land. In one such time, the king was so weighed down by this he sent out fewer and fewer knights to seek for wrongs to right, and so there were less petitioners who came to Camelot the Golden.

245

The knights of the Fellowship became idle, and some departed for other kingdoms, where they might find better use for their skills and their bravery. The greatest knights, Sir Lancelot, Sir Gawain, Sir Owein and others, remained, but sorrow walked the halls of Camelot the Golden in spite of this.

Perhaps the greatest sadness of all clung to the king himself, who took to wandering the halls, or remaining in his chambers in a state of silent contemplation. One day he found Queen Guinevere seated in a window staring out with eyes from which ran tears that coursed down her cheeks.

'Why do you weep, my love?' asked the king, knowing the answer.

'It seems to me that all we have built is falling into ruin,' answered Queen Guinevere. 'Our knights are deserting us and fewer adventures have come our way this year past. I fear that God has deserted us.'

King Arthur said. 'It is true, my lady. And because of this I also have no desire to seek adventure. I know not what to do. Since Merlin left I have no one to turn to but you, my love.'

At this Queen Guinevere smiled. 'I am no enchantress,' she said. 'But I have some wisdom, and I have heard tell of a place not far from here, within the Great Wood. It is known as the White Chapel, and I am told that a most wise man dwells there. It may be that he could advise you – or at least tell you why the land seems so wounded.'

His face alight with hope, the king said: 'I shall go there at first light tomorrow. No one but I may do this, or know of it. Therefore I shall go alone.'

'At least take a page with you,' urged the queen.

At first reluctant, King Arthur finally agreed. He chose a youth named Carhus and instructed him to prepare a mount for him at the break of day. This the boy promised to do, then settled down by the fire in the great hall to await the coming of dawn. He did not bother to go to bed, but instead fell asleep where he lay. In his sleep he had a dream: he thought that he had woken and that King Arthur had gone without him. Greatly troubled by this, he belted on his sword and ran to saddle a horse. Then he rode into the forest, following what seemed to be the hoofprints of the king's steed. For what seemed ages he hastened to catch his master, but as fast as he rode he could not see him. Soon, dreaming still, he came to a place where the path ended and he could find no more signs of the king. Then he saw where a chapel stood, its walls made of white marble, and thinking King Arthur must have gone there to pray, he galloped over and, having tied his horse to a tree, entered the chapel.

Within, all was silent and nothing moved save the flames of four candles that were set in golden candlesticks around a bed, upon which lay a dead knight most splendidly dressed. Then Carhus wondered greatly that this noble man should be left there without anyone to watch with him, and it came into his mind to take one of the golden candlesticks to give to the

The chapel in the Great Wood

king. He took it and placed it inside his doublet. Then he rode on, still looking for signs of his master's passing.

Before he had gone far he saw coming towards him a man of more than natural height – almost a giant indeed. Despite this, Carhus approached him and asked if he had seen the king.

'I have not,' answered the tall man grimly. 'But I see you, boy, and I know that you have taken one of the candlesticks from the chapel where a great man lies in state. Give it back at once, or suffer the consequences!'

Still in his dream, the boy answered that he would not, for he desired to give the candlestick to his king. At this, the tall man pulled a knife from its sheath and before the boy could say a word he plunged the blade into his side beneath the arm.

With a great cry, the page awoke, and found that a knife was indeed embedded in his side. Now he screamed in pain, calling out for a priest, for he knew his wound was mortal. At once men came running, and then the king and queen were summoned, for no one knew how the boy had received his terrible wound.

Barely able to speak, the page gasped out his story, begging them not to withdraw the knife until he had told King Arthur all that had occurred. By his side, lay the golden candlestick, still with a candle in it, and as he spoke the candle lit of its own accord.

Then the priest who had been summoned heard the boy's confession and gave him the last rites, and a surgeon withdrew the knife from his side. And with this his soul escaped from his body.

Both King Arthur and Queen Guinevere, along with all who had witnessed this, bewailed the death of the youth, who was much liked. His father was himself a knight of the Round

Table, Yvain l'Autre, and he too wept when he was shown the body of his son. King Arthur, thinking how he had himself intended to go where the page had visited in his dream, promised to avenge him.

'I shall depart in the morning,' he said, 'and follow the way Carhus went. If I can catch the one who wounded him, I will be sure to bring him to heel so that he may suffer the penalty of the law.'

Next day King Arthur was as good as his word. As dawn began he was already dressed, accoutred and armed, with his great sword Excalibur at his side and his finest steed saddled and ready. Several of the knights asked to go with him, but the king refused them all, declaring that the page had lost his life because he had served the king, and that the king would avenge him if God allowed.

Then he rode away into the forest and, watching him, all marvelled at the strength and stature of their lord, who seemed to them stronger and more certain of his place in the world than he had been for many a day.

✠ ✠ ✠

KING ARTHUR RODE deeply into the Great Wood, until he came to a wide clearing amid the trees, and there he saw a most beautiful chapel, its walls built of the whitest stone. Beside it was a hermitage, and the hermit himself, dressed in alb and dalmatic, was preparing to celebrate mass. The king, having tethered his steed to a tree, made to enter the chapel. There he found that he could not go in. Though the door was open and no one blocked his way, yet he could not even set foot within, and was forced to remain outside.

From there he saw a most wondrous and marvellous scene. The hermit stood before the altar and on his right side stood a most beautiful child, crowned with gold and dressed in robes of silk. To his left stood an equally beautiful woman, from whom shone a great light. And as the hermit began the *Confiteor*,[*] the lady sat on a throne next to the altar and the child sat upon her lap. And she said to him: 'Sire, you are my father, my son, and my guardian.'

When the king heard this he marvelled greatly, and again sought to enter the chapel. But once more he was prevented from doing so, though how and in what manner he could not say. Then he saw where a ray of sunlight pierced the window above the altar and shone down upon it, and there was for a moment a great flame, brighter than any King Arthur had ever seen, that danced there. And there was a great singing of many voices, though the king could see no other beings save the three before the altar.

Within, the mass progressed and when it came to the reading of the gospel, it seemed that many voices joined in, though the king saw no one there. At the *offertory*,[†] the lady took up her son in her arms and gave him to the hermit, who placed him upon the altar.

At this, King Arthur felt such sorrow that tears came to his eyes and he fell to his knees in the doorway of the chapel. And for a moment he could see nothing, but then he thought that he saw the hermit offering the child as if it were a sacrifice, but that it was no longer a child but a man who bore all the wounds of a crucified man. Then from every side King Arthur heard the song of angels, the most beautiful that he had ever heard, and there he saw again the

child, who raised his arms to his mother and was again seated in her lap.

Then it was, for so the story tells it, that King Arthur was allowed to see the Grail, and the five changes through which it passed. But of these none may speak save those who have themselves undertaken and achieved the search for the sacred vessel.

Then a great voice declared: *Ite missa est*,[‡] and the child took his mother's hand and all were gone from that place, save for the hermit. The flame that had danced upon the altar was also gone and it seemed to the king that, though he had seen none but the three figures of the hermit, the child and the lady, that a great host had been present and were there no longer.

The hermit turned to him and said: 'You may enter, King Arthur.' And at once that which had prevented him from going into the chapel was gone, so he knelt before the hermit and asked for his blessing.

'You shall have it indeed,' said the hermit. 'But I must tell you that all is not well in your kingdom. You have lost your purpose and allowed your dream of chivalry to fall into misuse.'

'That I know, all too well,' said King Arthur sadly. 'For that reason I came here to ask for your wisdom.'

The hermit looked at King Arthur with great solemnity. 'Your land is meant to be the home of the Holy Grail, but in this time it is lost to you. Soon will come many signs and wonders and your knights will go forth in search of the sacred vessel. You shall remain behind, for you are not yet ready to see the whole of the mysteries. Indeed, few of your people will do so

[*] Part of the Latin Mass in which the priest leads a general confession.
[†] The point in the Latin mass where the priest offers the wine and wafer.

[‡] 'It is ended.' The phrase spoken by the priest at the end of the Latin mass.

in this time, but the opportunity to go on the Great Quest shall be offered to all.'

Then the hermit blessed King Arthur and told him: 'In a place far from here is a great castle, the home of he who is called the Rich Fisherman, for he fishes for wisdom and guards that which is beyond price. Now he is wounded and cannot heal until the mystery is observed and the right question is asked as to its meaning. Until then there shall be no peace in this land, and parts of it shall be spoiled and become known as the Wasteland. If the whole of your noble kingdom is not to be made like this, you must hope that amongst your knights there are those who shall bring about the achieving of the Grail.'

Then he looked again at the king and said: 'It seems to me that you also are wounded, and that you shall not be restored to yourself until all those who have left your court are called upon to return.'

At this King Arthur felt a great weight upon his heart, but he swore upon his life that he would do all that he could to set things right, and with that he took his leave of the hermit and set out back the way he had come towards Camelot the Golden.

Now the story tells how, on his way, the king met with the tall man who had mortally wounded the page Carhus, and King Arthur challenged him and after a great battle, slew him. And on his return he had made a fitting tomb to the boy's honuor and set the golden candlestick upon it. And it is said that the candle burned bright for long days after, and that it never went out until all the lights of the city were doused when the king was taken into Avalon. Thereafter all the knights who had departed the realm returned, so that the Fellowship of the Round Table was whole again for that time.

THUS IT WAS that the Great Quest for the Grail began soon after. And at Camelot the Golden, as Sir Thomas Malory and others have told, there came the light of the Grail into the midst of the Fellowship, who declared that they would all follow that light – until Sir Galahad, Sir Perceval, and Sir Bors were granted the gift of seeing the mysteries openly. But of these matters I will not speak at this time, for most are known to those who have read the stories of King Arthur's realm. But this I will say. In time the Wasteland was healed, as was the Rich Fisherman, and for a time the land of Logres fared well, until the days when the Round Table Fellowship was broken for ever. And certain it is that King Arthur never forgot what he had witnessed in the White Chapel, but lived every day of his life to the full – as must any who love this world and long for another.

EXPLICIT KING ARTHUR'S QUEST.
INCIPIT THE CROWN OF THE GRAIL, WHEREIN MORE SHALL BE TOLD THAT WAS BUT HINTED AT ABOVE.

28: THE CROWN OF THE GRAIL

THOSE WHO HAVE READ SIR THOMAS MALORY'S ACCOUNT OF THE GREATEST QUEST UNDERTAKEN BY THE FELLOWSHIP OF THE ROUND TABLE – THAT OF THE SEARCH FOR THE HOLY GRAIL, WHICH IT IS SAID WAS USED BY OUR LORD TO CELEBRATE THE LAST SUPPER – WILL KNOW THAT IT WAS SIR GALAHAD, SON OF THE GREAT LANCELOT, WHO CAME AT LAST TO THE CASTLE OF THE GRAIL AND, WITH HIS TWO COMPANIONS, SIR PERCEVAL AND SIR BORS, SAW THERE THE SECRETS OF THE HOLY VESSEL UNVEILED. AMONG THOSE LISTED BY SIR THOMAS WHO SET FORTH ON THE GREAT QUEST, BUT WHO FAILED TO ACCOMPLISH IT, ARE SIR LANCELOT HIMSELF, WHO WAS FORBIDDEN THE GRAIL BECAUSE OF HIS ILLICIT LOVE FOR QUEEN GUINEVERE, AND SIR GAWAIN, WHO DESPITE HIS NOBLENESS AND STRENGTH WAS PREVENTED FROM ACHIEVING THE MYSTERY BECAUSE OF HIS GREAT LOVE FOR WOMEN. THUS, WHEN I CAME UPON THE TALE THAT FOLLOWS, WRITTEN BY ONE NAMED HEINRICH VON DEM TÜRLIN, I WAS AMAZED TO READ HOW SIR GAWAIN ACCOMPLISHED MUCH THAT HAS SINCE BEEN FORGOTTEN. I AM CERTAIN THAT, HAD HE KNOWN OF THIS VERSION OF EVENTS, MASTER THOMAS WOULD HAVE INCLUDED IT. THUS, I MAKE NO APOLOGY FOR TELLING IT HERE, FOR IT IS INDEED A MOST WONDROUS STORY.

✝ ✝ ✝

IN THOSE DAYS many wonders came to pass, and the Knights of the Round Table set forth on more adventures than ever before. The greatest adventure of all was the quest for the Grail, that holy vessel which some believed had been used to celebrate the first Eucharist on the occasion of the Last Supper. Others believed it a wonder out of Faery and sought it with great eagerness in their hunger for the marvels that attended so much of the world in that time.

Of those who set forth in quest of the

sacred vessel, many fell by the wayside, and were not heard from again. Nor were their bodies ever found, for they vanished without trace in the wilderness of the wasted land or the secret depths of the Great Wood of Broceliande – for both places were such that many who came there could not bear the power they possessed, and so were consumed by them utterly.

Amongst those who came closest to the discovery of the true nature of the Grail were Sir Perceval and Sir Galahad, and their adventures are well known and often told. Thus also in the instance of Sir Lancelot, whose sorrowful failure was because he loved King Arthur's queen more than life itself and thus was excluded from the quest. But amongst all those who sought the vessel that had no name, one other did so with such determination that he came as near as any to uncovering its secrets. This was Sir Gawain, who for all his impulsive nature and hot temper, yet brooded long on the nature of being, and when challenged gave all that he might to the quest.

Let us begin therefore with the great knight upon the road. Far from Camelot the Golden the king's nephew had ridden day and night, having sworn, before all the Knights of the Round Table, that he would not spend more than a single night in the same place until he found the Grail.

On this day he was so deep in thought that he did not notice where his steed Gringolet led him, or that he had turned aside from the road upon which he had been, following a narrow track that led into the depths of the Great Wood. There Gawain was brought to his senses by the sounds of battle somewhere amid the trees. Eagerly he followed the clash of arms, but as fast as he rode they seemed always to be as far ahead as before.

Then he saw where a lady rode on a white horse toward him. Across its saddle was the body of a dead knight, for whom the lady wept bitterly. When she saw Sir Gawain, she cried aloud: 'Ah! That I should suffer such a terrible evil! This was my love, who might have been spared or healed had not Sir Perceval failed to ask the question that was needed to heal all the Wasteland.'

Sir Gawain knew nothing of this, and the story has been often told, but for those who may not know of it, I will say that the brave knight Perceval had come to a strange castle whose lord suffered an unhealing wound. This could only be set right by the asking of a question about a strange procession which passed through the hall every night at the same time. Only if he who saw it asked the purpose of this would the lord be healed; and it is also said that if this occurred then the lands around, which were called the Wasted Lands, would flower again. Knowing nothing of this, Sir Gawain, like his brother in arms, failed to ask the mournful lady why she inveighed against Sir Perceval.

While he deliberated upon her words, the lady had ridden on, weeping as she went, and angrily crying out against the cruelty of the world. Gawain made up his mind to follow her, but as fast as he rode he found he could not overtake her, and in a while she was gone from sight.

At the same time he heard again the sounds of battle and soon emerged onto a wide plain where nothing, neither grass nor tree, or any other kind of growing thing, thrived. There, he saw a strange battle taking place. On the one hand a band of some fifty knights, all of them wearing white armour that gleamed as brightly as if it were reflecting the sun – though indeed there were only grey clouds over that place – fought against two horses whose riders could not be seen. Instead, a great spear and a mighty sword were wielded, as if by unseen hands. Nor could any of the white knights withstand them. Again and again the spear struck them down, or the sword cut deeply into them, so that their blood ran down and soaked the earth. Not one could damage either the horses or their unseen riders, whose spear and sword were soon covered in blood and yet suffered no damage.

These things Sir Gawain saw, and despite the pity he felt, he could do nothing but watch until all the white knights were slain. At which point the two horses departed at great speed, leaving Gawain to look with sorrow upon the field of the dead. Then a further wonder took place, for as he watched, the bodies began to smoke and then burst into flame. Every part of them, including their armour, was consumed, until there was nothing remaining but dust, which blew away in the air.

Shaken by this, Sir Gawain spurred his own steed to follow the two horses, but try as he might, they drew ever further away from him. At this point, as he rode deeper and deeper into the waste, he saw in these regions a number of strange things such as he had never witnessed in all his life and pursuit of adventure as a knight of the Round Table.

First he saw where a giant lay stretched out dead upon the earth, and how over it a great cloud of dark birds flew down to strip the flesh from its body. And there a naked woman flailed with a staff to drive the birds away, but in vain as they tore at the giant's flesh, consuming its heart and entrails and crying out all the time with their delight.

Though Gawain was shocked by the sight, he had in mind only to catch up with the two horses and their invisible riders, so that he looked ahead towards a range of mountains and made no move to stop or speak to the woman.

Only a little way beyond he saw another scene, that had he not been driven by his desire to catch the invisible knights, he would have sought to find a meaning for. He saw a strange and terrible beast which was the colour of the deepest green and had sprouting from its brow a long and spiralling horn. On its back rode a woman who was as strange to look upon as her steed. Long and ice-white was her hair, that fell to her waist. It was bound by a circlet of gold, and beneath it her face was yellow and desolate and shone like fire. In her left hand she held a hempen rope, at the end of which was tied a naked man, forced to run at her side, while she whipped him cruelly, drawing blood from his flesh.

It seemed then, that as far as Gawain went into this strange land, the more things he witnessed that would normally have caused him to stop or pursue them. But in each case his desire to overtake his quarry was such that he continued on his way.

Next a knight clad entirely in black armour came in sight. From his hand hung a maiden's head, dangling by its hair. A second knight followed, crying out to the first to stop and face him and show his worth as a knight should. But the black-clad man made no attempt to stop and both soon vanished from sight.

Still Sir Gawain rode on, and entered a deeper part of the forest. There, beneath a tree, he saw a grim sight. A broad shield was laid upon the ground, to which was tethered a fine horse. From its saddlebow hung a crested helmet and a richly decorated sword. Upon the shield was piled a rich hauberk, mailed stockings and other armour, and on top of these was placed a man's head. All were drenched in blood. As Gawain looked at this he heard the sound of three voices lamenting, but try as he would, he could see nothing of those who wept, and so he rode onwards.

Soon after he came to where a most beautiful mansion stood, but unlike anything he had seen before it was surrounded by a wall of clear crystal, at least as high as five tall men. He could see no way in, and paused to wonder at its purpose. As he did so he heard the sound of women's voices raised in song, and saw where several maidens played and sang together before the gates of the manor.

As he watched, out of the forest came a great churl, naked and hairy and at least as high as three men. In his hand he carried a mighty club, which Sir Gawain believed would have required at least four men to lift. Then the giant let out a great cry and struck the crystal wall, so that it shattered into a thousand pieces.

At once the manor began to burn, as did the ground around it. The maidens cried aloud as their clothing burst into flames and they were consumed in a matter of moments. As Gawain looked at this dreadful scene he longed to offer help, but so great was the conflagration he could do nothing but watch as the whole place was consumed. The churl meanwhile engaged in a strange, shuffling dance then, waving his huge club, he stalked off back into the forest, making no sign that he had even seen Sir Gawain. The knight, greatly saddened by these things, made himself continue his search for the horses and their unseen riders.

✛ ✛ ✛

THE LAND THROUGH which he rode now began to rise and in the distance he saw where a mountain rose high into the clouds. There it was that he caught sight of

the two horses and thus encouraged urged his mount to overtake them.

Still they remained beyond his reach, but the way now led into a wide meadow that was filled with roses. The scent they gave off was so powerful that it made Gawain feel light-of-head. After the dark and terrible scenes he had witnessed, this place seemed like a veritable paradise, and with each breath he grew stronger, the weariness of his long pursuit falling from him as if it had never been. Gringolet also seemed to gain strength and its speed increased.

Now it was that Gawain came to a rich-seeming castle, surrounded by a wide moat and protected by great walls. He rode up and called out to anyone who might hear, requesting admittance. At first there was no answer, but in a while a porter arrived. To Gawain's surprise he greeted the knight by name and invited him to enter. Pages came to take his horse to the stable and others to help him remove his armour. Then he went inside the keep and looked about him in wonder. The hall was vast indeed, but to his surprise it was empty except for a great bed on which sat a man with many winters upon him. So aged was he that he could no longer walk, but he smiled upon Gawain and told him that he was welcome and that supper would soon be served. Meanwhile he encouraged the knight to explore the castle.

This Gawain did, amazed to see how richly decorated it was. At length he found his way to a small chapel and decided to enter it so that he might offer prayers for those whom he had seen so cruelly killed on his journey. As he crossed the threshold the room became as dark as night, though the sun still stood high in the heavens. Then, several candles were suddenly lit around the walls and on the altar, though Gawain could not see who set them alight. At this moment a window opened in the roof of the chapel and through this descended a most beautiful naked sword. It came to rest before Gawain, who began to admire it. But almost at once it melted away as if it was merely a dream, leaving Gawain to wonder at its meaning.

Not without some trepidation he knelt down, but before he could begin his orisons, there came a great crash of thunder and all of the candles were doused. As Sir Gawain started to his feet, a gleam of light came from one of the walls and then he saw where a great spear, so long that no single man could have held it, emerged from within the stones. It was held by two hands, clad in gauntlets such as a knight would wear, and from its tip ran drops of blood that fell to the floor.

Then there came the sound of a voice lamenting. Gawain could not tell if it was a woman or a man, but its pain was such that it saddened him greatly. Looking around he saw no sign of the voice's owner. Then a gust of air passed through the chamber and once again the candles were doused.

After a while the voice ceased its lament and the candles were lit once again. Gawain looked around and saw neither the spear, nor any other person. With this he completed his prayers, crossed himself and left the chapel.

Beyond, the hall was now filled by people – knights and ladies and servants who were preparing for a great feast. Soon Sir Gawain was invited to be seated close to the frail old man on the bed. But before anyone could begin to eat there came into the hall a procession such as Gawain had never seen the like before.

The wondrous procession was led by four beautiful maidens carrying candles set into golden candelabra. Each one was as richly dressed as any the knight had seen, and all wore golden crowns such as might have belonged to queens. Following them came the most splendidly dressed lady of all. Golden hair spilled out from under a circlet of gold set with many jewels, and in her hands she carried a crystal vessel. As Gawain looked closer he saw that it was filled with fresh blood, and he watched in wonder as the maiden went to where the ancient man sat upon his bed. There the four candle bearers surrounded him and the maiden with the crystal cup held it out to the lord, who drank from it before lying back down on his bed and crossing both hands upon his breast. Then he seemed to sleep, while all around him the people of the castle filled their plates with food and their rich goblets with the finest wine and the maidens withdrew with the bright candles and the vessel of blood.

All of this Gawain watched and, more than once, was about to speak his thoughts aloud, asking for the meaning of the scene he had witnessed but, as was ever the way with the king's nephew, he decided to wait for a moment when it would be polite to ask such a question. So it was that the evening passed pleasantly with much merriment and music, so that not once did Sir Gawain feel that he could speak his thoughts aloud.

In time the feast ended and the people of the castle began to depart to their rest. Still Gawain sat and waited, until finally he was alone. No one spoke to him of the events that had taken place there, and he waited in vain for someone to show him to a place where he could sleep.

Finally, with the hall empty, Gawain approached the great bed where the ancient man lay, preparing to ask him the questions that plagued him – the meaning of the procession, the vessel of crystal and the blood it contained. Perhaps, he wondered, could this be the very Grail that he and his followers were seeking? But when he came close to the old lord he saw

PLATE 6: *'He saw a strange and terrible beast which was the colour of the deepest green and had sprouting from its brow a long and spiralling horn'*

that he no longer breathed, but lay peacefully in the great bed.

Now Gawain felt true fear, for he knew in his heart that these things were of great import, but he had missed the chance to question them. Surely he must find someone to ask when the new day came. He set forth to wander the passageways of the castle in search of a place to sleep, and found himself instead at the stables. There, he saw Gringolet in a stall with sufficient food for more than one night, and by its side a splendid bed had been set up, adorned with rich hangings and soft pillows. Here Gawain rested, and in the morning woke to find fresh food laid out beside him, but though he rose and made his way back to the great hall, he saw no living soul, and heard nothing but the soughing of the wind along the walls of the great castle. The body of the old lord was gone also, and Gawain wondered where it would be interred and how the passing of this ancient and noble man would be celebrated.

So it was that the king's nephew donned his armour and mounted his horse. Then, wondering still, he left the strange castle behind and resumed his search for the two steeds and their hidden riders.

✛ ✛ ✛

SO IT WAS that Sir Gawain set forth on a new series of adventures which, were I to tell them all, would delay the main purpose of this story – which concerns Gawain's objective in finding his way to the Grail, and learning the true meanings of the strange events to which he had been witness. Nor did he ever find the two knights who rode invisibly. Thus I shall pass over his battle with a dragon, whose blood was so hot that it melted much of Gawain's armour and would have consumed his great

steed had he not protected it with his shield. Finally he slew the beast with a borrowed sword which melted quite away in the dragon's hot flesh. Nor shall I speak of the number of knights who confronted him, and whom he fought and defeated, often with no little hurt to himself. But always he went onward, ever with the thought of the Grail and the strange procession he had witnessed in the castle of the ancient lord.

But one part of the tale I must tell, for it says much about the qualities possessed by Sir Gawain, and his many encounters with the women of Faery. I have heard it said before that the king's nephew served a goddess, and even that he was under her protection – but only in this tale have I found the truth of this.

So let me speak of how, after many adventures, Sir Gawain crossed the unseen border into the faery realm, where nothing is as it seems and no one who enters there leaves it unscathed or unchanged. From here came many of the challenges presented to the Round Table Fellowship, and it has been said – and I have no reason to doubt it – that King Arthur himself spent time in that place, so that, when the time came for his passing, he was taken into the place named Avalon, where his own half-sister, Morgana, herself of faery blood, rules supreme.

But these are matters for another time. Now I shall return to Sir Gawain, who followed a wandering path through woodlands, blossoming valleys and high crested peaks, until he came at last to where a great expanse of water lay cupped by the surrounding mountains. No road led around it, but in the distance Sir Gawain saw the sunlight flash from the walls and towers of a great castle.

Here he paused, wondering how he might gain entrance to this place, and it was at that moment that a knight clad in silver armour appeared. Ever wary, Gawain saluted him and the silver clad man greeted him pleasantly enough.

'How may I cross this water to the castle that lies beyond?' asked Gawain.

'Only by magic,' replied the knight. 'For that is the home of Dame Fortune herself, that no man may enter except at her invitation. No one may cross the water without a magical skein woven by faery women for this purpose.'

'Where may I find this skein?' asked Gawain.

'It is in my possession,' the silver clad knight told him. 'Only by facing me in battle can you receive it.'

'Then,' said Sir Gawain, 'we must do battle together, for I feel most strongly that my path lies to that castle and beyond.'

'Even if you defeat me and gain the magical rope, it is unlikely you will enter or leave the castle without the blessing of Dame Fortune, which is given to few,' said the other.

'Nevertheless, I must try,' answered Gawain.

So the two knights saluted each other and withdrew to prepare for battle. When they came together, both broke their spears, and the noise they made was loud enough to be heard many leagues away. All the birds in that place flew up, crying loudly, but even they could not drown out the clanging of the two knights' swords against shield and breastplate.

Gawain found the silver knight a mighty fighter indeed, perhaps the strongest he had encountered, but in the end his strength and skill with sword and poignard proved him the better of the two, and he felled the knight in the silver armour to the earth in such manner that he could not raise himself again.

Thus the man cried out for mercy and named Gawain the strongest opponent he had

ever met. 'Surely you must be protected by powers as great as those of my lady,' said the silver knight. 'For by no other means could I be beaten.'

'Well,' Gawain replied, 'it is my belief that muscle and sinew fuels my strength.' Then he demanded that the silver knight give him the magical skein.

'It is close by, in my house,' answered the beaten man. 'But I am not sure how I may get there, hurt as I am.'

So Sir Gawain helped the wounded knight to stand, and though he was no small man, the king's nephew lifted him up on his shoulders and bore him back to his house, which lay nearby, hidden among the trees. There, the knight gave into Gawain's hands the magical rope, which gleamed like silver and felt as if it were alive beneath his hands.

Bidding farewell to his opponent, whose servants had emerged and were ready to care for him, Sir Gawain returned to the edge of the lake, and as he had been bidden threw the rope out upon the water, which at once hardened as if to ice.

Greatly wondering, Sir Gawain mounted Gringolet and rode out across it, winding up the silvery rope behind him as he went. When he reached the other side of the lake he had all of the skein in his hands, and looking back saw that the water had returned to normal. Then he looked towards the castle and saw to his amazement that it seemed made entirely of precious stones, including emeralds, rubies, chrysoprase and mighty blocks of tourmaline, along with carnelians, amethysts, chalcedony and agate. Indeed, so much did it sparkle and glitter that it almost dazzled Sir Gawain.

Riding up to the entrance the king's nephew tied Gringolet to a fair cedar tree which grew there. Then he set aside his shield and hung his sword and helm from the pommel of his saddle – for in his heart he knew that he would suffer no attack in this place – though how he knew this he could not have said.

Now he heard voices raised in sweet song, and he walked slowly beneath the jewelled gatehouse and into a mighty hall, capped by a great dome on which were picked out constellations made of diamonds and agate. The walls were pierced by tall windows which seemed to reflect light, so that it was never wholly dark within, but changed constantly, making all that lay before him hard to see.

As his eyes became used to this, Sir Gawain saw before him a most wondrous sight. In the furthermost part of the hall stood a vast wheel, carved from the wood of many trees. It hung within a frame that allowed it to turn freely. But this was not all, for on either side of it were two thrones, in one of which sat she who could only be Dame Fortune herself. Such was her beauty that Gawain was once again dazzled, but as he approached the wheel he saw that while she was as lovely as the day, yet her look was stern also.

Then Sir Gawain saw that several men and women stood on either side of the wheel and as the lady herself crossed from one throne to another, so the wheel turned, and those who were upon its right side and seemed richly and splendidly garbed, became withered and dressed in rags – all their splendour gone, while those on the left were transformed into shimmering people of wealth and status.

From this Gawain knew that he looked upon the Wheel of Fortune itself – that all people, then and now, feared. For with its turning those who were wealthy became poor, and those who were beggars became rich. Such is the way even in this time, and though Dame Fortune is not often seen in these days it is still true that

✦ *The maiden with the cup* ✦

her wheel still shapes the lives of all who live upon this earth.

Then Gawain noticed another thing. While she sat upon the right-hand throne, Fortune was as beautiful as only a goddess may be, when she rose and passed to the left-hand throne she became stooped with age, and her face lined and ravaged and her beauty quite gone. And Sir Gawain understood that even Fortune herself was a plaything of her own power, subject to change as are all.

Gawain crossed the great hall and knelt before the goddess and she, seeing him, welcomed him by name.

'You are welcome here, Sir Gawain. Your story is known to me and I am aware of your devotion, that far exceeds that of any other man or woman now living.'

As she spoke, a great swelling sound of music filled the great hall. 'Do you hear this song, Sir Gawain?' said Dame Fortune. 'It is sung in your honour.'

And though Gawain hearkened to the song, he could not understand any of the words, which were, it may be, from another time or place.

'My lady, I salute you,' said Gawain. 'Long have I sought your presence, though I knew it not until this moment, and it is reward enough that I may look upon you.'

'That you have done, because I willed it so,' said the goddess. 'But it is not permitted that you stay here longer, else you may not depart at all. But, because you have come here, I will give you a gift for your uncle King Arthur. Say to him that while he possesses it, his kingdom and all those who serve him shall be under my protection, and no foe will ever succeed against him until the time comes when all things must change.'

So saying, she gave into Gawain's hands a golden ring in which an emerald sparkled. He took it with humility and wonder, and it is said that only when the king's own son stole it from his father's hand could the destruction of the Round Table and all of Camelot the Golden take place.

Then Dame Fortune gave Gawain her blessing and promised him that while the sun shone in the heavens he should grow stronger, and that none would be able to stand against him when it was at its height.

This and much more she told him, and warned him against the perils he might encounter upon his way. 'Soon you will come to a place full of wonder. You will see much that is a mystery, and it is most important that you ask the meaning of what you see.'

Also Dame Fortune told him to watch for her and five of her ladies, for their coming would be a sign that certain magical and wondrous events were about to occur.

So it was that Sir Gawain left the palace of Dame Fortune and returned to where he had left his horse. There he belted his sword around his waist and slung his shield at his back, and mounting Gringolet he rode away from that place. And this time he did not need the magical

rope, for the waters of the lake became as hard as the earth beneath his mount's hooves, and he was soon again on the shore of the lake. There he found the silver knight waiting for him, healed of his wounds, and expressing only wonder that Sir Gawain had indeed been blessed by Dame Fortune.

'Now I see that you have an even greater task to perform,' he said, taking back the magical skein. 'With the blessing of my lady it seems to me you cannot fail.'

'Of that I cannot speak,' replied Gawain. But in his heart he knew that the magic of the Grail reached out to him in that moment, and that his way would be guarded henceforth.

⊹ ⊹ ⊹

AND SO IT was – though not without further adventures, of which I will not speak at this time, since there are greater things to come – Gawain continued on his way. Once again he was plagued with strange events, and at one time he rode for a day surrounded by a ring of fire, which moved with him until night fell, after which it was seen no more.

So the knight once more took the road and followed it until he came at last to a mighty castle, that sat upon a high place, and there he was made welcome by all whom he met, who seemed to know him and to have awaited his coming.

Never in all his days had Gawain seen a richer or more beautiful place. It was decorated with precious stones and on its walls were painted scenes of strange adventures and brave deeds. How much I wish I could see these for myself, since I am certain they contained many secrets, and that they told stories such as I long to tell. But alas that cannot be, and so I must complete this tale of Sir Gawain.

In the castle the king's nephew met a most noble lord who greeted him kindly and offered to play chess with him. This Gawain accepted gratefully and played many games with the nobleman until it came time for supper to be served. And perhaps it may be that this was the very same magical board that Gawain himself had acquired for King Arthur long ago, but if this is so and how it came to the noble lord's possession the story does not say.* The feast, like everything in the castle, was rich and wonderful, served on plates of gold with wine in goblets of crystal.

At one point two squires entered the hall and laid the most wonderful and richly decorated sword before the noble lord. Gawain wondered what danger this might portend, but there was no threat made towards him by anyone present and the supper continued pleasantly.

As the feasting finally came to an end, there came into the hall a procession which reminded Gawain of another he had witnessed – long ago it seemed to him – in another castle.

First came two maidens bearing candlesticks and next two squires who bore between them a fabulous, richly decorated spear. Next came a woman of such beauty and grace that Gawain was at once filled with longing for her. In her hands she carried a shallow golden bowl wrapped in cloth of gold and she wore a crown of great splendour. Behind her came a second noble dame accompanied by four maidens, and Gawain at once recognised the goddess Fortune herself, together with her four handmaidens, whose coming she had told him would be a sign of great wonders.

As he watched, the beautiful crowned woman set the golden bowl on the table, and

* See 'Sir Gawain in the Land of Wonder' pp. 203–216.

the squires arranged it so the tip of the great spear sat above it. Then, wondrous indeed, drops of red blood flowed from the spearhead into the bowl. Finally, the noble lord lifted the vessel to his lips and drank from it.

At once Gawain remembered all that Dame Fortune had told him, and stood up and asked what these things meant.

For a moment there was silence, so that one might have heard birdsong from several leagues away. Then the entire company cried out with joy, and leapt to their feet and began to dance and sing.

The noble lord looked upon Gawain with a face that radiated joy, and said to him: 'Sir. You have done that which no other man could do. Others of your brethren have sat where you sat and observed what you saw. All of them failed to ask the question. Some even fell asleep! But most were overwhelmed by what they saw and could find no words to ask its purpose.

'Now I shall tell you. Though you have not seen it, both I and all those who dwell here are truly dead. Because of the use of the spear in anger to end the life of another, we were all cursed to stay in this place, half alive and half dead, until one came who asked the question. Until then I have been preserved by the blood from the spear, and through me my followers have lived a half-life such as no others known to me. And let me say too that the desolate place known as the Wasted Lands will now begin to blossom again, all because you asked this question. All here give thanks to you, and offer our blessings on your life.'

Then the noble lord took up the great sword that had been laid before him earlier and presented it to Gawain. 'This is a sword of great power and strength. While you carry it no harm shall come to you and all will fall before you.'

❖ *The cursed spear* ❖

With that the noble lord and all his men faded from sight, and the hall became silent. Only Dame Fortune and her ladies remained, and the goddess came forward and embraced Gawain, blessing him again for having achieved the greatest of mysteries. 'You see now that when you watched that other procession and witnessed the death of the old lord, it was but a shadow of these things. There are many aspects to the Grail Quest. Those who journey in search of it will find their way to other places, where they will be likewise tested. Only three will succeed as you have succeeded at this time.'

With these words the goddess led Sir Gawain into a rich chamber that had been prepared for him and within it he fell into the most profound sleep that he had ever known – though whether or not he dreamed I cannot say.

On the morrow he found fresh food set out for him, but of the goddess and her ladies there was no sign, and the castle seemed empty and deserted. Sir Gawain mounted his steed and rode away from the rich castle, wondering if some other knight would come there and witness marvels such as he had seen.

His journey to Camelot the Golden took many weeks, for he had wandered far in his quest. This time he saw none of the strange sights that had accompanied his coming to the castle of the Grail, and so he returned at last to the great city and was welcomed by King Arthur and Queen Guinevere and all of those knights who had already returned from their own quests. And then he gave into King Arthur's hand the ring that had been sent to him by Dame Fortune, and the king placed it upon his hand and wore it ever after until the ending of his rule in this world.

Later, Sir Bors returned with the story of how he and Sir Galahad and Sir Perceval had reached the great city of Sarras beyond the Nameless Sea, and there beheld the final wonders of the Grail. But of this Sir Thomas Malory has written, so I shall not repeat it here. Only I will say to those who believe there was but a single Grail, and that Galahad, Perceval and Bors alone found it and experienced its mysteries, that Sir Gawain also sought the mysteries of the nameless vessel and that he met Dame Fortune and was ever after her servant until the sad days of his quarrel with Sir Lancelot, which ended in his death. This too has Master Thomas told far more astutely than I, so I will end this tale here and offer a blessing upon those who serve the Grail, whose crown is the glory of this tale.

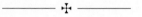

EXPLICIT THE CROWN OF THE GRAIL AND THE THIRD BOOK OF THIS COLLECTION.

INCIPIT THE POSTLUDES, IN WHICH THE STORIES OF THE REALM OF ARTHUR ARE EXTENDED BEYOND THEIR TIME.

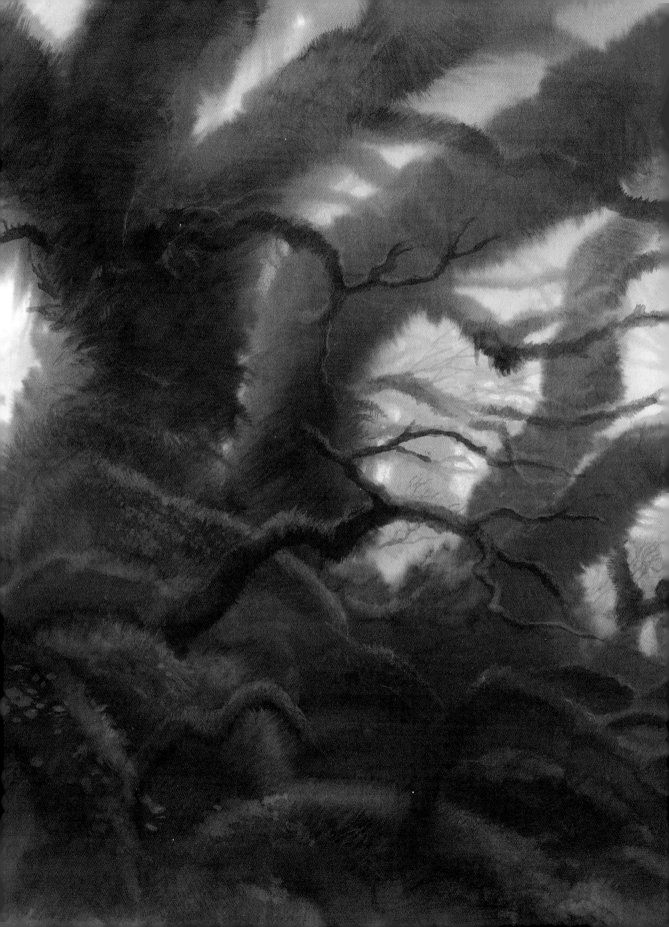

POSTLUDES

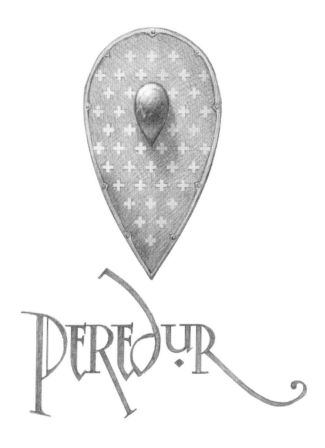

PEREDUR

29: THE PROPHECIES OF MERLIN AND THE LADY OF THE LAKE

IT IS A HARD TASK INDEED – SOME WOULD SAY BEYOND THE SKILL OF ANY MAN OR WOMAN – TO KNOW WHERE CERTAIN KINDS OF WISDOM ARE TO BE FOUND. ALL WE MAY SAY IS THAT SOME ARE HIDDEN FROM THE WORLD, WHILE OTHERS ARE PASSED DOWN FROM ONE PERSON TO ANOTHER UNTIL THE TIME FOR THEIR UNDERSTANDING. SUCH IS THE STORY OF HOW MERLIN'S PROPHECIES LIVED ON AFTER THE REALM OF ARTHUR WAS ENDED. THEN, ALL THAT WAS GOOD AND GREAT OF THAT TIME SEEMED TO HAVE PERISHED, SAVE PERHAPS FOR THE STORIES THAT HAVE PRESERVED SOME OF THESE THINGS AND UPON WHICH I HAVE DRAWN FOR THESE TELLINGS. ONLY LATELY HAS IT COME TO MY NOTICE THAT A MANUSCRIPT, LONG HIDDEN FROM THE WORLD, TELLS ANOTHER STORY. I CAN NO MORE SPEAK TO ITS TRUTH THAN I CAN OF ANY STORY IN WHICH THE ENCHANTER OR THE LADY OF THE LAKE ARE A PART. YET I FEEL IT IS A TALE WORTH THE TELLING, THAT HAS GONE UNKNOWN FOR MANY YEARS, SO WILL I TELL IT HERE FOR ALL TO READ.

✠ ✠ ✠

THE STORY OF Merlin begins and ends in mystery – as perhaps it should, given the nature of King Arthur's great advisor. At the beginning of the first of these collections of stories omitted by Master Thomas Malory, I told the story of Merlin as it was narrated by Master Geoffrey of Monmouth, and how also that he was not born of a human father, whether a faery or, as some have said, a demon. Rather it may be true that he was not born of any human, but emerged from within Broceliande itself, and that his sole purpose was to bring about the birth and deeds of the High King, of the Round Table Fellowship, and the quest for the Grail.

It seems fitting therefore that I should tell here a story that moves beyond the ordinary world into the realm of mystery and wonder that only Master Merlin himself could fully understand. Certainly, I make no claim to grasp these mysteries, which are part of the ageless

265

story of this land. Those who read the story of 'Sir Gawain in the Land of Wonder,'* may remember how the king's nephew slept in a bed on which the story of the world was carved upon the headpiece, and that Sir Gawain was never after able to remember what he had seen, save perhaps in his dreams. Of these things I may not comment, but I am sensible of links that may exist in the story I shall tell here.

Among all the great histories of King Arthur's realm, there are those that tell how Merlin became enamoured of Nimuë, one of the Ladies of the Lake – or indeed of that Lady herself. Some say that she took his life and, having enclosed him in a cavern beneath the earth, brought back his spirit so that he might prophesy all that would befall the realm of Arthur, as well as much more that was to occur in the world of men. Others say that, like King Arthur himself when he was taken to Avalon, Merlin was not dead, but remained in a state of suspended life. On this I cannot comment, but the story I tell here may answer some of these things.

Within this tale are hidden mysteries that do not always agree with each other. Of the prophecies themselves I will not write. In them, Merlin speaks of kings and queens, princes and princesses, lords and ladies, knights, squires, pages, and ordinary men and women. Often these words seem as if they had been written down by more than one wise clerk, who perhaps did not always understand what they read or heard, or that perhaps their writer was fearful of writing the truth that others might see as dark and even heretical.

✠ ✠ ✠

HE WHO HAD most to do with the preserving of Merlin's wisdom was one Meliadus, brother to the great knight Sir Tristan, both sons of a Scottish queen and the King of Lyonesse. Of Meliadus it is told how, following an attack upon his family, he was discovered floating in a small craft, and how this came to the attention of the Lady of the Lake.

As she had done with Sir Lancelot, she brought the boy into the country over which she ruled. There, where magic dwelled, as perhaps it still does, she raised him, and taught him some of her own wisdom, and thus he came to know the secret of Merlin's vanishment from the world of men. For as some say, the Enchanter was captured by Nimuë, a servant of the Lady of the Lake herself, whom he loved, and that it was she who placed him, still living, in a cavern below the earth. But others say that he retired to a tower built for him by his sister, Ganeida, who was as wise as he. Others still say it was the Lady herself who did this, as the tale here describes.

The story begins when Merlin was in conversation with a wise clerk named Tholomer, another of those to whom had been appointed the task of setting down his prophecies. To him Merlin told not only all that was to come in the days of King Arthur, but also elsewhere in the world.

On this occasion, Master Tholomer asked Merlin whom he thought was the wisest person that had ever lived.

'That is easy,' responded Merlin. 'It is beyond doubt the Lady of the Lake. In time all will come to know her for her wisdom and counsel, which extend even beyond my own. One day she will be as well known as Luscente, whom

---

* See pp. 203–216.

the wise poet Virgil spoke of in the time of the Emperor Augustus.'*

'What more can you tell me, Master Merlin?' asked Tholomer.

'I will tell you of the forest of Aurences, where I will shortly go, there to meet with the Lady. She will see to it that I do not return, but vanish from the sight of most men. However I shall continue to speak and to offer prophecies to those who visit me.'

After this, Merlin went walking in the forest. There he wandered for many days until he met with the Lady of the Lake herself. And there they found a house that was provided with everything a noble man and woman might want. There, they remained for a long while – some say as long as fifteen months, others longer – and in that time Merlin loved the Lady and shared with her his magic for though she secretly grew to hate him, for what reason the story does not tell, and sought ways that she might learn all his secrets.

In all that time they were together Merlin and the Lady behaved as lovers do, and shared much that remains unknown to this day. The Lady pretended to know little of magic so that she might learn all that the Enchanter knew. But he, for his part, saw that she knew as much or more than he, but that her magic was of a more recent time, while his was from an age long before hers, and indeed long before the coming of King Arthur.

Many of his spells and magics he hid within certain precious stones, and these glowed with the power he had stored there, so that they shone forth day and night – but these secrets

_____

* This reference is a curious one. It is possible that the writer of the original manuscript was making a reference to the Latin word for light, *lucent*, which would make her a lady of light.

he did not share with the Lady. Yet it seems that she learned from him two great skills – one was how to make a man sleep for a long while and dream while he slept, but that he could not awaken. The other was how to seal a tomb or chamber in such a way that no one could enter or leave it thereafter until the world ended.

One day Merlin said to her: 'Soon I shall be placed underground, and my tomb shall be sealed so that even I cannot open it. I shall not be dead, but simply held there. From this place I will continue to give prophecies and others will come from many places to hear me.'

'How can you know this?' asked the Lady of the Lake.

'Because I see what must be,' answered Merlin. 'And I see that it will be you who will do this.'

To this the Lady made no answer, but as Master Thomas and others have told, from that day forth no man has seen Merlin, though many have heard his voice.

✛ ✛ ✛

FOLLOWING THIS SAD departure of Merlin, Meliadus came to Camelot the Golden and lived quietly in the city, only occasionally emerging to offer words of wisdom to King Arthur. But because of the magic he had learned from the Lady of the Lake, he was able to journey to the site of Merlin's tomb, and there he learned much wisdom from the Enchanter. Much of what he learned, Meliadus wrote down in a book which he called the *Prophecies of Merlin* wherein was written much that I speak of here. Also Meliadus had in his possession the book of writings dictated by Merlin to Master Tholomer, who as we have heard, wrote them down while the Enchanter still walked abroad.

When word of these writings came to the

ears of other men, many came to Meliadus and asked to go to the site of Merlin's entombment, so that they might also learn from him. This Meliadus refused them all, but he permitted one amongst the petitioners to read the books. This man was named Raymond, a wise clerk who in later times became a bishop of Wales and afterwards a cardinal.

When he had read the books, Master Raymond was much excited. 'I wish to journey to where Merlin is hidden,' he said. But Meliadus would not allow this. Instead, he went himself to where the Enchanter was hidden and told him of Raymond.

To the wise clerk Merlin sent a message. 'Tell him to journey to King Arthur's court and there to await the coming of a knight named Perceval le Gallois. If he wishes to understand much that I have prophesied he will do so in this way. And another thing I will say,' added Merlin. 'When he arrives at Camelot the Golden he will find a round stone that is hidden there. If he stands upon it he may see many wonders, for within it is trapped the spirit of my father, whose knowledge and wisdom is even greater than mine.'

Here I must say that many believe Merlin was born to a princess of Dyfed from one who came to her in her chamber and then vanished away – and some have claimed that this was a demon, and others a being from the faery realm, but that soon after she gave birth to the wondrous child that was known thereafter as Merlin. I cannot say which of these things is true, and thus both the beginning and the end of Merlin are mysteries.

These things Meliadus conveyed to Raymond and he, in his eagerness to discover more of Merlin's wisdom, followed the instructions given to him concerning the mysterious stone. Thus he found his way to a certain tower,

within which he discovered the stone. Having studied it for some time, he read an inscription written there by Merlin himself, and only then did he venture to stand upon it.

At once he heard a voice that issued from the stone, which said that it belonged to the spirit of Merlin's father, and that it knew all the secrets of the Enchanter and where his tomb was hidden. And though he believed that Merlin's father was indeed a demon, Raymond asked again to be shown where Merlin could be found. And the voice of the stone spoke to him and told him that he would see everything under the light of the sun and the stars.

Then the voice told him to grasp the sides of the stone, which he did. And so it was that the foolhardy clerk got what he asked for, for the round stone lifted into the air and flew at great speed away from Camelot the Golden and across the world to many places Raymond had neither seen nor heard of.

And thus the stone came at last to the land of Ind, which was at that time ruled over by the mighty emperor, Prester John. There the stone landed in a garden where the emperor was much given to walk, and for a time Raymond was able to speak with him. When the priestly king heard that the wise clerk had come from Camelot the Golden in the realm of Arthur, he told how the great king's name was known even in this far-off land. Then he took from his shoulders a cloak of great richness and asked that Raymond greet the king and to give the cloak to him. And for a time thereafter the two men spoke together concerning many wonders that were to be found in Ind.

Following this, Raymond once again mounted the round stone, which flew on its way over mountains and seas, deserts and marshes, rivers and valleys, until it returned to Camelot the Golden. But at no point did

✦ *Raymond flies to Ind* ✦

the stone show Raymond where Merlin was entombed, so that he felt only great disappointment. But still he took the cloak of Prester John to King Arthur, who wore it afterwards and was recognised as the greatest king of his time.

Then Raymond again sought out Meliadus and told him all that had occurred and once again begged to be shown where the tomb of Merlin was.

'If the stone failed to show you, then it must be that you are not intended to do so,' answered Meliadus. 'But I will myself go to Merlin and ask him why this may be.'

Then Meliadus fetched his fastest horse and rode as quickly as he might until he came to the place where Merlin was hidden. At the entrance to the cavern there were many magpies, and these Meliadus drove away, since they are known to bring bad luck. Then he entered the cave and came to where a door was set in the rock that gave admittance to Merlin's tomb.

Whenever he came there the door remained closed, but he could still hear the voice of his wise master. Now he asked if all would be well in King Arthur's realm, both then and in time to come. And to this the Enchanter answered that it was, but that many things were yet to occur, beginning with the quest of the Grail.

'When will that happen?' asked Meliadus.

'The one who will lead the way is only lately born,'* said Merlin. 'But the knight who will accompany him will soon arrive at Camelot the Golden. His name is Perceval le Gallois, whom I have already told the wise clerk Raymond to await his coming.'

Then it is said that Merlin spoke many more prophecies, including the love Sir Lancelot had for King Arthur's queen, and how this would begin the breaking of the Round Table. 'But the search for the Grail shall be the point at which many things will change for ever, for many will go on that quest but few return, and thus there will

---

* This must refer to the coming of Sir Galahad, the son of Sir Lancelot and the Maiden of the Grail.

269

be fewer knights to sit at the Round Table. Then shall come the dark child who was born from the passion of Arthur and his half-sister Morgause, and he will come to Camelot the Golden and will break the Fellowship.* After that there will be a great war, and Sir Gawain and Sir Lancelot will do battle and Gawain will be wounded unto death. Then there will be a struggle by the shore of the sea between King Arthur and his son, and many will die there. And in the end the king will be taken into Avalon to be healed of his wounds – but even I cannot say if he will come again.'

Then Merlin spoke many more prophecies regarding the times after the departing of King Arthur, and of all these Meliadus recorded. But each time he asked: 'When will this be?' Merlin would only answer, 'It will be.' And he spoke of the rise and fall of kingdoms as yet unknown, and of the Serpent of Babylon, and the Beast with no Name, and of the loss of a great treasure, and the finding of another.

Of these and other things he spoke at length, and all of his words Meliadus took down, until he had a great book of prophecies. Then he bade farewell to Merlin and returned to Camelot the Golden, where he relayed all of the sayings of the Enchanter to Raymond, and once again reminded him to watch and wait for the coming of Perceval le Gallois.

⊹ ⊹ ⊹

NOW THE STORY tells us that not long after Master Raymond's return from his journey upon the round stone, there came a mysterious craft that sailed of its own accord without crew or oars, the wind filling its sails so that it sped like a bird across the water. It came to rest on the shoreline close to Camelot the Golden, and when he heard of this, King Arthur himself went there, and found a girl of no more than thirteen summers alone upon the craft. When he saw this, and certain symbols that appeared on the sail, the king grew afraid, for he knew that the ship came from Avalon, and he feared what this might portend.

Thus he enquired of the girl why she had come, and she told him that her name was Aglentine, and that her home was indeed in Avalon, where she served the Lady of the Lake. And she spoke also of the craft by which she had come, which had been made by Merlin himself not long after he made the Round Table, and which bore within it an inscription which said that it would one day carry King Arthur to Avalon.

'Why have you come at this time?' asked the king.

'I am come to bring you these letters,' said Aglentine, handing him a bundle wrapped in silk. 'They are from he who is called by many Prester John, and by others the Emperor of Ind. His wisdom is great, and the Lady of Avalon asks that you read these and remember what is to be found within them.'

Then she told how Merlin himself had journeyed many years before to the Kingdom of Ind, and there had spent many days talking of all manner of things with the emperor. And the story tells that it is for this reason, following the ending of the Quest for the Grail in that time, that the sacred vessel was brought to the realm of Ind and there entrusted to Prester John, as is told in the story of Titurel.†

Then King Arthur invited the girl to come with him into Camelot the Golden, but she refused, saying that she could not remain long upon the soil of Logres, but must return to

---

* Once again this must refer to Mordred.

† See pp. 239–244.

Avalon. Thus she went aboard the magical craft, the sails of which promptly filled, and which sped away from the shore.

King Arthur returned to the city with the letters and had them transcribed by the wise clerk Raymond, who read them to him. And it is said that they contained a description of the wondrous kingdom over which Prester John ruled, where he followed the teachings of the Apostle Thomas, and much besides. And at the end the priest-king wrote that he sent his greetings to the King of the West, and that his cloak, given to the wise clerk Raymond, would protect him in time of need. (Indeed, as I have read in another book, there is mention of the king's mantel, which protected King Arthur from harm and gave him the gift of understanding other tongues. Surely, this must be the very cloak once possessed by Prester John?)

⁜ ⁜ ⁜

NOW THE STORY turns to that very Perceval le Gallois of whom Merlin spoke. Much has been written of this great knight, including the story as I have told it already in the first of these books.* In the manuscript of the Prophecies, however, it is written that when he first came to Camelot the Golden, he met with Raymond, who told him of Merlin's words that he would follow the Knight of the Grail, and that afterwards he would become the guardian of the sacred vessel before it passed into the hands of the Emperor of Ind.

Much that Raymond told him Perceval did not understand, and he questioned him regarding what Merlin had foretold. But when he heard how his lineage was more ancient than he knew, and that it included kings and heroes, and that he himself would discover a great destiny, he shook his head in wonder.

'I do not know what this may mean,' he said. 'But my heart tells me I should seek out this Merlin.'

'I fear you may search for more years than any man's lifetime and that you will find no sign of Merlin,' said Raymond.

'Nevertheless I must try,' answered Perceval, and that very day he set out.

The way led him to a part of the Great Wood that was seldom visited. There he came upon a quiet glade wherein was a stone cell in which lived a greatly revered hermit named Helias. This saintly man had suffered many visions in his life, including those which told how the Grail would appear at Camelot the Golden and how three of King Arthur's knights would achieve its mysteries. Also he remembered the first coming of Merlin, in the shape of a child, and how he revealed the mystery of the dragons to King Vortigern in the days before the coming of Arthur.[†]

All of this Perceval heard in wonder, and declared that he would seek out the one whom he believed must be the wisest man in the world. To this Helias answered, much as had Meliadus, 'You may seek for ever and you will not find where Merlin is, unless he wishes it. Rather than this, let me give you his Book of Prophecies. Take this to the one named Meliadus and give it into his keeping.

So Perceval did as he was bidden, and returned to Camelot the Golden with the book,

---

* 'The Elucidation of the Grail and The Story of Perceval' in *The Great Book of King Arthur and his Knights of the Round Table*, pp. 363–396.

† See 'Merlin and the Dragons' in *The Great Book of King Arthur and his Knights of the Round Table*, pp. 21–7.

which he gave to Meliadus, who placed it with his own book of Merlin's prophetic wisdom. And after this the old hermit died, and was laid to rest beside his cell, as Merlin had foretold.

This all happened before the Quest of the Grail began, but everything came to pass as Merlin had said and which was recorded in his prophetic books. And in time Meliadus gave these to the wise clerk Raymond.

So it was that Merlin's prophecies were kept beyond the time of King Arthur, and whether the voice of Merlin is still heard from within his tomb, the story does not say, but here I will set down part of that book which the wise clerk Raymond read to the congregation of people who came to hear him. For these are words as wise and strange as any that I have heard, and as such deserve to be known.

'Know that those who show no mercy will be judged badly, and more men and women must suffer and become bitter because the grains of wheat they will sow on this earth will yield nothing. But those who have the law belonging to the earth and the stars of the sky, to the trees, the beasts, the birds and all things, will put their faith in the Lady of God.'

Others came after Master Raymond who were very great scholars and studied these writings at length. But such was their nature that many went away filled with confusion and doubt. For only someone of deep mind and virtuous soul could read these books with understanding. In the end Master Antoine Ver-art published them in the book which I have read and from which this story is drawn.

But wherever Merlin may yet lie – whether it be in a cavern beneath the earth, or in an airy tower, which some call his esplumoir or 'moulting cage' – his wisdom lives yet, and until he be released, or some greater prophet comes to read from his Book of Prophecies, those deep mysteries abide in the kist of the future.

✠ ✠ ✠

THUS IT MAY be seen that Merlin, despite being withdrawn from the world, was able to foresee the coming of many things, including the achieving of the Grail in the city of Sarras, beyond the Hidden Sea. So, also, we may understand how the priest-king John and King Arthur of Logres were linked through the wisdom of Merlin, who most clearly knew of these things, and how he prophesied all that was to happen in those times, and long after, as I have myself rehearsed here to the best of my ability.

30: KING ARTHUR AND THE DRAGON OF NORMANDY

✠

MASTER THOMAS MALORY FAMOUSLY WROTE, AT THE END OF HIS GREAT BOOK, THAT HE HAD HEARD HOW KING ARTHUR WENT INTO ANOTHER PLACE BUT, AS HE THEN WROTE, 'I WILL NOT SAY IT SHALL BE SO, BUT RATHER I WILL SAY: HERE IN THIS WORLD HE CHANGED HIS LIFE.' * MANY HAVE QUESTIONED THIS, AND HAVE NAMED IT FANCIFUL, AND LIKE SIR THOMAS I CANNOT COMMENT AS TO ITS REALITY. YET, AS THOSE WHO HAVE READ MY PREVIOUS COLLECTION OF THESE TALES OF THE GREAT KING MAY REMEMBER, A STORY THAT I FOUND THERE RELATED HOW THE AUTHOR, GUILLAUME DE TORELLA, MADE A JOURNEY TO THE ISLAND OF AVALON AND THERE MET THE KING HIMSELF, RECOVERED FROM HIS WOUNDS AND GIVEN HIS YOUTH AGAIN THROUGH THE MAGIC OF THAT PLACE. RECENTLY, THERE CAME TO ME AN HONOURABLE SCHOLAR, WHO GAVE INTO MY HANDS A CHRONICLE ASCRIBED TO ONE ETIENNE DE ROUEN, CONCERNING THE ATTACK OF KING HENRY THE YOUNGER[†] UPON THE LANDS AND PEOPLES OF BRITTANY, AND HOW KING ARTHUR HIMSELF PLAYED A PART IN THESE EVENTS. THIS GAVE ME CAUSE FOR WONDER, SINCE IT IS RARE INDEED TO FIND A STORY SET IN TIMES THAT WERE YET FRESH IN MEMORY IN THE DAYS OF MASTER THOMAS WHICH YET SPOKE OF ARTHUR AS RULING IN THE UNDERLANDS. THIS IS THE MOST EXTRAORDINARY AND WONDROUS ACCOUNT OF KING ARTHUR, OF HOW HE SURVIVED THE TERRIBLE WAR WITH HIS SON MORDRED, AND WAS TAKEN TO AVALON, THERE TO BECOME IMMORTAL. I TELL THIS BRIEF TALE HERE FOR THE INTEREST OF ALL WHO ASK IF THE GREAT KING DID INDEED

---

* *Le Morte D'Arthur*, Book XXI, Ch. vii.
† This is Henry II (5 March 1133–6 July 1189) King of England.

SURVIVE, AND IF HE MAY YET RETURN IN TIME OF NEED. WHETHER THESE THINGS BE TRUE OR NOT, I CANNOT SAY, BUT I BELIEVE IT TO BE IMPORTANT THAT THEY BE REMEMBERED FOR FUTURE DAYS.

✣ ✣ ✣

IT BEFELL IN the days when King Henry the Younger, known as the Dragon of Normandy, ruled over Britain and Gaul, and that he sought to extend his realms to include Brittany, which was neighbour to his own country. The king declared that certain Breton lords had rebelled against him, and in response to this he sent an army to ravage the kingdom.

At that time the Consul of Brittany was a man named Roland, who well knew the stories of King Arthur and the widely-held belief that he had not died but passed instead into the Realm of Faery, in particular the island of Avalon, where nine sisters ruled who were skilled in magic and the arts of healing. As the army of King Henry drew ever closer, this Roland commanded that a letter should be written and sent to the great king himself – for at that time the ways between the human realms to those of the faery race were not yet closed, so that his message could be delivered to King Arthur himself without let or hindrance.

In the letter, Roland told how the Norman king was invading the Breton lands and that he sought to kill or enslave all the people who, in a time before, had been subjects of the king who ruled from Camelot the Golden. And by dint of messengers who knew the ways between the worlds, the letter reached King Arthur in Avalon, whose anger was great upon reading it. He at once wrote in response to Roland, declaring that he knew of these events and that the fates had declared that the young king would soon be moved to withdraw his army and to retire to his own lands.

'Nevertheless,' King Arthur wrote, 'we shall send a letter to King Henry, bidding him depart from the Breton lands on pain of my wrath.'

This he did. The letter reminded King Henry that he, Arthur the Briton, had been made immortal through the magic of the faery race. Before that, he reminded King Henry, he had ruled not only over Britain, but also Brittany, Gaul and many other lands, as far as Rome itself. Also that he had fought a war against the Emperor Lucius and defeated him. Thus he warned the young king that he had best withdraw, for to attack without provocation was not the act of a true sovereign.

Then he spoke of other great warriors of history, including Alexander, Nebuchadnezzar, Constantine, and Charlemagne, all of whom seemed insignificant beside himself. 'Be aware,' he added, 'that the Lords of Wales, Scotland, Ireland and Norway, will all raise their banners in my name, and if called upon will bring down red war upon your head.'

Further, he wrote at length of his own passing, following the war with his sister's son, to the Isle of Avalon. There he had bathed in a fountain of immortal life, and was thus restored to his former strength. Then it was that the faery race gave him lordship over the underlands, where he remained until this time.

Thus he warned King Henry and promised that unless he ceased his war against the Bretons, Arthur himself, with all the immortal ranks of Faery, would rise up against him and not cease until the young king was destroyed and all his armies and his kingdoms with them.

❧ The Fountain of Barenton ❧

Then would the earth shake and the very stars clash in the heavens, as though Arthur and his warriors rode once again upon the earth.

When he received this letter King Henry was camped deep in the wards of Broceliande, the great forest which, in King Arthur's time, had been witness to so many of the deeds of the Round Table Fellowship. Indeed, so much was the ancient wood part of the realm of Faery, that even in King Henry's time it was yet filled with magic. Near to the camp of the Norman army was the Fountain of Barenton, where once Merlin the Enchanter, to whom Arthur had often turned in search of aid, was wont to wander, and whose voice, it was said, could still at times be heard.

All of this took root in the mind of the young king who, though angered by the intervention of King Arthur in his affairs, dared not ignore the letter. Thus he wrote to the great king that he believed himself to act according to the laws of the time, and that the rulership of the Breton lands were rightly his. 'Yet,' he wrote, 'I am mindful of your great power and the truth of the tales that are told of your realms and the knights who sat at your Round Table. Truly, you are worthy of all honour, and on this day I will do as I am bid, and depart from here. Thus shall I recognise your authority, even though you speak from the lands beneath, and I will make peace in your name.'

At this time news came to King Henry that his mother, the Empress Matilda, had died, and amid the sadness of this he saw a further sign that he should seek a peaceful outcome to his campaign.

So the attacking army withdrew, and the land of Brittany was made safe from conquest at that time, and in every part of that kingdom people rejoiced and praised the name of King Arthur.

And who shall say whether this be true or not? For I have heard tell many times that King Arthur is not dead, but went rather into the realm of Faery, where he lives yet, and watches over his own kingdoms of old with a fierce and watchful eye.

✠ ✠ ✠

THIS WAS THE relation of Etienne de Rouen. To my eyes it is but the first of many signs that Arthur will yet return and reign once more over the lands that were his in that olden time. I have heard it said also that Merlin has been seen abroad in Broceliande – and of that and more you have heard in the previous story.

CODA

+

THIS BOOK I dedicate to the memory of Master Thomas Malory, in honour of his great work, in which so many marvels and wonders are recorded. May God remember him and care for his soul, who was a knight prisoner, and may these stories be forever remembered in times to come, when it is said King Arthur himself may one day return.

    Deo Gracias.

**EXPLICIT LIBER TERTIUS, WRITTEN IN THE WARDS
OF BROCELIANDE BY MY HAND IN THIS TIME.
BLAISE SCRIPSIT.**

NOTES AND SOURCES

BOOK ONE:
THE BOOK OF THE KNIGHTS ADVENTUROUS

1: The Perilous Cemetery

L'Atre Périlleux, as it is known in French, is an anonymous romance dating from around the middle of the thirteenth century. It is found in a manuscript in the Bibliothèque National de France, numbered *français, 1433, f. 1r-60r.* ,which also contains several other stories of which Gawain is the hero. *The Perilous Cemetery* is a lengthy set of adventures, woven together in a technique known as *interlacement* (interlacing) in which a story is begun, interrupted by another, then another, and so on. This makes untangling the central tale difficult, and I had to make a number of decisions as to what I should include and what to cut, without altering the major strands of the story: Gawain's apparent death, and his adventure in the titular cemetery. To enable me to fit this lengthy tale into this collection I had to omit several adventures, and even, on occasion, blend two characters into one. (There were originally three knights who killed two men in the sub plot, but one of the knights disappeared later and it was really unnecessary to the plot to have two murdered men). Another of the things for which medieval story-tellers were famed was failing to give secondary characters names. Thus in the original both the damosel who arrives at the beginning of the story and the one whom Gawain rescues from the demonic knight, were nameless, and there are so many people called 'the knight' or 'the lady' or 'the damsel', that the reader could be forgiven for rapidly losing their way. Thus, I borrowed names from other Arthurian romances, via the essential *Arthurian Names Dictionary* by Christopher W. Bruce. (Garland Publishing, 1999). I also took the liberty of marrying off the lady in question (now called Alisand) to the redoubtable Tristan at the end, since otherwise they vanish from the scene and make for an untidy ending. The poem borrows a lot from other Gawain romances, including those by Raoul de Houdenc and Chrétien de Troyes, despite which it has several original lines of narrative which make it a tense and thoroughly enjoyable romance. The name of the dead knight who was said to resemble Gawain, is borrowed from an alternate French rendering of the story. My main source was the fine translation by Ross G. Arthur in his *Three Arthurian Romances* (J.M. Dent, 1996), augmented by *The Perilous Cemetery* (*L'âtre périlleux*) by Nancy B. Black (Garland Library of Medieval Literature, 104, 1994). Those wishing to read the missing adventures are recommended to seek out either of these editions.

2: The Tale of Hunbaut

The tale of Hunbaut is a curious confection. Composed around the middle of the thirteenth century in France, it sets out to show that its hero, the otherwise unknown Hunbaut, is a far superior man to the great Arthurian hero, Gawain. It does this by showing Gawain in his most impulsive and quick-tempered guise, while making Hunbaut a rather superior fellow, who constantly corrects his comrades of the Round Table. The text has never been translated into English, perhaps because of its daunting Picardie dialect, which makes even those familiar with medieval French turn pale. To include this tale, I resorted to the detailed summary given by its most recent editor Margaret Winters, which gave me the structure I needed while giving me the freedom to let my own imagination play its part. The text breaks off suddenly at a point which suggests that a new adventure is about to begin, but I felt that, to all intents and purposes, its author had gone as far as he could and possibly lost interest in his own story. For this reason I added my own ending, which I feel is much as it would have been if the poem was complete. As stories go, it perhaps has less to recommend it than others, but I was fascinated by the attempt to show up Gawain by setting him against the rather stuffy character of Hunbaut. I also love the references to the wooden statue of Gawain, perhaps intended as an in-joke, given his earlier statement that he was 'not made of wood', after giving in to the wiles of another lady! The only current edition is the one I used as the basis for my retelling. It was prepared by Margaret Winters and published as *The Romance of Hunbaut: An Arthurian Poem of the 13th Century*. (E.J. Brill, 1984).

3: The Red Rose Knight

This is one of the latest stories to be collected here. It gives the lie to the idea that after Malory interest in the Arthurian material was lost until the Victorians rediscovered it. There are, it is true, not so many stories, but this one suggests that there was still some interest, as indeed are the presence of Arthur and Merlin in Edmund Spencer's spectacular *Faerie Queen*, published in 1590, more than a hundred years after *Le Morte D'Arthur*. The text on which this story is based is attributed to the English writer Richard Johnson (1573–*c*.1659) of whom virtually nothing is known, despite the fact that he penned a number of successful stories and was something of a best-selling author at the time. The romance was published in two parts in 1599 and 1607 and was reprinted at least a dozen times before 1700 and even adapted as a stage-play early in the seventeenth century. I first came across this tale in a wonderful collection of *Early English Prose Romances* Ed. by William J. Thoms (George Routledge & Sons, *c*. 1910) and I have used this edition as the basis for the retelling.

The story of the Red Rose Knight is a strange, wandering tale, written in a florid style which I have stripped away to keep it in line with the other tales collected here. I also had to do quite a bit of rewriting to give more motivation to the various characters. Why, for instance, does the hero decide to become an outlaw? I think it's clear, but the text does not make it at all obvious. I also changed some of the names, again with the intention of linking this story to the others selected here. Thus Tom a Lincoln became Andret, a name I stole from the Tristan stories, because the name given to him by his foster-parents does not sit comfortably with his character. I also changed the shepherd's name from Antonio, which was in line with Italianate literature of the time, to Alanus.

The story as I have given it is only half the text. The rest concerns the life of Tom's son by Queen Caelia, who becomes known as The Faerie Knight. The story basically unravels in the first half, and is filled with bizarre episodes including ghosts, and a very unlikely death for Arthur, not to mention the murder of Tom a Lincoln himself. The most interesting aspect of the whole work is the encounter with Prester John. This shadowy figure, who was widely believed to have existed throughout much of the Middle Ages, is almost certainty fictional, or based on misunderstood accounts of Middle Eastern leaders, but his connections with Arthur have long fascinated me and are the subject of a book I am currently working on. Of the many Arthurian texts only three that I have found mention Prester John – this one, and the lengthy thirteenth-century epic *Der Jungerer Titurel,* as well as references in the thirteenth–fifteenth century *Prophecies of Merlin* which are incorporated into my retelling from this text (see pp. 239–244).

4: Sir Lancelot, Sir Gawain and the White-Foot Stag

There was considerable interest in the Arthurian legends among the people of the Netherlands, especially during the fourteenth century. Several large compilations were made from French and German texts, as well as individual romances.

One of the largest of these, known as *The Lancelot Compilation*, included five romances interpolated between editions of the *Quest del Saint Graal* and the *Mort D'Arthur* drawn from the thirteenth-century *Lancelot-Grail Cycle,* which was the ultimate source for most of Malory's book. Most of these do not appear anywhere else, and none of them are known of in English versions. I have included three of these here because of their originality, and the excellent narrative line possessed by each. The story of the quest for the White-Foot Stag is found elsewhere, but this version has a number of original features. I have included it here because of the vivid picture it paints of the friendship between the two major knights of the Round Table. Lancelot, who came on the scene well after Gawain, and more or less replaced him as the first knight of the Round Table, rarely appears in the same story, so this is of interest because of its serious interpretation of the chivalry of Arthur's court. The lady who declares her intent to marry only the knight who can bring her the stag's foot, is nameless in the text (as are so many characters in these romances) so I gave her the name Lady Blanche to distinguish her from all the other maidens and ladies thronging these pages. The text in English is to be found in one of the volumes of the wonderful Arthurian Archives series published by D. S. Brewer: *Dutch Romances vol III: Five Interpolated Romances from the Lancelot Compilation*, Edited and Translated by David F. Johnson and Geert H.M. Classens (with the assistance of Katty De Bundel and Geert Pallemans), (D.S. Brewer, 2003). This is the main source of my version.

5: The Boy and the Mantle

The story of 'The Boy and the Mantle' appears in numerous versions and in several languages, from which we may assume that it was a popular story – one of many which, under the guise of chivalric fiction, poked fun at both the institution of chivalry, and, by inference, at the moralisers who looked upon such tales as either frivolous or immoral.

Today we may well find this tale less to our liking than the medieval audience for whom it was written. But it is still a timeless story, since most men are jealous at heart, and the true hero, Sir Caradoc, is the only one with the faith not to care about the outcome of the test. Indeed, the fidelity and worth of his lady is borne out elsewhere, in 'The story of Caradoc of the Strong Arm' from volume one of this collection (*The Great Book of King Arthur*, pp. 117–193), in which both feature as leading characters, and in which the lady saves her husband with great courage. It is also worth noting that all the women, wives and sweethearts, are tested alike – this is not a test of fidelity to the vows of marriage, but to the love of man for woman and woman for man.

As so often in these tales the character of the boastful Sir Kay is contrasted with that of the nobler Sir Gawain (though even he is cast in a less sympathetic role here) while the attitude of the misogynist Geres the Little makes him the least sympathetic character of all. Griflet, who appears in several other Arthurian romances, is generally presented as a knight of courage and chivalry; here he is a jester figure, much like Malory's Dagonet, given to uttering home truths from the privileged position of courtly fool.

Earlier versions of the story exist in which the mantle is replaced by a horn; those who drink from it – generally the wives of the Round Table knights – are unable to help spilling its contents over themselves, and it is in this form that it appears in 'The Story of Caradoc'. In yet another variation, the mantle is poisoned, and anyone who wears it is at once either struck dead or consumed by fire. (Malory tells a version of this in Book 2 of *Le Morte D'Arthur*, where it is sent to Arthur by Morgan le Fay).

Generally, however, the object is to show up the hero's wife as both faithful and modest, always at the expense of the other noble ladies, who are forced to admit their own infidelities when they try on the all-revealing mantle. I have suggested that the lady who sends the youth to Camelot may well be the same as she who made it – an otherworldly woman of the type found extensively in Arthurian romances. Her function is ever, as here, to test the strength of Arthur's knights, not only in the physical realm, but in the moral as well.

The version used primarily in the telling of this story is the Old Norse *Saga of the Boy and the Mantle* translated by Marianne E. Kalinke from her own edition of the text *Mottuls Saga* and included in *The Romance of Arthur III* edited by James J. Wilhelm (Garland Publishing,1988). I have also made use of the fifteenth-century ballad included in *The Reliques of Ancient English Poetry* edited by Bishop Thomas Percy (Dodsley, 1765), and the Old French *Le Lai du Cort Mantle* (Lay of the Short Mantle) also included in Dr Kalinke's edition.

6: The Avenging of Raguidel

The Avenging of Raguidel is the second poem by the brilliant medieval poet Raoul de Houdenc to be included in this collection. Dating from around the middle of the thirteenth century, it tells a thrilling and detailed story of love gone astray and turning to hate. A second version, one of seven tales inserted into the main narrative of the Dutch version of the *Lancelot-Grail* cycle, adds to Raoul's version and includes some variants. In particular it tells us that the events narrated in the story take place after the achieving of the Grail, and the death of Galahad and Perceval and the return of Bors to Camelot. There are two further adventures inserted into this edition which emphasise the underlying theme of the story – how love can lead to death and disaster. Making Gawain the protagonist here is a stroke of genius. He is known as the most desirable figure among all of the Round Table knights, and the number of liaisons he has with both human and faery women are numerous. Here he stumbles around, trying to find the truth about a mysterious death, and in the process discovers that he is inadvertently the cause of the love-crazed behaviour of the Lady of Gaut Desert. As I worked on this retelling I realised that the text virtually repeats the same story twice, with variants, and in making the story shorter, while reflecting its original, I decided to conflate the two versions. This sadly meant much of the supplementary parts of the story had to be lost but, interestingly, there is a theory that Raoul de Houdenc may have only written the second part, following an anonymous earlier version. This may account for what appears to be the same story told twice over in different form. The ending in this version is partly mine, as the various loose ends left by the original seemed to require it. The two editions I worked from are the brilliant translation by Nigel Bryant of Raoul's original, (*Chrétien's Equal: Raoul de Houdenc: Complete Works.* D.S. Brewer, 2021) and the Dutch version which is included in the edition and translation made by David F. Johnson and Geert H.M. Claassens in: *Dutch Romances, Vol III: Five Interpolated Romances from the Lancelot Compilation* (D.S. Brewer, 2003).

7: Sir Garel and the Terrible Head

Most unusually, there are two distinct versions of the text known, respectively, as *Garel of the Blooming Valley* (written in the latter half of the thirteenth century, possibly in Austria) and *Daniel of the Blossoming Valley*. (c.1210–1225, also in Austria.) Of the two, I preferred the second of these, composed by the author known as Der Pleier, two of whose romances, *Meleranz* and *Tandareis and Flordibel*, are included in this collection. Though the two versions follow a similar storyline, 'Garel' is a much more sophisticated and well-written account, which adds many details not present in the earlier version. Der Pleier clearly thought the older version, by a poet hiding under the name of Der Stricker, was too crudely violent, and worse, that it presented a somewhat unchivalrous account of Arthur and his knights. Both romances really are just a long series of linked adventures, mostly involving huge set pieces describing wars and battles between rival kingdoms. Since this would have been out of keeping with most of this collection – and because Der Pleier borrowed from several other romances – including his own – making this too repetitive of others gathered here, I chose to focus my retelling on a single episode, which involves a somewhat Medusa-like head, attached to a shield, which causes everyone who sees it to fall dead. In the version by Der

Stricker the monster is defeated with the use of a mirror, following the pattern of the Classical Greek Perseus tale, but I preferred Der Pleier's more valorous battle against the monster – which also happened to resemble a centaur. Overall, it is such a well-drawn adventure that I decided to focus on this. The only detail I borrowed from Der Stricker was the fact that the monster drank the blood of its victims, apparently before devouring their flesh. The source was, as ever for Der Pleier's tales, the wonderful translations by J.W. Thomas, included in *The Pleier's Arthurian Romances* (Garland Publishing, 1992). Those wishing to explore the far wilder version can find it in an English translation by Michael Resler in *Der Sticker: Daniel of the Blossoming Valley* (Garland Publishing, 1990).

8: King Arthur and King Cornwall

This truly strange and original story is told in ballad metre and seems to date from the late fifteenth or early sixteenth centuries – making it one of the latest stories in this collection. Exact dating is impossible as it derives from the collection put together by Bishop Thomas Percy in his monumental collection *Relics of Ancient English Poetry*. This was published in 1765 and lacks sufficient information to date the work, but suggests the ballad is earlier than Percy's edition. However, the language is sufficiently archaic to suggest it could date from the late fifteenth century. It is, unfortunately, incomplete, due to the use of random pages by one of the original owner's servants to light fires! These missing leaves are mostly just half pages, so the extent of the lost detail is brief enough to enable the completion of the narrative – though it must be said that I exercised more than usual licence to make the story complete. In this I was helped by the fact that it is clearly based on an older French text, *Le Pèlerinage de Charlemagne*, dating from the thirteenth century, which tells more or less the same story. The anonymous author of 'King Arthur and King Cornwall' has replaced Charlemagne with Arthur, Oliver with Gawain, Roland with Tristan etc. The tone of the original work is much more religious, here replaced by touches of magic which make the Arthurian version a fascinating addition to the Round Table saga. Thus we have the enigmatic relic owned by Sir Bredbeddle, a knight whose name appears in the roster of the Round Table but is little known beyond this present tale. Curiously, his name is also applied to the otherworldly adversary in the poem of *Sir Gawain and the Green Knight*, which suggests an earlier association with magic. Here the character possesses the relic of a tiny book – possibly a reference to small metal codices discovered in more recent times and dating back to the earliest days of Christianity. This enables the overcoming of the demon named, in true ballad style, Berlo-Beanie. The final destruction of the second Round Table is not in the original, but is required since Arthur does not take the larger version home with him! The suggestion that Guinevere had a child by King Cornwall is unattested elsewhere, and seems to fit well as one of the boasts (called *gabs*) of the knights. There are various editions of the ballad, including Bishop Percy's – but I found the most accessible to be that included in Sir Frederick Madden's invaluable collection *Syr Gawayne*, originally published in 1839, reprinted by AMS Press in 1971. For an extremely helpful breakdown of the work, to which I am indebted, see 'King Arthur and King Cornwall' by William Dinsmore Briggs in *The Journal of Germanic Philology*, vol. 3, no. 3 (1901) pp. 342–351.

9: The Marvels of Rigomer

The Marvels of Rigomer dates from either the latter half of the twelfth or the early thirteenth centuries. We cannot be any more sure of this than we can say, with complete certainty, whether it was written by one man or two. It is ascribed to one Jehan, of whom nothing is known, but there is internal evidence which suggests that a later scribe reinterpreted, and possibly added to, an older version. As a piece of storytelling it is vivid and often delightfully detailed in its descriptions of places and people. In this it even at times equals the work of Chrétien de Troyes or Raoul de Houdenc. Also of note is the placing of Rigomer – and a number of additional adventures – in Ireland, which is described as a very wild place full of strange beings. The author seems to know a good deal about the geography of the country – though this could be derived from the *Topographia Hibernica* composed by Giraldus Cambrensis in the twelfth century.

As with so many of the stories retold here, it is lengthy and quite complicated. Its structure follows the usual style of interlacement, in which stories are constantly interrupted, to be returned to later. For a modern audience this can be frustrating, and in my retelling I had to make some difficult decisions regarding what to leave in and what to cut. There are some fabulous incidental adventures which would certainly repay reading, but happily, I believe, I managed to tease out the lines of the central story, which seems to exist partly to demonstrate that, while Sir Lancelot is indeed a mighty hero, Gawain is actually better! This is reflected in another tale included here 'Sir Lancelot, Sir Gawain, and the White-Foot Stag' (pp. 34–39). There are also a number of comparative ideas apparently taken from the Grail romances, but I was forced to omit these due to the considerations of space. There are a few places where the story is somewhat open-ended – the marriage of Lady Dionise, for example, is left unfinished, and I chose to complete it by marrying her to Sir Blioberis. Also the giant knight is not clearly associated with he who accompanies the rude girl at the beginning, but the story seemed to cry out for this identification. As ever, several characters are unnamed, and for the sake of unity I gave them names which I felt were appropriate. The very helpful nobleman who guides both Lancelot and Gawain is not named, so I borrowed one from a character in one of the adventures not included here. The exact intentions of the Faery in the romance is also somewhat vague, but I believe my solution is in keeping with the overall story.

The poem's editor and translator, Thomas E. Vesce, also produced an excellent edition as part of his dissertation for Fordham University in 1967 (Ann Arbor, Michigan University Microfilms, 1969). His excellent and lively translation *The Marvels of Rigomer (Les Mervelles de Rigomer)* was published by Garland Publishing, New York and London, in 1988, and is the basis for most of my retelling.

10: King Arthur and Gorlagon

Arthur and Gorlagon is one of several surviving Arthurian romances written in Latin in the thirteenth and fourteenth centuries, others being *The History of Meriadoc, King of Cambria* and *The Rise of Gawain, Nephew of Arthur* both retold in *The Great Book of King Arthur*. All these tales have a 'realistic' quality which puts them at variance with the more exotic works of the Romance writers. Nothing is known of the author of this little story, which is nonetheless a powerful tale in its own right.

It is certainly a grim tale, half morality and half horror story, with a shock ending worthy of a modern spinner of such tales. It is also a good deal less equivocal about the savagery of life in this time than most stories of its kind. Thus the wolf does not hesitate to kill the children of his former queen, while Gorlagon's punishment for his own faithless wife is barbaric in the extreme. Yet this reflects the true state of affairs at the time, when the situation of women was anything but happy, and they were frequently regarded as potentially evil.

Arthur's quest, prompted by Guinevere's response to his apparently innocent kiss, suggest a darker theme, while the end is far from conclusive since the obvious answer provided by Gorlagon's story is that all women are treacherous and deserve to be punished accordingly. Like the story of 'The Vows of King Arthur and His Knights' (*Great Book of King Arthur* pp. 31–41) this presents a heavily misogynistic view – though other tales, such as 'The Wedding of Sir Gawain and the Lady Ragnall' (*Great Book of King Arthur* pp. 352–9) where a similar question is asked, show another side of the coin.

The origins of the story are not hard to trace. It belongs to a series of 'werewolf' stories which include the Celtic folk tale of *Morraha*, and two medieval tales, *Melion* and *Bisclavaret*. Both these last named stories belong to the genre of the 'Lai' (Story) and possess strong evidence of Breton (hence Celtic) origin. The folk tale which may well have provided a common source for all these literary stories was in all probability far simpler, containing only one evil queen, one brother, and probably omitting the episode of the hidden child and the false accusation against the wolf, which derive from the Welsh story of *Gelert*, where a faithful dog is wrongfully accused of killing a child.

The three brothers, who appear to know nothing of each other until the end of the story, all bear names which can be traced back to the Welsh word for 'werewolf'. In both the Breton versions the role of the queen is different. She is usually a faery woman, or even a goddess who, having married a mortal, seeks to return to her own country and does so by discovering her husband's secret and turning him into a wolf. Apparently the anonymous Latin author heard the story and found within it a vehicle for his personal misogyny. As Alfred Nutt remarks in his notes to the story, 'The free self-centred goddess, regally prodigal of her love, jealously guarding her independence, becomes a capricious or faithless woman.'

I have added a final paragraph to the tale, which it seemed to require, and which I hope does not detract from the original intention of the author. Whether he intended to write more, perhaps to add some worthy comment concerning the subsequent betrayal of Arthur by Guinevere, we cannot know. It is reasonable to suppose that his audience would have been familiar enough with the Arthurian mythos to draw their own conclusions. In the text, Kay and Gawain are referred to by their Latin names Caius and Walwain; I have amended this to the more usual titles for the sake of harmony.

Arthur and Gorlagon is found in a late fifteenth-century manuscript, Rawlinson B.49, in the Bodleian Library, Oxford. It was edited by Professor G.L. Kittredge in *Harvard Studies and Notes In Philology and Literature* vol viii, (1903). It was translated by F.A. Milne with notes by A. Nutt in *Folk-Lore* vol 15,1904. pp. 40–67. I have made principal use of this version in preparing my own retelling.

11: Sir Cleges and the Christmas Court

Sir Cleges is an unusual and charming story based on a theme usually found in the medieval lives of the saints. It is one of the few tales set not in Arthur's own time but in that of his father, Uther Pendragon – though it assumes the existence of the Round Table even this early on in the cycle of tales. It is an English tale, from a single fifteenth-century manuscript preserved in the Advocate's Library in Edinburgh. It may be the work of a cleric with a sense of humour – presenting an unusual slant on the life of a knight. It is also a Christmas tale with a long history, dating back to an earlier period of the Middle Ages, if not earlier. It probably derives in part from the famous 'Cherry Tree Carol' in which the Virgin Mary asks Joseph for a cherry in midwinter and the tree obligingly flowers in order to provide the fruit. Rather than a romance it falls more exactly into the genre of a Lay – shorter poems aimed at a courtly audience – though it seems more likely that it was meant for a more homely listener, with its emphasis on the everyday life of the knight. There are thus a number of anomalies to this work, which is nevertheless worthy of re-discovery by a new audience.

I have made one very minor amendment to the story. In the original text it mentions that Uther gave some of the cherries to a certain Lady of Cornwall. I could not help wondering if this could be Igraine, the future mother of Arthur, whom Uther woos, thus instigating a war with the lady's husband and inadvertently bringing the entire epic of Arthur into being.

A much longer and very different story is told in the French romance *Cligès* by Chrétien de Troyes, but it seems unlikely that this is the same character as the one in this charming tale.

The text has been edited several times, notably by George H. McKnight in *Middle English Humorous Tales* (Heath, 1913) and in modern English by Jessie L. Weston in her *Sir Cleges and Sir Libeaus Desconus: Two Old English Metrical Romances Rendered into Prose.* (David Nutt, 1901). I have made primary use of this in preparing my own version.

12: The Turk and Sir Gawain

The original version of this curious tale dates to around *c.*1500 AD. It was collected by Bishop Percy in his extraordinary collection *The Relics of English Poetry*, published in 1765 and still in print to this day. (The most recent edition being that reprinted by The British Library, Edited by John W. Hales and Frederick J. Furnivall, in 2010). The poem, originally of an estimated 600 lines, was damaged in a fire and only 335 lines still exist. However, it is possible to guess at the content of the missing stanzas, and this I have done, following the guidelines of the poem's most recent editor, Thomas Hahn, while allowing my imagination to fill in some of the blanks. It's a strange tale, obviously related to the more famous *Sir Gawain and the Green Knight*, (edited and translated by J.R.R.Tolkien) but lacking the full Beheading Game episode and the attempted seduction of Gawain by the Green Knight's wife. In this version only a harmless blow is exchanged, and the beheading only occurs at the end, when the figure of the Turk (a general term which meant simply a pagan rather than someone from Turkey) is transformed into that of Sir Gromer Somer Jour (Man of the Summer's Day). This figure reappears in the story of 'The Wedding of Sir Gawain and the Lady Ragnall', retold in volume one of this collection, (*The Great Book of King Arthur*, pp. 299–307) which ends with Gawain marrying the otherworldly Lady Ragnall, Sir Gromer's sister. The story is clearly one of the many Arthurian tales that have a strong scent of the otherworld, and this

I have built up throughout my retellings. The original text makes a somewhat half-hearted attempt to Christianise a clearly pre-Christian story, but this I omitted as it seems far from in keeping with the subject matter. There are a number of editions of the original text, including that in the collection *Syr Gawayne*, edited by Frederic Madden and published originally in London in 1839, reprinted by AMS Press in 1971. More recently Thomas Hahn included it in his collection *Sir Gawain: Eleven Romances and Tales* published in 1995 by the Medieval Institute. Both these editions are in the original sixteenth-century English, but a modern translation was made by Dr Brian Gastle for the John Gower Society (*www://johngower.org*).

13: The Lady of the Fountain and the Knight of the Lion.

The story told here is based on a version found in the *Mabinogion* – the medieval Welsh myth-book which includes some of the oldest stories from this country, and several later Arthurian tales. Argument still rages as to whether these were the source for, or based upon, those of Chrétien de Troyes's romances. According to which opinion one accepts, they could be as early as 1060–1200, with Chrétien's versions not arriving until *c*.1160–1172. However, the dating of the surviving manuscripts to between 1350 and 1410 has led many scholars to opt for a later period for the creation of the Welsh stories. All one can say is that the mood of the stories and the folklore details – as, for example, the one-eyed, one-legged Lord of the Beasts – suggests an earlier date than the twelfth century. In my own view I believe they are likely to stem from the older Celtic material which was carried across to Brittany and Normandy by native storytellers following the Saxon incursions into Britain the sixth century. Whichever is true, I chose to follow the *Mabinogion* version, which feels to me much older than Chrétien's more polished, courtly poem. There are numerous editions of the *Mabinogion*, including the latest and best by Sionad Davis, published by the Oxford University Press in 2007, but for my version I chose to use Lady Guest's version in her edition of *The Mabinogion* from 1906. This is not always the most accurate of translations, but succeeds in capturing the mood of the original text better than most. As I worked on the retelling, I was struck by the way in which several characters from the first part of the story reoccurred, but without names, in the final adventure. I decided to adopt this reading in order to tie up a few inconsistencies within the original text. Those who wish to read the Lady Guest version will find numerous modern editions, based on the original publication by J.M. Dent in 1906. The best study of the Arthurian relationship to the Mabinogi in general is still *King Arthur and the Goddess of the Land* by Caitlín Matthews (Inner Traditions, 2002).

14: The Story of Geraint and Enid

This is another of the great Arthurian stories from the collection known as the *Mabinogion*, which assembles some of the earliest Welsh myths and legends. As noted above, there is still much debate among scholars as to whether these may have been a source for the romances of Chrétien de Troyes – in this instance to the romance entitled 'Erec and Enid'. My own belief is, that while we may never be able to prove one way or the other, the Welsh versions retains older material which both the anonymous authors of the *Mabinogion* and Chrétien drew upon when creating their stories.

This is indeed one of the most often told stories in the period between the twelfth and fourteenth centuries, with versions in German, Icelandic and Norwegian. It is also a difficult story for us to read today, and we can only keep in mind that attitudes were different in the medieval period to those of today. For this reason I hesitated over including it in this collection – but the details and twists and turns of the story are such, especially the handling of the relationship between the two main protagonists, that I felt I had to attempt it. Most of it is told straightforwardly, as it is in the original text, but I made changes to the end, which tails off rather abruptly after the long journey of Geraint and Enid, and the former's thoughtless behaviour towards the woman he loves.

I changed the ending slightly by making the iconic episode of the enchanted hedge and the Lady of the Tent – recognised as a symbol of sovereignty – the lead-up to Geraint's seeming death and sudden recovery. In the original text this is told as a rather basic battle with giants, after which the story fades out, with Geraint not even apologising to Enid. Joining it with the more powerful last adventure, with its enchanted hedge, seemed to bring the story to a more forceful conclusion. As with the previous story from this source, 'The Lady of the Fountain and the Knight of the Lion', I chose to use the translation in Lady Charlotte Guest's edition of the *Mabinogion*, which is still one of the best tellings. Those wishing to read the unaltered version should seek out one of the editions of the *Mabinogion*; the one used by myself being from the 1906 edition published in London by J. M. Dent and Co and in New York by E.P. Dutton and Co.

BOOK TWO: TALES OF LOVE AND HONOUR

15: Fergus of Galloway

There are two versions of this tale. The French romance *Roman de Fergus* attributed to Guillaume le Clerc, and an anonymous Dutch version, *Ferguut*, based upon it but with several differences of detail. I have drawn upon both of these, but the original French text provided me with almost everything I needed to retell the tale.

Uniquely amongst these stories of Arthur, the hero is named after an actual historical figure, though admittedly a rather shadowy one, who is believed to have ruled over Galloway after forming an alliance with the Norse Óláfar, King of the Isles, around the middle of the twelfth century. Fergus of Galloway (c.1096–1161) is believed to have married the illegitimate daughter of King Henry I, and thus to have allied himself to the English crown. The poem that bears his name may have been commissioned by his grandson, and dates from the beginning of the thirteenth century. Little or nothing is known of its author, Guillaume le Clerc, but it is clear that he was both a well-educated and literate man. His poem is sometimes seen as a parody of the Romance genre, but in fact the work is of a more serious intent – showing its hero, who is unusually of humble, peasant stock, rising to become a famed knight of the Round Table by dint of his courage and determination. The story is once again one of love found, lost and found again, and features some wonderful characters, such as the scythe-wielding hag and the wise dwarf. It is also full of references to the cultural history of the time, and to the writings of Chrétien de Troyes, whose characters and situations are frequently pillaged. Fergus is thus a parallel of Perceval in the way he encounters Arthur's knights and is immediately filled with the desire to become one of them, and his quest for the White Shield perhaps his version of the Grail search. Another figure, namely Fergus's father, Somerled, may be based on a second Norse-Gaelic hero who rose to power at roughly the same time.

In the version of the poem composed by Guillaume le Clerc, the setting of the story is largely in Scotland, and those who have studied the text have shown that the author knew the country well enough to enable us to identify many of the places known today. For this retelling I have kept more to the usual setting, with Camelot the centre of action and the Great Wood on all sides. This is for the sake of continuity with the other stories retold here. I have, however, retained the Scots names for the characters, including the hero wherever I could, and that of sites such as Roxburgh and Liddel Mount which are still extant.

The name of the site to which Fergus goes in search of the Black Knight is itself a mystery. *Nouquetran* is a name that has so far defied understanding. Since it is included with a reference to Merlin we may assume that, like the equally oddly titled *Esplumoir*, or 'Moulting Cage', to which Merlin is said to have retired, it may well stand for some magical chamber of the Otherworld. The poet seems to have believed it to be the name of a mountain peak, and the Arthurian scholar Nikolai Tolstoy in his seminal book *The Quest for Merlin* (Hamish Hamilton, 1985)

292

based much of his argument for an actual site associated with a sixth-century incarnation of the great enchanter on the geography of *Fergus*.

The comparison between the French and Dutch versions of the story reveals some interesting parallels. For those who wish to study this, the best source is an important essay: 'A Relaxed Knight and an Impatient Heroine: Ironizing the Love Quest in the second part of the Middle Dutch Ferguut' by Marjolein Hogenberk, in *Mediaeval English and Dutch literatures: the European context* (eds) L. Tracy, and G. H. M. Claassens (D.S. Brewer, 2022). Those wishing to read either text in English translation are recommended to *Fergus of Galloway: Knight of King Arthur* by Guillaume le Clerc, translated, with an introduction and notes by D.D.R. Owen (John Donald, 2018) *and Ferguut*, edited and translated by David F. Johnson and Geert H. H. Claassens (D.S.Brewer, 2000).

16: Meraugis and the Wounds of Love

This extraordinary poem, originally titled *Meraugis de la Portlesguez*, was composed sometime in the first quarter of the thirteenth century by an author named Raoul de Houdenc. Almost nothing is known about him, though the breadth of his written works, ranging from the mystical *Dream of Hell* and *Visit to Paradise*, a satirical commentary on knighthood (*The Romance of the Wings*) and the two Arthurian romances included here, suggest that he was a poet of some standing. Nigel Bryant, the first translator of his surviving complete works, describes him as 'Chrétien's Equal' (D.S. Brewer, 2021), referring to one of the greatest poets of the time, whose Arthurian poems are recognised as amongst the finest in the medieval corpus. There is some evidence that Raoul may have been a 'poor knight', perhaps the youngest son of a nobleman who became a wandering storyteller. This makes him, as our nameless cleric notes, a fitting companion for Sir Thomas Malory, the other great knightly author. The first of these two romances is a detailed study of love and chivalry – how one may affect the other, with often dramatic consequences. The treatment of female characters, especially the heroin Lidoine, is unusual for the time and the genre. The story turns upon the rivalry between two knights, once close friends, driven apart by their love for the same woman. Importantly, the hero, Meraugis, loves Lidoine for her beauty and her mind; while his rival, Gorvin Cadrus, is only interested in her outward beauty. The interplay between these two men and their different approaches to love, make the poem rich in modern correspondences. There is an element of the comedic in the story also, such as the episode when Meraugis dresses as a woman to lure his captors across to the island where he is imprisoned. His companion and fellow knight, Gawain, seems highly amused by the pretence, but goes along with it.

Inevitably, in a romance of almost 6,000 lines, I have had to lose a good deal of the wit and wisdom, as well as the detailed descriptions, of its author, especially Raoul's considerations on knighthood and chivalry, but we are fortunate that the translator of the poem, Nigel Bryant, has given us a vibrant and enjoyable edition, which I recommend to everyone, and which is the primary source of my version. Towards the end of the story, when matters become very complicated, I have simplified and largely rewritten the conclusion, hopefully in the spirit of Raoul, if not to the letter.

17: Meleranz and the Lady of the Fountain

Nothing is known of the identity of the poet calling himself 'The Pleier' (a word meaning someone who smelts metal; perhaps a reference to his ability to craft and shape his stories). His three works, all of them Arthurian, including 'Sir Garel and the Terrible Head' (pp. 56–60) and 'The Story of Tandereis and Flordibel' (pp. 217–225) all display a high level of poetic and storytelling skill. The dates for the Pleier's activities range from 1240 to 1280, and he makes use of other tales, especially those of Chrétien de Troyes, borrowing from *Yvain* in particular for the scenes relating to the Lady of the Fountain. Another possible source is the Breton Ley, *Graelent*, which follows the story here quite closely, but is completely revised and made over by Pleier. There is a very real sense of warmth and friendliness in all three of these romances, which are full of references to everyday medieval life (I especially love the way hospitality is described, with dressing gowns supplied to visitors, and cups of mulberry wine and snacks provided to Meleranz). But the real subject of the story is about the youth who grows up to be a great knight, and the steep learning curve to which he is subjected along the way. His clear devotion to his love is emphasised throughout, and brings him strength when he most needs it. The Pleier's name was widely known throughout Germany, and scenes from his works are still viewable at the castle of Runkelstein in the Southern Tyrol, added in 1400 to the thirteenth-century castle. The original edition was edited by Karl Bartsch in 1861, reprinted in 1974. The only English edition to date is that by J. W. Thomas, included in *The Pleier's Arthurian Romances* (Garland Publishing, 1992). My own version of the story draws on the latter, though I have diverted in several places, especially the ending, which Pleier extends over one hundred pages, most of them describing several extravagant weddings. I also added details to introduce a more magical sense to the story and to bring it in line with others gathered here.

18: The Madness of Sir Trystan

This story is based on the *Folie Tristan of Oxford* (so called to distinguish it from the *Folie Tristan of Bern,* from which it differs only in minor details). It is essentially an episode from a much longer tale, which relates the story of the doomed love of Tristan and Iseult (here called, in an older spelling, Trystan and Ysolt). Its author, who remains unknown, evidently knew the story in its entirety and expected his listeners to know as much as he. The abrupt beginning, which I have amended here for the benefit of those who do not know the whole story, simply refers to Tristan's sorrow and describes him as 'living in his land', which from internal evidence we may assume to be Brittany, though Tristan himself was from Cornwall. From this we can place the episode within the larger framework of the Tristan romance proper. Having discovered an undying passion for each other, the two lovers have sought to continue an affair under the nose of Iseult's husband, King Mark of Cornwall (who is also Tristan's uncle). Circumstances make it less and less easy for them to meet, and in order to protect her lover Iseult feigns coldness towards him. This has the effect of driving him away, and he undertakes a loveless marriage with the ironically named Iseult of Brittany, more out of spite for his mistress than for any better reason. Thus ensconced in Brittany, miserable and bereft of his love, Tristan languishes, and it is here that we first meet him in the *Folie Tristan.*

Tristan is the second great lover of Arthurian romance, the first being Lancelot, but there are few parallels between their stories. Lancelot is a far nobler figure than Tristan, who often behaves both savagely and without conscience. Mark, unlike Arthur, is a bad husband, as well as a bad king. The sly couplings of Tristan and Iseult are very unlike the noble passion of Lancelot and Guinevere, though it must be said that they were probably more popular among an audience whose fascination with Courtly Love led them to praise adultery while condemning it in the same breath. In more recent times, due largely to the success of Richard Wagner's opera *Tristan and Isolde*, their story has continued to overshadow that of Lancelot and Guinevere.

The *Folie* is essentially designed to rehearse the most important episodes from the saga of Trystan – the excuse to do so being that Ysolt is unable, or unwilling, to recognise her lover through his disguise. The fact that he continues to use the false voice of the fool, even when they are alone, has prompted one commentator to remark on his cruelty. It seems almost as though he is driven to draw out the torment of her failure to acknowledge him, but it would be a mistake to apply a modern psychological interpretation to the behaviour of a medieval man whose actions are described and set down by a medieval writer. Whoever composed the story was more interested in the game of words between the lovers, and to the device which enabled him to recall the best bits of the much longer cycle of tales about Trystan and Ysolt.

The *Folie Tristan of Oxford* was composed towards the beginning of the thirteenth century, though it is a very different work to the vast high romantic tale of passion written by Gottfried von Strasbourg in c1210 (*Tristan*, translated by A.T. Hatto. Penguin Books, 1960). It undoubtedly reflects the older Celtic origins of the story. It is a far earthier and more powerful evocation of the lovers' destructive desperation than Gottfried's, and as such deserves to be better known. It has been edited a number of times, notably by E. Hoepffner, who also edited the *Folie Tristan of Berne* (Paris, Les Belles Lettres, 1943 and 1949 respectively). The two versions have each been translated once before, the *Folie of Bern* by Alan S. Frederic, as part of his rendition of Beroul's *The Romance of Tristan* (Penguin Books, 1970) and the *Folie of Oxford* by Judith Weiss in her anthology of early medieval texts *The Birth of Romance* (Dent, 1992). I have referred to both these versions in preparing my own retelling.

19: Gismirante and the Lady with the Hair of Gold

The story of Gismirante was written by one Antonio Pucci (*c.*1310–1338), a native of Florence who held a variety of municipal roles including that of bell ringer, town crier and archivist. This last job may well have given him access to older stories, but the version given here is the only one that has survived. Pucci's output was extensive, running into hundreds of sonnets and a large number of *Cantari* (songs), a form of poetic romance, shorter than the great narratives of France, Germany and Holland, but often following the same strands of love and adventure which lie at the heart of this particular text. Stylistically, the story is competent, but lacks detail. Much of the action seems lightly motivated, and such details as the Lady with the Hair of Gold persuading the Wildman to admit the disguised hero, has no obvious purpose, so that I have given a reason for it that is not in the original. Pucci borrows liberally from a variety of sources – the story of the strand of hair that causes such a stir in Arthur's court, appears in the *Romance of Tristan*, where the mere sight of it causes King Mark to fall in love with its owner. The help received by Gismirante from the three creatures – gryphon, eagle and sparrowhawk (later revealed to be brothers to the faery who helps the hero) is a common one in folklore of various countries. The Wildman is reminiscent of the Green Knight from the poem *Sir Gawain and the Green Knight* and elsewhere in Arthurian literature, and the external hiding of his heart is found in many tales – usually applied to giants – where the hero must find the heart in order to kill or defeat his adversary. Here Pucci manages to weave these various stories into an enjoyable romance with a very human

296

hero and plenty of helpful faery magic. My retelling draws upon the edition by Maria Bendinelli Predelli translated by Joyce Myerson, Amanda Glover and Andrea Saunderson (British Rencesvals Publications 6, Edinburgh, 2013).

20: The Sweet Sorrow of Sir Gawain

This is one of the most unusual stories in this collection because it derives, not from a medieval romance, but from a Gaelic ballad known as *An Bròn Binn* (The Sweet Sorrow). At least thirty-one written versions of this ballad date from the early seventeenth century, but very clearly come from a much earlier time. What we have, I believe, is the fragmentary remembrance of a story of Gawain which no longer exists in any other form, but must have been heard, and remembered, by a ballad maker of the time. Thus it has preserved a now lost story which I believe would have added to our understanding of the Arthurian myth. It is a very tangled tale, with a cluster of variations between one version and another, but it was surprisingly easy to return it to a romance style of telling. For this I made my own ending, since the original was both fragmentary and contradictory.

I am grateful to my wife, Caitlín Matthews, for drawing this to my attention, and to making her own (unpublished) translation, elements of which I made use of in my retelling. For a complete, and fascinating, study of the mysterious text, I recommend *An Bròn Binn: an Arthurian ballad in Scottish Gaelic* by Linda Gowans (privately printed in Eastbourne in 1992).

21: Gauriel of Muntabel and the Faery Wife

This is perhaps one of my favourite stories in this collection. Not only is the original well written and lyrical, but it involves one of the most important themes in the Arthurian corpus – the relationship between the world of the Arthurian court and that of the realm of Faery. A study of the entire Arthurian corpus shows that as many as 80 per cent of the challenges issued to the Knights of the Round Table originate in the faery world. (see *Studies in the Fairy Mythology of Arthurian Romance* by Lucy Allen Paton (reprinted by Burt Franklin, New York, 1970). From this it is possible to posit that a kind of invisible war existed between the two worlds, and I have referenced this in my version of the story to show what is implicit in the original text. The story is also interesting in that it not only references such familiar texts as Chrétien's *Yvain, or the Knight of the Lion* (see 'The Lady of the Fountain and the Knight of the Lion', pp. 94–104) and that we find out what happened to the beast in question – but also reverses that story, in which a knight is initially accused of giving more attention to his wife than his knightly duties. Here Gauriel neglects his wife, who becomes someone to boast about. As ever, I had to make a number of cuts in what would otherwise have been far too long to include here. In between the recognition of Gauriel's abilities by his wife, there are several more adventures, and I recommend the fine translation by Siegfried Christoph (*Gauriel von Muntabel by Konrad von Stoffeln*, D.S. Brewer, 2007) to those who would like to read them. We know nothing about the author of this text, which was probably composed around the first half of the thirteenth century, possibly in what is today the southwestern area of Germany. It is very clear that Konrad was familiar with a wide number of Arthurian romances, which he references throughout.

I made certain changes to the names of the faery herself, and to her kingdom. In the original, her name is *Frîâpolatûse*, which is virtually unpronounceable today and largely untranslatable. From this I derived *Fatuse*, which both reflects the original and suggests her curious origin. Similarly, the land over which she rules is titled *Flûratrône*, which one editor has suggested derives from old French *flûrs* and *trôn* ('flower' and 'throne'). From this I decided to call her country the Land of the Flowering Throne. I also adopted the Welsh Owein rather than the German Iwein.

22: Wigamur, Knight of the Eagle

The romance of Wigamur was written in the thirteenth century in Middle High German by an unknown author. It's an extremely prolix story (over 60,000 lines) of a young man searching for his true identity, having been stolen away as a baby by a mermaid. I had to cut large amounts of description – mostly of tournaments and weddings and some very extravagant costumes, in order to tell it in a reasonable space. Joseph M. Sullivan, the editor and translator of the only complete English text, notes that it has been little studied due to a somewhat lukewarm critical response. In fact the poem, while at times rather long-drawn-out, has several original ideas – notably the presence of the sea creatures, and the eagle who becomes Wigamur's friend and companion. There is also an interesting aspect in the form of the moral stance exhibited by the hero, and his constant refusal to accept offers of employment and marriage until he has proved himself of worthy birth. More than one commentator has noted that this suggests a less well-born author, who at times pokes fun at the chivalry of Arthur and his knights. There is no complete manuscript as yet uncovered, but a number of fragmentary chapters have enabled the occasional gaps in the story to be added in. In one or two places I found it necessary to imagine what some of the missing parts might be, as much in keeping with the original as possible. As before, I have felt it appropriate to change some of the names for the sake of clarity. For example, the uncle of King Arthur, who appears in no other story, is spelled Yttra or Ittra. I changed this to Ettra, which is less difficult to say but still reflects the original. Of all the stories I have studied, the anonymous author made up some utterly strange names for his minor characters. In a lengthy tournament scene (omitted here) we find Zehattel, Fotoron, Triachta, Tubis and Pagofrical among others! The women's names are equally problematical for modern readers, but I have managed to retain these for the most part. For a full discussion of the sources for Wigamur, and its place in the ranks of the Fair Unknown narratives, I recommend 'The Sources of Wigamur and the German Reception of the Fair Unknown Tradition', by Neil Thomas (*Reading Medieval Studies* XIX (1993) pp. 97–111). For those wishing to read the entire story I recommend the edition and translation which was the main source for this retelling: *Wigamur*, Ed. and Trans. by Joseph M Sullivan (Boydell & Brewer, 2015). The most authoritative edition of the original is that edited by Michelle Szkilnik (H. Champion, 2004) .

23: Sir Gawain in the Land of Wonder

This is the longest, and to my mind one of the most fascinating, stories in this collection. Based on a medieval Dutch text, dating from the early thirteenth century, and entitled the *Roman van Walewein*, it has two authors: one named simply Penninc, and the other Pieter Vostaert, who completed the work begun by Penninc, possibly following his death. Nothing is known for certain of either author, though the presence of numerous religious references within the text suggests that they may have been clerics, possibly associated with either the court of the Count of Flanders or the Duke of Brabant. *Walewein* is certainly one of the most highly developed romances to emerge from the Dutch Middle Ages, which had a tremendous interest in all things Arthurian. Despite the initial borrowings from different sources, notably Chrétien de Troyes, it is actually a surprisingly original tale, containing many details not found anywhere else. Once again Gawain is the hero *par excellence*, whose chivalry is extreme – as is his love for women, none of whom seem able to resist him! Aside from the familiar romance style which forms the main content of the story, another aspect of it follows the outline of one of the most famous folk tales collected by the Brothers Grimm. In this, 'The Golden Bird', the hero succeeds in discovering the object of his search through encounters with several characters, each of whom needs the object he has just found and is therefore able to guide him to find the next. There are several other folkloric themes, such as the talking fox, to whom I gave a larger role than in the original in order to avoid a very lengthy sub-plot. In this, a knight killed by Gawain in the earlier part of the text reappears as a ghost and helps the knight on the final stages of his quest. In order to shorten the story, and because Rogier the fox seemed to deserve more of the action, I made him enable Gawain and his lady Ysabeau to escape. The concept of the Land of Wonder is particularly fascinating, as it very closely resembles descriptions of the mysterious kingdom of Prester John found in medieval accounts of the land ruled over by the mysterious priest-king. (see 'The Red Rose Knight' and 'The Prophecies of Merlin and the Lady of the Lake' in this collection). The magical chess board recalls one which appears in the *Mabinogion* story of 'The Dream of Rhonawby', in which the hero observes King Arthur and Owein ap Gwydion (the Sir Owein of the Arthurian Romances), playing an early type of chess called Gwyddbwyll, which I allowed the narrator to reference at the end of my retelling. I could not resist making a tentative connection with the game of chess played by Gawain in 'The Crown of the Grail' (pp. 250–261) The title, 'Sir Gawain in the Land of Wonder', is my own; there is no agreement as to the original title and this seemed to emphasise the most important element in the text. For those wishing to read the story in its entirety (it is over 11,000 lines long) I recommend the edition and translation of David F. Johnson and Geert H.M. Claassens (*Roman van Walewein*, D.S. Brewer, 2000).

24: The Tale of Tandereis and Flordibel

This is the third of three romances composed by the author known as Der Pleier (the Smelter) written between 1240 and 1280 in an area of modern-day Bavaria. All of these have a very natural and extraordinarily detailed quality, and I am sorry that I had to omit so much detail in order to make the story fit into this collection, and to work for a modern audience – who might have tired of the long descriptions of castles, costumes and armour. Interestingly, among these romances, there is much more detail of warfare than is usual. Arthur's army marches to Tandanas and we are treated to lengthy excursions on siege warfare. It is, above all (and like the other two stories) essentially a very moral tale, but the details are fascinating – the leopards that guard the villein Kerion, the dwarfish community of the Lady of the Wilderness, are gems I could not afford to lose. There is only one translation of the work to date, that by J.W. Thomas included in *The Pleier's Arthurian Romances* (Garland Publishing Inc., 1992). Professor Thomas's introduction and analysis of all three romances were exceedingly helpful in the composition of my own version.

25: The Story of Edern, the Son of the Bear

The story of Edern is one of the most unusual in this collection because of the way it shows a very different approach to Arthur's court and for that matter to the character of the king himself. Here, we see an Arthur who is jealous of the young hero for the way he is admired by Guinevere. Also he seems to put the normal requests for help from a beleaguered lady in the background as he goes to war with a knight who is less enthusiastic of becoming his liegeman and part of the realm. The story offers a view of courtly life that is quite modern in its style – suggesting the privileged lives of the knights and the importance of their financial status. Sir Kay once again serves as a failure, but in this instance his unprovoked attack on the hero is positively vicious. This is in line with his murder of Arthur's son, Loholt, in the *Lancelot-Grail* cycle.

The poem itself, entitled *le Roman d'Yder*, is only found in one manuscript, dating from the second half of the thirteenth century. The beginning is lost, possibly by as much as 1,000 lines, but this is easily recovered from internal evidence. Written in French, the style and accomplishment of the verse suggests a sophisticated and well-educated author. The poem itself is entitled *Yder* but its titular hero is an interesting character who may have played a more important part in the earlier stories of Arthur. Though most of the story told here comes from the thirteenth-century poem, there are references to its hero which led me to change the spelling of his name to Edern and to add in references from the older tradition in keeping with this collection. Edern, or Yder, is mentioned in the *Welsh Triads* and in the story of 'Culhwch and Olwen' from the *Mabinogion* collection, and is referenced on the Modena archivolt (a twelfth-century carving above the door of the church at Modena, Italy) as Isdernus, who is said to have kidnapped Guinevere. It is possible that echoes of this story would explain Arthur's untypical actions in sending the hero to a possible death. The only edition and translation of the text to date is by Alison Adams in *The Romance of Yder* (D.S. Brewer, 1983) and I have worked with this version throughout.

BOOK THREE: GUARDIANS OF THE GRAIL

26: Titurel's Dream

This story is taken from a huge and prolix work called *Der Jüngere Titurel* (The Later Titurel) attributed to Albrecht von Scharfenberg. Composed in the late thirteenth century, *c.*1270, it adds a number of important details both to the creation of an earthly home for the sacred relic, and to the growing family of Grail guardians. It thus connects to the equally little-known poem of *Sone de Nansay* which was included in the *Great Book of King Arthur* (pp. 397–411) and which also includes a description of the Castle of the Grail. The exact identity of the author of *Titurel* remains in question, even though he is routinely described as 'Albrecht von Scharfenberg'. Recent scholars have cast doubt on this. Charles E. Passage, the only recent editor of parts of the text, sums up his character as devout and '*Marked with an excessive concern with cult objects and religious symbolism.*' (*Titurel, Wolfram von Eschenbach. Translation and Studies* by Charles E. Passage. Frederic Ungar Publishing Co., 1984) An earlier editor of the poem believes that Albrecht may have become a churchman in later life. The poem is in fact a patchwork, based on several of Wolfram von Eschenbach's late works, including both *Parzifal* and a fragmentary poem called *Titurel*. The opening, a lengthy prayer in which Albrecht professes his faith, is based in part on the opening of Wolfram's non-Arthurian poem *Wilihalm*. Albrecht then adds some 6,300 lines to Wolfram's *Titurel*, which seems to represent his intention to write a pre-history of the Grail. In the end, Wolfram only managed approximately 170 stanzas (some of which are not definitively by him) that told the life of Schionatulander, the knight loved by Sigune, who is already dead in her arms in *Parzifal*. Possibly Wolfram intended this to be a more secular romance, balancing the spiritual intensity of his other work.

The third part of the text, currently unedited, contains a startling piece of information – that the Grail was taken and delivered into the hands of the almost certainly fictional priest-king Prester John, who was believed to rule a vast kingdom in the Far East. The whole fascinating story, which forms the second part of my retelling, has yet to be studied in detail, but for an account of the possible site of the Grail's home see my book: *Temples of the Grail*, co-authored with Gareth Knight, published by Llewellyn in 2001. The details included in both 'The Red Rose Knight' and 'The Prophecies of Merlin and the Lady of the Lake' in this collection, add further details. As with Chrétien's unfinished *Perceval*, the excitement generated by an unfinished poem supposed to be by the great Wolfram von Eschenbach produced a vastly extended completion by Albrecht, who pretended to *be* Wolfram until almost the very end of the poem. He was a lesser poet, though able to handle extremely difficult verse forms, but his imagination was much less distinctive than Wolfram's. The complexity, length and often impenetrable style of the work (*c.* 600,000 lines in length) have relegated *The Later Titurel* largely to the ranks of the forgotten texts; but a careful examination shows that, like *Sone*, it includes much that is important to an understanding of the Grail myth.

27: King Arthur's Quest

Perlesvaus, or the High Book of the Grail, the text from which this episode is taken is, to my mind, the finest Grail story of all. It is deeply spiritual, and blends this precisely with the adventure and chivalric ideas of the Arthurian realm. It is also one of the earliest of those that followed Chrétien de Troyes' poem, *The Story of the Grail*, which is often considered the first of its kind, but whose author seems to have known a far older story, on which he based his own. The anonymous author of *Perlesvaus* probably composed it during the first decade of the thirteenth century, and was clearly a highly spiritual man. Perhaps more directly than any of his contemporaries, he saw the parallels between the Rich Fisher (or Fisher King) who ruled over a wounded land, and Arthur himself, who is very clearly a wounded king himself – a detail I have done my best to draw out in my version of the story. The majority of the text deals with the quest of Perceval (Perlesvaus) for the Grail, but it is the only surviving text to give King Arthur a quest of his own, allowing him to see for himself the mysterious 'changes of the Grail' which remain as enigmatic today as when it was originally set down. There is a wonderfully spiritual aspect to this story missing even from the many hundreds of pages of theology in the *Lancelot-Grail* cycle, the longest of all the romances. I have kept as closely as I can to the strange narrative at the beginning of the text, adding only a few brief details for the benefit of those who may not be familiar with the Grail myth is totality. The wonderful translation by Nigel Bryant was the source for my version. It reads wonderfully for any modern audience, and I cannot recommend it highly enough. It can be found as *The High Book of the Grail: the translation of the 13th century romance of Perlesvaus*. (D.S. Brewer/Roman and Littlefield, 1978).

28: The Crown of the Grail

Diu Crone (The Crown) is one of the most unusual and powerful versions of the Grail myth. It is unusual because it makes Gawain successful in his quest, while all other versions have either Perceval (Chrétien de Troyes), or Galahad, accompanied by Perceval and Bors (in the *Lancelot-Grail* cycle). The reasons for this are complicated. Gawain is one of the oldest and most popular heroes of the Arthurian cycle, but he was replaced by Lancelot as the greatest of the Round Table knights, and when Lancelot himself was considered to love Arthur's queen more than he loved God, it passed to *his* son, Galahad, to achieve the quest. All of this is found in Malory's version. 'The Crown' takes us into another world where Gawain is a devotee of the Goddess Fortune (a theme which is found in other, older stories of the king's nephew) and where it is he, rather than the other knights, who actually asks the all-important question which brings about the healing of the Grail King and the Wasteland. As so often with these medieval romances, almost nothing is known about its author, Heinrich von dem Türlin. He probably came from Austria and the poem, of some 3,000 lines, is written in a Bavarian-Austrian dialect, sometime between 1210 and 1240. However, its only complete surviving manuscript dates from the fifteenth century and shows signs of rewriting. Inevitably, I had to leave out a good deal of the story, which follows Gawain's adventures over a much longer period of time than in my version. The text is also highly surreal in its use of imagery, and I have tried to retain as much of this as possible. Essentially, the Grail story appears in Book 2 of the poem, and I have therefore concentrated primarily on this. The translation is by a doyen of Arthurian scholars, J. W. Thomas, who captures the style and fluidity of Heinrich's text admirably. This version has provided the source for my own story, to which I have added references to several later texts for the sake of clarity. I strongly recommend reading the original text, which is a wonderful collection of Arthurian themes woven together by a master storyteller. (*The Crown: a Tale of Sir Gawain and King Arthur's Court* by Heinrich von dem Türlin, translated by J. W. Thomas. Nebraska University Press, Lincoln and London, 1989.)

POSTLUDES

29: The Prophecies of Merlin and the Lady of the Lake

The source for this story – which is perhaps hardly a story at all, but rather a collection of anecdotes designed to demonstrate the power and wisdom of Merlin – dates from the thirteenth century, and specifically to a French text written (or compiled) from a variety of older sources. It exists currently in roughly eighteen manuscripts, most still unedited, the most complete being published in Venice by Anthoine Verart in 1498. The earliest, written in *c.*1275, was kept in the monastery of San Francesco del Deserto in Venice at the same time as Marco Polo resided there. Despite its title, which implies a collection of prophecies attributed to Merlin, and which is only one of many such volumes written between the thirteenth and sixteenth centuries, the book is in fact far more. Sandwiched between the prophetic utterances are a number of fragmentary excerpts from the vast canon of Arthurian literature. In this way a number of unusual details have been preserved, in some instances deriving from texts which have not survived. The task of extracting these and of creating the story recounted here, was not easy. All those who have studied the text agree that it is confused and often contradictory, to a degree that makes it almost impossible to follow without a considerable familiarity with the stories of Arthur. I had no option but to add details from my own knowledge, and even from my personal understanding of the mythology underlying the romances, to flesh out the story. Without this we would have only a handful of fragments which would mean little or nothing to the general reader. I decided to include this as a tail-piece at the far end of the two volumes, which began with Geoffrey of Monmouth's *Vita Merlini* (*The Great Book of King Arthur and His Knights of the Round Table*, pp. 3–13). My attention to this remarkable document was first drawn by Maarten Haverkamp, who possesses a copy of the manuscript and is translating it into English. Much of what he discovered was startling – such as the connection between Arthurian mythology and the accounts of the fictitious King of India – Prester John. I have already spent several years exploring this link and have written about it in my book *Temples of the Grail* (Llewellyn, 2018), which is also attested in the later romance of 'The Red Rose Knight' (pp. 23–33) and the poem of *Der Jungerer Titurel*, (pp. 239–244) included here. I am grateful to Maarten for alerting me to this particular link in the chain. Without his translation I would not have been able to complete the story included here. Together we are currently working on a complete translation and commentary on this remarkable text. Those who wish to know more about it are recommended to read the essay 'Notes on Manuscripts of the Prophécies de Merlin' by Lucy Allen Paton in *Publications of the Modern Language Association of America*, Vol. XXI. 2., 1913. pp. 121–139, or to her more extended discussion in *Les Prophécies De Merlin* 2 Vols. Ed. and Trans. Lucy Allen Paton, (Heath, 1926).

30: King Arthur and the Dragon of Normandy

The *Draco Normannicus* or *Dragon of Normandy* is perhaps more of a satire than a romance, but the magical elements, which underlie Arthur's faery connections, make it a unique contribution to the Arthurian epic. Just as I ended the previous collection with 'A Voyage to Avalon', which told what happened to Arthur once he reached the Otherworld, so this brief story seemed the perfect ending to this collection. It comes from a chronicle attributed to one Etienne of Rouen, and was probably written around 1170. Essentially, it asks a series of questions: suppose Arthur really had been taken to Avalon and was somehow still living? Could he return to help the beleaguered Bretons – then under attack by Henry II of England, Normandy and Anjou (the 'dragon' of the title)? And how would an actual king respond to a letter sent to him (apparently by a form of mail delivery which included the underworld on its route)? The answers are written in elegant verse and are treated with absolute seriousness; and it is interesting to note that when Henry's mother, Matilda, died suddenly, the king did indeed withdraw his soldiers from Brittany for that time. The emphasis on Arthur living in the Otherworld, and that he could command armies of faery warriors at need, is fascinating and clearly reflects the folklore view of him at the time. I have taken the story as being of serious intent and have added a few comments in the guise of the unnamed scribe of this book. The only current translation is that by Mildred Leake Day, in her invaluable book, *Latin Arthurian Literature* published by D.S. Brewer in 2005. This, together with Dr Day's excellent notes, formed the basis of my version.

FURTHER READING

As in the previous volume, the sources of the individual stories included here are given within the notes for each text. What follows is a brief, eclectic list of additional titles, other texts as well as more general studies, intended to assist the interested reader in finding their way through the labyrinth of Arthurian lore and literature.

Adams, Max, *The First Kingdom* (London, Head of Zeus, 2021)

Barber, Richard, *King Arthur, Hero and Legend* (Suffolk, Boydell Press, 1986)

Besamusca, Bart & Frank Brandsma (eds.), *King Arthur of the Low Countries* (Cardiff, University of Wales Press, 2022)

Bromwich, Rachel *Triodd Ynys Prydein* (The Welsh Triads) (Cardiff, University of Wales Press, 1977)

Bromwich, Rachel, A.O.H. Jarman & B.F. Roberts (eds.), *The Arthur of the Welsh* (Cardiff, University of Wales Press, 1993)

Bryant, Nigel, (trans.) *The Complete Story of the Grail: Chrétien's Perceval and its Continuations* (Cambridge, D.S. Brewer, 2011)

Bryant, Nigel, (trans.) *Perceforest: The Prehistory of King Arthur's Britain* (Cambridge, D.S. Brewer, 2011)

Chrétien de Troyes, *Perceval, or the Story of the Grail*, (trans.) Nigel Bryant (Cambridge, D.S. Brewer, 1982)

Darrah, John, *Paganism in Arthurian Romance* (Suffolk, Boydell Press, 1994)

Dixon, Jeffrey John, *The Encyclopaedia of the Holy Grail* (North Carolina, McFarland & Co Ltd, 2023)

Geoffrey of Monmouth, *History of the Kings of Britain,* (trans.) Lewis Thorpe (London, Penguin Books, 1966)

Goodrich, Peter, (ed.) *The Romance of Merlin* (New York and London, Garland Publishing, 1990)

Grimbert, Joan Tasker & Carol J. Chase, *Chrétien de Troyes in Prose* (Cambridge, D.S. Brewer, 2011)

Guest, Charlotte, *The Mabinogion* (London, J.M. Dent, Everyman's Library, 1906)

Lacey, Norris J. et al. (trans.) *The Lancelot-Grail (10 Volume Set): The Old French Arthurian Vulgate and Post-Vulgate in Translation* (Cambridge, D.S. Brewer, 2010)

Logorio, Valerie, & Mildred Leake Day, *King Arthur Through the Ages* (2 vols) (Garland Publishing, London & New York, 1990)

Loomis, R.S., *The Grail: From Celtic Myth to Christian Symbol* (Cardiff: University of Wales Press, 1963)

Markale, Jean, *King Arthur King of Kings* (London, Gordon & Cremonesi, 1977)

Matthews, Caitlin, *King Arthur & the Goddess of the Land* (Rochester, VT, Inner Traditions, 2002)

Matthews, Caitlin, *Mabon & the Guardians of Celtic Britain* (Rochester, VT, Inner Traditions, 2002)

Matthews, Caitlin & John, *The Arthurian Book of Days* (London, Sidgewick & Jackson, New York, St Martins, 1990)

Matthews, Caitlin & John, *The Complete King Arthur* (Rochester, VT, Inner Traditions, 2018)

Matthews, Caitlin & John, *Ladies of the Lake* (Wellingborough, Aquarian Press, 1992)

Matthews, John, (ed.) *An Arthurian Reader* (Wellingborough, Aquarian Press, 1988)

Matthews, John, (ed.) *At the Table of the Grail* (London, Watkins Publishing, 2002)

Matthews, John, *Gawain, Knight of the Goddess* (Rochester, VT, Inner Traditions, 2002)

Matthews, John, *The Great Book of King Arthur and his Knights of the Round Table* (London, HarperCollins, 2022)

Matthews, John, *The Grail: Quest for the Eternal* (London, Thames & Hudson, 1981, Crossroads, 1990)

Matthews, John, *King Arthur: from Dark Age Warrior to Medieval King* (London, Carlton Books, 2003)

Matthews, John, & Gareth Knight, *Temples of the Grail* (Woodbury, Minnesota, Llewellyn, 2018)

Matthews, John & Maarten Havercamp, (eds. and trans.) *The Prophecies of Merlin* (Rochester, VT, Inner Traditions, 2025)

Morris, John, *The Age of Arthur* (London, Weidenfeld & Nicolson, 1973)

Paton, Lucy Allen, *Studies in the Fairy Mythology of Arthurian Romance* (New York, Burt Franklin, 1970)

Stewart, R.J., *The Prophetic Life of Merlin* (London, Arkana, 1986)

Tolstoy, Nikolai, *The Quest for Merlin* (London, Hamish Hamilton, 1985)

Venning, Timothy, *The King Arthur Mysteries* (Barnsley, South Yorkshire, Pen & Sword History, 2021)

von Eschenbach, Wolfram, *Parzival* (trans.) A.T. Hatto (London, Penguin Books, 1980)